Praise for *There's Something About Mira*

"It's so rare to find edge-of-your-seat drama that also cracks your humanity open. There's truly something about Sonali Dev's *There's Something About Mira*—it's a book with so much heart you'll want to wrap every character in a hug and never let them go."

—Ali Rosen, author of *Alternate Endings*

"Love, adventure, mystery, and Sonali's signature wit—you can't go wrong with this one. I got so carried away with this story that I read it in one sitting. Lose yourself in this mystery that explores what it means to love and be loved."

—Sally Kilpatrick, *USA Today* bestselling author

"Sonali Dev knows how to deliver a punch to the gut while making her reader laugh at the same time. Her characters are masterfully constructed, their emotions raw, their relationships real no matter how desperate or trivial their situation. Mira Salvi's journey to restore a lost ring to its rightful owner while also trying to plan a wedding with Dr. Right, and trying not to fall in love with Mr. Unexpected, is both heartrending and heart-healing. I read it in one sitting and came away breathless. A must read!"

—Trisha Das, author of *Never Meant to Stay*

"*There's Something About Mira* is everything that makes Sonali Dev's work special: swoon-worthy romantic elements, nuanced social themes around the consequences of other people's expectations and influences on who and how we should love, and beautifully rendered characters. I loved every minute of this story and am jealous of those who get to read it for the first time."

—Jamie Beck, *Wall Street Journal* bestselling author

"Simply put, a masterpiece. Only Sonali Dev could create an achingly beautiful, sob-and-laugh-out-loud, best-banter-ever story of healing, courage, family, and the most magical coincidence ever. Absolutely extraordinary, and Dev's best book to date."

—Kristan Higgins, *New York Times* bestselling author

"Sonali Dev is a master of the craft, and every time I open up one of her novels, I know I'm in for something special! *There's Something About Mira* absolutely captured my heart, and Mira was a delight to root for. Her journey to uncover the truth—about the ring and herself—takes the reader on a gorgeous, layered exploration of family, self-discovery and acceptance, and love. Warm and brilliant, with Sonali Dev's trademark wit and lush prose, this is an absolute must-read!"

—Naina Kumar, *USA Today* bestselling author of *Say You'll Be Mine*

Praise for Sonali Dev & Her Novels

"A joyful and fun read, but also a timely tale."

—Mindy Kaling

"How do we define love between friends, and how far would we go for that love? Sonali Dev's book peels back one unexpected surprise after another as she blurs the lines between the family we make and the family we are born into, between altruism and selfishness, and between truth and lies."

—Jodi Picoult, #1 *New York Times* bestselling author

"*Lies and Other Love Languages* is a tender and compelling novel about how women navigate their relationships with families, friends, careers, and their pasts. Mallika's disappearance and Rani's emergence set the story on a path of intrigue and revelation. The contrast between Vandy's carefully crafted public persona and her inner turmoil will resonate with many women. This is a story about discovering who we are."

—Balli Kaur Jaswal, internationally bestselling author of *Erotic Stories for Punjabi Widows*

"Sonali Dev pulls the reader as deep as one can go into the hearts of the exceptionally well-drawn, relatable characters. I was emotionally invested from beginning to end, and I can't recommend this gem of a novel highly enough."

—Julianne MacLean, bestselling author of *Beyond the Moonlit Sea*

"*Lies and Other Love Languages* is a gripping mystery cloaked in a rich family drama. It's full of unexpected twists and turns, and Sonali Dev did a masterful job weaving a tangled web of secrets, lies, love, and devotion. I found myself lost in the pages and wonderfully satisfied when the last one was turned."

—Suzanne Redfearn, bestselling author of *In an Instant*

"Vivid and deliciously enticing, Dev's storytelling is layered with emotional depth . . . a flavorful harmony of cross-cultural unions, familial love, and an entertaining ensemble of characters that will leave readers with a serious craving for more."

—NPR

"These Indian American women and their struggles will appeal to readers from every age and culture."

—*Washington Post*

"Dev weaves humor and romance through her tale of three generations of women."

—Audible

"A super-fun, bingeable story about three generations of vibrant women navigating relationships, friendships, mishaps, and ambitions."

—*Ms.*

"A cozy cup of chai for the soul."

—*Kirkus Reviews*

"Sonali Dev's trademark character depth and beautiful writing really makes *The Vibrant Years* shine. A gorgeous story of evolving female relationships and how love, hilarity, and the bonds between three generations of women help them thrive in even the fiercest winds of change."

—Christina Lauren, *New York Times* bestselling author

"Dev writes with such rare empathy and humor that I often found myself holding my breath on one page only to be giggling by the next. This is the kind of book you finish with a whole-body, happy sigh and a warm ache in your chest where the characters will live on."

—Emily Henry, *New York Times* bestselling author

"No one writes like Sonali Dev. A rich, delicious tale."

—Barbara O'Neal, *Wall Street Journal* and
#1 Amazon Charts bestselling author

THERE'S SOMETHING ABOUT MIRA

ALSO BY SONALI DEV

Lies and Other Love Languages

The Vibrant Years

The Wedding Setup

The Emma Project

Incense and Sensibility

Recipe for Persuasion

Pride, Prejudice, and Other Flavors

A Distant Heart

A Change of Heart

The Bollywood Bride

A Bollywood Affair

THERE'S SOMETHING ABOUT MIRA

A Novel

SONALI DEV

LAKE UNION
PUBLISHING

Published by Lake Union Publishing, Seattle

www.apub.com

ISBN-13: 9781662524271 (hardcover)
ISBN-13: 9781662524264 (paperback)
ISBN-13: 9781662524257 (digital)

Cover design and illustration by Kimberly Glyder

Printed in the United States of America
First edition

For Swati, for always helping me dig deep and holding my hand as I stumble through what I find. I would not have made it through the hardest times without your wisdom, generosity, and love. Thank you.

CHAPTER ONE

There's something especially embarrassing about having to reschedule a trip with your fiancé to celebrate your engagement. My future mother-in-law calls it an *engagement-moon* (which is only slightly less embarrassing), and I just spent an hour on the phone rescheduling mine, for the second time.

"This is the last change allowed," Shay, the lovely airline employee, warns with finality, and I smile into the phone as I speed walk along the Naperville river trail, getting my steps in for the day. Shay's own engagement broke up last week, so I spent the first half of our conversation convincing her that her life is far from over and that someone even more perfect for her is out there waiting.

I've known Druv since middle school, but I only *found him–found him* a year and a half ago, at the ripe old age of twenty-eight, so I know a thing or two about second chances.

"You're the luckiest girl in the world," Shay says wistfully, voice equal parts envy and hope, as she lets me go. It's a sentiment I've heard repeated so many times since my engagement six months ago that my brain tends to skip over it. So I take a moment now to count my blessings and to really let myself feel gratitude for being such an incredibly lucky person. Whose fiancé has canceled on our engagement-moon twice.

Your orthopedic surgeon fiancé, my mother's chiding voice says in my ear. My mother's guiding force is the fear of tempting the fates. In her mind, all good fortune is precariously balanced on the knife-edge of bad fortune and under constant threat from the evil eye of those who want what you have. The only path to preventing my gifts from disappearing, as miraculously as they appeared, lies somewhere between never acknowledging them out loud (*Do not put happy pictures of yourself with Druv on the Instagram!*) and never letting anyone forget exactly how lucky I am (*If we do not invite the entire community to the engagement party, how will everyone know you got Druv?*).

Most important: I am never ever to forget how very lucky I am to have bagged Dr. Druv Kalra, MD, or how critical an orthopedic surgeon's commitments are. I don't disagree. I'm proud of how wholeheartedly Druv gives himself to his work. Obviously, rebuilding spines takes precedence over a trip to New York with someone he's going to spend the rest of his life with anyway. I do get the irony in celebrating our first step into domesticity by getting away from our families and responsibilities.

Not that the cancellations matter anymore. We're going to New York. We get another chance at not losing the $5,000 my parents and Druv's have so generously spent on gifting us the trip.

I'm going to New York! Anticipation races up my spine.

Druv loves New York. He finds it preposterous that I've never been, and wants to fix that ASAP. Or as soon as his surgical schedule opens up, which he's assured me it has next week. He's got his partner covering him for emergencies. All the scheduling, and the rescheduling, and the re-rescheduling that I've done was worth it. I'm good at that. At taking everyone's needs into consideration and making things work out, especially when no one else knows how.

It's why I love being a pain management therapist. What's more rewarding than finding a way to soothe physical pain? There's nothing more universally human than pain. And yet, identifying what causes it, then understanding how to address it: there's nothing more individual than that. The search for sources of discomfort comes easily to me, of tracking the clues the mind and body hand us, of acknowledging the trauma that's always at the root of pain.

Unfortunately, most of my clients have no interest in digging into sources. They just want the pain gone. *Now.* Bandaging festered wounds always makes them worse in the long term. You have to open them up, let them breathe, treat the infection.

I stop in my tracks and drop onto a wooden bench facing the DuPage River where it slips under a curved bridge. Should I worry about the fact that Druv has canceled our getaway twice? Do I need to dig into the why a little more?

Before I can give that thought more oxygen, Druv calls. "Hey, beautiful," he says in that lovely tranquilizer voice that I swear takes away half his patients' pain even before they tell him what's wrong. I know this because a lot of my patients are his patients too. Yet another reason we work so well. An orthopedic surgeon and a pain management therapist: a match made in heaven for this accident-prone earth.

"Hey yourself," I say, already calmer. "How was the laminectomy?"

"Straightforward. The patient's age was a concern, but I'm not expecting complications." He takes a breath, and I know the word *complications* was not used in vain. "Speaking of complications," he adds, "you know how I said next week was taken care of for our trip?" He barely pauses, but my heart finds the gap and drops in my chest. "Well, Jake can't fill in for me anymore. He tripped down the stairs this morning and broke his arm."

"Oh no! Is he okay?" Suddenly our stupid engagement-moon feels insignificant. At least Druv didn't topple down a staircase.

"It's barely a hairline crack. But no surgeries for a month at least."

"Poor Jake," I say as my brain starts making plans to bake the lemon cookies Jake loves so much. I'll take them over to his place later when I go check on him.

"Can we reschedule for next month?" Druv brings me back to the problem at hand.

"Next month is the wedding shopping trip, remember?" I'm going to India with our mothers. No one even asked Druv to come, because: surgical schedule. "Also, neither the airline nor the hotel will let us change the dates again."

"I'm sorry, babe," he says. "I know how hard you've worked to make the trip happen."

I have. I've spent hours on the rescheduling alone. But that's not why disappointment squeezes my chest so hard I can't make words.

I breathe through it. Druv didn't break Jake's arm, and he can't leave his practice when his partner is unable to perform surgeries. I should say something soothing, but nothing comes out.

"Mira," he says, the regret in his voice making everything worse, "I'll make it up to you."

How? I want to ask him. I already feel like I don't deserve him. "Druv, is there something else? Do you even want to go?" The engagement-moon was his idea, not mine. Actually, it was his mother's idea, wholeheartedly backed up by my own mother. But Druv was the one who got excited and ran with it. I only got excited when we chose New York.

"That's not fair, babe," he says. "Spending time with you is my oasis, you know that. You're the only stress-free thing in my life." He sounds so tired. I've never known anyone who pushes himself harder. "But getting away for five days? I don't know what I was thinking."

"I'm sorry," I say. I wish we were having this conversation in person so I could comfort him. "We don't need to get away. Isn't that the best part of being each other's oasis?"

"I love you," he says, his voice hoarse with emotion. "Maybe you can ask them to roll the refunds over for our honeymoon. You can make it happen. You're impossible to say no to."

That should make me feel good. It shouldn't rattle me. Druv's mother loves to tell the story of how Druv was absolutely not interested in marriage until we met at that wedding. *Look at her! She was impossible to say no to,* my future mother-in-law loves to say. Everyone loves that story; no one cares that I never offered myself up for him to say yes or no to. Even Druv, for all his thoughtfulness, has always assumed that I was available and interested.

I was, but that doesn't excuse the fact that everyone assumed that I would be. I'm almost thirty and not married. Obviously, either I'm not impossible to say no to, or I haven't been interested. Or both. Not that any of it matters anymore. Truth is I've never met anyone gentler or more sincere than Druv. Everyone else might see him as "the catch of the community" I won like some lottery, but Druv is the first man around whom I can breathe.

"I'll see what I can do," I say, knowing that the money for the trip is already lost. I get off the bench and start walking again, working to shake off my disappointment.

I was looking forward to Central Park, to Times Square, to the Empire State Building. All the romantic comedy hallmarks I grew up with. In my head Deborah Kerr from *An Affair to Remember* presses an elegant hand to her throat and silently sobs for me. Meg Ryan's wispy blond bangs fly around her face as she tries to cheer me up with that brave-sad imp's smile. I've internalized that smile as the language of my soul. I flash it at an older man who jogs past me, and he brightens.

Much as I will miss seeing New York City, that's not what's at the heart of my disappointment. That would be Rumi, my twin brother.

I haven't seen Rumi since he moved to New York two years ago. I understand why he hasn't spoken to our parents in more than five years, but he's been avoiding me, too, lately. He hasn't RSVP'd to our wedding invitation, which is a punch to my heart. I can't imagine getting married without him. This was my chance to convince him to come. Something I can only do in person, because it's too complicated to do over the phone so long as the phone has a disconnect button.

"Thanks," Druv says, "for being so understanding. Every other woman I know would have pitched a fit. I love how you manage to keep things so zero-drama. I hope you know how much I value it."

"Thanks," I say because how can I not be grateful for someone who values the thing I cherish most about myself? It's why I'm with Druv, why our first conversation led to the next and then the next, because with Druv everything is always even keeled, and I like even keeled. It makes me feel safe.

"Mira?" he says in his kind way. "What I just said, I didn't mean you can't tell me when things upset you. If something is bothering you, you'll tell me, right?"

The fact that we're not going to New York *is* bothering me, but he already knows that. Neither one of us can do anything about it, and I'm not going to make him feel worse than he already does. I turn down the street that leads to the house I live in with my parents and take a breath.

"Are you saying you'd like more drama?" I say in my best teasing voice.

"God no," he says, his relief obvious.

"Because at your mom's dinner party tonight we're going to have to tell our parents that the trip is off. So, you're going to get that wish. The Two Moms are going to go into total Tragedy Queen mode."

He groans dramatically and laughs. "How will we survive this, beta?" he says, doing his mother's voice.

"Cue the weeping violins," I say. And just like that, I'm laughing, too, because I did manage to comfort him after all.

CHAPTER TWO

My mother, Ajita Salvi, and Druv's mother, Romona Kalra, have been besties for the past year and a half, and all Naperville's tight-knit South Asian community, a.k.a. Brown Town, knows it. My parents have lived here since before my birth, but the Salvis weren't always part of the establishment. We aren't the norm here. My parents aren't doctors, partners in consulting firms, or IT company bigwigs. They own Bombay Masala, our town's oldest South Asian grocery store.

My father came here thirty-five years ago with big dreams and the fabled eight dollars in his pocket—and even those were borrowed. A distantly related uncle needed someone to run his grocery store and he sponsored my parents' visas. For almost twenty years, Aie and Baba ran the store, barely making minimum wage. The uncle always took the "distantly" in "distantly related" very seriously. Right from the start, he made it crystal clear that they were employees, the hired help, and not family.

My parents worked around the clock and raised us in the apartment above the store. Aie also made and sold rotis and snacks and cooked and cleaned for private parties. And Baba probably cooked the books a little, because just before his uncle died, they were able to buy the store.

Until then we'd stayed on the fringes of uppity Brown Town. Rumi and I were never invited to the birthday parties or even to playdates at the McMansions. Sometimes when Aie helped serve and clean at the parties, she took me with her, and the hostesses, bedecked in designer wear and diamonds, sliced up giant pieces of cake for me with that benevolent look that tried for generosity but couldn't help but give off charity. When I was very young, I loved going because the cake was always incredible. Baked by an auntie who'd taken a baking class and started an artisan cake business focused on nostalgic flavors like mango, saffron, and pistachio. As I got older, run-ins with the kids I went to school with became progressively more awkward, and I started to beg Aie to let me stay home, cake notwithstanding.

When my parents bought the store, I was thirteen years old. Within two years of buying the store, my parents bought a McMansion of their own in one of the aspirational subdivisions. Suddenly, the Salvis slid from the fringes to inside the hallowed circle.

Aie and Baba took to their new status with the zeal of converts. They replaced our secondhand Chevy Caravan with his-and-hers luxury cars: a Mercedes and a BMW (which have now been replaced by matching Teslas). My mother started getting keratin treatments and gel manicures and bought a Louis Vuitton bag with the unmistakable monogram proclaiming our hard-won bougieness. Rumi and I were expected to be models of good behavior, always well turned out in identifiable brands, always excelling at school, always volunteering at the temple in our finest Indian designer wear.

We were expected to guard the family's position with the fierceness of children who understood the sacrifices our parents had made so we could have the life they gave us.

Back then it felt like a lot, but now I know how ungrateful we were. My parents could have let my teenage rebellion destroy me, but they cleaned up my mess and set me back on my feet. Rumi doesn't see it that way. Maybe because what they see as his rebellion, unlike mine, isn't rebellion at all. It's simply who he is. Someday they'll see that. They usually see things in the end. It just takes them time. The chasm between how they grew up and the world in which they raised us isn't an easy one to cross.

As far as Rumi is concerned, they're out of time, and he's angry with me because he thinks I'm making excuses for them.

I watch them now, entirely at home in the high-ceilinged great room of Druv's parents' house. There's an understated elegance to the Kalra home—all subtle accent walls and moody art pieces. Masks, mirrors, and bells cover entire walls in perfectly arranged clusters. Books, lamps, and lush fabrics work together to turn furniture into statement pieces. Old money, my aie calls the Kalras. Based on the pictures Druv's mom loves to share, the houses they grew up in back in Delhi are just as grand as this. I've never understood why people like that would leave their home to be outsiders in someone else's land.

Druv says his parents craved the adventure and independence. They grew up with American music, movies, and clothes, so it called to them. My parents, on the other hand, obviously craved the ability to feed their family. Which they have. They educated all the children in their extended families back in their village in India; they bought homes for their parents; they even bought Baba's cousin a new hip last year.

I watch him, my rail-thin father, his shoulders permanently stooped from years of leaning over a cash register. His silver hair is still thick, he sports a goatee, and he's wearing the lilac Brooks Brothers polo I gave him last Father's Day. All the men he's talking to are similarly dressed: the golf uncles in branded polos humblebragging about their handicaps and bragging-bragging about the courses they've played. Druv's father belly laughs at something Baba says, and they slap each other on the back. I try to remember a time in my childhood when I saw my father laughing and I can't, so this is nice.

Aie is with the aunties in the kitchen. Even though Druv's mom has two people helping her serve and clean, I'm certain the aunties are in there proving their domestic-goddess cred by helping the helpers. I try to imagine my life like this: entertaining, keeping house, raising family, building community. The details are startlingly clear, but the entirety of it, the bigger picture, that part I can't seem to visualize.

"Here comes the bride," Ariana, Druv's younger sister, announces as she wraps me in a hug. She's wearing a perfectly fitted ribbed tank dress that's bright red and ends a couple of inches below her butt. It's something my mother might strangle me for wearing. A Van Cleef & Arpels pendant that reminds me of a four-leaf clover hangs delicately around her neck, just the way it hangs around the necks of several of the girls she grew up with. Druv's mother gave me one when we got engaged. Mine is tucked under my gray linen jumpsuit with cap sleeves and a cowl-neck. On my earlobes are the sensible but absurdly pricey solitaires my parents gave me for the same occasion (*Three-quarters of a carat because we don't want to look like we're trying too hard*).

Ariana and I hold hands and compliment each other's clothing.

"I'm guessing Dr. Kalra-the-Second isn't here yet," she says, calling it. Druv *is* running late. Which is perfectly understandable, given Jake's hairline fracture situation.

Before I can respond, she rolls her eyes and turns to the woman standing behind her, and my stomach drops. Priyanka Joshi. I didn't notice her standing there. Possibly because she was trying to make her escape so she didn't have to talk to me.

Priyanka and I went to high school together. We were friends for a few months our junior year until she quit the Young Feminist Leaders club. Or more accurately, until I caused her to be removed from her position as club president. My face turns hot. She's refused to look at me since the incident.

Her disgust is as thickly palpable as it was when we were seventeen. Without acknowledging me, she hands one of the two glasses she's holding to Ariana. They were obviously hanging out before Ariana noticed my presence. My presence, which is enough to make Priyanka drop an air-kiss on Ariana and walk away, head held high, not even a flicker of recognition in my direction.

She's as stunning as she was as a teenager. No awkward phase for Priyanka Joshi. While the rest of us brown girls stumbled into freshman year with unwaxed upper lips, unibrows, frizzy hair, and acne stubble,

Priyanka breezed in looking like a Bratz doll. All glossy hair, long-lashed eyes, petite frame, and the kind of comfort in her own skin that baffled the rest of us.

As she walks away, I notice she still has that self-possession that flashes me back a decade. I haven't seen her since then, but what I did to her is a nudging splinter of guilt that's been stuck under my skin. Now it pushes against a nerve, and I want to run after her and apologize, but the disdain in her demeanor was so clear that I'm frozen.

"I didn't realize you were friends," I say to Ariana, and despite my best effort not to give anything away, I study her to see if she knows what happened between Priyanka and me.

"We used to live next door to each other until her parents moved to the city. I was much younger. She and Druv were the ones who were inseparable." A flash of doubt passes in her eyes. She's not sure she should have said that, and she rushes on. "She went to college out of state. She just got a job in Chicago and moved back, so Mom invited her over." Her gaze follows Priyanka until she disappears out of the room. "I wanted to be her when I grew up."

I think I did, too, but I can't admit it. Priyanka was the only girl I knew who didn't care about what anyone else wanted her to be. Until they—we—found a way to break her.

"She was always so badass, I could never have imagined . . ." Ariana catches herself. "I'm so glad she's okay now."

"What happened?" I ask, and the splinter turns sharp.

"She's been pretty open about it, so I guess it's not a secret. She was in and out of rehab for a while." Suddenly she looks guilty. "I'm not gossiping, I swear." Ariana is just twenty-five, a good ten years younger than Druv, but she has his inherent kindness, that same intentional commitment to being a good person and doing the right thing that I love about him.

"It's okay," I say, but I feel anything but okay.

Priyanka's voice from a long time ago echoes in my head. *That club was my whole life. I hope someone ruins your life too.*

"What's wrong, Mira?" Poor Ariana looks worried, so I push away the ancient memories and smile.

"Nothing, I'm fine," I say. But I can't leave it at that. "Can you excuse me a minute?" It's been thirteen years. And yet I'm knocked off balance by the clarity with which I remember the expression on Priyanka's face when she told me to go to hell. "There's something I need to take care of."

Fortunately, an auntie accosts Ariana and starts gushing about how great she looks, so I slip away and follow Priyanka.

I have no idea what I'm doing or what I hope to accomplish, but I also can't believe I've let all this time go by without an apology.

"Priyanka!" I call after her in the empty corridor that connects the living room with the kitchen.

She stops but doesn't turn around. Her stance tells me she was hoping I wouldn't chase her. I walk around her, and she looks at me with utter incredulousness.

"It's . . . it's been a long time. It's good to see you looking so well."

"I'll bet it is," she says and starts walking away.

"I wanted to . . . I wanted to apologize," I say, almost relieved that she seems to have no interest in making this easy for me. "I never meant for you to lose your—"

"Please don't." Her face is entirely expressionless when she turns to me. None of the hurt from years ago, just a blank calmness. A look people often get when they recall past pain that they've worked hard not to feel anymore. "I'm sure you want to vomit your feelings all over me so you can feel better about being a vicious little shit. Maybe go to your mommy and she can fix this for you too? I'm not interested in your catharsis, so leave me out of it." She turns away again but then stops. "If this is about me telling poor Druv who you really are, don't worry. I'm not in the business of crushing other people's dreams."

This time she does walk away, and I feel like I'll never move again, like she just hammered me right into the floor.

I don't know how long I've been standing there when Ariana finds me. "There you are. Did you need something?"

I shake my head. "No. I was just going to check on Druv." I hold up my phone. My limbs have gone cold and stiff, and I pray that she doesn't see it.

"Good luck finding any privacy around here." She winks. "Did Priyanka go this way?"

I point at the kitchen.

"Oh no! She just walked straight into the coven of aunties. They're going to attack her with a hype fest of all the single guys in Brown Town. I have to go rescue her." With that she traces Priyanka's footsteps and is gone.

I force myself to move and return to the living room, where Druv's mother and Arti Auntie, one of her girl gang, find me.

"Were you talking to the Joshi girl earlier?" Arti says, looking over my shoulder. "She looked remarkably normal."

Druv's mom frowns, albeit gently. "She's a good girl, Arti. She's been through a lot. Give her a break."

"Right," Arti says. "Now that Druv is all settled with someone else, it's easy for you to say." Before Druv's mom responds, Arti puts both hands up. "I'm only joking. All I mean is that I'm glad she's done with her wild phase. Her poor mother must be relieved. I just want all the kids to be happy." With that she turns her focus on me. "Look at this one here. Always been such a good girl. None of that attention-seeking nonsense." She squeezes my shoulder, and the cold, sick feeling Priyanka's words left inside me bloats. "So, I hear Druv is taking you to the Ritz-Carlton for your engagement honeymoon." She wiggles her perfectly filled-in brows.

"Mira deserves no less, and my Druv knows it." Druv's mom puts her well-sculpted arm (*Three days of Zumba and two days of weight machines, thank you very much*) around me and engulfs me in a cloud of White Linen. I haven't told her yet that the trip is canceled. She's been so excited about it, I just didn't know how to break it to her. "And it's called an engagement-moon, Arti!"

Arti Auntie chuckles bawdily. "Oy hoi, look at you making sure your son and daughter-in-law don't do honeymoon before marriage."

I almost choke on my wine. Ever since Druv and I got engaged, it takes the aunties and uncles precisely five minutes to maneuver every conversation with us toward sexual innuendo.

"Mira knows I'm the kind of mother-in-law who wants her to have a healthy sex life, right, Mira? We're friends first." She smiles at me in commiseration.

Mortification steamrolls over all the other emotions raging inside me. That's an upside, I guess. A furious blush warms my cheeks. Which makes the two of them so happy they burst into delighted laughter and pat my cheeks.

"Romona, your daughter-in-law might be the only modest girl we have left in the community. How precious! I can't remember the last time I saw a young woman blushing."

Until I got engaged to Druv, everyone treated me like I was an old-world spinster on the shelf. Not exactly done at almost thirty (because everyone is progressive now) but with my chances of "settling down" pretty much dismal (because everyone is also still a "realist"). Druv's a man *and* he went to med school, so the same standards don't apply to him around here. Since my engagement to Druv, however, I'm treated like a bud in first bloom.

Druv's mother is possibly the most sensible person I know, but even she looks proud and doting about what she sees as my modesty. What it is, in fact, is just me being a grade A dork.

"I would have killed for my mother-in-law to look at me like that." My mother joins us, and her face is bursting with so much smug satisfaction that my flush deepens to a different shade of embarrassment. She presses her knuckles into her temples to ward off the evil eye and pats my cheek with the kind of affection I've hungered for all my life. "Did you know Mira has had her bag packed for weeks? I've never seen her this excited about anything. I told her, 'Calm down, you have a lifetime with your Druv.' So eager."

All three women burst into more of those innuendo-laced giggles.

I know they mean well. I know they didn't grow up with this kind of freedom. They probably think they're being generous with me right now, because their elders gave them nothing but rules and shaming. My mind still slips to my childhood, to the things I've heard said about me and Priyanka and every other girl I grew up with. *Slutty . . . too dark . . . too plain . . . chubby . . . skinny . . . mousy . . . bossy . . . damaged goods . . . past her prime. Not in his league.*

I try not to think about their reactions when they find out that Druv canceled the trip again.

I try to manufacture a smile, but I can't seem to manage it. My chest feels tight. The pressure of things I don't want to remember squeezes like a corset, cutting off my breath. Before I can figure out what's happening to me, Druv enters the party, a good two hours late.

He's startlingly handsome in his midnight blue button-down and slim-fit dark jeans. His hair is freshly washed and slicked back. He stopped at his place to clean up even when he knew he was late. I can practically smell his bodywash and cologne even from this far away, and his confidence that no one will call him out for his lack of punctuality.

"Excuse me a moment," I say to the aunties.

"Of course," Romona says and winks at her son as his face breaks into a smile at the sight of me.

Every single person in the crowded room seems to be watching us as we make our way to each other. Druv takes my hand and places a kiss on my cheek. Playing to the gallery but also keeping it intimate.

"What's wrong?" he asks near my ear, picking up on the discomfort churning inside me.

"I need air," I whisper even as I fight to understand my rioting emotions.

"Hey, can you help me grab something from the car?" he says loud enough for our audience to hear and leads me out the front door to some good-natured hooting.

As soon as the front door shuts behind us, I press my hands to my face. I'm shaking. "I'm so sorry," I say.

Druv pulls my hands away from my face with so much gentleness that some of what I'm feeling settles.

"Mira, honey, what's the matter?"

"I don't know," I squeak. I want to scream it. Everything is so great, so great, but I can't seem to shake off this pressure in my chest. I want to say that, but I don't know how to.

"Did our moms say something about the canceled trip?"

I force myself to breathe. I've been avoiding it, but he finds the source of my discomfort, my panic, and I'm immensely grateful to have that thread to hold on to. "I didn't tell them. And I haven't canceled yet. I haven't had the time."

He rubs my back. "That's fine. We'll tell them together." He throws a look over his shoulder at the line of cars in the sweeping driveway. The din of music and laughter spills from inside the house.

"They'll never understand," I say, surprised at how despondent I sound.

What's even more surprising is the realization that it's not about whether they'll understand or not. I don't want to cancel. As soon as I admit it to myself, the knot of panic in my chest eases.

I want to go to New York. I need to. I need to see the Statue of Liberty and ride a subway and eat pizza and buy kababs from a food truck. I need to see my brother. I *have to* see my brother.

I've never left Illinois by myself. But I have to see Rumi.

"I can't leave the practice with Jake's arm broken, Mira," Druv says.

"I know. Don't you think I know that?"

He glances at the gigantic lead glass front door, then at the landscape lights casting halos around trees. When his gaze returns to me, there's an odd expression on his face. "What if you don't cancel?"

My heart skips a beat and fills with hope a little too fast.

"It's already paid for. What if you just go by yourself?"

"You'd be okay with that?" As soon as I say it, something gathers inside me, and I stand up straighter.

"I think so." There's so much kindness in the way he looks at me, I know exactly what his patients feel like. Why they let him dig up their spines. "It's not like you broke Jake's arm."

"You didn't either," I say. "I'd much rather go with you. But . . . but I've already taken the time off."

He runs his hand through his perfectly cut hair. "That's true," he says as though he hadn't thought about that until this moment. "You've been working so hard."

I have. I just finished my postgraduate work in post-op care for spinal surgery, which I managed with a full-time job and while doing all the wedding planning myself because no one has expected Druv to have the time. I also still help my parents out at the store. No wonder I almost had that totally out-of-character breakdown just now. I also just quit my job at the pain center so I can join Druv's practice next month after my trip to India. The timing for our engagement-moon was supposed to be perfect.

The timing is still perfect for me. "You sure you're okay with that?" I ask.

"Yes!" he says without a moment of hesitation. "I want you to go have fun. Get away from the moms and their wedding obsession. You need this."

I do. Recklessness grips me. I'm doing this. I'm going to New York by myself.

I kiss him. A quick but fierce peck on the lips. Everyone is right. How did I ever get lucky enough to find him?

He looks surprised but delighted. I'm not exactly comfortable with physical affection. He's been immensely patient with me in that too. He looks like he might lean in for another kiss, eyes aglow with hope, but

I pull away and turn to the gigantic door. One step at a time. It's how I've always lived my life. This moment. Then the next.

Telling everyone we're canceling our trip was going to be hard enough. I can't even imagine telling them that I'm going by myself.

I ignore the disappointment on Druv's face and brace myself for the avalanche of disappointment that awaits us on the other side of the door.

CHAPTER THREE

Whoever came up with the phrase "all hell broke loose" must've known my parents. As expected, Druv's parents recovered quickly and gracefully. After an appropriate amount of disappointment, Romona was entirely chill about me turning the engagement trip into a solo trip and going off to New York on my own.

"No point waiting around for my son for every little thing. If I waited around for his father to make time to do things, I'd never leave home," she said, then followed it up with a list of *darling* stores and restaurants that she and her girlfriends *adored* during their girls' weekends.

My mother, on the other hand, has been acting like I'm handing Druv a *Goodbye, it was nice knowing you* card. Over the past two days, every mistake I've ever made in my entire life has been dredged up from the depths of my parents' vault of woes. They've accused me of being irresponsible and overconfident, as though Druv is a priceless, fragile artifact I'm lucky enough to get to hold and I've decided to bounce him in the air, with oil on my hands.

As soon as the last of the guests at the dinner party left, Druv broke the news to our parents. He went for it quickly and precisely, just like slicing a scalpel through skin. Taking my hand, he announced that I was off to New York City by myself because he refused to let me waste that much money. A brilliant approach because it relied on our parents' favorite motivation: economics.

The announcement was greeted with an entire minute of silence, the kind that's usually observed to commemorate the death of a world leader. After the initial shock, Druv's parents rallied and mine pretended to rally for Druv's benefit. As soon as we left the Kalras', my aie practically pounced on me to change my mind as Baba goaded her in her rant with approving grunts (for her) and disapproving growls (for me). When I didn't change my mind, the silent treatment ensued. It lasted all yesterday.

Today, on the day of my departure, Aie has dragged me to the temple to beg Ganesha for blessings and protection. She even paid the priest for an extra ritual to ward away the evil eye. My flight leaves in a few hours, and I think she's trying to get me to miss it. But I know her only too well, so I've lied about the departure time by a good three hours. Plus, the idea of flying makes me nervous and a trip to the temple helps me relax.

"You know what the definition of stupidity is?" Aie asks as soon as we're alone, her Marathi so sharp edged with anger the words land on me like slaps.

It's taken us half an hour to leave the temple because we've stopped to say hello to a substantial chunk of the Indian population of the western Chicago suburbs. It's Sunday and the dosas at the temple cafeteria are incredible, so everyone is here.

Naturally, I wasn't brave enough to suggest getting food, given my mother's mood, which hasn't improved even after bribing the gods to protect her daughter from her own stupidity. Nonetheless, the smell of the crisp, buttery dosas lingers in my head like a reminder of missed joy.

I don't answer, because she needs to get this out of her system and the only way past it is to let her. I remind myself that it's just her worrying about my happiness.

"Stupidity," she continues, "is not recognizing how fortunate you are. Do you know why you get away with it?"

I take her cane from her and help her into the passenger seat without responding. Rhetorical questions are my mother's favored mode of communication.

"It's because everything has come too easily to you. Stuff falls in your lap no matter what you do to kick it away," she says when I slide into the driver's seat. "Don't you think it's time to grow up and stop pushing your luck?"

"Druv was the one who suggested it, Aie." I should have been the one to suggest it. But until he said it, it hadn't felt like an option. Mostly because I knew exactly how virulent my mother's reaction would be, and I refuse to feel ashamed for using Druv now to get around it. "It makes no sense to waste all that money." I stay the course with the monetary motivation.

"You're willing to sacrifice a life-changing marriage to save five grands?" she says in English, and I suppress the urge to correct her grammar. "Do you know the most common trait in smart people?"

I pull out of the parking space and find my way around the line of cars waiting to nab the coveted spot we just vacated. Finding parking at the temple on a Sunday might be harder than finding God. Between that and my mother's feelings about my ungratefulness for Druv falling in my lap, much like a prime parking spot, the metaphors are making my head spin.

"Smart people learn from their mistakes," she says, voice heavy with meaning.

If I were a different person, I might laugh. Everything I know, I've learned from my mistakes. It's been twelve years since I went to that party and almost ruined myself and my family. *I was seventeen!* I want to say, but my shame is so acute and debilitating, my tongue knots up.

"I haven't seen Rumi in two years," I say instead.

She goes still and silent.

I much prefer her in scolding mode. Aie in despair mode is something I've dreaded for as long as I can remember. Her sadness is much harder to navigate than her anger.

She gathers herself, shuttering her face. It's her turn to not know how to respond. I should feel good about turning the tables, but all I feel is guilt and more shame.

"He's my twin brother. Druv and his family would never understand if he didn't come to our wedding."

She turns to me, horrified. "Your father will die of shame, Miru. You know that." She takes my hand. "Promise me. Promise me you won't do something stupid."

"Don't you miss him, Aie?" I ask, suddenly exhausted enough for the both of us.

A tear slips from her eye, and she swipes it away angrily. "You kids are so American. Taking advantage of your parents' love. Not caring about your part. Rights and responsibilities are two sides of the same coin. We didn't do our part against all odds so you could become self-indulgent and think anything you do is okay. Obviously I miss him. I carried him for thirty-four weeks, I stayed up half the night for three years when he couldn't sleep from colic. Your father and I starved so you two could eat. That doesn't mean you get to emotionally blackmail us into getting your way. There are standards in the Salvi family. If you can't live up to them, you're dead to us."

My mind and body separate, as they often do when I'm arguing with my parents. I think it started when I was seventeen and my father slapped me across the face, then emptied a bottle of sleeping pills down his own throat and almost died because I was stupid enough to forget who I was.

Aie isn't just being dramatic anymore. She means every word. My body reacts as it is conditioned to do. I squeeze her arm and smile placatingly. "Druv is not going to leave me over this, Aie, I swear." Saying the words makes me sick to my stomach. No matter how wonderful Druv is, and he truly is, this belief every person around me holds, that he's a prize I've ended up winning by some stroke of luck, makes me want to roll up in a ball.

"This is what your baba and I worked for. So you could have this life. A husband like Druv. A family like the Kalras. I spent so many hours standing, I can't walk without a cane, Miru!" She throws a look at her carved rosewood cane propped against the back of my seat, and unshed tears gleam in her eyes. "We have no hopes for Rumi. Our son is already lost to us. You're all we have."

"It's a trip to New York. A two-hour flight. You're not losing me. I just need a little time off. Can't you be happy for me?"

She scoffs. She's always found the concept of time off amusing: just another irony for the privileged. *Time off from what? Your pampered life?* That's what she's thinking right now.

"The only thing I've ever wanted was happiness for your brother and you," she says. "But I know how fragile happiness is."

"Why is it so hard for you to believe that Druv loves me?" I slide through another green light. The surprising lack of traffic is disconcerting, like the universe is trying to reinforce Aie's point.

She looks at me like I'm being deliberately ignorant. "What does love have to do with anything? But sure, if we want to speak in simplistic terms, of course Druv loves you right now. You're a beautiful, well-behaved young woman, and he's a hot-blooded young man eager to start a family. In youth, before real life intrudes, love is easy. The question is, are you smart enough to build a good life on that? The life you build, that's what makes marriage last. When hard times come along, when temptations arise, that's what will keep him from walking away. The investment in what you build together: a home, children, a family, a place in society. The fear of losing *that* is what tides a marriage through life's storms. Not *love*."

Our wedding is four months away, and her words fill the car. The light I'm approaching turns amber. I step on the gas, knowing I have no chance of making it. Then, ten feet from the stoplight, I slam the brakes as it turns red. My poor old Prius bounces to a screeching halt, unused to my sudden recklessness.

Aie presses her hand against the dashboard and shakes her head as though I'm a child throwing a tantrum. Maybe I am. She turns to me with the look that always kept me from ever actually throwing a tantrum. Then she says the one thing that makes everything worse. "Just make sure you understand this, Mira. You are not to meet your brother when you're in New York."

CHAPTER FOUR

It's obvious that my brother isn't the one who wanted to pick me up from the airport. I'm glad his stubbornness doesn't work on his boyfriend, who happens to love me. The drive from LaGuardia to their semidetached house in Queens is barely twenty minutes. It's one of those beautiful early-May days that make you forget that the skies here could ever be gray, or that the sidewalks could ever be sprinkled with snow. The untainted spring air gives everything a crisp freshness and reminds me of Chicago, and that causes a prickle of homesickness in my heart.

As though he senses this, Saket, the love of my brother's life, twists in the passenger seat and reaches for my hand in the back seat. "We're so glad you're here," he says. "We've missed you."

Rumi, who is driving Saket's golden Mercedes convertible, rolls his eyes. But there's a smile deep inside them, a joy that's entirely new to my twin's personality, and I soak it up.

"Me too," I say. I love Saket Dixit.

Yes, that's his name, and unfortunate as that is, it's the reason they're together. The first words my brother said to him were *You're actually called Suck-it Dick-shit?* and then he laughed for a good five minutes straight because that's the kind of heartless monster my brother is. To Saket's credit, he'd been so mesmerized by the laugh, he'd asked Rumi if he actually did want to suck it. The rest, as they say, is history. A long bloody history of coming out when you have the Salvis of Naperville for parents.

Saket, on the other hand, doesn't have a coming-out story. He doesn't even remember telling his parents. They knew before he did. Sometimes I wonder how people like Saket and Druv, who've only ever been showered by unconditional acceptance by their parents, could ever understand people like Rumi and me. But it's their deep sense of being enough that seems to capture us.

Saket Dixit is relentlessly and inescapably lovable. And my brother is felled all the way to his soul. I keep Saket's hand (perfectly manicured with frosty pink-tipped nails) in mine as we drive past the idyllic homes with their front steps leading to quiet porches, each almost identical yet unique. My brother pulls into the garage a little too fast, and Saket claps as though we're on a plane and Rumi just stuck a flawless landing. Then he pulls Rumi's face to him and kisses him, hot and quick, before using his thickly kohl-lined eyes to wordlessly tell Rumi to relax.

My brother gives him a tortured smile that I feel deep inside me, because, well, it's our twin curse to feel each other's pain and joy.

"I wish you were staying with us. I'm also kinda jealous of the Ritz-Carlton, Ms. Fancy-Pants." Saket leads me into the house.

"Whoa! Forget the Ritz!" I say as we step inside. It's impossible not to gasp at the dramatic, luxuriant beauty I've just stepped into. A low white linen couch is artfully scattered with embroidered cushions in jewel tones. Woven rugs tell stories in color. An unbroken band of clustered paintings stretches across the living room walls and into the dining area and around the walls of the entire floor. I follow it in awe.

"Mom helped pick out most of the furnishings." Saket's mother is Binita Dixit, designer to the stars. Zendaya wore her on the Cannes red carpet last year. "But the art had to be me and Rooh. They're pieces we've picked up from street artists over the years. No investment art for us. Yuck." He shakes the offensive thought of art as commerce off his shoulders like a bad feeling.

Saket's family owns one of the biggest jewelry brands in the world. They have stores in every major city from Mumbai to Berlin to Dubai. Saket runs their flagship store on Fifth Avenue.

"This is absolutely gorgeous," I say, still trying to grasp the decadent artistry of it all.

Rumi follows us in. "It's true. Some stereotypes are based on fact. American desi gays have impeccable taste." He wraps Saket in a hug from behind, and I try to picture this with Druv. Will I ever be someone who won't cringe at being wrapped up like this?

"How is Dr. Drum-Roll-Please?" my brother asks.

I smile what I hope is a dreamy smile. Because despite my complicated feelings about back-hugs, Druv is perfect, and I tell Rumi that.

"So perfect he missed your engagement-shag trip?" Saket spent part of his childhood in London, and Rumi has obviously picked up his Briticisms.

I've been waiting for my brother to start, so I'm almost relieved to get it out of the way.

"So perfect he wanted our girl to have some fun by herself," Saket says. "Dr. Drup-Dead-Gorgeous, am I right?"

Even Rumi laughs at that.

"Exactly," I say and follow the two of them into the white-and-gold kitchen. The most beautiful glazed fruit tart sits under a glass dome on the mosaic dining table. Fruit is my weakness. Especially in baked goods. The table is tucked into a bay window under a gigantic skylight. I'm in heaven. This is where I want to come to die.

Rumi starts the espresso machine as Saket makes a production of lifting the dome and slicing up the tart. The kitchen fills with the aroma of fresh coffee, and every cell in my body relaxes as we sink into the most comfortable dining chairs I've ever had the pleasure of resting my butt on.

"If you tell me you made this tart yourself, I will murder my brother and marry you myself," I say.

Saket wiggles his dramatically arched brows. "You'd have to get in line, sweetheart. We get that a lot!"

Rumi and I both laugh our identical laughs, and our eyes meet. He looks away. Saket's sunniness might have brightened his edges, but the rage he's always carried simmers close to the surface. Or maybe it's just my presence digging things up.

Saket feeds a piece of mango into Rumi's mouth, and his restlessness settles. We sit there like that, tucked into the nook, the orange rays of the setting sun flooding in through the skylight and bay window and tinting the absurdly extravagant kitchen golden. The tart is everything food should be, suffused with the pure essence of its ingredients, soulful. Saket didn't make it. He knows this French patisserie around the corner. He has an eye for finding things, obviously. My Rumi is a jewel, but his anger and cynicism are a patina not many can see past. Saket has always seemed entirely unfazed by his thorny armor.

Rumi's hair has grown out. He's always had the most beautiful hair. Thick and so inky black it shines silver in the light. People say I have the same hair, but mine's curlier, frizzier, the unrefined version. Much like everything else about our appearance. His skin, his eyes, all his features are finer, more artistic versions of mine, like I was the mold and he the finished product.

He's cut his hair in layers. His jaw is shaved to smoothness. He's more well groomed than I've ever known him to be, but it's how comfortable he is in his skin that fills me up.

My heart cramps as a memory of him with a shaved head slashes through me. The bleeding cuts on his scalp from struggling as our father ran a razor blade over it. I push it away. This isn't the time for ugly memories. This is a moment of unbearable beauty. Sunshine and flavors and aromas and smooth surfaces, and love. All our senses bathed and caressed and wrapped up at once. Seemingly healable.

The look Rumi throws me is all sorts of smug. This is the kind of life our parents didn't even know to want for us. Even more than the *more* they've always pushed toward.

"Isn't it weird how Aie and Baba always went on and on about us ending up with Indian people? Now here I am. Sak is not just Indian, he's Marathi—even you, the golden child, didn't pull that off."

Druv's family is from South Delhi. Culturally, a different galaxy from the outer reaches of the northeastern suburbs of Mumbai my parents grew up in.

"That makes it sound like you're only with me because I'm Marathi," Sak says, pretending to be offended as they link fingers and exchange another intimate look.

I've missed Rumi more than I can put into words, but it's painfully obvious that moving to New York to be with Saket was the best thing he's ever done. It's something he almost didn't do, because Saket wasn't interested in any relationship that involved hiding. Which in turn involved Rumi having to look our parents in the eye and tell them he was in love with a man. Which in turn meant our parents declaring that he was dead to them.

Rumi's reaction was more relief than sadness. Laying down a weight that had been crushing his spine crack by crack. He might've been done with me, too, when he left Chicago if not for Saket.

"I mean, it *is* pretty hot to be able to talk about people behind their backs in public in our own secret language," Rumi says.

"Eighty million people speak it. Hardly a secret language, love." Saket picks up another piece of mango from Rumi's slice of tart and pops it in his own mouth, and I'm filled with that sense of wholeness I only ever experience when I'm around my twin, even when he obviously wishes I wasn't here.

"True," Rumi says, "but that's not the point, is it?" Another spark passes between them before he switches personalities again and turns to me. "The point I was making with Mira was that you're practically perfect, Sak, and my parents are assholes."

His words hit me straight in a part of my heart that's raw and vulnerable. Excuses for my parents' homophobia leap to my tongue and fill me with shame. I push them away. He's happy. Isn't that all that matters? That and my brother coming to my wedding.

"Go ahead," Rumi says, studying me over his hand-glazed coffee cup. "Tell me I'm going to hell for not thinking of my parents as gods."

"I've never said that." I don't idolize our parents, but that doesn't mean I can erase all they've had to overcome to give us the life they did. Why is cutting them some slack until they come around such a terrible thing?

"You don't have to say the words, Mira. Your actions are as loud as a wail in the night."

"Dramatic much?" I say.

"Definitely dramatic," Saket says and rubs my shoulders. They've been feeling like rock, and they immediately relax.

"Don't you want Sak at your stupid wedding?" Rumi's glare is relentless.

"Of course I do. He's invited. You know how much I love him."

"I love you too." Saket gets up and stands behind me and starts to knead my shoulders in earnest. "What the hell have you been doing with these shoulders, sweetheart? They're concrete."

"You love him but not enough for him to be at your wedding as my fiancé." My brother is in that place where he's lost his ability to see past his feelings. When my patients are in this place where their pain imprisons them, it's my job to dig a hole through those walls and insert a breathing tube.

"Then come home. Maybe if you bring Sak home before the wedding, Aie and Baba will get a chance to know him."

"Right, and they'll fall in love with him the way they're in love with your straight-as-nails doctor. You're an idiot, Miru. And absurdly naive. They would poison his dinner. Then I'd die of a broken heart, and it would all be very Romeo and Juliet."

"Romeo and Julien. Or Ramu and Jay—the Indian gay version." Saket keeps burrowing circles into my deltoids with one hand even as he reaches out and strokes Rumi's puckered brow with the other.

"Plus they already told me I'm dead to them for being unnatural. So, no, I'm not coming to your wedding and pretending to be your *natural* brother."

I don't want him to pretend to be anything. I just want him to be there. "Can you imagine getting married without me there?" I ask. Until I was four, if you took me out of the same room as Rumi, I would scream and scream until I could see him again. They had to put us in separate preschools to train us to be apart. It took us half a year to stop crying all day for the other.

"I would absolutely understand if you chose not to come to my wedding because you're only allowed to be there if you pretend to be someone you're not." Rumi obviously had an easier time with our separation.

"Saket is invited," I say. "Why can't that be enough?"

"Because it's fucking not. Saket's not going to pretend to be your random friend. The only way we will be there is if Saket gets to be in every single one of those idiotic posed family photos with my hand around him or on his ass if I choose." He shoves his chair back and stands. "He will come as the other half of me or neither of us will."

I turn to Saket. Tears are running down his cheeks and into his perfectly lined-up stubble.

"Don't you dare say a single word," Rumi snaps at Saket, who closes his mouth and swallows what he's about to say. What he's said before, that Rumi should go to my wedding without him because this is about me and no one else. Then Rumi turns to me again. "When will you grow a spine, Mira?" There's so much disgust in his voice that I fold inward.

"Rooh!" Saket says. "Enough."

Without another word, Rumi storms to the front door and leaves the house, slamming it so hard the bells on the doorknob jangle in protest.

"I'm sorry," I say, and Saket wraps his arms around my shoulders. He smells of sandalwood and lavender, like cosmetics and hair product, but a little bit like my brother, too, as though he's soaked some of Rumi's spirit up.

"It will be okay, love. Everything will work out. Life has a way of falling into place."

"Do you really believe that?" I say.

"With my whole heart. The universe is magic. It's working to set things right. My dad used to say that. He had a theory that for centuries humans have tried to control the world by forcing everyone into matching molds by getting them to close their minds. It's why the pressure of discontent has turned humanity into a ticking bomb. The only way to defuse it is to change one heart at a time. Every time a single person opens their heart, the magic gets stronger. And your heart is one of the most beautiful, most wide-open ones I've ever known, Mira. You're filled with magic. All you have to do is let your fear go and believe."

His words pierce me. The word *magic* burrows deep into me, all the way to the part where I hold all my pain. All I know is what life has shown me. I want to believe, but I don't know how. This is the only way I know how to feel, as though this helplessness in the face of everyone else's pain is my story and it's the only one I'll ever get to live.

CHAPTER FIVE

New York is every single thing you said it would be," I say to Druv, and I sound so excited he chuckles. After spending most of the night tossing and turning because of the way I left things with Rumi, I'm determined to focus on Sak's words and look for the universe's magic. It's surprisingly easy in a city that seems to buzz with human energy. Even the buildings seem to be whispering to each other as they reach for the sky.

"I'm so happy for you, babe." Druv sounds exhausted, and my heart squeezes. Here I am, walking down Broadway, munching a bagel that sticks to the roof of my mouth like a yeasty cloud slathered in cream cheese with little bits of crunchy garlic. And everyone I love is in pain.

"Have you been doing your shoulder exercises?" I ask when I know the answer. Druv is as bad at being a patient as he is good at being a doctor. Ever since he injured his shoulder while wrestling in high school, it's been achy. Being a gym rat in college (his words, not mine) didn't help. He keeps all that under wraps because *who wants an orthopedic surgeon with an achy shoulder?*

He grumbles something about not having time. The thing about pain management is that treatments work better when the person in pain is the one doing the work to make it stop. This usually involves walking right into your pain to get to the other side. Often sitting on the edges of your pain, with the discomfort you're used to, is easier than digging into the unknown root of it where its unbearable intensity lives.

My patients can be divided into two groups: the kicking-and-screaming ones, and the let's-do-this ones. When it comes to his own ailments, Druv is most definitely a kicker-screamer.

"You just did a seven-hour surgery, Druv. Did you at least stretch before?" Our first date was a coffee setup orchestrated by our mothers after Druv and I ran into each other at a wedding and spent some time talking at the open bar. That was it. That had been enough encouragement for the Two Moms: us having a twenty-minute conversation, making lame jokes about the floral notes in the wedding wine, while politely catching up on our college experiences after having been casual acquaintances through middle and high school.

On our coffee date, Druv seemed to be holding his shoulder at an uncomfortable angle, and I asked him about it. He was surprised that I noticed, but seeking out pain in people is my superpower. Then he was even more surprised at himself for telling me about his injury and the constant pain.

"I need you to be here to do your woo-woo poke-me-like-a-pincushion thing," he says. "I miss you so much."

"Me too," I say, irrationally happy that acupuncture helps him enough that he's asking for it after how hard I had to work to convince him to try it. "I can set you up with someone else at the pain center."

"I'm not letting anyone else stab my shoulder, Mira. I can't risk my arm. And, well . . ." He clears his throat and whispers the next part. "You know I'm a big baby about needles."

I laugh. He is. He slices through the human body like a machine, but he can't watch needles go into his own shoulder. And he lets me see that vulnerable part of him without a whit of self-consciousness.

"Druv," I say. "I can find you someone who will help you through the trypanophobia."

"I already have someone who helps with it, and she's coming home to me in five days. We'll do it then. Now tell me your plan for today."

I don't push anymore. I know he won't trust anyone else with this, and I've been dying to tell him about my plans for today. "The top of the Empire State Building," I say, and I can't keep the excitement out of my voice.

It was supposed to be our trip's romantic kickoff, to start out with the most iconic part. I've never been up on the 102nd floor, with its 360-degree view of the city, but I feel like I have. I know the criss-crossing diamond-patterned railings that prevent people from flinging themselves off. I've looked through the binocular-viewers shaped like alien faces and identified the city's landmarks. I've felt the wind in my face as I waited like Meg Ryan for the man she's never met but who makes her feel exactly the way she was meant to feel when she was put on this earth.

Druv's chuckle brings me back to our conversation. He knows I've floated away. "God, I wish I could see your face right now," he says. "Go have fun. Take lots of pictures."

"You know I will. I'll try not to blow up your phone with them."

"Please please blow up my phone," he says. "I need something to sustain me through a triple spinal fusion."

I imagine him in surgery, every cell in his body focused on his work. I've observed him in the OR, and I think it's the hottest thing about him. "Deal," I say. "It is my duty to have fabulous experiences so I can share them with you and sustain you through your work."

"Such a giver," he says.

"Acts of service. It's how I show love."

He laughs. "I miss you, Mira. You're not allowed to love New York more than you love me, okay?"

"Never. New York doesn't look as hot as you in surgical scrubs."

"To be fair, who does?"

It's my turn to laugh. "I wish you were here," I say before I can stop myself.

There's an aching sweetness in his responding silence, and it's like we're both acknowledging something essential, another stitch we're weaving into the fabric of each other's lives and hearts.

"Mira." His voice is quiet now. "I promise we'll go back again, together. Maybe we'll make it a tradition. New York every spring."

"That sounds perfect," I whisper. Then I let him go and I speed up. The Empire State awaits.

I watched *An Affair to Remember* for the first time in my junior year of high school, when Rumi took a film appreciation class. The teacher was a fan of iconic romances, and Rumi and I became obsessed with them. *Buona Sera, Mrs. Campbell, From Here to Eternity, Pillow Talk, Come September, Roman Holiday*: we watched them over and over again, lost in the grayscale and comic-book-toned color images moving slow and intense. The deliberate movements, the close-ups highlighting every nuance of the large, hyperfocused emotions, all of it so pure and heartfelt and undistracted by the complex background imagery of today's movies.

I'd been especially felled by Deborah Kerr's simplicity and playfulness and how Cary Grant *saw* her. Like really saw her all the way down to her soul. I think Druv sees me that way, the way I want to be seen. It's why when he first showed an interest in me, I didn't run and hide, the way I've always done.

Suddenly the air around me tightens with energy, and a rightness fills my chest. I make my way across the intersecting crossroads that make up Times Square. The gigantic flashing billboards pull my attention in all directions at once. A smoky-eyed model winks as she bites into the plumpest strawberry with the glossiest, reddest lips. A bobtail rabbit does a cartwheel, and a vintage bottle of cola pops open as bubbles fizz and overflow down the thick, frosty glass. I turn a full circle like an enchanted princess in a Disney film, the billboards spinning magic around me.

In my head Cary Grant smiles knowingly at me as I hop onto the sidewalk over a manhole. My long knit skirt swishes around my cute leather boots as I leave Times Square behind and stride toward the Empire State Building. Meg Ryan tendrils of hair dance around my face as I walk and walk, skipping to dodge the crowds. I can feel it getting closer. My eyes sparkle like Deborah Kerr's when it comes into view. My gaze travels to the very top, where the ornate concrete rises in a steeple and crescendos into the iconic antenna. Christopher Reeve as Superman winks at me as he replants the antenna at the top of the tower.

I'm walking on air. Saket's words from yesterday spin in my head. The magic of the universe feels strong inside me. It spins like a tornado. I'm flying. Falling into myself. Then I'm actually falling. Knocked off my feet as something hurtles into me. A child. He comes at me out of nowhere, a torpedo that hits me above the knees, tipping me back on my butt, then tripping and landing on top of me.

Instinctively I wrap my arms around him, protecting him from hitting the pavement. I sit there, winded, my arms full of a strange child, my heart racing in my chest. He's laughing, black curls spilling around his face, big brown eyes crinkling in glee. He touches my face, and I pull my arms away. A sick sensation wobbles in the pit of my stomach. I usually avoid children. I'm not a fan of their smell, or the grime that sticks around their noses, or their fragility.

I don't take them on as clients. Their pain feels different, like I'm not enough to handle it.

A woman scoops him up, and relief floods through me.

"I'm so sorry," she says. "Kyle! I told you not to run. You hurt the lady."

The child throws his head back and tries to free himself from her hold. He's evidently not done with his sprint across New York City. "Kyle run!" he yells, completely unaffected by his mother's scolding, and the fact that I'm sitting on the pavement and a crowd has gathered around us.

"I'm fine," I say, trying to stand up. Pain shoots through my ankle when I put weight on it, but when I wiggle my foot, it eases.

The crowd starts to dissolve, disappearing like the possibility of this being any sort of real tragedy.

"You sure?" the woman asks as she squats in front of a stroller and tries to strap a wiggling Kyle into it. "That's enough! You stay in there until you calm down."

She's wearing a beige trench coat and red heels that I'm amazed she can squat in so gracefully.

"I'm sure," I say. "Those shoes are gorgeous!"

She smiles, and we both stand all the way up. Kyle starts screaming again. "Out! Out! Out!"

I can still feel his weight on me, and I try to push the feeling away.

"I really am sorry. He's usually not like this. He's just overstimulated," the woman says as Kyle's volume rises. "Let me help you?" She looks at my bag lying on its side on the ground.

Oh no! My stuff has spilled out. It's touching the gross pavement. "I'm fine," I say, again throwing a look at her shrieking child. "Please. I've got this."

She senses my discomfort at Kyle's screaming and leaves.

I'm still a little winded from the fall, but I squat next to my bag. Not a single person stops to help me. I should be offended, but there's something freeing about feeling this invisible. In Naperville I can rarely ever leave the house and not run into someone I know. I straighten the bag and dust it off. It's a beachy thing that Druv's mom got me for my birthday, made from plastic fished out of the world's oceans.

I pick up the lip balm and granola bars that have fallen out and toss them into the trash can next to me. My water bottle, also made from recycled aluminum cans, has rolled off and lodged itself against a lamppost. For a moment I consider not retrieving it and throwing the bottle away too. But what's the point of making the effort to buy recycled things if you're going to treat them the way people treat the things that cause the need for recycling, as disposable?

I can wash the bottle. I can take it to Rumi's place and run it through a dishwasher to disinfect it. I try not to think of all the gross things the ground it's lying on has seen. I try not to imagine dogs peeing and humans throwing up, but my mind takes a sweeping dive into all the unsavory visuals I'm trying to avoid. I steel myself and reach for it. My skin crawls when I pick it up. Then I forget everything else, because there's something shiny lying right under it.

I lean closer. It looks like a piece of jewelry. I look around, but no one spares me a glance as they hurry past. It's almost as though women in cute skirts routinely squat on the sidewalk and forage for things.

I try to pick it up, but it sticks. It's a ring made of gold, and it seems to be tethered to the base of the lamppost with a gold chain. I jimmy the chain and tug at it. After resisting me for a second, it pops out. And just like that, a ring and a chain sit in the palm of my hand.

I stand and pour all the water in my bottle over it, scrubbing with my fingers until the layer of dirt washes off. Then I dab the wetness against my skirt. The ring is a thick polished gold band with a notched, swirling, flame-like bezel that forms a pointy end that catches in the knit of my skirt and rips a few threads loose. It seems to have a piece missing. I look around for it and find nothing more. Maybe that notch in the bezel is part of the design, because as I study it, I realize that it doesn't appear broken. The workmanship is beautiful. I've never seen anything like it. The chain hanging from it is broken. Someone had to have been wearing it around their neck when they dropped it. Something about that image makes me melt.

The flashes of joy I've felt today, the ancient discomfort I've carried all my life, all of it pulses inside me in time with the slightly off kilter beating of my heart. I hold the ring up, and it frames the very tip of the Empire State Building's crown just as the sun slides red and fiery behind it. My breath catches. The moment stops around me. I can feel the earth spinning beneath my feet.

"Your ring is beautiful!" a man with a camera hanging around his neck says as he stops to admire it.

"Thank you," I say, pulling it back when he leans in to look at it more closely.

He reads something in my body language and backs up and walks away.

My heart is racing. "It's not mine," I whisper, but he's already out of earshot.

Whose is it? The words whisper in my ears.

I squeeze it in my hand and look up and down Fifth Avenue as humanity whizzes past me in all its mismatched yet cohesive glory. Couples holding hands, solitary people speaking animatedly into their headphones, everyone moving with purpose around everyone else.

Everything that just happened already in the past. Gone. Was I really just sitting on the pavement on my butt? Did a child just knock me down? Here, in the least child-friendly place on earth. A place that should be no more than a concrete jungle but is filled with stories of romance and human connection. All these things that shouldn't fit but do. The ring and chain dig into my palm. I open my hand and let the ring dangle on the chain. A ring on a chain: two more things that shouldn't make sense together but do.

I squeeze my eyes shut, and every romantic comedy moment I've ever escaped into fills me. Something slides down my spine, something urgent and ravenous. The anger in my brother's eyes when he talks to me, the love that spins around Saket and him when they're near each other. The infinite chasm between those two versions of him.

The kind of discontent I've never allowed myself to feel scrapes underneath my skin.

Why did I find it? Why me?

The ring hangs from my hand, the oddest glow emanating from it, like an answer I can't interpret.

I'm not someone given to wanting. Wanting things always leads to hurt. I've avoided it with all I'm worth my entire adult life. Now it grips me, fills me from the tips of my toes to the crown of my head. I want to know where the ring came from. I have to know.

CHAPTER SIX

Vasudha Patil
Garware Ladies Hostel
Fergusson College, Pune, India
January 1983

Sureva Bhalekar
St. Mary's Ladies Hostel
Charni Road, Bombay, India

Dear Suru,

Last night I dreamed that you lost your ring and I woke up so scared because it felt like we had lost each other. It was one of those dreams that feel no different from reality and the sensation in my heart was exactly the same as when we both moved to college, when we were separated from each other for the first time in our lives. I had to remind myself that unlike our rings, our friendship isn't something that can just slip from us. You were right, living in different cities for a few years can't be bigger than a friendship that started when we were born.

I do wish I liked living in Pune as much as you like living in Bombay. I'm sitting at my window as I write to you and looking out at the street and Pune feels so ordinary now. Remember how awestruck we were when my appa first visited the city? I think we were five. When he got home, we jumped and jumped until he let us sit on his lap, you and me on each side, and he told us how truly big the big cities were. How the roads were coated with black tar that turned sticky in the afternoon sun and smelled of coal and metal, how lamps hung along the streets on high poles, and how water flowed out of bronze taps at will? All of it sounded to us like stories he was making up.

And yesterday I got a letter from my aie which was filled with nothing but her complaining about how the water in the house had to be shut off for some repairs. She seems to have completely forgotten that there was no running water in our village just ten years ago. Remember when that Tanaji plumber came to lay pipes and installed a tap over the drain in the kitchen and a toilet in the main house and in your quarters? We followed him around and watched him work the entire time.

Remember how scared I was to squat over the new ceramic hole-in-the ground toilet and you couldn't stop laughing at me? But then you showed me how and I stopped being scared. How quickly we forgot what life was like before water came to us through pipes and electricity through wires. Now my aie acts like the sky is falling on her head when it's gone for a few hours.

I suppose I'm no different because I just called Pune ordinary.

How big it seemed in Appa's stories—like a foreign country. Now look at us. I'm here at one of the biggest colleges in the world and you're in Bombay, where everything about Pune must feel small to you. Is everything in life a matter of scale? Is anything actually large or small?

I dream of visiting you in Bombay some day. I dream of seeing all the friends you write about. Thanks for sending those pictures in your last letter. I love the one from your visit to the Taraporewala Aquarium. The statue of the shark made me laugh. How do you think they got the fish into the tanks? They had to have put them in other tanks and then put those on trucks and driven them to the aquarium then transferred them from tank to tank. Your scientist brain had to have asked that question the moment you entered the aquarium. I'm right, am I not?

You keep asking in your letters why I haven't made any friends yet. Why do you ask when you know the answer? You know how that goes for me. The girls who sound like us, like village girls, are too scared to talk to me because they're from where we're from and they already know how big a man Appa is in our district and they assume I'm a spoilt brat with my nose up in the air. The ones who wear Western dresses and Hindi-movie saris and speak English are embarrassed by the way I speak and dress. Or maybe I'm the one who's embarrassed. I know that's what you'd say. You'd purse your lips and furrow your brow and you'd scold me for projecting my feelings on others. You'd tell me to be more bold. So I've done it myself, pretended to be you as I scold myself in your voice. I supposed I'm not used to being you for me by myself yet, even after two years apart.

I can see you shake your head at my silliness. But you're smiling, aren't you? Making you smile used to be the best part of my day. Now the best part of my day is writing to you and looking at the photos you send me.

I know it isn't cheap to take photographs and have them processed and I have to be patient until the roll is finished. But I'm including twenty rupees so you can buy more film rolls. Please don't be angry with me for sending money. I know you have a scholarship and a stipend, but I also know you send everything you can to your aie. Appa and my aie keep sending me things and food and I don't have anyone here to share it with. I'm sending you one of the two salwar suits Aie had stitched for me. Green looks better on you than me. I look like a giant raw mango in green. And there are rava laadoos. Please don't share those. Those are just for you. I'll send more next time and you can give some to your friends. Even to Varsha, who is in all your pictures. Does she like rava laadoos as much as we do? Do you know the things she likes to eat? Don't frown. I'm happy that you've made new friends. I really am. Who can resist you, Suru?

Fine, I'll stop being cranky now. I'm probably only being this way because of the cold. I dislike Pune in the winter. Why is it so cold here? But don't worry, I have a woolen blanket that the Home Minister sent Appa from Delhi. Appa says the Pune cold is nothing compared to the Delhi cold. Does Bombay get cold at least in December? Actually, I know you will not tell me because you think I'll send the blanket to you.

And I know what you're thinking—how will I know if you're cold if you don't tell me? You know I always know when you lie (but there's also the *Times of India* that I can check for the Bombay weather). Actually why am I asking you? I'm going to put this letter away and go to the library to find out how cold Bombay is.

See, you did what you always try to do: got me to leave the house (or my hostel room in this case). I do try, you know. I try to do the things that would make you proud of me. Like studying (it's just not as easy for us mere mortals as it is for the brilliant science scholar Sureva Bhalekar), and trying to enjoy it (who other than you enjoys filling their brain with overly complicated information?), and going outdoors (where I'll only get dark and then Aie will cane me before washing me in milk and baking soda until the tan washes off), and keeping up with my music (but what's the point? Aie and Appa will kill me if I sing outside the house).

Turns out you were right, my life is a prison. You thought if I studied and let Appa send me to Fergusson College I'd leave the prison behind. But can we ever leave our prisons behind? They built them into us. It's all they've ever done from the day we were born, turn us into our own prison cells. It didn't work with you. But you know it worked with me. I know you wish it hadn't. I know you wish I was stronger, cleverer. But at least I made it here. I never would have if I hadn't believed that you would be here with me. You were supposed to be here with me. I'm not angry that you went to Bombay instead. I'm really not. Like everything else, I just wish it weren't so.

I wish I were you, Suru. I know you hate to hear me say it, but all I've ever wanted was to be you. To hide away in your shadow. Sometimes I think that's the problem. That I never learned to live as separate from you and I don't know how to change that. We're like our rings. They were forged to fit together. Now we've separated them and each one just looks and feels odd without the other half. Sometimes I stare at my half and I'm filled with a sense of its incompleteness. Then I think of you wearing your half and everything falls back in place. You do wear yours, don't you? I know you do. I know it's not actually lost.

Now, don't be sad because I said all this. Please. I'm not sad, I promise. This is the happiest of moments because I'm writing to you. If I don't say these things and remove them from my heart and hand them to you the way I've always done, they'll turn to acid inside me and eat my flesh. So, thank you for letting me.

All right, now I must go to the library and check on the temperature in Bombay.

Yours lovingly,

Your friend,

Vasu

CHAPTER SEVEN

I cannot believe you posted that video on social media! What the hell is wrong with you, Miru?" Rumi says, his livid tone even more over the top than usual. His oversize lemur eyes—nearly identical to mine—are practically popping out of his skull.

"What else was I supposed to do? I know this ring is special, and I want to return it to the person it belongs to." I squeeze the ring, and the cool, heavy metal digs into the palm of my hand in the most satisfying way.

Rumi's eyes roll all the way up into his head. "There is absolutely no way on earth you could possibly know that there's anything special about that stupid ring."

But I do know it. I can feel something. I feel different since I found it. I can't even get myself to put it down. "Can you think of anything more romantic than a ring on a chain, Rumi? Remember Amamma used to wear one?"

Rumi groans and starts pacing across his beautiful kitchen as though he really needs to get away from me but doesn't know how. "Our grand-aunt? She was a mean old witch who told me I was going to burn in hell because I tried on Aie's lipstick. When I was eight!"

"True, but she was only mean and bitter because she had her heart broken when her husband died in the war." I press the ring to my chest, and Saket pats my arm. He seems to be on my side, even though his gaze bounces between Rumi and me like someone's tearing him in half.

"The man probably went to war only to get away from the nasty old crone."

"Rumi! She never married again, and she wore his wedding ring on a chain for the rest of her life. Her children spread her ashes in the Krishna River, where her husband's ashes were. It was her dying wish." When our mother told us the story, it made me cry so hard I remember having a headache for days. Rumi had been so kind to me then. He'd always been kind to me whenever I had what our parents called my *oversensitivity episodes*.

He isn't kind now. "How are you such an idiot?" He turns to Saket. "How can my twin be so dumb? How do we share the same DNA?" When Saket glares at him, albeit gently, as though he empathizes with the pain of having a dumb twin, Rumi turns his glare on me again. "You're getting threatening messages from psychopaths, and you're here spinning all these fantasies. Best of times you're too afraid to do anything, and this is where you decide to be reckless? How can you not understand what a brutal jungle social media is?"

How could he not understand that this isn't about social media? It's about the ring. "It's a ring on a chain! They're not fantasies. No one wears a ring on a chain unless it's special. A love of a lifetime." No one can convince me that wearing a ring on a chain around your neck isn't the most romantic thing. There's no greater symbol of longing and loss, of love cherished beyond its earthly existence. I can still remember the ring of hearts that hung around our great-aunt's neck. So what if on the outside she was the most unromantic human in all the world? True love and cynicism can coexist in this world. It's one of the universe's great ironies, and my brother here is another great example of it.

"More likely someone was running away from an abusive partner and wanted to get rid of it. More *Sleeping with the Enemy* than *An Affair to Remember*. They probably spat on it as they tossed it away."

Saket makes a pained sound. "You are one damaged little boy, aren't you, baby?"

Rumi lets out a long-suffering sigh. I know he's angry with me for reasons that have nothing to do with the ring or my posted video. Which, by the way, only went viral because it was so heartfelt and real. I wish he'd be reasonable and help me find the owner.

"Can you just hand the damn ring over to the cops and be done with it?" he says a little too meanly. At least he doesn't say *Keep it like you want to*, the way so many other eye-rolling cynics on the internet have.

"No one who's forced into an unpleasant relationship wears a ring on a chain. There's a broken chain attached to it. See! It reeks of love." I hold the ring with its ripped-apart chain in his face. That means it meant something to the wearer! I know the person is going to see the ring and reach out. I just know it. "Also, it couldn't have been that long since they lost it. It was dusty, but it hadn't been lying on that pavement for that long. Saket, who's an expert, said it was recently polished. Right, Saket?"

Saket gives my arm another pat and takes the ring from me. "It is a beautiful piece." He sits down at the mosaic dining table, unable to hide his reverence. "Definitely created by one of the old masters. Possibly dating back to the last century, possibly with some sort of royal lineage."

Rumi harrumphs.

Saket throws him a warning glance. "I know my work, Rooh. Don't be scoffing at my two master's degrees, in art history and design. I've handled antique jewelry from the day I was born."

Before Rumi can say something rude, I cut him off. "Is there any way to find out where it came from? Like the name of a jeweler or a marking or logo? If we can find the jeweler, maybe they keep records of customers."

Saket twists it between his fingers and holds it up against the light, studying it again, and ignores Rumi, who resumes his pacing. "It's definitely crafted in India, and it dates back to the early 1900s, based on the hue of the gold and the wear on the metal, even though it's been recently polished. As for the design, I've only seen one other piece that resembles this one, and based on the difference in the cut on the inner and outer rim, and the puzzle-like flame bezel, I'm pretty sure it's part of an interlocking set."

I gasp. "Why didn't you tell me that before?"

"Because I had to look up the details some more." He throws my brother a quick glance to make sure he isn't melting down over the betrayal. "Also, you're kinda right." He clears his throat and lowers his voice. "I agree that wearing a ring on a chain is the most romantic thing ever. And if it's an interlocking ring, there's another piece just like it somewhere else in the world." His eyes sparkle in the exact way I'm feeling, and we both let out identical sighs and leave the last part unsaid. Somewhere out there, someone else is wearing the other half.

Rumi grabs his head with both hands and lets out the longest, most pained grunt. He loves the theater so much that he left his job as an architect to work on designing sets. He can be very dramatic.

He whips out his phone (very dramatically) and turns the phone toward Saket and me. "Have you two forgotten these messages?"

He starts flipping through the horrid messages I've gotten in response to my post since I sent it out last afternoon. Of course he took screenshots and sent them to himself precisely so he can rub them in my face.

"Psycho One: 'What you've done is stolen someone's ring. Women like you deserve to be'—I can't even get myself to read the rest. What the hell is wrong with this person?" Rumi's eyes fill with despair.

I get it. People can be horrid, and Rumi has suffered the worst of it when he was cyberbullied in high school. But this is not the same thing.

He isn't done, of course. He's just settling into stage-reading the messages. He's even doing voices.

"Psychopath Two: 'That's mice. I dropd it.'" He's pronouncing the shortened and misspelled words exactly the way they're spelled. "Mira: 'Hello there. Could you tell me what the inscription says?'

"Psycho Two: 'Bitch. Frst U stills ring. ThN U'—the letter *U*—'wants 4'—the number four—'me to tell. Gv'—that's a *G* and

V—'Back.'" Rumi's on a roll now. He moves on to the next one, then the next.

"Psychopath Twenty-One: 'I can do things to you with that ring that will make you scream.'" Rumi raises his hands. "I don't even know what he means by that."

I shrug. "I don't want to know. How does it matter?" It is not fun to read people's rage fantasies directed at you for absolutely no reason. It's been shocking, actually. But not hurtful, per se, because I can't take it personally. And because there are also hundreds of lovely emotional messages that prove that people still care. I'm choosing to focus on those.

"You've received four hundred responses. In less than twenty-four hours. What is wrong with this world?" Rumi asks as though I'm in any way qualified to answer that question. He reads off another particularly ugly message.

"Stop it, Rooh," Saket says. "Quit being a jerk."

"*I'm* being a jerk? Did I write these heinous things? Did I open myself up to an attack like this?"

"All I want is to find the person the ring belongs to. Social media just happens to be the way to reach the most people."

"Of course! So simple!" He smacks his forehead and bats his eyelashes and pouts in what I know is his entirely offensive, not to mention inaccurate, imitation of me. "It's my first trip to the Big Apple, and guess what happens?" He raises the pitch of his voice in what he thinks is an impression of me on the video I posted. "Here I am walking along, and I fall, like actually butt plant. I'm lucky I didn't break my ankle falling on those heels. My stuff scatters all over, and as I'm gathering it up, what do I find?" He pauses breathlessly. "This am-AY-zing ring. Isn't it gorgeous!" He sniffs and pretends to tear up. "And it's on a chain! Isn't that the most romantic thing ever? I'd love to reunite you with it if it's yours. Oh, and it has an inscription on it. Message me with what that is, and let's meet." He signs off with blowing kisses. He really should move from the back of the theater to the stage.

"I did not blow kisses. You're being totally offensive right now." Despite myself, my eyes fill with tears. Only Rumi can do this to me. Make me cry at the drop of a hat. Will I always feel four years old around him?

"I'm being offensive? What if one of these psychos finds you?" His eyes sparkle with moisture too. When he was the victim of cyberbullying in high school, it ended with a mob attacking him outside our parents' store. He had three broken ribs and a ruptured lung, and our parents refused to believe him when he said it was premeditated and planned on the internet, or even to press charges. Actually, they refused to talk about it. Period. They didn't want bad publicity for the store.

Rumi has always believed that they thought he deserved it and that they hoped the incident would teach him a lesson. Make him see that there are "consequences" to what they've always seen as his choices.

My heart hurts. I can see his beaten-up face, the purple skin around his swollen-shut eye, like it was yesterday. I understand why he hates social media, why he detests our hometown. I'd hate it, too, if I let myself. But unlike him, I haven't been able to leave. Our parents have no one else, and despite everything, I can't abandon them in their most vulnerable years. Baba is a heart patient, and Aie can't get around without assistance. None of that has anything to do with what I'm doing. My quest to use the internet to find the ring's owner is completely unrelated to what happened to Rumi.

"How could you knowingly open yourself up to attack like this?" There's so much anguish in his voice, I almost apologize and offer to take the post down. But before I can respond, the doorbell rings, startling us.

Saket jumps and lets out a squeak and presses a hand to his mouth.

Rumi turns to him with unabashed suspicion. "Are we expecting a package?"

Color spreads across Saket's face under his perfectly applied bronzer. "Um . . . ," he mumbles, wringing his hands in the most uncharacteristic way. "I . . . okay, this isn't how it looks. Maybe I didn't think this through. But you have to trust me that my intentions were good."

Rumi looks like he wants to do several things, none of which involve trusting anyone. "What did you do?"

"Excuse me!" Saket says. "Do not take that tone with me."

The last thing I want is for the two of them to fight because of me.

"Please," I say to Rumi, and he all but snarls at me to butt out.

"Someone contacted me about the ring." Saket raises his chin but doesn't quite achieve the indignation he's going for.

"The ring?" both Rumi and I say at once.

Just like that, Saket's moment of nervousness passes, and he presses a hand into his waist as if to tell us to stop our nonsense. "Yes, the one Mira found. The one she wants to return to the owner. Which, by the way, I think is very sweet." He smiles at me, overtly ignoring Rumi. "I want that for you too, sweetheart."

I take a step closer to him and squeeze his arm. "Thanks."

"What did you do?" Rumi asks again, tone ice cold. He's nothing if not a dog with a bone when it comes to being pissed off.

Saket somehow manages to look both placating and scolding at once. "Well, it's someone I know. I met him at a wedding. He's my mom's friend's sister's son's friend. And he . . . he can help us find the owner of the ring."

Rumi makes a sound that manages to be both a groan and a growl. "How did he know to reach out to you?"

The doorbell rings again.

Rumi storms toward the door, and Saket grabs his arm. "This is someone I know, and you will not be rude to him in our home."

"I'll get it," I say. "Please, Rumi, calm down." I rush past them down the long corridor and pull open the door. The smell of skunk washes over me. And I'm fully aware what smells of skunk, despite the protests of those who don't agree that it does. It's a smell I know well from having grown up with Rumi, and combined with the memories and feelings his anger is digging up, it triggers a bout of my worst teenage anxiety. I feel unsteady on my feet.

The man standing there gives a pursed-lipped smile. I wonder if he's heard the entire fight inside, but he looks too bored to care. He's wearing a faded gray Henley and jeans frayed at the knees. But it's not in a fashion statement sort of way. His jaw is covered in stubble. But it's not the sexy groomed kind. More someone who hasn't bothered to shave. His hair, grown out all the way down to his shoulders, is thick and curly, but it doesn't seem to have met a hairbrush recently. Dark aviators cover his eyes, so I don't know how I know that he's studying me and picking up all my thoughts, but I do.

"Hello, Mira," he says in a voice so bass and polished it takes me a moment to reconcile it with the rest of him.

I startle out of my study. "How do you know my name?"

His hands stay where they are, dug into his pockets. "Four hundred thousand people know your name. That's how viral posts work." His flat tone is like a splash of ice water.

I have an entirely uncharacteristic urge to kick him in the shins and slam the door in his face.

Behind me Saket clears his throat, and I turn around. Rumi and Saket have come up behind me.

"Sak," the man says over my shoulder. "Thanks for setting this up." He finally pulls a hand out of his pocket and reaches over me to shake Saket's hand.

"Of course," Saket says. "Come on in."

He does come on in, squeezing past me when I don't move out of the way.

"This is Krish," Saket throws out before leading the way into the living room.

The man slips off his white sneakers at the door without untying his laces and follows without bothering to remove his sunglasses or waiting for me and Rumi to acknowledge the introduction.

Saket invites him to sit, and he drops into the linen couch. Rumi and I fold our arms across our chests striking identical poses, and it makes Saket smile. He turns to Krish. "It's good to see you. But this is where I step out of the picture, okay? Mira gets to decide if she wants to do this or not."

"Wants to do what?" Rumi and I say together. Our twin thing has a way of popping up at the most inopportune times, so naturally it's in overdrive right now.

Saket and the man named Krish look at each other. I've never watched *Survivor*, but I've heard of alliances, and that word pops into my head.

"I think I can help you find the ring's owner," Krish says. The heavy texture and refined clip of his voice that was so jarring a moment ago clicks in place and settles into him as he makes the claim. His tone is so casually confident it's almost insouciant, like he has every right to be here, be anywhere he wishes to be.

Without meaning to I find myself leaning in to listen, because obviously there's more.

When he says the next part, it's with the kind of sense of entitlement I've rarely ever encountered before. He looks straight at me and says, "But I have conditions."

CHAPTER EIGHT

There's something especially annoying about a person who clearly wants something from you but acts like you're the one who needs their help.

It's obvious Krish Hale is the kind of person who thinks he's doing the world a favor simply by existing. He's sitting there with his legs stretched out, leaning into all those gorgeous embroidered silk cushions as though they've been laid out just for him.

His comfort in his place in the world is vaguely familiar. I've seen it before, I just can't remember where. And I have no idea why it's annoying me this much.

"Why do you think you can help me find the ring's owner?" I ask as Rumi, Saket, and I settle into the sectional across from him. He seems unmoved by the breathtaking beauty of their home, and that takes even more points off. At least the skunky weed smell hasn't followed him into the house.

"Because I've been a reporter in New York City for several years. And I know how to follow a trail."

"Fine, then tell me where you would go first with this trail."

He laughs. *Laughs!* "Sure. I can't wait to. But as I said, I have conditions."

"He did say he had conditions," Saket says.

Rumi is still glowering like he's the hero of a gothic novel. Although honestly, I've never understood why gothic heroes brood quite so much.

At least with Rumi, I know why he glowers. He hasn't said a word, and I want him to keep it that way.

He doesn't. "I can't believe you're encouraging Mira in this nonsense. How much do you even know this guy?" he says to Saket as though the guy in question isn't sitting right there.

I'm not sure I like the idea of Saket bringing a stranger into this without asking me. But I like what Rumi just said even less. "I'm not a child who gets carried away with a little encouragement."

"To be fair, how much does anyone really know anyone?" Saket says.

"He's literally a total stranger!" Rumi says.

"Sak and I have met," the stranger says even though no one asked him. "At least I'm pretty sure it was Sak. You were at Mini Patel's daughter's wedding, correct?"

"Yes! Beautiful wedding!" Saket says. "Great lehenga."

"Sure," the guy says. "Purple with yellow peacocks."

Saket sits up, clearly impressed. "My God, you're right! Although that purple was a bit dark for a morning wedding, now that it's coming back to me. How on earth do you remember? It was five years ago."

"Photographic memory," Krish says the way someone else might say *diabetes* while turning down chocolate cake. When they aren't particularly fond of chocolate, or cake.

"Do you remember what the groom was wearing?" Saket asks excitedly.

"A yellow sherwani with purple palm trees," the guy says without missing a beat and without any visible signs of humor or irony. He looks South Asian, but he says the word *sherwani* with a heavy East Coast drawl, and again it bothers me more than it should. There's nothing more annoying than an Indian person who thinks they're not. That's when it strikes me: the thing that's been *off* about this guy is that he looks South Asian but something about his demeanor, the way he talks, the way he holds himself, doesn't match that.

Saket practically bounces in his seat. "Yes! Oh my gosh, I remember now. It was that whole birds-on-the-bride, trees-on-the-groom theme. A little obvious, even for a nature motif, if you ask me. But you'd love it, Rooh, with your obsession with symbolism."

Rumi is about to burst the vein popping ominously in his forehead. He glares at Saket like he can't believe they're having this conversation. For the first time in a very long time, I agree with my brother.

"What are your conditions?" I say quickly before Saket causes my brother's head to explode with more talk of wedding dress themes.

Krish turns to me. Again, without a whit of gratitude or humor. "I want to be part of the search. That's my condition."

I'm confused. Obviously if he's going to help me find the owner of the ring, he's going to be part of the search.

He picks up on my confusion and leans forward and places his elbows on his knees. I have the urge to ask him to remove his sunglasses. I hadn't realized how much I hate not being able to study eyes. How much I count on them to get a read on people so I know what to do with them.

"That's it. We track down the owner together." There's the subtlest pause. "And I get to do a story about it."

Ah. Now it makes sense. He wants to write about it. He wants to use the story to further his career.

"No, thank you," I say. I know for sure that I don't want this to turn into something to squeeze mileage out of. It feels personal, getting this ring back in the hands of the person who wore it on a chain, possibly for years, based on how old Saket says the ring is. I feel oddly protective. Not that anyone would understand that. Plus, the Salvis shun the media.

Back when my parents first started to work at Bombay Masala, the local newspaper did a story about the "awful curry smell" in the store. It was the nineties, so saying ugly things about ethnic communities was perfectly acceptable and pretty ubiquitous. The store owner threatened to fire my parents, but then Naperville's Indian community got livid and fought back and thronged the store and made the paper apologize. But my family embraced the fear of the media like second nature. They also embraced an industrial exhaust system and every form of deodorizing spray, candle, and incense. Bombay Masala now smells like a Bath & Body Works with a hint of cumin.

Putting my video on social media isn't the same thing. That was me trying to reach as many people as possible to maximize the chances of reuniting the ring with its owner. That doesn't mean I'm going to let some journalist turn it into a piece of entertainment.

"May I ask why?" Krish says without much feeling.

I shrug, mirroring his nonchalance. I never, ever dislike people on sight. I'm almost embarrassed by how much this guy rubs me the wrong way.

He keeps looking at me from behind those aviators, and the rudeness of someone who wears sunglasses indoors is taking everything else over. "I have no reason to believe you can actually help me."

He pauses, thoughtfully weighing my accusation. "I found you, didn't I? No one else has found you after that post, correct? Although I'm guessing there's hundreds of responses with people wanting to meet you to see, or steal, the ring."

Rumi gives me a pointed look, and the reason for his worry descends on me in one fell swoop. Maybe putting that video out wasn't the safest thing to do.

Saket reaches over and squeezes my hand. He's looking curious, but he remains silent, so I bite. "How did you find me?"

Krish considers that for a long moment, as though pondering whether or not to share his investigative tricks with me. The urge to kick his shins returns.

"I simply dug through your social media until I found someone you're friends with who I could trace a connection to. Saket and you follow each other on all platforms, and you comment on each other's stuff a lot. And Saket and I happened to have a few common friends. It's New York."

"Plus we're both desis. All desis know each other, am I right?" Saket says. "Over a billion people and usually, like, what, four degrees of separation? Six at the most."

Krish gives a tight smile that reinforces my sense of his discomfort with his heritage.

"Do you see how creepy this is?" I say. "You stalked me instead of just reaching out and offering to help."

"I'm here in your friend's home. Even with a personal connection, you're still saying no. Why would you have picked me as the one to believe from the hundreds of trolling messages?"

"So, you didn't even try."

"I believe in working smart. I don't waste my time on dead ends. Which is why you need me. I'm guessing you're only here for a few days and you need to get back to Naperville and your wedding preparations."

He probably throws that in to make some sort of point about social media and how easy it is for people to know everything about you. Well, duh. That's hardly news.

But I do need to get back. It's my third day in New York. Thus far all I've seen is Times Square and the pavement outside the Empire State Building, which my butt got to become intimately acquainted with. I can't bring myself to care. All I want is to find the ring's owner before going back home. That gives me two and a half days, but this guy doesn't need to know any of that.

"Maybe," I say. "But I do have another question. Why would you go through all this trouble to seek me out? Why is the ring important to you?"

His jaw tightens. Without access to his eyes, I have no way of knowing what that means.

"I already told you. It's not the ring. It's the story." He points his phone in my general direction. "It's you. Well-meaning midwesterner becomes obsessed with a lost ring she finds in the big city. This seems to matter to you. And that's irresistible to the audience these days. Everyone wants everything to matter, and yet nothing matters to anyone for more than moments. At least not in any meaningful way. Then there's the fact that you're brown. So the diversity checkbox checks." He smiles in that way where a smile isn't a smile but a raised middle finger.

"I'm from Chicago," I say, and it's infuriating how indignant that comes out. "Not quite the country mouse in the big city."

His expression doesn't change. Apparently Chicago *is* the country to him.

"Well, it was nice meeting you," I say with a smile. I am a midwesterner, after all, and I *will* be nice, damn it. "I'd rather do this without turning it into clickbait. Or ticking any checkboxes." Or having my parents kill me. I'm already starting to dread their reaction when they find out about the social media post.

This time when his jaw tightens, I know it's frustration. But he doesn't push. "May I at least look at the ring?" he asks after a long pause. His voice is soft, and for the first time I feel like I glimpse the human being behind all that swagger.

I want to say no, but that entirely unexpected flash of nervousness stops me. Even with the rude sunglasses I recognize the pursing of his lips. It's the face of someone who's being stoic in the presence of pain. Until a second ago, this person seemed untouchable, unreachable. Now I sense a blast of emotion like a shark senses blood in the water. It's only a drop, barely even there. I've never ignored it, this inner gauge I have for suffering. I pull the ring from my pocket and put it in front of him on the lacquered mahogany coffee table.

He doesn't pick it up immediately. There's the barest tremor in his fingers when he reaches for it. I'm trained to pick up the nuances of discomfort from a person's body, and his is screaming discomfort right now. At least a six on the pain scale.

It's like I just jumped from not being able to read him at all to learning a new language. The language of the jaw and mouth instead of the eyes.

Finally he touches it. Not tentatively but like someone who refuses to be intimidated by something. He picks it up and runs his finger along the sharper edge. The interesting thing about the ring is that the two rims are different. One is sharp and flat, and the other is rounded. It's subtle yet unique. Once Saket pointed it out, it was obvious that another ring is meant to fit against the flat part and snap into the curved notch like a jigsaw puzzle. He turns it around and finds the inscription, which looks like a scribble of three vertical lines and one diagonal line. Even with Saket's help I haven't been able to decipher what it might mean.

"Thanks," Krish says and puts it back on the table. Quickly, like suddenly it's too hot to hold.

Then with nothing more than a bye, he gets up, slips his shoes back on, and leaves.

"That wasn't weird at all," Rumi says, and Saket makes a sound of agreement.

I'm barely listening. Because from my perch on the couch I can see him through the window as he jogs down the steps. I slip behind the half-open curtains. He doesn't turn around and look at the house. He seems too lost inside his head to check if he's being watched. As soon as he leaves the front yard and crosses the street, his entire demeanor changes.

He squeezes his forehead with his fingers. For almost an entire minute he stands there like that, head squeezed. If I hadn't just met him, I'd think he was a man who'd lost something precious. When he finally drops his hand, his body goes limp, his limbs letting whatever he's just felt go. For a moment I think he's going to come back to the house, to persuade me, to push harder. He doesn't.

He walks away, just like that, leaving me wondering if I was wrong in my judgment. The search for the ring obviously does mean something to him. Then why act like it doesn't? I guess I'll never know, because there is no way I'm chasing him down to call him back.

CHAPTER NINE

Sureva Bhalekar
St. Mary's Ladies Hostel
Charni Road, Bombay
February 1983

Vasudha Patil
Garware Ladies Hostel
Fergusson College, Pune

Dear Vasu,
I hope this letter finds you in good health and spirits.

I cannot believe you sent me a woolen blanket. How could you? I've asked you before to stop sending me things and you promised to listen. I thought we kept our promises. And if that's not enough reason, here are some more reasons why you shouldn't have:

1) *Weather.* Bombay is only cold for three days in a year. If that. Pune is cold all winter. Which is why Appa-saheb acquired the blanket for you.

2) *Space.* Bombay has no space, ergo the hostel dorms are tiny. I share one cupboard with seven girls.

Now I have the blanket and I don't have any place to put it.

3) *Economics (and Nutrition).* You know I don't have the money to send it back to you. You too should not be spending so much money sending me packages. The laadoos were delicious (but unnecessary). Your aie sends you the laadoos because your blood sugar drops when you don't eat. You live by yourself now. You have to be the one to take care of yourself. Our aies and I cannot be the ones doing that anymore. What if you have a hypoglycemic episode? Do any of your friends know what to do when you black out?

Now on to other things:

1) *Debt.* What will happen when Appa-saheb finds out that you no longer have the blanket? Your father is already paying for my college and has paid for my entire education. I cannot take more charity from your family. You know I have to return it all someday and I will, but if you keep adding to it, it's going to keep getting harder to repay the debt. And until I've repaid it we can never be equals. I understand the village girls in your college who are scared to talk to you because they know who your father is. I wish I didn't understand them, but I do.

2) *Health.* I wish you'd send me photos instead of laadoos. I wish the photos I sent didn't make you sad. I wish we weren't miles apart, but the photos are my way of removing the distance that separates us. Stop sending me money for film and save it for a camera. And, yes, Varsha is my friend but that's not why she's in the photos. It's because the photographs come from her camera. She just makes duplicate copies and lets us pay for them when her uncle's photo studio in

King's Circle processes them. Also, the term "friendship" is what we call in light theory a spectrum: every component of the beam is not equal. Some parts of the spectrum are brilliant, blinding, can vaporize you with their intensity. Others simply exist to make the brilliant parts bearable.

3) *Education.* I know you don't enjoy studies. But you *are* cleverer than anyone I know. It's in everything you do. You have this ability, Vasu, to understand and to grasp things even those who claim to be scholars can't. People like me, we can fill our heads with facts and hopefully someday that can help us fix material things. We might make things that make the world easier to live in, but people like you create a world that's better for us to live in. You see people. You don't believe what you're told about them, about how you should feel about others and about yourself. I know that causes you pain, but you have the courage to do it despite that. If there's anyone who isn't in a prison it's you because your mind is free and it's untrainable, unchainable, unmoldable. If I may dare to speak the truth, I find that terrifying. I lie awake some nights thinking about things you say and I'm afraid of what could happen if someone found out that you can think like that, in ways that could destroy the world it's taken them millennia to build and keep in their control.

You think I'm the brave one. But I'm a coward. I'm terrified of them finding out all that you hold inside you. And yet I want everyone to know all the things that seem so naturally possible inside your mind no matter how hard they try to snuff them out.

Don't let them see, Vasu. Protect yourself. For me if not for yourself. Because I cannot live in a world where you've been hurt.

(Sorry, I digressed from the subtopic of Education. But the words just wouldn't stop. I should white them out but I can't.)

4) *Music.* I'm sending you the name and address of a certain Mrs. Ashatai Athavale. She is a music teacher who runs a music school out of her home on Prabhat Road. She's Varsha's sister and she can be trusted. She teaches several girls whose parents do not want them to learn music and is discreet about it. I've also included a telephone number. If you decide to telephone her, remember to use a public phone booth. If you use the hostel phone, the number will show up on the phone bill that will be sent to your parents.

Please go to her, Vasu. She is expecting you. Please keep singing. When you sing, the world makes sense.

5) *Miscellaneous.* You're obviously worried about the ring. I wish you hadn't given it to me. It belonged to your grandmother and if Appa-saheb and your aie found out that you had parted with it they would be hurt. If my aie found out, she would kill me. As it is, she feels buried under the weight of everything your family has done for us. If they hadn't taken her in and given her a job when she was eighteen and still wet from bearing me, she wouldn't have been able to feed us.

You know how afraid my aie was of me coming to Bombay to study. She's been waiting for something disastrous to happen. Can you imagine what will happen if she finds out I'm studying to be an engineer and not a teacher, as she thinks I'm doing? To her even me becoming a teacher feels like I'm reaching past the limits of our station in society as she sees it. She thinks I should respect those boundaries. To her my taking the ring would be stealing. She'd think I've taken advantage of you, been greedy. (Have I?) But yes, I do wear it. And everything falls in place for me too when I think of you wearing yours. Sometimes I feel like we are the same person. But how is it possible to miss someone so much if they are part of you?

Why is it that I start to write a letter promising myself that I will fill you in on the things happening in my life but by the time I'm done, I've become a newer version of myself?

Next time I'll stick to the subtopics, I promise.

Please care for yourself for me.

Yours lovingly,

Your friend,

Suru

CHAPTER TEN

"You can stop staring out that window now." Rumi growls me out of my trance.

I've been standing here for heaven knows how long doing exactly what he just accused me of doing. The sun was on its way down when Krish left, and now it's dark and the streetlamps are casting eddies of light onto the sidewalks.

"You're not going to conjure him out of thin air by sheer force of will. If you've changed your mind about wanting his help, just call him back." Rumi is holding two steaming cups of chai in his hands, and of course the aroma is like a drug and the cups themselves look like an artist glazed them with the essence of their soul.

"I thought you wanted me to give up the search."

"I do. But I know you're not going to." Obviously he knows this. "You might as well have someone who knows what they're doing helping you." He does it grudgingly, but for the barest moment he lets me have my Rumi back, the one I've lost somewhere inside this angry one.

"I agree with Rooh." Saket joins us, bringing a plate of Parle-G biscuits to the party. Which makes me smile because the four-packets-for-a-dollar cookies that Rumi loves more than life itself are such a sweet misfit in the ethos of all this decadent luxury. "I think you should call Krish back and take his help. He was right. It was brilliant how he found you."

"It's hardly brilliant to stalk someone on social media." Especially if that someone took no steps to protect herself. I'm going to have to go through everything that's out there and clean it up.

"And yet he's right, no one else thought of it," Saket says.

"Shouldn't we be relieved that more people don't think of stalking as their first course of action?"

Saket looks at me like I'm being obtuse on purpose. He has gray-green eyes set against dark skin and dramatically chiseled features that magnify all his expressions. "Going through your social media to look for common friends might be borderline creepy, but it isn't the same as being a stalker. He reached out to me—someone he knows, not you—then showed up at the door and laid out his cards. And when you said no, he left. No stalker behaves that way. I should know."

When I raise a curious brow, he shrugs and says simply, "Three restraining orders. Trust me, I know stalkers."

Rumi hands me a cup of chai, and I take a sip. It's pure unfiltered heaven. "You did not make this, brother of mine."

"Guilty as charged. Sak makes the world's best chai. His aunt makes the blend of spices from scratch and sends it to us."

"What does she put in it? The tears of angels?" Because this is like having a spiritual experience.

"Or good old marijuana," Saket says, and I have no idea if he's being ironic. "Because seriously, no one who takes a sip is ever unhappy." All three of us take a happy sip and sigh. "Plus every time I've met Veena Maasi, she's seemed high."

A laugh spurts out of me.

"Sak calls it Happy Tea." Rumi hands me a napkin, allowing his first smile of the day to escape. My relief at that is so huge, I don't even care what brought on the change, although I suspect Saket had a hand in it. I imagine a whispered lecture on my behalf happening when they were in the kitchen making the chai.

I take a shamelessly slurping sip and drop into the couch. There's definitely something different about this chai. It could just be the perfect balance between cardamom and ginger, but it's magical. I'm definitely happier than I was before I drank it.

"Speaking of marijuana, did your friend actually smoke weed on your porch before ringing the doorbell?"

"Did he?" Saket says as though I've just accused Krish of still using Axe deodorant as a grown man.

"There was a distinct whiff when I opened the door."

"Really? I smelled nothing. Maybe it was an actual skunk," Saket says. "Or the kid from next door."

I roll my eyes. "I'm Rumi's twin. I know what weed smells like." In high school and college I had to secretly buy Costco-size bottles of laundry fragrance beads for his clothes to make sure our parents never found out.

"Ah, yes. The smell of weed is a trigger for some happy memories for Mira." Rumi picks up my cup and takes a sip now that he's drained his own. "Is that why you didn't like this Krish guy?"

I snatch the cup back. "Who said I didn't like him?"

Rumi's eyes practically roll out of his head. "Come on, Miru, seriously? The disdain was coming off you in tidal waves."

"Not true." I look at Saket for support.

He shrugs guiltily. "You basically glowered at him the entire time. It was like he'd walked in off the street to tell you he'd run over your pet hamster. Honestly, I couldn't have imagined you throwing shade at anyone. But you're kinda a Division One shade thrower."

Rumi sits up straight, something our aie would have paid him good money to do when we were younger. "Hah! You have the hots for him!"

"Excuse me?" I squeeze the cup hard. If the white linen of the couch weren't so beautiful, I'd dump the chai on Rumi's head.

"Oh, gosh, this is exactly how you were with that nemesis of yours. That jock you had a crush on in middle school. What was his name? Jack, John, Josh, something. You walked around looking like you wanted to kick his locker. Didn't you kick his locker once?" He's grinning like an oaf now. Obviously harassing me with embarrassing memories was what he needed to get to his happy place. "It's actually a thing. Some people use anger as an outlet when they don't know how to process feelings of horniness."

"Rumi!" I throw a pillow at him. "I'm getting married in less than four months."

"Which might be exactly why you're so pissed off. Being reminded of how it feels to actually be hot for someone has got to suck when that someone isn't your fiancé." He makes a serious face, but his eyes are twinkling with humor instead of his recently more commonplace meanness. "Anger in place of the inability to process attraction is pretty classic in children. And repressed people."

Saket laughs and then turns it into a cough and apologizes.

"I'm not repressed." But even I can't infuse any honesty into that declaration. I'm at least self-aware enough to know exactly how repressed I am. "He wasn't even that attractive," I say with more feeling.

"Whoa!" Saket says, raising both arms. "Come now. Let's not resort to lies. That was a ten-on-ten ass if I've ever seen one, and a twelve-on-ten jaw. And that whole rumpled vibe like he just rolled out of bed and couldn't care less? Holy hell!" He fans himself.

I look at Rumi, expecting him to be glowering, but he takes a calm sip of my chai, the last sip. And smiles! "Facts are facts. I'd say twelve-on-ten ass *and* twelve-on-ten jaw. And that mouth?"

"Fifteen on ten," Saket says, and they both nod.

"You're both weird. Maybe the smell of weed was coming from *inside* the house," I snap. "And you know who's a fifteen on ten?"

"Let me guess. Dr. Druv-His-Girlfriend-into-Another-Man's-Arms-Because-He's-Surgerying?" Rumi looks far too thrilled with himself.

Saket looks at my face, then back at Rumi. "Okay, too far, Rooh."

Rumi sighs dramatically. "Fine. Druv's a solid seven, and if he stopped trying so hard, he'd be an eight. Maybe."

"You've never even met him after we grew up." Rumi had already moved to New York when Druv and I got together. And they haven't spoken since then because Druv thinks we're estranged.

"God knows you've sent us enough pictures. And I know his type. A demigod of the overachieving model minority worshipped by the aunties and the uncles alike. Seven is generous." I guess my respite with my brother is over. The angry spark in his eyes is back. Is it Druv? Is that what brought his anger back?

"Who rates human beings? It's such a problematic thing to do," I say, standing up and going back to the window. My hand finds the ring in my pocket, and I play with the smooth, cool weight of it. Maybe I should call Krish, because I have no idea where to start other than that.

"You know a sure sign that someone has lost their sense of humor?" my brother says. "When they misuse the word *problematic* because a truth hurt their feelings." I don't respond because I'm angry and tired and I'm on vacation and until an hour ago I felt like something magical had happened to me.

Rumi makes a frustrated sound when I don't give him the fight he's looking for. "Just call the guy," he says. "You don't have to sleep with him. Just let him tell you what to do. That should be easy enough for you."

CHAPTER ELEVEN

"What is this I hear about you putting things on the Phase Book? I knew we shouldn't have allowed you to go to New York by yourself," my mother says on the phone. I haven't told anyone back home about the ring or the video. Not even Druv. Only because he's been in marathon surgeries back to back, and when we checked in, he was so exhausted and sleepy he was slurring his words.

"That Phase Book is not a safe place. You should know that." Fortunately Aie is really good at carrying on a conversation by herself. At least when it comes to her children. With everyone else, she's famed for being a good listener.

"It's Facebook, Aie," I say. I've never been happier that my parents shun social media and instead prefer to get their misinformation exclusively from WhatsApp.

"What?" she says as though I've said something totally off topic.

"Not Phase Book. Facebook."

"Like your face? The one on your head?"

The very one. "Yes."

"That makes no sense. Why did I always think it was *phase*, like going through a phase and sharing it with the world?"

"That's actually not bad, Aie."

"Right? Anyway, never mind all those things. What were you thinking?" Apparently, some auntie saw the video (it's at a million views now) and sent it to my mother on WhatsApp. Which is scary, because once something is on WhatsApp, every single Indian person on earth, across the entire diaspora, which is represented in every nation on the earth's surface, is going to get it sooner or later. There's even a half life. When I'm fifty, someone who knows someone who knows me is going to discover it and send it to my mother. She's right: What was I thinking?

"I just found a *gold* ring." I emphasize the word *gold*, because losing gold jewelry is probably one of my mother's top-five life disasters. "And I wanted to return it to its owner."

She gasps. "You picked up something that doesn't belong to you? From the street? What if they arrest you for stealing?" Ugh, I've miscalculated, because having a cop pull you over or even look in your general direction is far higher on her life-disaster scale. "That, too, over there in New York. You know, last year in New York one person pushed a young Indian boy in front of a train because they didn't like foreigners. Obviously they don't like foreigners there."

My head is starting to hurt. I do remember that news story and how terribly sad it made me. Generalized hate toward groups of people for being those groups of people is possibly the scariest thing when you're a minority.

I take a sip of my *chai tea latte*. Yes, I've done the unforgivable and ordered the carelessly named drink, even though finding it called that on a menu in a New York café knocked down my wide-eyed wonder at the city a few notches. America remains America across America in some ways, I guess. Usually it makes me want to run to all the Italian restaurants and change the menus to read *spaghetti noodles*. But no, instead I was so homesick for Saket's aunt's chai after drinking it once that I ordered chai.

Sidenote: this syrupy concoction does not taste like Saket and Rumi's Happy Tea. Also, my brother and I are never speaking again, so I'm going to die with this craving. Also, my mother is still talking about her version of New York where I'm about to be arrested for stealing because I'm a *foreigner*. Side sidenote: I was born in Naperville, Illinois, and have never left the USA, not even to go to Canada or Mexico. Yes, very foreign, I know.

"It was on the street between a lamppost and a garbage can. Why would anyone think I stole it?" As soon as I've said it, I know exactly which part she just caught even before she responds.

"Mira! You touched a public garbage can?" My mother has never let me use a public toilet. She still reminds me to make sure that I use the bathroom every single time I leave the house. Even though I'm almost thirty years old. She might sincerely believe that I've never had to answer nature's call by myself in school or college. She carried hand sanitizer and alcohol wipes and wiped our hands down the second we touched anything at the mall long before the pandemic.

"I fell, and it was right there."

"You fell!"

Okay, this tragedy is building on itself. It's time to draw Aie back from the edge.

"Everything is okay, Aie. I was carrying wipes, and I've sanitized the ring, and I'm going to take the video down because I think I've found the owner. As a matter of fact, I have to go, sorry, because I need to take care of that now."

Before she can protest, I promise to call her soon and disconnect the phone. She immediately calls back. It's not easy, but I don't answer.

A man in a black hoodie and workout shorts just walked right past me where I'm sitting at a bistro table on the sidewalk on Fifth Avenue and went into the coffee shop. To be fair, I ducked behind my phone and my hair, which is twice the size of my head today and works handily for hiding.

I'm not sure he's the person who messaged me this morning, but he did say he would be wearing a black hoodie. I had almost given up on anyone legit reaching out and was about to take my video down when his message came in. After what Rumi said to me yesterday, I stormed out of his home. I wasn't able to stop crying as I took the train back to the 9/11 Memorial and then walked all the way across Manhattan to my hotel.

I'm so angry with him I can barely breathe when I think about it, but not calling Krish felt like cutting off my nose to spite my face—one of my mother's favorite sayings. So, after getting back to the hotel, when Saket texted me to make sure I was okay, I asked him for Krish's number. He sent it to me and then asked me to come back and have a conversation with Rumi. I can't. Not after what Rumi said. I'm not spineless. I hate when he says that when I'm the only one here trying to hold our family together.

I get why he had to leave, but how can he not get that both of us can't abandon our parents? Not only am I the only family my brother has left, but I'm also the only child my parents have left. I'm basically stuck overcompensating in both roles because no one else will give even an inch.

Just as I started to type a text to Krish last night, the message from Rajesh Pandya came through.

Hi Mira,

I hope it's okay to reach out to you like this. I'm sure you're inundated with messages from all sorts of creeps. I happened to come across your post about the ring and I couldn't believe what I was seeing. That's my ring. My grandmother gave it to me when I left India to come to New York. My Naani practically raised me. She died last month and I dropped it on Broadway across from the Empire state building the day I found out. I was heartbroken. It felt like a sign. Like punishment for not going to see her before she was gone. Please please if you've found it let me have it back. I'll pay you whatever you want for it. It's my last memory of her. She died before I could see her and losing the ring means I'll never forgive myself.

Thank you so so much for finding it,
Rajesh Pandya

I had tears in my eyes reading the message. After all the creepy messages, this one was jarringly normal.

I messaged back immediately, thanking him for reaching out and telling him how sorry I was to read about his grandmother. I never met my grandparents. My father's parents died before I was born. My mother's parents lived in Dombivali, outside Mumbai, back when it was still called Bombay. They died when I was in elementary school, before my parents had enough money to visit them or have them visit us. I've never been to India. I only ever knew them through letters that my parents read aloud to us. My mother made Rumi and me write to them twice a year, once for Diwali, to wish them happy Diwali, and once on our birthdays, telling them how our year had been.

Rajesh's message hit a nerve already raw from my fight with Rumi. I was tired and vulnerable, but contrary to what Rumi might think, I'm not an idiot. I went through Rajesh Pandya's social media to hunt for signs of assholery but found none. Just selfies all over New York, most with plates of food. His greatest social media sin seems to be that he's trying a little too hard, which makes him like everyone else.

When I asked him about the inscription, his response had been Those may seem like just some random lines, they may be meaningless to you, but to me they mean everything.

He knew about the lines etched into the inside of the ring and that they were seemingly without meaning. The curiosity to know what they meant has been overwhelming. Now I would find out.

After all that due diligence, I sent him a message asking him to meet me at the coffee shop across from my hotel and deleted my text to Krish Hale, incredibly grateful to be saved from the fate of apologizing to a man who seemed far too certain that I couldn't do this without him.

I study the black-hoodie guy, who's obviously looking for someone. He's stocky, with hairy bowlegs, and his orange sneakers are scruffy and worn. I usually work hard not to judge people based on their appearance, but there's something about the quick, jerky movements with which he's peering at tables that sends a little frisson of discomfort through me. Before I can decide if I should get up and leave, he catches my eye through the glass and rushes out to the sidewalk.

"Mira?" he asks. There's an odd squeak to his voice.

I'm tempted to say "No, I'm not her." I don't even know why. "Who's asking," I say instead, surprising myself with my calm tone.

He smiles a plaque-y smile and sits down. An odd feeling I haven't felt in a very long time nudges at the back of my neck, where my body meets my brain at the top of my spine.

"I'm Rajesh. Rajesh Pandya?" he says as though we're old friends and I've had the nerve to forget him.

I continue to look confused. I have no idea why I'm pretending to have no idea who he is, but it just happens. He's obviously watched the video and knows what I look like.

Four hundred thousand people know your name. That's how viral posts work.

"You have the ring?" Rajesh Pandya leans forward in his chair. "My ring."

My reptilian brain shivers again, ever so slightly. Am I being paranoid? All my life I've been taught to ignore my feelings and instincts on one hand, and then taught to trust nothing and no one on the other. Until this moment I've never processed quite how much I've been trained to be dependent. I've developed no instincts that could help me rely on myself. I've been equipped only to follow, never to lead.

The ring is clutched in my hand, and I tighten my hold. The end of the chain is dangling from my fist. I should have put it away until I'd confirmed that I'd found the owner.

His eyes drop to it, and suddenly I feel naked. "May I see it?"

I study his eyes—something I've always considered my superpower—and open my fist a little. Just enough for him to glimpse the ring. There should be grief in his eyes at worst and recognition at least. Instead there's something else. Something I recognize only too well. Greed.

Before I can pull back, he snatches the ring from my hand.

"It's beautiful, isn't it?" he says and squeezes it against his chest, making the effort to soften his eyes and to smile. Until he realizes that I haven't let the chain go.

I pull the ring back, and it starts to slide from his hand. He tightens his hold. Now we're playing tug-of-war with the chain and ring, and I know I've made a terrible mistake. My reptilian brain might be stunted, but it's not dead.

"What do the lines on the inscription mean?" I ask. It comes out a whisper.

His answering breath sounds loud because we're a little too close over the bistro table. His eyes widen, but he attempts another smile. "It's something that was very special to my daadi."

"Let the ring go," I say and throw a quick look around. No one is paying any attention to us, but the rest of the tables are occupied, and there's a substantial amount of pedestrian traffic passing us.

"What's wrong?" he has the gall to say.

"I thought it was your naani," I say.

In the message he sent me, he said the ring belonged to his naani. There's a linguistic distinction between how paternal and maternal grandmothers are addressed in Hindi, as I know from being engaged to a man whose family is from New Delhi. My heart is starting to beat faster now.

He grips the ring tighter, and the chain digs into my fingers.

Shock flashes in his face. He's surprised that I'm holding on so tight. Before my eyes, he transforms from greasy and simpering to stone cold.

"Two things are going to happen now," he says quietly. "You're going to let go, and I'm going to walk away." His grip tightens even more; his nostrils flare as though he can smell my fear. Déjà vu fills me. "If you don't let the ring go, I'm going to pull out the knife I have in my pocket and stick it in your gut under this table. Or maybe I'll hold it to your back and take you with me to the alley behind the building, and then I'll make you regret posting that video even more than you're doing now. You're even softer and juicier than I imagined. Also dumber, if you don't let go."

There's something so ugly in his face, horrible memories hiss at the edge of my consciousness. Dark shadows dance before my eyes. I've pushed these shadows away too many times. Today they paralyze me. I gasp for breath, but I can't get one in. My hand goes limp.

In that second he stands up while shoving me with such force my chair topples back. I land on the sidewalk, and my head hits something with a whack. Pain, sharp and bright, steals the breath from my lungs. Lights flash before my eyes.

I hear screams and scraping chairs as the crowd grasps what is going on. I force myself to focus. He has the ring. He breaks into a run, just as a tall, lanky figure in a leather jacket flies at him out of nowhere and grabs his hoodie, stopping him midair. We're suddenly in an action film with choreographed fight scenes. More screams erupt around us as both men tumble to the pavement.

Explosions of pain are still going off in my head, but two things strike me at once. This is the second time I've been sprawled on my butt on a New York sidewalk. And the person who just attacked my attacker is Krish Hale.

CHAPTER TWELVE

Vasudha Patil
Garware Ladies Hostel
Fergusson College, Pune, India
April 1983

Sureva Bhalekar
St. Mary's Ladies Hostel
Charni Road, Bombay

Dear Suru,
I'm sorry it's taken me so long to reply. While I've been writing to you in my head every day, I couldn't put pen to paper because I broke my spectacles soon after I received your last letter and they had to make me new ones. Why does it take a whole month to make new spectacles? It was the most frustrating thing I've ever experienced to have read your letter and to not be able to respond. Isn't it funny that you're the scholar but I'm the one who can't see without glasses? I did start to write to you by feel, but then I couldn't read it back and I didn't want to worry you by writing gibberish.

I have my new spectacles now and you shall not be spared my letters anymore.

Your letter was so beautiful, Suru, I never want to wait weeks before responding to your words again. (I've ordered an extra pair of spectacles, just in case this happens again.)

Please don't stick to the subtopics. Even though I love your subtopics—they cheer me up immensely—I love you meandering off even more. It feels like being with you, like we're lying by the river talking, the way we did all the years of our lives until we left our home.

How can you keep saying my family took you in and gave you charity? Your aie has worked every minute of every day for the past twenty years. No one *gave* her or you anything. She earned it. If anything my family is in your aie's debt for raising me and my brother and feeding us and taking care of Aie every time she got sick. Which both of us know was pretty much all the time. Remember how we overheard Appa telling my aie once that if it wasn't for your aie keeping our household going, he would have had to find another wife.

I know we had laughed and imagined all the women Appa might ask to come run his household. Your impression of him proposing to other women had almost made me die from laughing. "My children need herding. My house needs managing. My cook needs directing. My self needs tending . . ." That fake mustache you made with the end of your braid held above your lip was hilarious. Remember how it kept getting in your nose and making you sneeze?

But now when I think about what Appa said, it makes me sad. How must Aie have felt? I suspect she was just glad that your aie had made sure it didn't come to that. So you see, my family owes yours far more than yours owes ours. Money is easy to repay. A life and a million acts of nurturing and kindness aren't.

Please don't ever say I don't keep my promises. That caused me to cry. You had to know that. Actually, no you didn't, I'm sorry I said that. You thought you were scolding me as you always do, for my own good. But you know keeping my word is important to me. All we have is our loyalty and character. Isn't that what your aie taught us? We won't take jewels and land to our grave, but our souls will carry the choices we made and how we lived to the next life.

You were wrong in your accusation. I never promised not to send you things. You asked me to not send you things, but I never agreed. If I didn't send you things I would be buried under the weight of all I have. If I didn't have you to share things with I would be too alone to comprehend. I'd become locked up inside my aloneness. A mountain would grow around me and trees upon that and no one would ever find me buried under how distant I feel from all of humanity because you aren't here to connect me with it.

Please don't take that away from me.

Oh, and help me out with a very important question. Where did you put the blanket? I know you found a solution. You always do. Did you lay it out beneath your mattress? I can imagine you doing that. Rolling it out where it would not take up space while still taking care of it. I am sorry that I inconvenienced you by sending it. I do wish I thought more before I acted. Do you think I've never had to think about the consequences of my actions because you've always done that for the both of us?

In any case I am sorry. I am now fully aware of how hot Bombay is. I made the mistake of asking our hostel warden about the temperatures in Bombay and she has not stopped complaining about her years there when she only remembers swimming in sweat every day of the year. She came to Pune when she married her husband twenty years ago and she talks about the Pune weather like it is Kashmir. In truth the weather has turned quite hot here too after the few months of cold.

I will not be offended if you bring the blanket with you when you come to Pune in two months for the youth festival. I am so eager to see you, my excitement doesn't feel like it can fit inside my heart. There is so much I want to show you and tell you. I called Ashatai Athavale immediately upon receiving your letter. She might have the most beautiful voice you've ever heard. I've been singing with her every day. I know you will be felled by her voice. We've been preparing a thumri for the youth festival. It's in raag megh malhaar, so it will be perfect to celebrate the start of the monsoon. But you won't believe what happened the other day. I was practicing and the strains of music that match the rhythm of the rain so perfectly filled me up so tightly that I started to cry. And when I looked out of my window, it was drizzling. An entirely unseasonal shower that sprinkled the city and was gone in a breath. It was so beautiful. I wish you'd been here to see it. That was my first thought. I sing to you, Suru, when you are not here. Do you hear me?

Stop shaking your head. I am too silly by half. I do know that. You are not wrong when you call me the most self-aware yet most fanciful girl. One would think those two things would cancel each other out. Are you truly silly if you know you're silly? It would take some smartness to know silliness, and how can a smart person be silly? Maybe you could devise an experiment in your lab to figure me out? Slice up my brain like one of your rats.

I suspect you're the only person on earth who has a prayer of a chance of doing it, of determining why my brain won't let me be all the things I'm supposed to be. Please don't be afraid for me, I don't show what is inside me to anyone but you. You get to be the keeper of my true self. You once told me that they cannot hurt what they do not know.

But please never again say that you do not feel like we are equal. You understand much, my dear Suru, but you do not understand the meaning of equality if you can see a difference between us. Why do you think humans need to use all these scales to gauge our worth when we all drop onto the earth from a birth canal in exactly the same state and return to dirt that crumbles beneath our feet and feeds the roots of plants in exactly the same way too? How can something as transient as money define our equality? Our opportunities, yes. Our possessions definitely, but certainly not how equal we are in any sense that is human. How can there be equality and inequality between things that are one and the same?

I've done it again. Come to the end of the page when I have so much more to say. But you are Suru and you know the rest without me having to say more.

Writing this last part above all else gives me the greatest joy: I will see you soon, my friend.

Yours lovingly,

Your Silly Vasu

CHAPTER THIRTEEN

I feel like I'm never going to see the ring again. That makes me so sad I don't know what to do with it.

At least New Yorkers are nicer than their reputation because a bunch of strangers help me up and ask if I'm okay. Then again, maybe they're tourists. The waitstaff shoo them away and get my chair up and help me into it and bring me water. The manager asks if she should call the cops. I see no point in it. What are they going to do, chase down a man who ran off with something that didn't belong to me? After I practically invited him to?

I tell the manager I'm fine. I am, except for a sharp pain in my neck. I know I haven't broken anything or torn any soft tissue. I also know it's going to hurt like a bitch tomorrow. I'll take an anti-inflammatory soon, and that should help.

The manager brings me the biggest frothy concoction I've ever seen, piled high with whipped cream, and then blessedly leaves me alone to lick my wounds.

The good news is that I fell right. Falls can be disastrous or harmless, depending on how someone falls. Generally, it's hard to plan your fall, but having a strong core helps. Being young helps. All those years of yoga and suspension exercises help.

Nothing helps the bruised ego, though.

How could I have been so stupid?

I, Mira Salvi, the girl who always manages her expectations, who always overthinks consequences, who never trusts anyone, how could I have gotten so carried away? *This will not end well for you if you're not careful* is a line my parents have fed me so much it's coded into my DNA.

A spot of blood rises where the chain cut my finger when the bastard ripped it from my hand, and my stupid throat clogs with tears. For some reason the child who hurtled into me and sent me flying flashes into my memory. The look on his mother's face when she put him in the stroller as he struggled for freedom: fiercely protective even when she was scolding him. That look weighs on me even as his fragile body and barely there weight knocks me down afresh.

Humiliated as I am, it's the loneliness of this moment that truly crushes me. There's no one I can call without being told exactly how much of a fool I am or being told that I have no one but myself to blame. I don't. I exposed myself on social media. I got excited about a love story I made up in my head. I opened myself up to crime in a city known for crime. I invited it in with a big flashing welcome sign.

The last time I did something that was out of character, I paid for it by putting away every bit of recklessness. I made sure I learned from my mistakes. I still live with my parents. Sure, they need help with the business and their health issues, but I also went to college in Naperville. Between work and school and helping my parents at the store, I've carefully created a safe and stable life. I'm not made to go hurtling after things without thought. How did I forget? Why did I think this would be different?

There's no doubt that my parents and Rumi would shake their heads in disappointment. If I tell Druv, he'll know it too, how good I am at messing things up when I'm not careful. Something I've managed to keep from him.

The leap of hope in my heart when Krish grabbed Rajesh's hoodie and took him down makes me feel like a supersize idiot all over again.

With the wind knocked out of me, I wasn't exactly sure what was happening when the two men started rolling around on the sidewalk. Rajesh made his way to his feet first, but Krish didn't let his hoodie go and ended up being dragged up to standing too. Rajesh tried to shake, punch, and kick Krish away, but the man was like a leech, refusing to let go. Obviously neither man was a fighter, let alone adept enough for the choreographed fight promised by that first leap. My heart does an odd little hop when I remember Krish flying through the air at the bastard.

The entire episode felt like an eternity but was actually over in a few moments. Despite Krish's tenacious clinging, Rajesh managed to struggle free and took off. Krish shot after him, not even sparing me a glance as I sat there on the pavement.

It's been at least twenty minutes, so Krish obviously didn't catch the man. Unless he did and decided not to come back. The sadness I'm feeling tightens around me. The person who lost the ring will never be reunited with it. And it's my fault. I was given the chance to right a wrong, and I botched it. Between that and the physical pain radiating from the back of my neck, I lose my battle against the tears I've been holding back. The chaos of heartbreak and disappointment dancing inside me takes over, and I let the tears flow. I have no idea how long they've been running down my cheeks when a white paper napkin flaps in my peripheral vision like a flag.

Krish.

He's back. Does that mean he got the ring? Hope leaps again, and I shove it down and snatch the tissue from him and wipe my eyes. "What are you doing here?"

"What are *you* still doing here? You should be at the hospital."

"Why?"

"Because you took quite a hit to the head when you fell."

And he just left me lying there. Which is a stupid thought to have, because of course he had to chase the thief. "I'm fine." I study his face.

He says nothing about the ring, and I'm so disappointed I don't want to think about it anymore.

"We should let a doctor decide that," he says instead.

"Or someone who's trained to gauge injuries."

"Sure. We can find you one of those holistic healers after we go to the ER."

Despite myself I snort out a laugh. "I'm a physical therapist, with all sorts of graduate degrees in pain management and rehab, and I'm pretty sure I'm going to live." I have no idea why I feel the need to wave my credentials in his face, but I do.

"Did your degrees also give you x-ray vision?"

"No. But they do qualify me to know if I need an x-ray."

"Fair enough. Can I at least get you ice?" Without waiting for an answer, he goes into the café. His step is actually jaunty. He's feeling none of the loss I'm feeling. Unless he found the ring and won't tell me.

I blow my nose, wipe my face, and contemplate leaving. But I'm still sore from the fall, and suddenly I'm less despondent and more angry, and it feels like a relief.

By the time he returns with a baggie of ice, my rage is at a good simmer.

He holds out the ice. Having to look up at him sends a shot of pain through the back of my neck. He's at least six feet tall and so lean that he appears far taller than that. I snatch it from him and put it on the table between us. I don't need his ice. I need that ring. But an odd sort of pride keeps me from asking what happened.

"You really should ice that," he says, and I fold my arms across my chest.

He picks up the baggie and walks around me but then just stands there. I can see him reflected in the glass of the café window, a loose-limbed form behind my scrunched-up-in-pain form. He's holding up the ice, but my hair is in the way. There's a strange sort of elasticity to the air that makes it impossible for me to move, to be myself, like I have rubber bands wrapped around me.

"Please lift your hair so I can take a look." He says the words formally, but there's also an impatience to them. Irritation that I'm not making this easier for him.

"Why did you come back?" I don't lift my hair, which is hanging down my back in a mop of curls I didn't bother to straighten this morning because I was in too much of a hurry to meet the ring's owner. I can't remember the last time I left home without straightening my hair.

"Please, Mira."

I lean into my purse, pull out a clip, then roll my hair into a bun and fasten it. I watch his reflection study the back of my neck. "There's no bruising."

"It's not the kind of injury that bruises." There is, however, a bump at the base of my skull that isn't going to be fun tomorrow. I take the baggie he's hovering over the nape of my neck and push it against the tender spot that took the impact. It hurts like a sledgehammer but also feels good. I refuse to flinch. He sits down across from me and studies me. Not that I can see the results of his study. He's wearing dark glasses again today.

"Do you ever take those off?" I ask as he leans back in his chair away from me, relaxed as ever.

His lips twist with confusion.

"Your sunglasses. Do you ever take them off?"

"They're prescription. I can't see without them," he says in a tone that says he has no idea how his glasses are any of my concern. "They're transitions, and we're in the sun."

"You were wearing sunglasses yesterday too. Indoors." And those weren't these same ones.

"My glasses were in the shop being repaired yesterday. I broke them."

"How?"

"How's your neck?"

"Why did you come back?"

"What possessed you to meet a stranger from social media?"

"How did you know I was meeting him here?"

"How could you hand him the ring?"

"Why did you come back?"

"What kind of question is that?"

We're both winded from the questions that fly from us and drop between us without answers, the question I'm dying to ask still unspoken.

The silence stretches. He shifts in his seat. It's the first sign of discomfort I've seen from him. Actually, it's the second. The memory of him on the sidewalk outside Rumi's place comes back to me. It's impossible to reconcile this relaxed-to-a-point-of-ennui man with that tortured soul I know I wasn't supposed to see.

"You took a bad fall," he says in that tone where he seems mildly impatient that he's having to explain obvious things.

I'm perfectly aware of how bad my fall was. I wait in silence for him to answer the question I haven't asked, mirroring his disinterest.

"I came back to make sure you were okay." Again, the word *obviously* remains unsaid, but he communicates it loud and clear. "I couldn't very well let the bastard run off with the ring. Is that what you wanted, for him to get the ring? I thought you cared about finding the owner."

I sit up, every bit of disinterest gone. "You got the ring!" An absurd amount of glee fills me. I don't care about anything else.

He looks even more confused now.

"And you still came back." I have no idea why I say that, but it just flies out, and something suspiciously like anger slips past his apathy.

"You thought if I'd gotten the ring, I would have run away with it? You think I'm a thief." He says it as though it's an observation. Him piecing my thought process together.

I didn't think that, but I also seem to have no idea what I am thinking. And I sure as hell don't need to explain any of that to him. "I don't know you."

He pulls the ring out of his pocket, picks up my hand from the table, and puts it and the chain on my palm. Just as he's about to let go and walk away, he notices the cut.

"Do you happen to have a bandage in that humongous bag?"

"Yes," I say and squeeze the ring. The relief of seeing it again is completely out of proportion to my normal scale of feelings. "And it's not humongous."

"You're right. It's gargantuan." He leans toward the bag. "May I?" he says and waits until I nod to pick it up and hand it to me. Is politeness his weapon or his shield? I hate that it feels so familiar because of course it's mine too.

I put the ice down on the table and retrieve a bandage from my bag. "I didn't think you were a thief."

Without so much as a twitch of emotion on his face, he takes it from me and hands me the ice again.

"Keep the ice on it." He rips the cover off the bandage. "You expected me to run away with the ring. That sounds like something you'd expect a thief to do." His tone is as calm as ever.

He holds up the bandage, and I stick out my finger. It's stopped bleeding, but the cut looks tender. He wipes it with a clean napkin. I'm not good with letting people I know touch me, let alone strangers. Maybe it's the fact that he's so clinical and distant about it, but the frisson of discomfort I'm expecting when he holds my hand and wraps my finger never comes.

"You can help me," I say before I can stop myself.

He returns my hand to the table, crumples the wrapping and pushes it into his pocket, and raises a brow.

"You can help me find the ring's owner."

"No, thank you."

"Excuse me?"

"I'm no longer interested."

"Why?"

"It wouldn't work." He stands. "You sure you don't need me to take you to the hospital, or call Sak or your brother before I go?" So polite.

He's just going to leave, just like that. After he chased a criminal down and retrieved the ring. Because I called him a thief.

When I don't answer, he flicks me a two-fingered salute and turns to leave.

"Why did you chase the guy down if you didn't want to find the owner anymore? Actually, how did you know I was here meeting with him?" I almost ask if he was stalking me, but I might have been too free with my accusations already. Another accusation may not be my best move if I want to get him to help me. Suddenly, I really badly want his help. It feels like my only option now.

He turns around. "Do you always make all your choices backwards?"

It's my turn to look confused.

"You asked me to help you before you asked me how I knew you were meeting this guy. I'd think figuring out my stalker status would come first."

"Then answer that first."

"Sak told me. I spoke with him this morning, and he told me that you had found the owner and that you were meeting him here. So I rushed here." He studies me again and pauses. "You were obviously being tricked." Then, with that matter-of-factness I already know is his trademark, he adds, "I have very good instincts."

He doesn't come out and say that I obviously don't, but it's there on his face.

"I misunderstood something the guy said about the inscription on the ring."

His brow furrows. He's piecing together the plot again. "He knew about the lines."

"I thought he did." It was stupid of me. "Will you help me? Please." This isn't like me. Asking for something so clearly. I search my brain, and I can't think of the last time I asked anyone for anything. But this

I have to have. Maybe it's because he's a stranger who stands to benefit, too, but asking Krish Hale for help is easier than I expected.

He sits back down, not even a hint of gloating. "Why is it so important to you?" he asks. "Finding this person."

"Honestly, I have no idea. But I've never really left Illinois. I've barely ever left Chicago. Why would I come all the way to New York and fall down exactly in the place where the ring was lost and find it?" I haven't told anyone that a child knocked me down or that I didn't see him because I was looking up at the Empire State Building and thinking about *An Affair to Remember*. "It feels like it can't be for nothing."

"So, it's because you believe in signs."

"I've never thought about signs before." I've never thought about what I do and don't believe in. I've only ever thought about what I needed to do. "But I do believe that I found it for a reason. I have to find out what that reason is. I don't know why, but I have to." And I have to find out before it's too late. Even though I don't know what I'm afraid of it being too late for.

For a long time he says nothing. A deep shadow has fallen over our table, and his glasses aren't as dark anymore. I still can't see his eyes enough to tell what he's thinking, but I know that he's still here.

"I can't help you if I can't write the story," he says finally, his voice still flat but not unkind, and my heart does another one of those unfamiliar leaps of hope. He's going to help me. We're going to find the ring's owner. Despite my best efforts, a smile escapes my lips. Much like it does for Meg Ryan and Deborah Kerr, and every spunky romantic comedy heroine who's ever found herself in the middle of contrived coincidences.

"Are you at least a good writer?" I ask.

And for the first time since I met him, I make Krish Hale laugh.

CHAPTER FOURTEEN

My mother-in-law-to-be would absolutely love this place," I say as Saket squeezes me in a hug and then stands back and sweeps his arms in a mix of *Welcome* and *This is where the magic happens.*

Krish and I follow Saket into the store. I'm practically skipping with joy while Krish remains unmoved.

Navri by VND, Saket's store, feels a lot like Tiffany and the Taj Mahal had a baby girl. "*Navri* means 'bride' in Marathi," Sak explains to Krish, who nods in that well-meaning way polite people nod when presented with a foreign concept. No one says *exotic* anymore, but it's what I got called all the time back in school, even by my teachers. I didn't know any of the baggage the word came with until much later, but even back then I knew something was off about it, a stamp pressed into my skin that marked me as different in a seemingly desirable way that didn't feel desirable at all.

It's the word that comes to mind when Krish's face, for all its polite interest, takes in the gold-and-ivory palace-chic decor and the heavily embellished jewelry arranged tastefully in glossy brocade-lined glass cases. He seems to be thinking the word. Which is very confusing. Not only does he look South Asian, but he's named Krish, which is as Indian as a name can get, the name of, arguably, the most beloved Hindu god. And yet one would think he's never seen a piece of Indian jewelry up close.

Saket fits into the store as though it was designed expressly with the intention of him fitting into it so seamlessly. It probably was. He's wearing a black silk tunic with subtle gold embroidery around the neck and black and gold flowy pants that I'm seriously coveting.

"My great-great—I forget how many *great*s exactly—grandfather built the first VN Dixit store in Pune when the Peshwas were still in power back in the 1700s," Sak says with the kind of pride I can immediately relate to because I love my work. "They survived the Mughal invasion and colonization. Which simply means they were sleazy bastards who knew how to work the system. Definitely true of my grandfather, who would die if he knew his grandson models his own jewelry." He winks irreverently with his mile-long lash extensions.

He introduces us to the elegantly dressed staff, men and women wearing burgundy silk shirts with black silk pants. Then he leads us to the inner sanctum of the store, where the gold and silver in the display cases changes to diamonds, cut and uncut, in sizes so large they can't possibly be real. My aie and Druv's mom have been sending me pictures of jewelry for my bridal outfits for months now. Even with those being costume jewelry (my mom's word for fakes), they've been absurdly expensive. I can't even hazard a guess as to what this stuff must cost.

Saket rearranges a locket the size of my palm that's hanging by a twisted rope of pearls so it catches the lighting better. "My dad was the apple that fell pretty far from the family tree, thank God. But he almost bankrupted the business because he didn't have a wily bone in his body. I've brought us back. This last year we recorded our highest sales in the history of the business. Good thing I'm as wily as my dick grandpa and the rest of our ancestors."

I can't imagine Sak hurting a fly or ever doing anything wily. "Not true," I say, and he squeezes my hand gratefully.

"Obviously, I'm not an evil bastard obsessed with oppressive power structures, but I do know what people want and how to sell it to them."

A stunningly beautiful woman in a balloon-sleeved linen top over super-slim white slacks is sitting at one of the counters with a younger woman, also dressed all in white but less couture. She's in a white silk tank and a fitted skirt. Both women are wearing those shoes that are supposed to "pull an outfit together"—a concept I'm only aware of because of *Cosmo*. The kind of shoes you throw on when you want to go from day to night—another *Cosmo* concept I've never had the opportunity to practice in real life. Who are these people who spend an entire day at work dressed like a goddess and then take off a jacket, slip on a necklace, and switch out their shoes to look instantly like a whole different kind of goddess? I work in scrubs, and I'm so exhausted after a ten-hour shift that going from day to night involves swapping scrubs out for pajamas in my room after avoiding my parents.

Today I'm wearing a pale-yellow sleeveless eyelet dress I bought at Ann Taylor Loft for this trip, and until five seconds ago I felt over-dressed for a research-and-recon mission at a friend's jewelry store for a mystery ring.

The woman's eyes light up when she sees Sak. "Oh my gosh, I can't believe it. Sak Dixit!" she practically squeals.

"In the flesh!" Saket says and sashays over to the two women, his patent leather ankle boots clicking against the mirror-bright floor.

They jump out of their seats.

"I've literally been following you since day one! I love you so much! *We* love you so much!" The older woman turns to the younger one. "Don't we love him so much?"

"Mom's right. We love you. You're, like, so inspiring." The daughter tears up.

Her mom has one of those faces that doesn't move much and doesn't have a single wrinkle. Druv's mom calls it Muppet Face, from a meme about how Miss Piggy was way ahead of her time with her puffed lips and high cheeks, which everyone seems to be aspiring to these days. It's mean, but what meme isn't?

Saket blinks as though he's trying not to tear up, too, and pats his heart. "You're both so sweet. I appreciate the support. It means everything. And so beautiful. Ah, gorgeousness. Look at that skin tone. What shade of highlighter is that?"

For a few minutes they go off into a discussion about makeup that makes me feel entirely lost.

Finally, Saket turns his attention to the pieces they've been looking at. "What are we here for today?"

"My baby girl is getting married." A tear spills from the mother's eye.

Sak gasps. And it's so heartfelt I almost gasp too. "Lucky bastard! What a gorgeous bride you're going to be. Let me guess. Destination? Lake Como?"

The bride-to-be glows and bounces on her feet. "Lake Champlain in Vermont." She's only slightly embarrassed.

"We wanted to stay stateside," her mother adds. "It's important to support local."

"I love that. So important," Sak gushes. "And Vermont is the best. Just as beautiful as Tuscany, if you ask me, and so much more real. Do you have your lehenga picked out?" He throws an excited glance at their phones.

The girl beams and pulls her phone to her chest. "I have options, but I haven't been able to choose." She seems despondent about this, and for the first time I can relate. The Two Moms have sent me so many "inspiration pieces" over the past months I'm entirely overwhelmed. I'm also terrified of making the wrong choice.

"Oh honey," Sak says. "It's such an important day, and the lehenga is everything. Have you considered a theme? Trees for your groom and peacocks for you." He throws a quick glance at Krish and me. "Birds and their habitat. So beautifully allegorical for marriage."

Krish's usually immobile mouth quirks. I'm all-out trying not to laugh. Sak's so good even I want a lehenga with peacocks and am ready to fight Druv to put trees on his sherwani.

"Did you just come up with that? That's brilliant!" the mother says, and her sky-high cheekbones push up into her eyes.

"Or stars and the moon," Sak says.

The bride squeals. "I love that idea. How did you know how much I love stars?" She lifts her hair and shows him the spray of stars tattooed on the back of her neck.

Sak's eyes brighten, genuine joy glistening in them, and I realize he isn't working these people. Well, maybe a little bit, but that's not his main angle. He's actually connecting with them. Seeing them, letting them in. It's generous and vulnerable, but also he's not afraid to use his own power.

He looks at the salesperson who was helping the mother and daughter. She's looking as awed as I'm feeling. "Have we put the Chanda-Tare collection out on display yet?" he asks.

"Not yet," the salesperson answers. "Oh, those are beautiful. They would've been perfect," she says to the bride and her mother.

The two women look like they might be on the edge of winning the lottery as their expectant gaze flits from the salesperson to Saket.

"The pieces have arrived in the store, though, right?" Saket says.

The salesperson nods, and Sak turns his attention back to the shoppers. "These are the headlining pieces in our summer collection. We did the photoshoot at the Lake Palace in Udaipur last month, and the campaign is just about ready for release. I think this might be my favorite collection yet. My fiancé says I say that with every collection, but these are my heart. My babies. I think I put all the magic he makes me feel into them."

The bride is in tears again. I think I am too. "When will they be displayed? We can come back."

"Oh, honey, I'd never do that to you. Would you like to see them?"

They jump at the offer with heartbreaking enthusiasm, and Sak turns to the salesperson. "Perna, would you bring them out? Xiang, would you help Perna?" He beckons another staff member. "Champagne?" he asks the ladies. "It's a special day!"

As everyone gets to work retrieving the new collection and champagne, Sak wraps an arm around me and introduces us.

"This is my fiancé's sister, Mira, and this is Krish."

The mother and daughter introduce themselves as Reena and Nimi. We shake hands.

"You look familiar. Have we met?" Nimi, the daughter, asks, trying to place me.

"Are you on social media?" Krish deadpans.

I hate that I want to smile. Sak fills them in on the ring saga, playing up the sidewalk fight and Krish's heroic rescue of the ring as we accept champagne flutes from Xiang.

"Well, Mira found it and hurt herself trying to save it. She's the one who's given up her vacation to find the owner. I'm just along for the ride," Krish says.

I can't tell if he's being facetious or if he means it. His eyes are no longer obscured by dark glasses. This is less of a relief than I was expecting because it's not easy to look into his eyes. The overhead lights are creating a glare on his glasses, and that, of all things, is a relief.

I work to not flush at the possible praise.

"You were both badasses fighting that monster." Naturally Sak says the most Sak thing ever. "Isn't it amazing? They're going to search for the ring's owner."

The two women gush over the romanticism of finding the ring. They ask to look at it. But this time I have it tucked away in a zippered pouch at the bottom of my bag, and I lie about having left it in my hotel room.

Saket and Krish look the tiniest bit impressed and relieved. They both know that I have the ring because we're here so Saket can help us. When Saket looked at it yesterday, he said that it looks like it had recently been repaired and polished. Krish and I spent an hour brainstorming the next steps at the café where our alliance started. We'd decided that visiting the local jewelers to check if they've seen the ring is the best place to start.

Our hope is that the ring was repaired by a local New York City jeweler. Unless it was a tourist wearing it, in which case we might as well give up. It's also obviously an Indian piece of jewelry, and we're hoping that it was taken to an Indian jeweler. Unless it was taken to India and then brought back, in which case we might as well give up.

I pull my mind away from the nay-saying spiral. I know we're going to find the owner. I just know it. I have to hang on to that belief and focus on finding the jeweler who might have worked on the ring.

I know Saket's store is a little too high end for small repairs. There's a better chance of it being one of the smaller jewelry businesses, and we're hoping he can point us in the right direction.

"Where would you even start to look?" Reena says. "You found it in the most crowded part of New York. Literally millions of people walk through Times Square every week."

"But half of those people could be native New Yorkers, Mom. The cool thing is that Sak could identify the country of origin as India. That's got to be a sign, right? Anyone could have found it, but Mira did."

"Right?" I say and glance at Krish, who's watching the unfolding action as though he's already writing the story in his head. "And Sak was also able to identify that the ring was damaged and has been repaired. So there's a chance that a local jeweler has seen the ring and might be able to give us some clues."

"Mom, what was that place Naani goes to in Jackson Heights? The place she wanted us to—"

"Nolandas," Reena says, cutting her daughter off. "They do repairs and polishing. They repaired my wedding set."

"There are about twenty jewelry stores along Seventy-Fourth," Sak says. "Nolandas is one of them. If the repair was done here in New York, then there's a good chance it's one of those stores."

Across the room, the salespeople finish setting up the new collection and beckon us over. Sak was right: it's spectacular. Breathtaking, and wildly over the top. Stars and moons formed of uncut diamonds, emeralds, and sapphires the size of blueberries, on growth hormones. If true love were opulence, this is a story that spans lifetimes.

The idea that Saket's feelings for my brother resulted in this makes me choke up. Rumi deserves it. He would throw himself in front of several speeding trains for Saket. He would walk away from every other person on the planet. He's walked away from our parents without a backward glance.

It's big, visible love, the kind of love that's not meant for everyone. I'm glad my brother has it. I have no idea how he's become the person who owns it so completely and feels so entirely deserving of it, and returns it with such fearless force. While I've spent the past year marveling at how I could possibly have been lucky enough to be with Druv.

Reena places a diamond-and-ruby piece around Nimi's neck and hooks it in the back. It starts as a choker around her neck, then cascades in a wide, deep triangle of a hundred stars to her cleavage and ends with a fringe of tiny moons. She looks like she just stepped out of a royal period drama or a mythical fantasy. I've just met her, but a vision of her as a bride springs into my head.

The mother breaks down first, then the daughter. They hold each other and sob. Their emotions are contagious, and tears push at my eyes. The pictures of wedding jewelry that Aie has been sending me have been accompanied by notes about what looks "rich but not like we're trying too hard" and what kind of color and design wouldn't emphasize my "dark coloring."

"Done?" Reena asks in the softest voice.

"It's the one," Nimi whispers back.

Both women throw their arms around Saket as he congratulates them and tells them he couldn't have had a more special first sale for the collection of his heart.

"I hope your naani likes it more than the piece she wanted you to get at Nolandas," Saket says, and we all laugh.

CHAPTER FIFTEEN

Sureva Bhalekar
St. Mary's Ladies Hostel
Charni Road, Bombay
July 1983

Vasudha Patil
Garware Ladies Hostel
Fergusson College, Pune

Dear Vasu,
I have done something terrible. I am so sorry. Please know that I'm doing everything to make it better. Please trust me and don't worry. Aie found the ring.

I was so happy when she surprised me with a visit last week. Now I feel so stupid. I should have known my happiness would have a price. It was kind of your father to bring Aie with him on his business trip so she could see me. I was careful to remove the ring from around my neck as soon as she arrived and hide it in a secret pocket in my handbag. But it all turned out to be useless.

She had to stay with her second cousin, since we can't have overnight visitors in the hostel. I went to see her every day and took her around Bombay to show her all the sights. We were having a lovely time, turning our hearts into Bombay, as the saying goes.

You say that Aie and I don't owe your family anything, but without your father neither Aie nor I would ever have been able to see Bombay in our lives. Appa-saheb practically had to force Aie to sit in the car and come to Bombay with him. No other employer treats their servants in this manner, like family. You should know that. He was coming to the Sachivalaya for a congress session, for heaven's sake! He had more important things on his mind. I wish you would understand my gratitude and not fill my head with nonsense just because you feel a certain way about me. Our friendship and your family's charity toward mine are two separate issues. You have to stop conflating them.

Coming back to the ring, Aie inspected my bag when I went to the bathroom. It was the one time I got careless and forgot to take the bag with me. She kept telling me that something was different about me and that I was hiding something from her (you know how good she always was at discovering mischief we tried to hide). She kept saying that I was not acting like a girl who was studying to be a teacher. I kept trying to tell her that nothing was different, that living by myself had obviously made me more worldly. She didn't believe me and said I should remember my place and not become too big for my shoes and ruin everything she's worked for.

You know how angry that makes me. Her fear, her lack of faith in me. How can she not understand that this engineering degree is going to give us a life she can't even imagine? It's going to let her repay all her debts and live free. I can hear all the excuses you're making on her behalf and I am not interested in them. If I weren't afraid for you and me, I would not be speaking to her right now.

I even almost told her that I was studying engineering and not teaching. I know you think I shouldn't lie to her. I would have told her if I weren't one hundred percent sure that she would make me quit and go back to Yevla and force me to get married off. You know that's no longer possible, Vasu. Not after last month.

My degree isn't the only thing she's suspicious about. She thinks I have something going on with some man. She thinks I have a lover. I should never have let her see me just after I spoke to you on the phone. That might be what ruined everything. After that, she kept pushing me and asking why I was looking the way I was. My own mother suspicious of my happiness. Can you believe such a thing?

Maybe you should never have sung to me at the youth festival. You were wrong. Ashatai Athavale does not have the most beautiful voice in the world. You do. I know you were supposed to have been singing for the audience, but I know you were not. It was in your eyes, which stayed on me the entire time. That was the thing that changed me, it changed my life. Maybe I should not have allowed everything that followed to happen, but are we born to turn away meaning when it finds us? Everything that happened was like light filling the sky when the sun rises, natural and inevitable.

I know we promised not to speak of this in our letters. But I cannot wait for you to call me on the phone to say this. If something goes wrong and we cannot reach each other, you have to know this. I will not be able to live this life without you, Vasu. What happened between us is the most beautiful thing I have ever experienced. Every breath I have taken since then has been more beautiful. And every breath I take in your presence is more beautiful than one where I am without you. If everything else were lost to me, every one of my senses gone, I would not trade how I feel when I'm with you to get it back. They can have everything, but they cannot have the piece of me that is you.

I am so sorry for how horrible I was to you after the first time. Of course you were braver, of course you knew better than me what this was. I was afraid. I'm always a coward at the start of anything new. You know that. I cannot bear the idea of you being hurt. If I let myself think about how much this could hurt you, I'll never be able to stand up again and go on living.

I should never have called what happened between us the ugly names I did. Thank you for not believing me. Thank you for giving me another chance. I am forever incomplete without you and I will never again forget it. Who we are when we're with each other cannot be anything but God's gift. No, they cannot take that from us.

I know we cannot do this without lies. I will tell a million lies for us.

The lie I told my aie feels like the first of those million we're going to have to tell. She obviously knew that it was your ring and that there's another one in the set. I told her that you forgot it in my bag when I visited you and you gave it to me for safekeeping. She didn't believe me. "Why would Vasu-baby only put one of the two rings in your bag?" she asked. "Where is the other one?" "Why is there a thread tied to it?"

But the question that hurt the most was "How could you steal from the family we owe everything to?"

She thinks I'm a thief, Vasu.

I, who have never asked her for anything. Not even new clothes on Diwali. Did you know that I let her sell the clothes your family bought me for Diwali? I never told anyone. I understood that we needed the money and I didn't need the clothes. Your used clothes that your mother gave me were as good as any. I am in one of the world's best engineering colleges, on a full scholarship, studying to change the world we live in (that's what Professor Pai said to me last week). Why would I ever steal?

But I don't care that she thinks that. What I do care about, what I'm terrified of, is the fact that I know she will not rest until she has told Appa-saheb and confessed on my behalf and begged for forgiveness. I've begged her not to. I've assured her I'm going to return the ring to you. I've told her I would die of shame if Appa-saheb and your aie think me a thief too. I don't think that will stop her for too long.

I have thought and thought but I don't know how to stop her, so I am turning to you. What should we do?

I might be a coward at the start of any change, but as you often remind me, I find my courage eventually (thank you for believing that even when I have a hard time believing it myself). I've been thinking about how we can be together forever without letting the world stop us and call us ugly. I do have a plan for that, but we'll never get that far if we don't come up with a plan to convince my aie that her suspicions are unfounded. Since our brains work in entirely different ways, I know you will find a solution where I see none.

Yours and only always yours,

Suru

CHAPTER SIXTEEN

Jackson Heights reminds me of Devon Avenue in Chicago. Every Saturday of my childhood my mother took us there to pick up Indian fruits and vegetables from the grocery stores in Little India to stock at Bombay Masala for a markup. One of my oldest memories is Rumi and me helping her carry cardboard boxes filled with sharp-smelling curry leaves, curly-skinned bitter melon, extra-hot Thai green chilies, hairy brown taro root, young green mango, and bunches of fenugreek and cilantro with the dirt they were pulled from still clinging to their roots. I'd wait eagerly to get everything loaded into the trunk of our van so we could have our special treat. One plate of pani puri split between the three of us. Two pieces for each of us.

I've never been to India, but in my head Devon's Little India always stood in for visits to where my parents are from, even though I'm pretty sure Indian towns don't look and feel anything like that. Or like this: shop windows with gold-embellished ghagras and saris, interspersed with grocery stores and restaurants that fill the air with the aroma of smoky tandoori chicken and buttery samosas.

In the Indian movies I've watched, the teeming heat, dust, color, and crowds captured on screen make these streets seem like an anemic shadow of what they're aspiring to be. It's a bubble, an island, still intrinsically New York, with different skin and clothes. Or the other way around: Indian on the inside but placed firmly in a foreign context. A little like me. I don't know which of those two I am either.

I've been nervous about my visit to India next month, but suddenly I'm curious. An entire country and culture that's a significant part of my identity, and I have no idea what its reality is.

As Krish and I stop outside the Jackson Heights subway station and study our phones for where to start, I wonder if he's ever been to the land of our ancestors. He doesn't seem to be experiencing the existential thoughts crowding my brain.

He's also not nearly as rumpled as he was yesterday. His stubble is gone, and his clean-shaven jaw is smooth and angular. His hair is pulled back into a simple elastic tie, and the result is the strangest combination of nerdy and outdoorsy.

"So which way?" I ask.

He looks up from his phone. "I think we go that way."

On the subway ride here, we identified the route we would follow to cover all the jewelry stores. Until we got off the train and took the stairs up, he seemed as loose limbed and at home in his skin as ever. Now behind him is a giant store sign for **Meena Bazaar** written in five different Indian languages, and he looks like a martian who's just made an Earth landing.

This isn't the first time I've noticed it, the minuscule ways in which his body language screams *unfamiliar* when he's presented with anything from the Indian subcontinent. It reminds me of the way the kids at my school looked at the dal and rice in my lunch, even though that was my lunch every single day. Not so much discomfort as distance.

"Have you never been to Jackson Heights before?" I ask.

"Not a whole lot." That's it. That's all he says. No anecdotes of coming here with his family, or food memories, or any nostalgic associations.

There's a very particular way in which he seems to protect information about himself. Maybe it has to do with the fact that as a reporter he spends a lot of time digging information out of others and that's made him conscious of how to keep information to himself. His disconnection is subtle, but my superpower for homing in on any kind of discomfort goes into overdrive.

"Did you grow up in New York?"

"Connecticut," he says. "New Canaan." The word fills his mouth the way the names of our hometowns always fill our mouths, as though we can taste them.

I've never heard of it, but I've obviously heard the most common stereotype about Connecticut: that a lot of rich people who work in New York live there.

"Are there a lot of Indian families there?" I don't even know why I ask that, except I'm feeling inexplicably curious, and evidently ungenerous. Most brown kids I grew up with got over their brown-discomfort by high school, or at least by college.

He laughs and says no, but he's really saying *Hell, no*.

"Was that hard?" I say. Rumi and I were one of about ten Indian kids across our grade in elementary school. There was still a strange isolating spotlight I remember feeling when I was surrounded by the hundred kids who looked different from me and seemed to know it. How I felt wasn't so much conscious but a sensation under my skin. I never really identified the feeling until much later.

I can't imagine what being the only one might feel like. "How did your family decide to live there?" To this day, my parents act noticeably strange when "foreigners" walk into the store. It's almost as though, like their ancestors, they're still living in colonized India, and a colonizer just walked in.

"My family has lived there since they got off the *Mayflower*," he says flatly. "Can we start on our list of jewelers? You have less than two days to do this."

"Your family came here on the *Mayflower*? The *Mayflower-Mayflower*, or is that code for some sort of visa I don't know about?"

His face does a thing where he doesn't seem to know if I'm joking or serious. "I wouldn't have pegged you for someone so nosy."

"I wouldn't have pegged you for such a fortress." Truth is I'm never nosy unless I'm interrogating my patients for sources of pain.

"Let's start with Nolandas. That's at the northern end of Seventy-Fourth. It's going to take us a while to hit them all."

He's right: we don't have time for anything else. Why do I care, anyway, that his family chose to move to a place that's made him this uncomfortable with his heritage? I start walking. He shoves his hands into his pockets and falls in step next to me. He might have cleaned up his appearance, but he's wearing the same worn-in dark jeans he's had on since I met him. I imagine him with a closet full of identical clothes and want to smile.

Instead of a gray Henley, he's in an olive green quarter-zip fleece. It's a good twenty degrees cooler today than yesterday, and I forgot to carry my hoodie. I packed mostly summer dresses that I picked up when Druv and I first bought our tickets. I also bought dressy evening outfits, which I'm glad I left at home.

The first time we rescheduled, I canceled our dinner reservations at all the fancy New York restaurants Druv wanted to take me to. I haven't had a chance to give much thought to the itinerary Druv and I so painstakingly put together. This trip hasn't exactly been the engagement-moon we'd planned, but my heart is still racing with excitement as we head to the first jewelry store.

~

It takes three hours to visit twelve stores, with no luck.

Krish sinks into a bench outside a boba shop, which, much like him, feels entirely out of place here.

I sit down next to him. "Was it really necessary to be so rude to the salesperson?" I ask.

"You've answered questions about your wedding in each store. I wasn't rude, I just left before I had to hear the answers for the twelfth time."

"Jewelers are in the business of weddings. They're interested. It breaks the ice."

"Okay."

"It wasn't like I was planning to spend my vacation visiting jewelry shops." With a grumpy reporter in tow. "I haven't seen one single thing on my checklist."

"Let me guess," he says in the most patronizing tone ever. "Central Park, Times Square, the Empire State, the Statue of Liberty, the *Friends* coffee shop . . . What did I miss?"

My chin goes up, but I refuse to be this petulant child I'm feeling like, and I lower it. "The MoMA. I love Van Gogh, and I've only seen what they have at the Art Institute in Chicago." In third grade we did a project on Van Gogh's paintings, and I remember becoming obsessed with drawing the blue swirling sky of his *Starry Night* over and over again. It felt like a portal sucking me out of where I was, and sucking things out of me. I also remember throwing the art away so Aie wouldn't yell at me for wasting my time. "And I've never watched *Friends*."

Of all things, his eyebrows shoot up at that.

"I tried. But it felt fake. Or it made me feel odd, like my life was too far from normal."

He doesn't respond. Just looks at me through his frameless glasses with an odd kind of curiosity. His eyes are the translucent brown of beer bottles, and his lashes are so long and thick they seem to crisscross and clump together.

"What happens if we can't find the ring's owner?" he asks finally.

"You don't think we will."

"It is a possibility. Actually it's more of a probability."

Technically, he's not wrong, but disappointment grips me, and his expression softens into something too close to sympathy.

"It would be such a waste," I say. "For me to fall, for me to find the ring, for me to post that video, for you to find me. It would all be such a waste if the person who lost the ring doesn't get it back. It's almost like the universe is conspiring for something to happen, and I can't figure out how to do my part."

"So, this person not getting their ring back is your fault?" He smiles. Like the rest of him, his smile is restrained. As though he's being observed, being photographed when he smiles. Actually, it's not just restrained, it's performative. I know because I've seen my own smile in pictures.

"It feels that way. How can two million people have watched that video and no one who knows anything about the ring has seen it? It's not a common design. If I saw it on someone, I'd remember. I just don't get it."

"Do you always take responsibility for everything that goes wrong in the world? There are several wars going on right now that no one wants to take blame for. They might need you."

"Funny you say that. It's quite the opposite, actually. I'm usually accused of not taking responsibility for my own life."

"Really? I was getting a more hyperresponsible vibe."

"You should talk to Rumi. Or my mom and dad. It's a totally fake vibe."

"And the fiancé? Does he blame you for everything too?"

"I never said they blame me for everything," I snap. "It's just that . . . never mind. Let's just go back to looking, please."

Without another word he stands and starts walking toward the next jeweler on our list. Heera Mahal. The Diamond Palace.

"What if you're right and it's the end of the road?" I fall in step next to him.

"It won't be. You're right. It would be an awful waste of coincidences if you had fallen and found the ring for nothing."

I'm so surprised I stop in my tracks. He doesn't seem like someone who's so easily convinced.

Last night in my hotel room I fell down the rabbit hole of looking up Krish's work. Every one of his stories proves he's a hard-ass. Everything I found was unapologetically weighty: political lobbying and gerrymandering, corruption on Wall Street, corporate cover-ups. I don't even know why he's interested in this little-ole-me story. Maybe it's a bet?

"Why are you being like this?" I ask.

"Being like what?"

"Why do you suddenly believe me?"

He looks at me as though he has no idea what I mean, so I elaborate. "The things I said about there being a reason why I found the ring. I wasn't even that convincing. Why are you suddenly convinced?"

"You were convincing. That's the whole story. Your belief that you are meant to . . . that you are *going to* find the owner. If we don't believe that, why are we even here?"

"So you're waiting for the crash and burn?"

"Mira, you believe in this. You've believed it with such passion from the start. Why are you letting how I feel get in the way of that?"

"So you don't believe we're going to find it. You're just doing this for the story."

"I don't know if we're going to find it. I do know that we're going to try our damndest." He turns to me. "The only thing I can tell you for sure is that I'm not doing it only for the story." With that cryptic pronouncement, he steps up to the glass door of Heera Mahal and waits for me to give him a sign that I'm still in.

I nod, and we enter the thirteenth store on our list.

Unlike all the other stores, this one isn't brightly lit. Like all the other stores we've visited already, this one hasn't been updated in a while. Honestly, at this point it's impossible to tell one store from the other. They all have blue or maroon velvet-lined shelves that carry nearly identical necklace-and-earring sets that are large enough to be seen across a room. They do have more delicate wares, but those are arranged in display cases under the glass countertops.

"May I help you?" a salesperson says for the thirteenth time. This one is wearing a pink silk kurta. I feel a little weary.

"I'm Krish Hale," Krish says. "I'm a reporter with the *New York Times*. We're trying to track down the owner of a lost ring." We've started each interaction exactly this way.

The man looks baffled. "We don't know anything about lost rings," he says, sticking out his chest and looking at once terrified and brave. This, too, has been the pattern: an initial reaction of fear and suspicion. Half the salespeople relaxed and turned friendly soon enough, asking questions and trying to sell us things. The other half looked at the ring, told us they'd never seen it before, and rushed to get us out of the store. Only half of those cracked when I tried to make small talk about my wedding to get them to relax.

"Could you take a look at it for us? We have reason to believe it was recently repaired." Krish looks at me, and I pull the pouch out of my bag, unzip it, and hold the ring out.

Without taking the ring, the guy leads us to the counter and moves to the other side. He puts a velvet-lined tray on the glass between us and waits.

I put the ring on the tray. I think I've just been chastised for not treating jewelry with the respect it deserves. I want to smile, but I don't, and I notice that Krish isn't smiling, either, but behind his glasses, his eyes definitely are.

The salesman picks up the ring. He looks as impressed as the others have. "It's antique. Over a hundred years old. They don't make gold like this anymore. It's twenty-four karats. They don't make jewelry with twenty-four karats anymore because pure gold is too soft, and it doesn't hold shape." He indicates some curving along the ring where the ring has lost its form.

"We were wondering if there's any way to know if it was brought here for repairs," I say.

He examines the ring again. "This repair?" He points at the part where the flame-shaped bezel has the finest line on it where it might have broken off and been reattached. "This was done years ago, at least forty years ago. This isn't a new repair job. No one uses this kind of soldering anymore. And this was done in India. This is a one hundred percent desi technique of repair that needs a master goldsmith to do it."

"Are you sure?" I ask and get a haughty look in return.

"I've been working with gold for fifty years. I started apprenticing for my dad in Zaveri Bazaar in Mumbai when I was twelve. I can recognize the origin of any piece of jewelry." He looks at my ears. "Those solitaires are from Costco. The design is from about two years ago. Point seven-two carats, VVS1, and G color." Then he throws my engagement ring a glance. "That's Tiffany. Two carats." He turns to Krish. "Good eye, sir. You were going for the big gesture, ha? But the same diamond, better quality, from us would have saved you at least two thousand dollar."

Krish slides me a glance but leaves how I want to respond to me.

"He's not my fiancé," I say quickly. "He's just helping me find the ring's owner."

"Oh. Sorry. My mistake. I can match a jewel with its store, but I guess I can't match human jewels as skillfully." He laughs. "But I did get your other jewels correct, did I not?"

"You did. I'm impressed," I say.

"I am renowned for it. Maybe if your fiancé was here, I wouldn't have gotten that wrong either." He points at Krish. "I guess I was looking at the wrong piece." He laughs, far too thrilled with his own joke, and I smile politely.

Suddenly Krish sits up. "Can I see the chain?"

When I don't respond because it takes me a moment to figure out what he's talking about, he adds, "The chain with the ring."

"Of course." I pull the chain from the pouch, and a light bulb goes on in my head as I realize what Krish is thinking. Maybe we've been showing them the wrong piece.

I place it on the velvet tray. "Can you tell us anything about this chain?"

The jeweler picks up the chain and studies it. "Easy, this is from Anderson's in Brooklyn. They've been there for a hundred years, I think, but this is a newer design. Maybe 2015 or so. But it's a faulty design. See . . ." He shows us where the link is broken as though that should tell us something. "Sooner or later this kind of twisted wire snaps. Especially when someone wears it every day. Was the chain used to wear the ring around the neck?"

"Yes," both Krish and I say together.

He tut-tuts disapprovingly. "That chain is not strong enough for the weight of that ring. The jeweler should have told the customer that."

"Does the store have multiple locations?" Krish asks.

"No, it's family owned, and the old man still runs the store. One of his sons was working with him to take over from him. Then he died last year. Very sad. The other son is a waste of space, no interest in the family legacy. I think he sings in some bar or something."

Krish lets him finish with the most absorbed expression. I'm practically bouncing in my seat. Krish starts tapping on his phone. "Did you say Anderson's?"

"Yes, they're in Williamsburg. They close in half an hour. I don't think you can make it there with this traffic. And with the subway line disruptions, it will take at least an hour to make it there by subway."

"So, we can't make it there until tomorrow morning?" I say, and my heart all but sinks.

"It would appear that way," the man says kindly.

Krish's eyes are searching the street through the shop windows. He picks up the ring and chain and hands it to me. Then goes to the door, steps out on the street, looks around, and comes back in. "There's a motorcycle parked outside the store. Does that belong to any of your guys?" He throws a glance at the two other salespeople.

"It's mine," the younger man says.

"Two hundred dollars if you let us borrow it for the evening. We'll drop it off at the store tomorrow morning. You can look me up on the internet. I work at the *New York Times*. Krish Hale. I'm not going to disappear."

"Two hundred dollars?" the young man and I say together.

"Yes, and I'll leave my watch as collateral. You can keep it if I don't come back." He removes his very expensive-looking watch and holds it up.

The man pulls the keys from his pocket and tosses them at Krish, who naturally catches them midair, because suddenly we're in some sort of dude-bro movie.

"Thank you, man." Krish manufactures two hundred-dollar notes and slaps them, along with the watch, on the counter in front of the man, and they do some sort of testosterone-laced shoulder bump.

"Let's go," Krish says to me. "We have half an hour to make it to Brooklyn."

CHAPTER SEVENTEEN

What exactly are we doing?" I ask, following Krish out into the street.

"Going to Anderson's Jewelers before they close."

"How?" I refuse to look at the motorcycle he's standing beside, his stance suddenly all Power Ranger–y.

He unsnaps the helmet from the handle and hands it to me. "I'm riding a motorcycle, and you're riding behind me."

"I don't think so."

He straddles the bike's thorax-like body. It looks a little like a garden ant was magnified and metallized. It rumbles like thunder when he turns it on.

"Do you even know how to ride that thing?"

He looks at me patiently. "I'm a better rider than I am a writer. Does that help?"

"That makes me very nervous about letting you write this story."

He's trying not to smile. "Well, a motorcycle race just got added to the story, so really, how can it go wrong? Hop on."

"Ah, you're being ironic," I say, unable to move. "Also, how does one hop on this thing? What am I, a rabbit?"

He laughs, and it's really weird to feel good about making someone laugh when you're gripped by panic. "You just saw me get on. Do what I did. Take a step closer and throw one leg over the way I just did."

"Can I throw you off it instead, and then we can take a cab?"

He laughs again. Suddenly Mr. Broody is all Mr. Amused. "Sure, if you want to get there after it closes."

Ugh. "Fine. Can it take both our weight?"

"Mira, they close in twenty-five minutes. I'm a good rider. Trust me. Do you really want to wait until tomorrow when your flight leaves tomorrow afternoon?"

"Stop pressuring me. I'm terrified of heights." I know that sounds unrelated, but it's why I don't get on roller coasters, and this feels a lot like that.

Another laugh. He takes the helmet, puts it on my head, and secures the strap. "We're going to stay on the ground, I promise. No wheelies until we know who dropped the ring."

I groan. I'm going to have to do this. I try to channel *Charlie's Angels*, and I mount the growling machine. It's the weirdest feeling I've ever experienced in my life.

"You've seriously never ridden a motorcycle?" he says, as though it's a normal thing for people to ride killing machines where your breakable body is entirely exposed while flying through the air.

"I like a metal box around me when I'm traveling at high speeds. Do you know how many bike accident survivors I've treated?"

"I'm going to try my best to make sure that doesn't happen to us. Okay?"

I squeak an affirmative-ish sound, and the motorcycle bounces as he takes it off the stand. I squeak again.

"Still okay?" There's a smile in his voice but also kindness.

"There's literally metal vibrating between my legs," I say.

This time his laugh is big and free. "That's what she said."

That's when I learn that when embarrassment and fear live together inside you, fear wins. "Why the hell would anyone want to do this voluntarily?" But I'm on, and I grab his shoulders because even though we're not yet moving I feel off balance.

"Hold on, close your eyes, and imagine something soothing. Like shopping for your wedding." And with that he takes off.

~

Krish helps me off the bike and leaves his hand cupping my elbow until my legs steady. "You did good. It's normal to have shaky legs after riding."

He's totally patronizing me, but I haven't caught my breath enough to be snarky in response. To be honest, it wasn't bad. He did seem to know what he was doing, and it was more weaving through traffic and riding between lanes of cars than a 007-style thriller chase.

"I might throw up," I say.

He bends down to study my face. When he determines that I will not actually be bringing up my guts, he looks at his phone. "They close in ten minutes."

"We got here in fifteen minutes?"

He shrugs. "Bikes can be handy."

I start walking, but I stumble, and he holds out a bent arm instead of taking mine.

"There's something weirdly gallant about you, you know that?" I say and use his arm to steady myself.

"That might be the first nice thing you've said to me. Unless you're calling me old."

"How old are you?"

"Thirty-eight."

"Really?"

"How old did you think I was?"

"I thought you were younger than me. Closer to twenty-eight."

"There's an advantage, I guess, to not hitting puberty until college." A particular kind of sadness flashes in his eyes. For the first time since we met, it seems like he's forgotten to pull on his nonchalant mask.

He grew up the only Indian kid in his town, and he didn't hit puberty until college. I would never call my childhood easy, but his doesn't sound like a breeze either.

"That's got to be the male equivalent of me being the first and only girl in my elementary school to hit puberty." I've never verbalized childhood discomfort to anyone ever, and for a moment, I'm even more disoriented than I was flying across New York on a motorcycle.

We're under the maroon awning of the store. He pulls his arm away from me, holds open the door, and does a gallant, gentlemanly bow.

I hate admitting this, but it's freaking adorable.

This store is entirely different from anything we've seen today. For one, it's small. There's a single long counter that runs along the far wall. It's the standard glass-topped case displaying pieces of jewelry that are nowhere near the scale of what we've seen everywhere else. There are a few mannequin heads on shelves lining the wall, which display classic Western pieces. Pendants of diamonds around sapphires and rubies, with understated drops for earrings. It's much more Hollywood than Bollywood.

"May I help you?" a man asks from behind the counter, and Krish and I exchange a smile. That's number fourteen today.

"I'm so glad you're still open," I say, more excitedly than I intended, and the man smiles a few-teeth-missing smile.

Krish introduces us in the exact same way he's done all the times before and asks if someone can help with identifying if the chain came from this store.

The man, who looks almost exactly like the Albert Einstein photograph from one of my physics textbooks, beckons us to his glass case. More déjà vu makes me throw a glance Krish's way, just as he does the same. It's weird that we've only been at this for a day. It feels like this day has spanned a few years.

The man pushes a velvet tray toward us, and I place the chain on it.

He picks it up. "Ah, it's our Marilyn. Beautiful. My late wife designed it. But it never caught on because it kept breaking when customers put a locket on it, especially a heavy one." He stares regretfully at the chain. "We had to discontinue it."

Krish and I look at each other again. Did we just do it?

"That was my wife's name," the man says. "Marilyn. She had black hair and brown eyes. An angular little woman." He smiles wistfully. "She was named after everyone's favorite bombshell, her mother's favorite actress. Marilyn—my Marilyn, not Monroe—never understood why her parents named her that, given that she was black haired and brown eyed at birth."

There's a framed picture of a stern-faced woman, wearing a black dress buttoned all the way up to her neck, with hair so tightly tied back just looking at it gives me a headache. My own messy bun has really leaned into its name after that bike ride.

"How did you meet her?" I ask. "Your Marilyn?"

"She worked in my father's workshop after her family moved here from Romania. The best metalworker I'd ever seen. I used to design pieces, and she would turn them into magic. Knew exactly how to tweak each piece to make it even more eye catching. There was nothing more beautiful than her when she was working on a piece. It used to make me breathless. All the way till the end, seeing her make jewelry made me breathless."

"That's beautiful," I say.

He makes a sound that's suspiciously close to *pfft*. "Outside the workshop she had an inferno of a temper. Couldn't get along with no one. Not her own parents, not mine, not even our kids. Told everyone to go to hell. Except me. For thirty-five years."

"Why do you think that is?" Krish asks. No wonder he's won all those journalistic awards.

Mr. Anderson, which is what I assume the man's name is, presses a finger to his lips. "Shutting up. I don't enjoy talking much. When you shut up, nobody gets to tell you to shut up."

Krish makes a sympathetic sound. Mr. Anderson has just talked for fifteen minutes straight without taking a breath.

"What about you two?" His gaze bounces between us. "She do all the talking, or do you get a word in?"

Once again Krish waits for me to respond.

"He's a chatterbox," I say. "Couldn't get the man to shut up if I tried."

Krish shakes his head, and I notice for the first time that he has the hint of a dimple that softens the sharp angles of his face when he smiles and he's trying not to.

"I thought that's why you fell in love with me, because you couldn't get enough of what I had to say."

"It's true. It's handy at night. He starts talking, and I fall right to sleep."

His smile widens, and the dimple deepens.

Mr. Anderson looks like he just met someone who speaks his language in a foreign country. "Exactly. No insomnia when Mar was around. Now I can't sleep without one of those gummies." He pats the chest pocket of his white shirt.

"When's the wedding?" he asks, pointing to my engagement ring. "Is it going to be one of those big Indian weddings? Based on that ring, I'm thinking it is."

Before I can answer, he tells us about an Indian wedding he and his wife went to in 1999. A diamond-merchant friend had rented out all of Yankee Stadium. Obviously, it left an impression. "Heartburn for days from the food, but Mar got drunk, and we danced until two in the morning. They had flown in all your Indian film stars to do those dances. Will you be wearing one of those red-and-gold sari dresses? Will he be riding an elephant?"

Suddenly my cheeks are flaming.

"Would you know who might have bought this chain?" Krish asks, sliding a quick glance at me.

Mr. Anderson looks at the chain. "Mar was really good at keeping records of customers. We only sold this model when she was alive."

"If someone brought it in to repair, would there be any way to find out? We think the repair was done fairly recently."

His bushy-browed eyes light up. He presses a finger to his temple. "I think last week . . ." He trails off and walks away, leaving us alone in the tiny little space filled with priceless merchandise. We could easily swipe something and make a run for it.

Krish points to the cameras and the locks on the display cases. "Everything's secured. He's done this long enough that he knows what he's doing. He isn't as frail and helpless as he seems." he says softly, as though he assumes that the man is listening to us from wherever he's gone off to.

"He seems lonely," I whisper, close and soft too.

"Who isn't?" he says.

Before I can quite absorb that, the man returns, his arms full of leather-bound ledgers.

"You've got to be kidding me," Krish says, also under his breath. But he steps forward and helps the man put the ledgers down.

"We'll have to look, but I think an old customer came in a week or so ago. I only remember because I recognize the Marilyn. Not easy to forget the piece you named for the love of your life."

For the first time since the ring landed in my hand, I feel my heart beating in a completely different way. Although I've felt hopeful from the moment I found it, the hope has felt like it belongs to someone else, a character I'm playing. This time my hope feels real, like it's mine. I bounce on my heels and lean over the counter. "Would you have her name in one of these?"

"Every single person who's ever bought anything from us over the last seventy years we have a record of. But don't worry, this is just the last few months. I brought it all out just to be safe. Also because they all look the same." He opens a few ledgers until he finds the one he's looking for. "This one's from last month." He starts poring over the neatly written entries.

A part of me is thrilled that they sell so much at the store. When I first walked in, I was a little sad about how run down the place looked.

When I look closely, I see that each page has only one entry with a lot of notes and drawings.

He flips through the pages, looking at the headings, which are words and phrases like *Lightbulb*, *Cleopatra's Eyes*, *Tiger's Breath*, and so forth.

"Mar liked to name our pieces," he says as he flips pages, and it strikes me that it's been half an hour since closing time. He hasn't said anything, and so I don't either.

Finally, I know he's found something when Krish's entire body language changes. He's been reading the ledger upside down. I had forgotten about his photographic memory, which is ironic. I wonder if being able to read upside down goes with having a brain like a computer.

Mr. Anderson puts a finger on the center of the page. "That's it. This one. It was the fifteenth of last month. The lady lives right here in Brooklyn. She bought the Marilyn many years ago to replace an old fake chain that was giving her a rash. I think she developed a nickel allergy. She said she had to have it because of its name."

When I look impressed, he points to the notes. "Most of this information is here, but I also remember because we were not used to those types back then, so it stands out. I was uncomfortable serving her, but then Mar looked like she would take my head off, and I never went against my Mar."

I'm about to ask what he means by *those types* when he says, "And we don't get a whole lot of Indian customers. They tend to go to the guys in Jackson Heights. So, I remember."

"Can we know her name and address?" I ask, but I already know that Krish has it memorized upside down.

Mr. Anderson pulls the ledger toward himself. "There are privacy laws, young lady. But I can call her for you and tell her you have the chain and the ring and ask if it's hers."

CHAPTER EIGHTEEN

Vasudha Patil
Garware Ladies Hostel
Fergusson College, Pune
July 1983

Sureva Bhalekar
St. Mary's Ladies Hostel
Charni Road, Bombay

Dear Suru,
I know things are bad when you send me a letter that doesn't have numbered points and subheadings. I hope this new us doesn't change the old us. I love that word you used: conflate. Is it a combination of contain and inflate? That's how I feel. Like our love always contained us into one being, but what has happened between us—the hunger to feel each other's physical being—inflates us into something higher, something even more beautiful.

Of course I was singing to you. Every song I've ever sung has been for you. I think I've always known,

Suru. I've always loved you. In every way it is possible to love. Welcome, I have been waiting here for you.

I know you've blamed yourself for touching me that way first. The moment when you came to see me in the greenroom after the show, tears shining in your eyes from the sound of my singing, and pulled me to yourself. It will always be the most beautiful moment of my life (if life's beauty can be turned into a scale and superlatives apply). If I could put into words the relief of that moment I would, but I suspect you do not need my words, you felt that relief too. It felt like being allowed an entire lake after burning in the desert without a drop for so long I'd forgotten the taste of water.

I can still feel the softness of your lips, see the fire in your eyes. It makes me unafraid now. I've thought about this a lot, I used to be afraid of losing you. But now when you are inside me and I have felt your touch, even tearing my body open cannot take it away.

You've studied the universe, from its tiniest elements to their place on this massive rock, and you know that there is always a reason why things—atoms and molecules?—are placed in each other's vicinity, because forces outside their control bring them together and tear them apart. It cannot be a coincidence that your aie found her way to my parents' home when she'd had you but a week and your home had been destroyed in the fire. Imagine the courage it took for her to leave her village so soon after your father died and knock on doors to find work with an infant strapped to her breast.

It cannot be a coincidence that my aie had just had me and was unable to make milk for me and I would vomit up any other milk they tried to feed me. I would have died if you hadn't been born. That cannot be a coincidence. We are covalent atoms. Without your existence mine would not have been possible.

Why would any of that have happened for no reason? And if the highest power itself has willed us to be together, why should we be afraid? I have already told my aie on the phone that I left one of the rings in your bag when I gave it to you for safekeeping in the crowded college auditorium. They know that you were visiting Pune for the Youth Cultural Festival. (Naturally, I have not told them that I sang onstage. You know that I would be immediately shipped back to Yevla if Aie and Appa found that out.) (Oh, and Aie was very happy to learn that you are doing well in school and keeping good health. Actually, she was grateful that you had the rings for safekeeping because you are so much more responsible than I am.)

I also told her that in my hurry to take the rings back from your purse before you left, I forgot one of them in there. She was not surprised. Obviously, this is what she would expect me to do. She was surprised that you did not check that I had both rings. To which I told her that you did remind me and I still forgot. Also, a pattern she was not surprised by. So all is well, dear Suru. We are safe for now.

I am eager to hear your plan for the rest of our lives. I have one too, but I suspect it is more simple and less viable than yours. Which obviously means we will be following yours rather than mine. Which obviously makes me hopeful and happy (a pretty constant state for me these days).

I'm looking right now at that Darwin book you left me. It's interesting enough. The man seems to understand the world in a way the world needs to be understood. There is also an added advantage to reading it: as soon as I read a few pages I get the best sleep. I almost want to give it to my aie. Instead of taking her pill to sleep she could use this. (Of course I know she cannot read English. Which is why I think she is so terrified that I can.) Actually there is another advantage, the photograph of yourself you left in it. Tell the truth, you left it in there as a test to see if I would read it, did you not? The photograph is beautiful.

Did I tell you that you look like Marilyn Monroe with your new haircut? Thank you so much for forcing me to go to the screening of *The Seven Year Itch* at the National Film Institute. I was afraid I would not understand the spoken English (although thanks to you forcing me to write these letters in English, my written English is greatly improved), but with your translation (how is your spoken English so much better than mine?) I could understand most of it. Not that infidelity is terribly complex. The film itself was like any other film, but I have not been able to get Marilyn out of my mind. I know what you are thinking. It isn't that (there is only place for one bombshell in my heart, even though mine isn't blond).

As I sat there watching Ms. Monroe filling up the screen, I kept thinking how, of all the people in the world, she was the one who seemed to look straight at us and understand us.

I could not put my finger on it until now. I think I know now why a woman who looks and acts nothing like anyone we know, let alone us ourselves, would feel so familiar. It's because what she is on the outside keeps everyone from paying any attention to who she is on the inside. To everyone who looks upon her, especially men, she is a shell inside which they can place whatever they want to believe. I think it's an experience all women relate to. Because of the way we're made on the outside, we've already been told who we are on the inside: what we can think, what we can do. Our shells, our bodies, they are vessels they have stuffed with their own beliefs. They've decided for us who we are. Who we actually are seems of

September 1983

Sorry I had to leave the letter in the middle of writing it because the girl in the next room rushed over to say that Appa had just arrived at the hostel. Usually men are not allowed here in the girls' hostel, but rules do not apply to men like my appa. In my panic I tucked the letter in my bra. Which was a fortunate thing because he was in a rage and searched my room. I know it's been months, but they've brought me back to Yevla and locked me in my room and taken away all my pens. I was able to steal one from the guard and now I can finally finish it, albeit not in the manner in which I wanted to and not at leisure either.

Everything is over, Suru.

Appa came looking for your letters and found them. He hit me so hard, across my face, I wasn't able to see out of my right eye for weeks. Even now I can only see clearly with my left one. Which is enough to be able to write to you. I hope this letter reaches you. I gave Ranjana the gardener's wife my silver anklets in return for her secretly taking this letter to the post office. I can only hope that she will do as she promised. I am sorry the handwriting is so terrible. Aie broke the fingers of my right hand by slamming a book into my hand.

We've always said that you are the smarter one and I the braver one. I never understood what you were afraid of. You always said only a girl who had never lost anything or wanted for anything could be as brave as me. Now I could lose you—and I've never wanted anything as much as I want to be with you. If I lost you I wouldn't know what to live for. For the first time I am terrified.

Your name means the rain and mine the earth, how can anyone want to keep us apart?

Appa said we were filthy. He said he should have listened to Aie and never let me out of the house because when you let girls study and live alone and don't marry them off young they do dirty things for sex. Aie spat on my face when Appa brought me home. She refuses to look at me. Who would have thought the breaking of a heart makes the breaking of bones feel insignificant?

In the movies we watched, when men love women they fight for them. They get beaten up to prove their love. Then they hit back. What happens to us? Who do we smash so we can have each other? How is it fair that they get to beat us both down, crush us both. Our love is as strong as theirs, isn't it, Suru? They just never let us strengthen our bodies enough to fight them.

When I gave you the ring and you hung it by your neck to hide it, I remember wishing you didn't have to. I wanted everyone to know that we wore two halves of the same ring. That we are part of a whole, one and the same. Now I want to hide. I'll hide forever. I'll do anything so they leave us alone.

I wish I could go on writing but I do not have time to say anything more than this: Do not come home. Do not try to reach me. Not yet. I will find a way to escape and be with you. I will never let anyone else touch me. I cannot.

If Appa sends anyone to find you, hide. Don't even go anywhere with your aie. I thought she at least would understand me but she hasn't come to see me or help me while I've been locked up in my room. I suspect she was the one who told Appa about the ring and caused him to come looking for your letters.

I know you have friends, but if you can think of nowhere else to hide when he comes for you, go to Ashatai Athavale. She is the bravest person I know. She has friends who hide women hunted by their families. I will make my way there ultimately. Wait for me.

Please do not forget how much I love you.

Forever only yours,

Vasu

CHAPTER NINETEEN

Her name is Reva Smith," Krish announces in a tone even more broody than normal as we leave Anderson's.

Actually, I leave. *He* storms out with the curtest thanks. That stick up his behind is truly whimsical. He's been perfectly pleasant all day. Or at least as pleasant as one can expect from a generally distant person. Mr. Anderson (whose actual name, it turns out, is Andrew Barr; his father was Anderson Barr) called her and left a message. Because of course when you've lost something precious and someone calls with information about it, you'll miss their call. It's Murphy's law.

I tried to convince Mr. Barr to give me the customer's phone number and name, but he politely reminded us that in this country we follow the law. Which was a little impolitely phrased. However, he did take my number and promised to give it to her when she got back to him. Which is fair but doesn't help with the impatience doing cartwheels inside me.

Krish has barely been interested in anything since Andrew Barr placed his finger on the name in the ledger. The emotionless mask has fallen over Krish's face again, reminding me of the first time we met.

"How do you know her name?" I ask, even though I know the answer.

He gives me a look that tells me he knows I know how already.

"She lives in Park Slope." He looks at his phone, mapping her address, which he's obviously memorized. "It's twenty minutes away."

"We can't just show up on her doorstep without warning."

When he doesn't answer, I second-guess myself. "Can we?"

Usually he'd smile at that, I think, but he seems preoccupied, almost nervous.

"What's the matter? Is there something you're not telling me?"

He startles out of his trance and focuses on me with an intensity that makes me yearn for his indifference. "What do you mean?"

"A question in response to a question. Now you're scaring me."

"It's your story. We don't have to go." Sulky *and* nervous? This isn't the same guy who goaded me to hop onto a killing machine and then flew with stone-cold glee across Queens. Something about him is suddenly different.

"We can also just wait for her to call back. Because how can she not? She's probably been in a panic over losing the ring."

The dimple doesn't just make an appearance when he smiles. It makes an appearance when he frowns too. "Or maybe she doesn't care as much as you do."

"Of course she cares." If it turns out that she doesn't care, I'll feel like a grade A idiot. Which is a judgment everyone I know has unanimously passed about me since I found that ring.

"You have no way of knowing that. Not everyone makes attachments the way you seem to think they do. Most people forget about things when they're out of sight."

"You said earlier that you have good instincts. That means you believe in instinct, right?"

"I'm a reporter. Of course I believe in instinct."

"And I deal with people's pain all day, every day. Instinct is what helps me get from what they're able to identify to what is truly causing them pain. I know there's something here, and I know your instinct is telling you that too. Isn't that why you're still here? Isn't that why you paid two hundred dollars for this bike and left your watch with a stranger?" I point at the motorcycle. "Because mine is screaming it."

Then I go quiet because something strikes me. I lean heavily, almost desperately, into my inner voice at work. But in my personal life, all anyone has ever told me is that I have no instincts for self-preservation. That I don't know how to take care of myself. And I've believed them, because a long time ago I proved them right. Now I want to be right. I want this raging belief that's taken hold of me to be right. I want it so badly I'm trembling.

Krish is watching me like he knows exactly what I'm talking about. "That's why I think we should just go there and see what this is all about."

I smile through the stupid tears that just sprung into my eyes. "Are you always like this?"

He looks confused.

"Is everything always about the story for you?"

He takes a quick step back and away from me, but before he can deny the accusation, my phone buzzes.

"Sorry, I have to take this." It's Druv. I clear my throat and answer. "Hi, Druv. What's up?"

"Hey, babe. Are you with someone?"

"Yes, why?"

"You sound different, that's all."

"You sound rested," I say. "For the first time in days."

"I love how you do that. How you can tell so easily how I'm feeling."

"Thank you," I say, and there's an awkward silence because that was a nonsensical response to what he just said. "That was a nice thing to say," I add, and that comes out even more awkward. Krish is staring at his phone, and I can't tell if he's listening, but he's pretending not to, and for that I'm grateful.

"What all did you see today?" Druv asks.

"I'm in Brooklyn right now." I throw a glance around me. "It's nice."

"You're still trying to find the owner of that ring?" I can't tell if he's annoyed, but I can't blame him because I haven't had a chance to explain how much it means to me. All I've told him is that I found it and I'm looking for the owner. He's been so busy and tired these past few days, he probably barely even registered it.

"I think we might already have."

"We? Has your brother put you up to this?"

"What is that supposed to mean?"

"Come on, Mira. You know how your family is."

"Excuse me?" I say to him, and apparently also to Krish, because he looks up and I put up a finger to signal needing a moment and take my phone across the alley we're parked in.

"You know your family manipulates you. You've said so yourself. One of the reasons I wanted to take you on this trip was so you could loosen up and relax away from them."

My heart is beating so hard I'm not sure I can make words. "I have never said that to you." The most basic thing about me is that I never say anything negative about my family out loud, no matter what. It's something that's been hardwired into me. It's like a gag I have been breathing around my entire life. It's the thing even my twin loathes about me. It's practically a flashing neon sign I carry around: **Never Criticize Your Family.**

"You don't have to say it in so many words." Druv uses his Dr. Druv voice, and as always, it tranquilizes me a little. Maybe I'm overreacting. It's probably the excitement from everything that's happened with the ring.

"They don't manipulate me," I say with a firmness bred into me. "My parents are more protective and strict than yours. But they come from a tougher background."

"I'm sorry. I shouldn't have said that. I know how hard they've worked. It's admirable to break the cycle of poverty. I respect them for that. It's just that I planned this trip so you could do something just for yourself. A happy Mira is a beautiful Mira to me."

Dr. Drum-Roll-Please, Rumi's voice says in my ear.

No, I will not let Rumi's cynicism ruin the best thing that's ever happened to me. Druv *is* the best thing that's ever happened to me. He just apologized for not even doing anything terrible. I've never heard my father apologize for anything in my entire life, except to customers.

"I *am* doing something for myself." For the first time in my life.

I look across the alley at Krish, who's leaning against the bike with his hands dug in his pockets. Ready to chase down what we started.

I give him my most endearing smile, apologizing for making him wait. He doesn't smile back. Which only proves how lucky I am to have found a man like Druv when the world is filled with jerks.

"Then go see the Statue of Liberty," Druv says. "Go stroll in Central Park. I want to hear you gushing over all your rom-com associations. Nothing fun has happened in my life in days. Let me live vicariously. Throw a man a bone."

He's being charming. I would be an idiot to not be charmed. Those were all things I wanted to do. There's nothing wrong with him suggesting that I do them. But all I want to do right now is find Reva Smith. Across the street Krish throws the ring in the air and catches it, then throws it again and catches it.

"Stop that!" I shout. "What is wrong with you?"

"Mira? What did I say?" Druv says on the phone. Krish stops tossing the ring. "I was just kidding. I didn't mean to tease you about the rom-com thing." He sounds placating instead of offended.

I want to groan, but Krish is watching, expression as dry as ever. I turn away from him and face the donut-shop window, filled with more donuts than anyone could ever eat. "I didn't mean to yell at you," I say into the phone. "You can tease me about the rom-com thing all you want. I'm not ashamed." I channel his charm.

He laughs. "What is going on with you? I've never heard you be like this."

"I'm sorry," I say. God, it's been a long day.

"No, I like it. You've never yelled at me before. I guess we just took a step forward in our relationship."

I turn to find Krish slipping the ring back in his pocket and going into his stick-up-his-behind stance. Suddenly I want this to be over. I want the ring where it belongs, and I want to be back with Druv, where I belong.

"I have to go," I say and tell Druv that I'll call him later. Then I march across the alley.

Krish doesn't move.

"Let's go," I say, walking straight to the motorcycle and throwing my leg over it. "You're right. There's no point in waiting until Reva calls us if you already have the address."

CHAPTER TWENTY

Park Slope is gorgeous. The vibe is somewhere between Chicago's Wicker Park and Gold Coast neighborhoods, but at a somewhat grander yet more intimate scale. We ride past a huge park and through narrow streets lined with brownstones that are at once grand and cozy.

I'm a lot more comfortable on the bike this time. My hands on Krish's shoulders aren't cutting off his circulation. When we were trying to make it to Anderson's in time, I was filled with fear—of being on a motorcycle for the first time, of not knowing if there was any way on earth we could actually find the ring's owner, of being physically so close to a stranger.

Or maybe I wasn't afraid of that last one. I hadn't given a thought to the fact that I had grabbed onto a strange man for dear life. But there's that gentlemanly thing Krish has going on. Even now his body language is so reserved, so nonthreatening, so entirely unaffected by our nearness in this deeply respectful way, that my natural distaste at the nearness of men feels eased, maybe even erased.

"Thank you," I say as we turn into a lane lined with wide-canopied trees.

"For?" Krish says, and we pull to a stop in front of the quirkiest brownstone on the block. For the most part it's like all the other attached town houses surrounding it, but the steps leading up to the front stoop are painted in all the colors of the rainbow.

Krish waits for me to get off the bike, then puts it on its stand and hops off himself. When he turns to me, there's a storm in his eyes that takes me by surprise. We've obviously not arrived here in the same state of mind. Did I do something?

"What were you thanking me for?" he asks with some force, spinning away from the house, and I take a step back.

He immediately softens. "Mira?" He wants something from me, and I don't know what it is.

I step closer because I can feel pain rolling from him in waves. "Just for everything. For . . . for being so kind."

He laughs. "I just snapped at you for no reason. Do you always have such low standards?"

"What is that supposed to mean?"

"Exactly that. You're impressed with me when I show the bare minimum courteousness and decency."

"You don't, though. You show above-average courteousness and decency. Even if you're a bit . . . How do I put this? Moody?"

"Moody?" His eyebrows tend to furrow when he's amused.

"As moody as a menopausal woman and as broody as a menopausal man."

"Okay then. Mira is a poet."

"She was. Did you not know that? Rumi and I are both named after spiritual poets." I laugh because our parents might be the two least poetic *or* spiritual people in the world. We were named by my father's uncle, the man who brought them to America. Baba asked him to name us as a sign of his subservience. Although he likes to call it respect.

"My mom would love your names. She lived for poetry. Read it to me every night growing up. Everything from Robert Frost to Mary Oliver to Kahlil Gibran and Rumi."

It's the first time he's mentioned his family. He looks even more surprised about it than I am.

"Your mom must've gone to one of those fancy private schools in India. Oh, or are you third generation?" I don't think I know many

Indian people in my generation whose parents were born here. But I know they exist. I went to a museum exhibit once that traced the history of immigrants from the Indian subcontinent to the United States as far back as the 1800s.

Maybe he's only half-Indian, since he did say his ancestors came here on the *Mayflower*. His skin is a few shades lighter than mine, but almost everyone's is. That might explain some of his awkwardness around the culture.

"I was adopted." He says it quickly, like he's not used to saying the words. "My parents are white. Good old British-from-the-motherland white."

I react in the worst way possible. I go speechless. Not because there's anything at all the matter with being adopted, but because I've been so horribly clueless, so unkind. I've made so many assumptions. Even judgments.

Shame warms my cheeks as my mind runs through all possible responses and settles on "That explains so much." The second-most obvious thing about me, after the fact that I never say anything negative about my family in public, is that I never say what pops in my head unless I've overthought it. Something is very wrong with me.

He laughs. A big, incredulous laugh that's filled with relief. "Have you been judging me this entire time?" The fading sun is reflecting off his glasses, but behind the lenses his eyes are crinkled with his laughter.

"Maybe it started when you mentioned the *Mayflower*. No, wait, maybe it was when you didn't know what a jalebi was."

"That never happened."

"It's a metaphor for how you were in Jackson Heights. Like an alien."

"An Englishman in New York?" he says just as the Sting song pops in my head.

"You listen to Sting?"

"My parents were all about British bands."

"Were?" I ask, knowing full well it's terribly rude and nosy.

"How did Mira from Naperville start listening to Sting? Is it a *Brown Town* thing?" Naturally he remembers everything I've ever said.

"Rumi." My twin has always existed in a time and place different from the one we lived in.

He raises his chin in an *ah*. Neither one of us acknowledges that he's done talking about his parents. I turn to the town house looming behind us.

"You think it's hers?"

"The ring?"

I nod.

He shrugs.

We stand there looking at the rainbow-colored steps leading up to the buttercup yellow door with a lion head knocker.

"It would all be an awful waste of coincidences if it weren't, wouldn't it?" he says, and I smile.

"Shall we?" I ask.

Instead of giving me his arm, as I'm picturing in my head, he stays rooted to the spot. "Maybe we should wait for her to call us."

"Really?" Now he has cold feet?

"No. Let's do it," he says, and we take the steps up.

"Knocker or bell?" I say.

"Decisions, decisions," he says, and I knock and he rings.

CHAPTER TWENTY-ONE

No one answers the door.

So we repeat the ringing and knocking.

When the door still doesn't open, I look at Krish. "That's anticlimactic." But given that Reva Smith didn't answer the phone when Mr. Barr called her, maybe we should have expected it.

He doesn't answer. He has that look again where something is going on inside him that has nothing to do with this moment. It's like he's not even here, like he's disappeared into another time. I'm getting intense *Time Traveler's Wife* vibes.

"What's going on, Krish?" I ask, not for the first time.

Not for the first time, he looks at me in that way where it's almost like he's forgotten I'm here.

"You're right," he says, snapping out of it. "That was anticlimactic."

I sit down on the steps.

"What are you doing?" he asks.

"I don't know. Trying to figure out what to do next."

He sits down next to me.

"Are you ever going to tell me why this means so much to you?" I ask.

"I take my work seriously."

I point at his face. "That's not it."

He makes an *Excuse me?* face. "Do you ever stop making assumptions about people?"

"That's not what I'm doing."

"You assumed I had the same kind of Brown Town childhood as you did just because I look like you."

"I look like you? That's below the belt."

He makes a *Haha, very funny* face.

"Fine. But that's not what I'm doing this time. And I never assumed your childhood was anything like mine. I doubt anyone's was, even in Brown Town." I don't know why my voice shakes when I say it, but I hug my knees and look away.

"I'm guessing you're just going to let that sit there without any explanation."

"Says the man who never explains any of his own behavior."

"Fine. What do you want to know? Ask me."

Wow. I was not expecting that. There's so much I want to know, but I have to pick the right question because he's wily and he's not actually interested in telling me anything. Either he's deflecting from whatever is going on with him or this is a trick to get me to let him ask me the same thing so he can find out things about me for his precious story.

"You said earlier that the only thing you could tell me for sure is that you were not doing this only for the story. What did you mean by that? Why are you doing it, then?"

He looks surprised, impressed by how I framed that. I make a face that tells him I don't enjoy being underestimated. I have more experience with it than he could ever imagine.

"The same reason you're doing it. To find out who the ring belongs to."

He is wily. Because he's not lying. He's just telling a part of the truth: another thing I'm a master at. "But why?" I ask.

Before I can figure out if he's going to answer me, a woman comes jogging down the sidewalk. She stops in front of us. There's a moment when all three of us freeze. Then I realize that she was headed to the door we were just knocking on and we're blocking her way.

"Hi." She's lean and tall with dark kohl lining her eyes. The word that comes to mind is *statuesque*. Her dark skin and leanly muscled body are glistening with sweat, and her angular, faintly lined face is framed with sweaty silver curls that have escaped her ponytail. She's obviously just returned from a run. Black running tights, black running tank, and bright-white sneakers. She emanates power in a way I've only seen in the movies.

"Hi," I say and stand up. "I'm Mira Salvi. Do you live here?"

"I thought that was you," she says, and I notice that she has the kindest eyes.

I must look surprised because she smiles. "Andrew Barr from Anderson's jewelers left me a message. I usually don't check my messages until I'm on my last mile. I'm Reva."

She shakes my hand, then turns to Krish as he stands up. His quicksilver mood has turned again. He looks like he's seen a ghost and he's disappeared deep inside himself to get away from it. Something very strange is going on with him.

He introduces himself. With his usual "reporter for the *New York Times*." The dark lenses of his glasses obscure most of his face.

"You're doing a story on this?" Reva's eyes study him. "Why?"

"A tourist finds a ring near the Empire State Building and tries to return it to the owner," he says, as though that's answer enough.

She smiles. "Well, I'm seriously grateful she did. It's been like being naked without it. I haven't been separated from it since I was a child." She looks at me with those kind eyes again. "Thank you."

"Can you describe it for us?" Krish says in the coldest voice I've heard come out of him.

I want to stomp on his foot, but Reva meets the challenge on his face with such withering haughtiness it's a miracle he doesn't crumble to dust. "You know I could just watch the video and describe it, right?" She jogs around us to her front porch. "Barr told me about the video, and I watched it." She reaches out and squeezes my shoulder. "You're really something special. I hope you know that."

She's barely met me, but it's still rude, the way Krish scoffs. She turns her attention to him. "I guess you want to know what's inscribed on the inside."

His response is to fold his arms across his chest.

"Would you like to come in?"

I say yes just as Krish says "No, thank you."

She gives us a curious look. "It's part of a . . ." She releases a breath. Talking about the ring obviously isn't easy for her. "It's part of a set. There's the Sanskrit *shree* symbol inscribed into the inside, which spans both bands. My band has the lower half, which looks like one diagonal line and two horizontal lines."

She's exactly right, and my relief is so huge it's like breath filling my lungs. Reva reaches out and squeezes my arm and gives me a smile that can only be described as fierce. I'm dazzled.

Krish seems anything but. "Where's the other ring? The pair."

Her eyes harden in a way that's brutal and so stark she obviously doesn't care that we see it. "I have no idea."

"Where did you get the ring?" Even when he was distant, Krish has been nothing but polite. Now he's rude to the point of meanness, and I have no idea who this person is.

"Krish!" I say. "That's not our business."

"It isn't? So after all this you're just going to hand it over to someone who doesn't even know where she got it from?"

"I didn't say I don't know where I got it from."

"Where did you get it from?" Krish asks.

"I don't believe that's any of your business. I'm old enough to be your mother, young man, and I see that your mother forgot to teach you manners."

Krish takes a step back. "My mother taught me to be smart about who I trust."

"Well, congratulations to her. Fortunately for me I couldn't care less if you trust me or not. Just do what you came here to do and you never have to see me again." She looks at me. A deep sadness is back in her eyes. "Could I see it, please?"

I reach for the ring in my bag, and Krish puts a hand on my arm. "What are you doing?"

"What we came here to do. It's obviously her ring."

"I can show you pictures of myself with it hanging around my neck over the years," Reva says.

"That won't be necessary," I say, although I'm overwhelmed with the desire to know what she was like over the years.

"I thought you were eager to learn the story behind the ring," he says incredulously. "Now you don't care?"

"Only if she was comfortable sharing it. She's obviously not."

The way Reva's been looking at me changes. "Why don't you both come in," she says. "Please."

I take Krish's arm and drag him in. "Just for a minute."

He goes with me, even though there's a new coldness to him. He's a completely different person. He was obviously more interested in the ring's story than mine. Everything else was just an act. I'm too filled with wonder at having found Reva to care about the betrayal the realization sparks. I can't believe I did it. I found her.

Magic, Saket's voice whispers inside me. *Magic. Magic. Magic.*

The inside of the house is warm and welcoming. It smells of lavender and peace. Soothing gray-blue wainscoting covers walls that are hung with architectural renderings.

"Are you an architect?" I ask, taking everything in with unconcealed admiration.

"My partner was."

"I'm sorry. Is he . . . ?"

She smiles. "She. She died five years ago. A boating accident. We were visiting Alaska. It was her favorite place on earth."

"I'm sorry."

She has the faraway look in her eyes I recognize as grief. "Thank you. Loss is part of life."

I take the pouch from my purse, slip the ring and chain onto my palm, and offer it to her. As soon as her eyes see it, something shifts in the air. Her entire body sags with relief, and her already sad eyes glaze with moisture.

After the barest pause, she takes it from me with impatience and reverence, and that makes me tear up too.

"Thank you," we both say together and then smile.

Krish remains unmoved. "Did the other ring belong to her, to your partner?"

"No," she says simply.

He's obviously not ready to give up. "But you know who it belonged to."

Something in her face changes as she studies him. She swallows, and her jaw tightens. I know what people look like when pain flashes through them. That's what just happened. "Why are you so interested in the other ring? Did you know it was part of a pair before you came here?"

"My brother's fiancé, he's a jewelry designer, and he told us it was part of a set," I say.

"That's amazing that they can tell like that, just by looking at it." She says it casually, but she's watching Krish with an expression I can't decipher. It's suspicious but also scared, and yet not quite either of those things. "I haven't seen the other ring in forty years."

Krish's head snaps up, and their eyes meet. We're indoors, and his glasses are no longer opaque. It's almost like she loses her balance. She grips the back of the couch hard enough that it stretches between her fingers.

"I'm sorry, I totally forgot that I have to get on a call, and I'm already late." She hurries toward us and nudges me to the door. "Truly, I'm so grateful." Her voice is sincere, even though she's obviously shaken. "I would love to send you a little something as a thank-you. I have your number from Barr. I'll text you for your address. I'm sorry to be rude, but I have to take this."

Her breathing has turned erratic. There's an edge of panic to it. I put a hand on her shoulder. "Are you okay? Can I do something?"

She laughs. I almost believe it's real. "Maybe your reporter friend needs some help leaving?"

Finally Krish unfreezes. He's gone from rude to angry. His anger is raw and palpable as he strides past me and out the door. "It was nice meeting you, Ms. Smith," he throws over his shoulder. "Have a nice life."

"What the hell was that?" I ask, racing down the steps after him, because honestly, what the hell was that?

"That was my story ending up being a damp squib." He stops at the bottom of the steps and runs his hand through his hair, pulling it from the tie at his nape.

"Excuse me? We just did something nearly impossible! No one believed we could find the owner of the ring, and we did. There is nothing even a little damp-squiby about that!"

I turn away from him and start walking. This should be such a great moment. My heart feels like it's swooping around the skies. There's also steam coming out of my ears.

Krish falls in step next to me. "I don't understand why you're angry with me. The least she could have done is be more gracious to you. You were so invested in her story without even knowing her. Now you've got nothing."

"She was absolutely lovely to me! I have everything I hoped to have. You are the one who thinks he's got nothing. But if you can't make something from a story like this, I don't know how you've won all those awards. You're giving me whiplash. One moment you're Mr. Gallant, the next moment you're a jerk to a lovely woman for a stupid story!"

"I did not win all those awards by thinking of my stories as stupid."

"Fine, then go ahead and put your story ahead of real human beings and go brood somewhere else. I just did an amazing thing, and I'm going to go celebrate!"

"Let me guess, a horse carriage ride in Central Park. Just like in *When Harry Met Sally*."

"Great, so you lied about the photographic memory too. Because there's no horse carriage ride in *When Harry Met Sally*."

"The sacrilege," he mumbles.

Obviously he's never even watched the film. Which is the real sacrilege. "You know when I thanked you for being above-average courteous and decent? I'm taking that—"

"You cannot take compliments back. What are you, two years old?"

"You're fighting with me about taking back what's not even a real compliment, and you think *I'm* two?"

We're both breathing hard. We just speed walked across Park Slope, but that has nothing to do with it. Then I crack a smile. I can't help it. This argument is just so incredibly stupid, and I'm just so incredibly happy that Reva has her ring.

"We did it!" I say in a small voice.

I want to tell everyone I know, and I have no one I can tell who cares. And I could never have done it without him. He's been with me every step of the way, even though it's for entirely selfish reasons.

He's staring at me, and I could swear he heard everything I just said in my head. "You did it," he says, just as softly, and there's true wonder in his voice for the first time since I met him. Suddenly he takes my elbow and starts walking back to the bike. "You know what, you're right. You deserve to celebrate."

CHAPTER TWENTY-TWO

Sureva Bhalekar
St. Mary's Ladies Hostel
Charni Road, Bombay
October 1983

Vasudha Patil
[Address left blank]

Dear Vasu,
Where are you? Is your eye better? Have your fingers healed? Please tell me they're not hurting you. (If someone else is reading this, please please don't hurt her.)

For the past three months, I've been begging the gods for some sign that you're okay. But after getting your letter, I know they're not listening. I miss you so much it's like I can't feel myself. Sometimes I slap my own limbs to make sure I'm here. But I will leave you alone, I will let you go, if that makes them stop hurting you.

Why am I even writing this letter? I don't know where I'm going to send it. Are you still in Yevla? I don't know where you are, Vasu! How can that be? For the entirety of my life I've always known exactly where you are.

You probably already know this, but Appa-saheb came to me and asked for all the letters you'd sent me. When I told him I always throw all my letters away because I don't want the girls in the hostel to read my business, I saw a flash of rage in his eyes. He knew I was lying and couldn't believe that I had the arrogance to deny his orders. He concealed it immediately, but I have a sense that will not be the end of it. The hostel warden was standing just outside the open door so he couldn't do much more then. He knows I have the letters. I'll die before I give them to him. But he knows everything between us. I saw it in his eyes. Did he read my letter to you? The one I should never have written.

I suspect my aie knows all of it too. He fired her for my actions.

Or she left because she's ashamed of me. I no longer recognize my own mother. She refuses to hear any mention of you. She seems terrified, as though she knows someone is going to hurt us. She's livid with me. She blames me for taking away her home. Was it ever her home, though, if they threw her out so easily? They think separating our families means separating us. They're breaking every connection between us. I know Appa-saheb is punishing me, but throwing Aie out when she has nowhere to go feels like a threat, like he's not done.

January 1984

Vasu, I just found out. How could you do this? You told me no one but me would ever touch you and you got married? I feel destroyed, ripped up. I don't know how I can live through this.

Everything that has ever happened to me in my life has been bearable because you showed me how to get through it. Because you knew who I was even when I had no idea. Now who will tell me what to do? How will I know who I am?

No, this cannot be. They've forced you to do this and I wasn't there to protect you. What did they say to you? Did they threaten to hurt me?

I'm safe. Do you hear me? I'm safe. Don't do anything because you think you're protecting me. They're lying to you.

February 1984

Vasu, I don't know why I'm still writing because I know for sure now that I have nowhere to send this letter. But if ever I find a way I want you to know what happened. I want you to not believe whatever lies they've told you. Yesterday, my aie and I moved in with a friend of Ashatai Athavale in Thane after some thugs followed me into an alley. They pushed a knife to my throat. Do not worry, I'm unharmed, their aim was to scare me and give me a message from your appa. He wanted me to know that if I ever tried to contact you or your new family or told anyone about what he calls our sickness he would set my aie on fire. When I came home I found my aie waiting at my hostel. Her shanty in Yevla where she moved after she left your parents' house was burned down in the night. She escaped with minimal burns and ran to me in Bombay and I had to get her to safety.

Being angry should have made my sadness less but a boulder sits on my heart. I will carry it for the rest of my life, Vasu. My yearning for you will only die with me. But how will I last from this day until that one?

April 1984

I haven't heard from you in six months. It's felt like six years. Today was the day I was waiting for. The day I know you saw so clearly for me. Columbia University in America has admitted me into their biomedical engineering graduate program on a full scholarship. I also have a teaching assistantship, which means I can support us now. This was always my plan. To take you with me to New York, where I'm told death does not await those who are made by the creator the way we are.

In New York we have a chance. Please tell me it is not too late. It cannot be too late. I know you're married now but it cannot be a real marriage. I don't think I can leave India without you.

With every beat of my heart I pray that you come back to me.

Yours and only yours,
Suru

CHAPTER TWENTY-THREE

I cannot believe that I was ever afraid of a motorcycle.

"I don't understand why more people don't ride motorcycles," I scream into Krish's ear as we race across the Brooklyn Bridge back into Manhattan.

He throws his head back and laughs.

"Where are we going?"

"I can't hear you," he shouts back, hearing me just fine. "Hang on and trust me."

We float past steel, glass, and concrete, the faintly acrid smell of the Hudson chasing us as we weave through traffic. He pulls over by the edge of a park and points to the Statue of Liberty across the water. Before I can catch my breath, he takes off again and slows down as we pass the High Line, then the *Charging Bull* on Wall Street and the 9/11 Memorial. We drive through Tribeca, SoHo, Greenwich Village, and Chelsea Market. Before I can process the fact that he's just shown me all the places on my checklist and more, he stops near a food truck with unnaturally red kababs painted across it. There's a line of people staring down at their phones. He squeezes the bike into a spot between two cars that I'm not sure is legal. I follow him to the line.

"What are we doing?" I ask.

He looks at the truck. "Grabbing kababs." He pauses, with the most faux-serious expression. "A food truck should be part of every New York checklist."

"Krish." An embarrassed flush creeps up my cheeks. "You don't have to do this."

"I know. But I'm hungry. We haven't eaten anything all day."

As if on cue, my belly lets out a nice long growl. I'm not the kind of person who forgets to eat. We totally forgot to eat.

"Fine. I'm sorry that I took back calling you above-average courteous and decent. You can have it back. You can stop being nice now."

He makes a relieved face. "Great. So, we'll pick up the world's best kababs and go our separate ways."

My disappointment must show on my face because he smiles and steps up to the food truck window, where a sweaty guy with impressively abundant facial hair throws us a silent demand for our order.

Krish asks for chicken without a moment's thought, and I read through the entire menu painted on the side of the truck before ordering lamb and asking for extra hot sauce. We wait in silence as the guy ladles our food into a foil container with a mumbled warning about the hot sauce. Krish takes the white plastic bag, and we both reach for our wallets.

"Let me get this, please," I say, expecting a macho fight, but he puts his wallet away and thanks me.

"That's just one bag," I say. "We'll need two to go our separate ways."

"Damn," he says. "Then let's stay together until the bag issue is resolved."

I roll my eyes and follow him into a park.

I know this is Central Park even without knowing it's Central Park from all the movies I've seen it in, a rolling green plateau in a valley of skyscraper mountains. It's past eight and a pink twilight sky floats over the buzz of activity. It's exactly as bustling and idyllic as it looks in the movies.

We find an empty bench and settle into it.

"I'm sorry I didn't ask if you like kababs," Krish says, handing me my box.

"It's my favorite food." I peel the lid off, take a deep inhale of the intoxicating charred meat smell, and dump the entire cup of hot sauce on it.

Krish raises a brow. "I'd go easy with that."

I laugh. "The Salvis can eat more hot food than anyone else we know. I think my family ate as many hot green chilies in one day as all our customers put together bought from the store in a week." I don't mean for it to be a flex, but it is a little bit.

Krish is right. These kababs are fantastic, and eating them on a bench in Central Park as runners jog past us feels unreal. It's possibly the most fanciful thing I've ever done. Like being Audrey Hepburn in *Roman Holiday* and getting to escape real life and spend one day straight out of someone else's life.

We're so hungry that we attack the food with wordless focus. I'm usually a slow eater, and I don't realize how fast I'm scarfing the deliciousness down until the burn from the hot sauce hits me with an unholy force and I stop. Before I can grasp what's happening, my lips are being skinned, doused with acid, and set on fire. It's like my mouth is a volcano, my lips the ripped-up crater.

I'm trying not to whimper in pain when Krish gets up and disappears down the path. As soon as he leaves, I start licking my lips and dabbing them with the napkin. Instead of helping, it makes things worse because my tongue is also burning and my face is hot and my skin is melting. It's so bad that tears flow from my eyes and nose. I quickly wipe them against my shoulder because as a Salvi I cannot be someone who cries from burning her lips on too much hot sauce.

In my family there's no such thing as too much hot sauce.

I'm dying.

Before I pass out from the pain, Krish returns with a bottle of water that I grab and down in great graceless gulps. When water dribbles down my chin (which I might or might not have planned), I rub the moisture into my lips. It doesn't even touch the burn.

If Krish is laughing at me, I don't know because I refuse to look his way. And even if I could, I wouldn't be able to see past the pain. He hands me a Popsicle.

As I suck on it for dear life, he soaks a napkin in water and hands it to me. By now I'm beyond embarrassment, and I rub the Popsicle into my lips until the burning finally eases and I practically moan in relief when I press the wet napkin to my lips.

"You might as well say it," I say when I can speak again. My lips are swollen and sore but also numb, and I couldn't be more grateful.

"No longer the undisputed Hot Sauce Queen of Brown Town?"

Smiling hurts. I don't think I'm ever going to eat hot sauce again. "What on earth was in that?"

"I believe the man said it was five times hotter than ghost peppers just before you scoffed at him."

"I thought you promised to be nice to me."

"I believe your words were *You can stop being nice now*."

"Who knew being able to remember everything could be so annoying?" Now that I can breathe again, I take the Popsicle stick and both our empty take-out boxes to a trash can, and he follows, hands unsurprisingly dug into his pockets. "Seriously, though. This was great. Thank you. Now you can stop being so nice for real."

He gets a look.

"What?"

"I would've canceled if I'd known you were serious about not wanting me to be nice. It might be too late." The dimple also makes an appearance when he's teasing me.

Another smile slips onto my lips and makes them sting. "What did you do?"

"Let's go find out."

~

Krish won't tell me where we're going, and honestly I don't care. I feel weightless, as though we're still on our motorcycle, bouncing in slow motion between cars and tourist buses. But we're walking, and soon we stop next to low, wide steps leading up to a wall of glass.

I press my hand to my mouth. "Is this the MoMA?"

"No," he says with the strangest expression. I obviously amuse the man. "It's MoMA."

"Sorry?"

"Not *the* MoMA, just MoMA. It's *the Met* and *MoMA*." He trails off.

"You New Yorkers are weird," I say, looking at the hours of operation on the door, which tell me that the museum is closed, which I knew. It's still great to be able to see it, and I thank him. "This is the sweetest thing anyone's ever done for me."

Instead of telling me I'm welcome, he looks embarrassed.

"It's not," he says, and he looks unsure in a way I haven't seen yet. I don't even know what he's unsure about.

That's when a woman with flaming-red hair in a pastel-yellow pantsuit walks up to us. I'm about to apologize for trespassing and leave when she hugs Krish. Long and hard, with affection that doesn't seem casual.

"Hi," she says to me. "You must be Mira."

"Mira, this is my Auntie Anne. She's the director of the museum."

I'm not quite sure what's happening, but Auntie Anne shakes my hand, then turns and walks toward the side of the building. She flashes a card at a reader to unlock a door and lets us into the closed museum.

I have no idea what is happening right now, but the phrase *I'm so excited I might pee my pants* doesn't feel as ridiculous as it always has. Because *what is happening right now*?

Krish's aunt walks us down a corridor and stops next to an elevator. "It's on the fifth floor. Take your time," she says. "I'll be in my office. I have to get something finished. John will go with you." A uniformed museum employee walks up to us and nods.

"Thanks," Krish says, and she hugs him again.

"We missed you at Karl's birthday brunch." She gives him a pointed yet gentle look, and his face does that thing again where a mask slips over it.

She waits, but he doesn't respond. She gives him another moment, then pats his cheek. "I love you. We all do."

"I do too," he says, and it's so flat he might as well have said *ditto.*

To her credit she seems not to notice. "It was lovely meeting you, Mira," she says to me before she clicks away in her heels.

I have so many questions, but the way Krish looks, I'm wondering if he's regretting this incredibly kind thing I still can't believe he's done for me.

John leads us into the elevator, and Krish and he fall into a deep discussion about the late-spring weather. One of them declares the temperature (eighty degrees yesterday, sixty today), the other declares the humidity (sixty percent). They nod their joint disapproval at the temperamental weather gods.

Evidently, New Yorkers aren't great at small talk. A Chicago version of John would have talked without pause. By now we'd know what his wife made for breakfast today and what his retirement plans are. New York John, now silent, leads us to a room, and there it is: the swirling sky I've seen in my dreams since I was eight years old.

At the edge of my consciousness, I notice that John falls back and Krish excuses himself. I step up to it. An odd turmoil grips me. What must it have been like to see the world this way? Every stroke is restless, all those tiny splotches of color coming together in a tidal wave of chaos and beauty. I'm rooted and shaken. I never want to look away. It's how my lips burned, how my hair flew in the wind. It's how I felt when I found the ring, how the rough pavement scraped the skin of my palms. An experience that traps my body and squeezes my heart, takes up all of me. I am the swirling blue sky, the steady yet nebulous flames of foliage, the bleeding glow of the stars and moon. For a moment, I am every painful experience I've ever had. I'm all my yearning for joy. Eddies of pain and pleasure burst inside me.

I close my eyes and dissolve into all I'm feeling.

"Mira?" It's a whisper that startles me. When I open my eyes, I expect to see Krish's teasing face, but he's looking like a man who has never smiled in his life. Like someone who doesn't know how.

"You okay?" I ask him because he looks so sad.

He laughs his most humorless laugh and points to my cheeks. "You're the one crying."

I wipe my face.

"You've been looking at one painting for the past twenty minutes?"

"Sorry," I say.

"For what? For liking a piece of art?"

I know I apologize a lot and I shouldn't, and I want to apologize for that. "For keeping you waiting."

"I just got here. I was talking to my aunt."

"I'm glad you went and spoke to her. She looked like she wanted to talk to you."

The intense look in his eyes cools instantly. He steps back.

I know I've violated some sort of boundary again. But when you've known someone for all of one day and they feel like the only friend you've ever had, boundaries feel fuzzy.

"Anything else you'd like to see?"

I shake my head. Suddenly I want to be back in my hotel room. By myself. Where no one knows me.

John leads us out, and we thank him.

Krish starts walking, and I follow in silence.

Just let him tell you what to do. That should be easy enough for you, my brother's voice says in my ear. Every bit of warmth I've felt today goes cold inside me.

I wrap my arms around myself. We go back into Central Park and follow one of the meandering paths.

"Do you live far?" I ask when the silence stretches into awkwardness.

He points across the park at a French-style stone-and-brick building.

"No way! You live in Central Park?" I practically squeal.

"Technically it's outside Central Park."

"Well, excuse me, Mr. Fancy-Pants."

He doesn't smile. "It was my grandmother's apartment. She left it to me."

"I'm sorry."

"Why are you sorry this time?"

"Because if she left it to you, it means she loved you and that she died."

Fair enough, his face says. "She is dead. So, thanks. But I'm not sure she was built to love anyone."

"Who leaves someone they don't love a place in Central Park?"

"Someone who has no use for the place after they're dead. And my mother probably forced her to leave it to me."

He sounds sad again.

"Was it hard?" It slips out.

"Having someone leave me an apartment? Or having a grandmother who hated me?"

Without thinking about it, I touch his arm. "I didn't mean to intrude. It's just that . . ."

"I know. It's been a weird couple days. Of course it was hard. All of it was hard. But no one ever gets it." He looks at me with all his focus again. "Everyone expects me to be grateful. Because my parents chose me after I was given away by my birth parents. As though I was meant not to have the life I got to have."

I know exactly what he means, and it makes me sick to my stomach.

"You're the first person who's ever picked up on it. How it must've been to be the only one who looked like me in my town. To look nothing like the rest of my family." He swallows.

"That's ridiculous. How could your friends not pick up on it?" He's a journalist, for God's sake, and his pain has been raging at me.

He gets that odd look again, as though I've said something unexpected; then he smiles his teasing smile. "Maybe none of them were this comfortable being nosy."

"What was it like?" I ask instead of responding to that.

For a few minutes we walk in silence. "When I was very young, I had no idea," he says finally. "The first time I noticed was when we were taking family pictures one Christmas and my grandmother said *Move the brown one to the back*. I didn't realize she was talking about me until someone took me by the shoulders and moved me to the back row. I never forgot again. If it ever receded to the back of my mind, everyone who saw me with my parents reminded me with the way they looked at us."

"What about your parents?"

"Mom never saw it. I think she was actually color blind. Or at least she was so determined to create a color-blind world for me, she refused any other reality. Dad was too in love with her to not think her reality was reality."

"They sound really sweet."

He laughs his sad laugh. "They were. When it was just us, it was amazing. The best childhood ever."

Now I laugh.

"What?" he says.

"We were the opposite. When it was just my parents and us, I could barely breathe. Outside the house, we could at least experiment with being ourselves." As soon as I say it, I realize what I just did.

"Don't say sorry again. Please."

"Okay. But I've never said that out loud before."

"I know. I've never said any of this out loud before either." He scrubs a hand across his face. Then looks up at the sky. "Except to my mom. The last time I saw her. She passed away last year."

"Oh, Krish," I say. I want to wrap an arm around him, but I have no idea how one comforts a friend physically.

"Yeah, that's me. The guy who told the best mother in the world that she was too clueless to understand what she put me through with her family my whole life. Two days after that, her car was hit by a drunk driver. I never got to tell her I didn't mean what I said."

"And your dad?"

"We don't talk much anymore. I think he blames me for her death."

"Is his name Karl?"

He huffs out a laugh. "You might be the most perceptive person I've ever met. Yes, that's him."

I'm about to open my mouth, but he says, "Please don't say sorry again."

"Can I say thank you?"

"What is it for this time?"

"For everything? For teaching me the right way to say *MoMA* and *the Met*. For telling me what you just did. For helping me find the ring. For completing the checklist."

"You came all the way here. How could you go back without seeing the checklist?" A smile returns to his eyes.

A harsh knot gathers in my throat, and for a moment I feel like I'll never be able to speak around it again. Every time I've wished for something today, wanted something, he's been there with the answer. I've never had to ask.

"Can I ask you something?" he says, and I feel like he's imitating me.

There's that not-being-able-to-speak-around-the-lump-in-my-throat thing, so I nod. Or I nod inside my head, and he sees it.

"Earlier, when you said me driving you around New York was the sweetest thing anyone has ever done for you, were you serious?"

Is that pity in his voice? "No." He just got me into the frickin' Museum of Modern Art after hours, so it isn't a fair bar anyway. I don't want him feeling bad for me. "I shouldn't have said that. My family does nice things for me all the time." That comes out much more defensive than I intended.

He has the gall to look skeptical. How dare he? My parents got me back on my feet when I screwed up. I shove away the voice that says they did that for themselves too. They were protecting their own public image, their reputation, their "good name." That's not the point.

"My fiancé gifted me this trip," I say, "because I've always wanted to see New York." It's a small lie. So what if Druv is the one who loved New York and chose it? Now I love it even more than he does.

"Is that why he didn't bother to join you?"

I step back. An irrational amount of anger gathers inside me.

"He's too busy saving lives." Druv fixes spines, which is close enough.

Krish barely nods. "All I meant was that they should be. Everyone should be making you feel special, Mira. Because you . . . well, because everyone deserves that."

I start walking, and he follows in silence. Too soon we're back at the motorcycle by the kabab truck, and suddenly I'm sad again. Is this it? Will I never see him again?

"What about the story?" I say. "Are you really going to drop it?"

He shrugs. "There's really no story. There's also something else I didn't tell you." He takes a breath. "I haven't written anything in a year."

"Since your mom died."

He makes a *yup* face.

"You thought this story would help you break through the block."

"Something like that."

"I wish you'd told me this before."

"Why?"

"Because I would have tried harder to get the story of the ring out of Reva."

"She wasn't going to give us more. No matter how hard you tried."

"You have no way of knowing that."

He shrugs again.

"There's something more you're not telling me, isn't there?"

"It doesn't matter." He holds out his hand. "It's been a pleasure chasing a dud story with you. Thank you, Mira. Take it easy with the hot sauce, okay?"

I have the urge to cry, but there's also the sweetest warmth inside me, like a hot compress on an achy spot. I shake his hand. The firmness of his grip is absurdly comforting. "You can't thank me. I'm the one who can never thank you enough." I think this might've been the best day of my entire life.

"We're even, then." He pats the motorcycle. "Where can I drop you off on my noble steed?"

Wanting to laugh on top of wanting to cry doesn't help with how I'm feeling. "My hotel is a few blocks away. I think I want to walk."

For a few moments we stand there like that, looking at each other. I don't want to go. In the end, it's that realization that makes me turn around and walk away.

CHAPTER TWENTY-FOUR

As I walk toward my hotel, I can't stop thinking about Krish's face when he told me about his childhood. I see him clearly, a boy with those somber, thickly lashed eyes and that dimple. It's like I'm there. What a beautiful baby he must've been. What must it have been like for his birth mother to give him away? What must it have been like for his adoptive mother to find him?

An old pain lances through me. It's been so long since I let myself think about babies and mothers. My abortion is something I never let myself think about. I've never spoken of it to a soul. My parents know because they arranged the whole thing. Rumi knows, but I don't know how he found out. Probably from hearing Aie and Baba screaming at me when they found out about the pregnancy.

I don't even know why I'm thinking about all this now, but the face of the nurse who prepped me is back in my head, clear as day. Her family was from the Philippines. I remember this because she told me. *I understand how you're feeling. My parents are Filipino. I know how Asian parents can be. If they're forcing you, you should know that you can have the baby and put it up for adoption. You have that choice.*

I was seventeen. And I really didn't.

I've never thought about this before, but would I have made a different choice were I given it? I don't think so. The idea of me, at seventeen, being a mother is impossible to contemplate. Just being me at seventeen was so painful I want to double up at the memory. I remember considering taking my own life before I considered telling my parents.

I look at my phone, where I've been following the map to the hotel. I can see the imposing facade down the block. Instead of following the path, I hail a cab. I'm not leaving New York without talking to my brother.

When I get to Rumi and Saket's place, I see that the lights in the house are on. I ring the doorbell, but no one answers. It's a moonless night and there's no one on the street except a kid smoking by the neighbor's garage. He disappears into the house when he sees me. A skunky smell wafts over, triggering those ugly memories from my childhood that turn me inside out and still hold me in their grip. I think about Krish standing on this porch for the first time and how careless I was with my judgments. How very wrong I've been about so many things.

I try the doorbell again. I've been standing here for a good five minutes, but I can't make myself leave. Just as I'm about to give up, the door opens and a slightly flustered Saket stands before me, looking faintly embarrassed. His hair is disheveled, and his bright-red kimono with giant white lilies is hanging open as though pulled on in a hurry.

Great. Just great.

"Mira? Hi, honey!" He steps out onto the porch and hugs me. "Sorry to make you wait. Come on in." He says not a word about me showing up at their doorstep at ten o'clock without any warning and pulls me into the house.

My brother is standing at the bottom of the stairs, hair also disheveled and in nothing but his boxers.

I want to die of mortification.

"Excellent timing, Miru," he says flatly. "Come on in."

"I'm sorry," I say. "I didn't mean to barge in like this. But I had to come."

"Don't be absurd," Saket says. "Mi casa es su casa." He hugs me again. "You are always welcome here. If you ever need a place to go, this is where you come, okay? Always."

Tears threaten, and I will them away. I can't believe how much I've cried today, and it's been the best day of my life.

Rumi takes a step down into the foyer and studies my face. "Holy shit. You found the ring's owner."

"Oh my God!" Saket says. "Is this true?"

I nod.

"That's flippin' phenomenal. This calls for a celebration. Wine? A Barolo okay?"

"I have no idea what that is," I say. "But it sounds fantastic."

Saket hurries away, and Rumi grabs the shirt strewed across the back of the couch and pulls it on.

"That is phenomenal, Miru," Rumi says with an old kindness I haven't heard in a very long time. "How the hell did you manage that?" His voice is filled with the same wonder I've been feeling since I saw Reva look at the ring.

Over wine that's so good it makes me feel like I'm someone else, I tell them about my day.

Saket listens with unbridled excitement, and it doubles my own excitement. I'm practically levitating. How the hell did we manage it?

As he watches me recount the events, my brother's wonder turns to incredulousness, then disbelief. "You rode on a motorcycle?" he says. "Yeah, right!"

I guess the old kindness was just my imagination.

My twin, who knows what I'm thinking without me saying a word, can't believe that I rode on a motorcycle.

"And that's the least wild thing I've done today," I say smugly.

He starts to laugh. But it's not a happy laugh. It's mean, and he doesn't stop.

"Rooh," Saket says. "Stop it."

"What?" Rumi says, finishing his wine in one large gulp. "I just never thought I'd see the day when Uptight Mira would have some fun."

Uptight Mira.

I want to throw the wine in his face.

"Fun? You mean the thing you were having when we were growing up, while I was running around trying to save your ass?" And keeping him from being killed by our parents.

He looks surprised that I reacted and slams the empty glass on the coffee table. "Oh, sorry, should I also have been holed up at home, toeing the line? Too chicken to do anything?"

These were the exact words that goaded me into going to that party. Into having my disastrous rebellious phase that lasted all of one evening and ruined my life.

I stand and grab my bag. Why the hell did I come here? I can't be around him anymore or I'll say things I'll regret. "You're a jerk, you know that?"

He leans back on the couch. He doesn't care that I'm upset. He doesn't care that I've been throwing myself at the glass wall he's put between us. He couldn't care less if I stayed or left.

"At least I'm a jerk who's living his life. At least I'm not so apathetic, so cautious, such a damn coward I might as well be dead."

Before Saket can reprimand him again, I throw my bag back on the couch. I've had enough. "A coward?" My voice is loud and hot. "Have you ever considered why I might be such a damn coward?"

Instead of answering, he makes a rude sound.

"Do you not remember how many times I lied so you wouldn't get in trouble? Have you forgotten how many times I sneaked you into the house after Aie and Baba went to bed and you could barely walk? How many nights I didn't sleep so you wouldn't get caught? Apathetic? I can't stop seeking out people's pain and discomfort even when I try because I had to be so tuned in to you! *Uptight?* Do you know how many things Uptight Mira didn't get to try because you had to do what you had to do? You know how many things I didn't get to be so you could be you?"

He looks shocked. As though having me react when he's lashing out at me is somehow impossible for him to comprehend.

Saket picks up our empty glasses and stands. "I'll be in the kitchen if you need me."

Neither of us acknowledges him.

Finally Rumi looks like I feel, punched in the heart. "You resent me," he says. "You've always resented me. *You.* The one person on earth I didn't have to worry about loving me has hated who I am all along."

"Stop, Rumi. Stop it. This isn't about love. Don't make this about love." Because there isn't a soul on earth I could ever love more than I love him. It's the kind of DNA-deep love I could never explain. More than my love for my parents or my friends or the man I'm supposed to be spending the rest of my life with. There is nothing of this seamlessness, this deep knowing, in any of those loves. "This is about you constantly jabbing at me for how I never got to be this version of me you want me to be. Stop manipulating me. Because I'm sick of it. I'm sick of being blamed for everything. I'm sick of being told who to be. By every single person in my life."

He pushes off the couch and faces me, eye to eye. "I don't want you to be anyone other than who you are."

"And who the hell is that, Rumi?"

"Don't you want to find out? Don't you want to be someone other than this person who never stands up for anything? You say you never got to be you. Is it my fault that you never even tried to find out who that was?"

I shove him. I've never in my life been physically aggressive with anyone. Even when I should have been. Even though I still have lucid graphic dreams about bludgeoning the person who took advantage of my physical weakness. But I shove my brother.

"Call me a coward again and I will punch your face."

He looks so stunned that if I weren't having rage palpitations, I'd laugh.

"Yes, I'm a coward. Yes, I'm uptight, I'm spineless. I had to be. I had to contort myself into this person Aie Baba wanted, because—" His face drains of color, and I stop.

Now I want to take everything back. Every ugly word I've said, every word I've thought, I want to swallow it back.

"Because of me. Because I can never be who they want me to be." His curls are wild about his face, his eyes even wilder. I suspect I look much the same. Like we got caught in a windstorm and are only now realizing it.

"I'm sorry," I say. But I know it's not my fault. So I make myself say that too. "I am sorry. It's the ugliest thing, but our parents being the way they are isn't my fault. You are the world's most perfect being, Rumi. My world rests on you being you. I've never wanted you to be anyone but you. But the fact that Aie Baba did, how can you blame me for that?"

"I don't. I blame *them* for that. I just wish you understood." He looks away, then back at me, and I brace myself for what he's about to say next. "I just wish you'd stood up for me once. Not just shielded and deflected, but stood up."

He's right. The sick thing is that I've always known this. I've always understood how wrong our parents were, how cruel. But until this moment I've never been able to admit it. I've made excuses upon excuses. I've compensated for their behavior by contorting myself into the shapes that might make them love me enough to listen, to change, so I might make them see Rumi for who he is. It's the most convoluted logic, but up until now it's felt like the only choice I had.

"I'm so sorry," I say. The shame inside me is so sharp it's an actual ache. An eleven on my beloved pain scale.

"Oh, Miru." Rumi is the first to move. He puts his arm around me and pulls me close, and I go easily. I've missed him. The way he's holding me means he's missed me too. "Maybe I do understand why you felt like you couldn't stand up for me," he says. "I think I've always known that it wasn't because you were weak."

"I wasn't?" I feel so damn weak right now.

"Maybe you were protecting me in the smartest, most pragmatic way possible. At first you were just keeping them from throwing me out. Then you thought you were keeping our family together for when you hoped they'd finally see sense."

I didn't think it was possible, but the tight knot of pain inside me loosens at that. "Thank you," I say.

"I understand why you're you, Miru," he says with a sigh. "But we're adults now, and it's painful to watch you still doing it. It's like watching Mrs. Incredible tying herself in knots." His voice softens. "You still live at home. You schedule your days around their needs. And . . . and well, you're getting into this marriage to make them look good."

Just like that, I'm shaking again. How can he stand there so clean, flinging all the dirt of our ugly history at me?

I pull away and face him. "Druv has nothing to do with this. But you do. What about your role in all this? If you always knew, why didn't you say something? I know I chose to do it, let myself twist into knots to suit them. It might have been because I thought that would make it easier for you, or it might have been because I didn't know any other way. But if you saw it, then instead of stopping me, you let me. You let me be the scapegoat. You left me to it and walked away. You abandoned me."

Shock vibrates through me. I've never thought about him this way. I've never thought about me this way.

Instead of reflecting my anger, he looks sad. "I tried," he says, and his voice is quiet. He's not shouting. We're talking, like adults. "It wasn't in the kindest way, but when I figured it out, I tried. I'm sorry too. I should have tried harder, but you were always so convinced that you were happy. It felt cruel to take that from you."

I drop down on the couch because it's a lot. All of it is a lot.

"Are you happy?" I ask. "Is that even a real thing?"

Before Rumi can answer, Saket comes back in. "That's a lot for one day," he says and wraps his arms around Rumi.

A laugh escapes me. "Okay, stupid question."

Rumi presses a kiss into Saket's cheek. It's unbearably tender. His smile is everything I've ever wanted for him.

Saket sits down next to me and puts an arm around me. Rumi does the same. They're holding me from both sides, squeezing me back into myself. I put my head on Rumi's shoulder. It feels good. It feels like amid the debris of everything we just blew up, we're fine. For the first time in a long time, we're fine.

"I think I might actually be happy," Rumi says. "It's not all the time. God knows, I'm not that evolved. But when I am, I just am, and it's so much simpler than I thought it would be." His voice changes again, turns the slightest bit more vulnerable. "But it didn't happen until I stopped being afraid, Miru. Until I stopped believing everything I'd been taught about myself. It didn't happen until I learned to follow my heart. It's terrifying, but you have to learn to listen to what your heart is saying."

His words hit me slowly, one painful jab at a time, and something I've been trying to push away floats its way to the top of my mind.

CHAPTER TWENTY-FIVE

I'm going back to Reva's house. I've been waiting all night to send that text to Krish. I finally hit send on it and get out of bed.

Despite the deeply luxurious hotel mattress, I haven't slept well. Not in a restless way, but in a filled-with-anticipation way. It takes me twenty minutes to shower, pack, and make my way to check out. It's seven o'clock. My flight leaves at noon. If I make it to Park Slope by eight and leave by ten, I'll still make it.

On the train I check my phone to see if Krish responded.

Please don't. That's his response from twenty minutes ago.

Wasn't asking. Just letting you know. Already on the train, I type. Then I call Druv.

He's in surgery, so I leave a message. He left me one earlier telling me how much he misses me and that he'll be at the airport to pick me up. Something I know won't happen, because he just started a complicated lumbar fusion and there's a good chance it will go eight to nine hours. He also said that he's upgraded the Two Moms and me to business class for our wedding shopping trip to India next month. He sounded so excited about it that I smile. I like that he leaves voice messages in the age of texts. I like the sound of his voice when he's excited.

Then I call my mother, and she spends the entire conversation raving about Druv and how generous he is and how lucky I am. She doesn't ask about my trip, or the ring, or Rumi. She's assumed that I haven't reached out to Rumi because she ordered me not to. She's that certain of my obedience.

As soon as we get off the call, she WhatsApps me a hundred and twelve pictures of bridal lehengas and bridegroom sherwanis from the designer we're going to meet in India. She and Druv's mom have already filtered these down before sending them to me.

I'll look at them on the plane ride home, I message back.

Why can't you look at them now? What's more important than your wedding?

Instead of answering, I check Krish's messages. He hasn't responded. This doesn't surprise me, but I have no time to think about it because the train pulls into the Seventh Avenue station, where Google instructs me to get off.

The station is as crowded as Chicago on Saint Patrick's Day. Suitcase in hand, I dodge the crowd and set off on the path my phone maps for me to Reva's home. It's cloudier but slightly warmer than yesterday. It's strange to walk these streets without Krish by my side. I have to be more present and aware. It's stunning to me how easy it was to trust him.

As I turn the corner onto Reva's street, I see a figure leaning on a motorcycle next to the rainbow-stepped house. Did I just conjure him out of thin air?

His hands are dug deep in his pockets, and he doesn't move. I think he's going for a disapproving vibe.

"Hi!" I can't help but smile. It's just so great to see him again. "Why do you still have the bike?"

"I was going to return it this morning, but then I had to rush here."

He didn't have to rush here. But I'm glad he did.

"What are you doing?" he says, jaw tightly clenched, obviously not glad about anything.

I turn up the steps. "Finishing what we started."

"We did that already. We returned the ring."

"There's more. I want the whole story."

"Mira," he says, still on the street. "You don't have to do this. I'll write a different story."

"No, you'll write this one." I'm about to ring the doorbell.

"Please, can you come down? Please." There's an odd desperation in his voice, and I stop. He clears his throat. "You're right. There's more. I haven't told you everything."

I come back down the steps.

"Can we walk?"

I nod, and we start walking. He's quiet, and I don't push.

"I didn't come to you just to write a story."

I stop walking and turn to him. He looks like he's swallowed a storm again.

"Please tell me you weren't actually stalking me."

I know exactly how he's going to react, and he does. He huffs a humorless laugh. I'm still relieved it wasn't that.

"There's something about the ring that I haven't told you." He looks off balance. Like he can't believe he's saying the words. There's been a lot of that between us.

"Krish, it's okay." I squeeze his arm. He grabs my hand and leans on it. I don't think he has any idea what he's doing. He's lost deep inside himself. He lets my hand go and sits down heavily on the ledge of the sidewalk.

I lower myself next to him. "Breathe. In for four and out for six." I count the breaths and breathe with him.

I expect him to scoff at that, too, but he does as I say.

"Shit, that actually works," he says after a few cycles of breathing.

I wait. This isn't going to be good. I know that. I hate how distraught he looks. "Just say it, Krish."

"I have the other ring."

"What?"

Now, *that* I was not expecting. "What are you talking about?" That can't possibly be true. "What do you mean you have the other ring?"

He takes another breath. His fists clench and unclench. His jaw, all of him, is wound tight. He's lied to me this entire time.

I want to get up and leave, but I can't move. I want the whole story. I deserve the whole story.

"Your video . . . when I watched it . . . ," he says. "I . . . my mom . . ."

"Start with her," I say, and it's not gentle. "Start with your mom."

"That fight with my mom I told you about. I asked her about my birth mother." He takes a breath. "It was my thirty-seventh birthday. My grandmother had just died and left me the apartment. I didn't want it. I didn't want anything that belonged to her, and my mother tried to explain to me how that was throwing the baby out with the bathwater." A sad smile shines like pain in his eyes. "She used to love her old idioms."

He goes quiet again. I wait.

"My parents never talked about my birth parents, not ever. I think I remember first identifying the need to ask about them when I was in elementary school. I never did, but it stayed at the back of my mind. Mom was . . . she was sensitive. My dad always said she was a heart without an armor, exposed nerves. She could spend days in bed, unable to stop crying, when something sad happened to someone she knew. Like a neighbor's pet dying, or like when my fifth-grade teacher got cancer. Every once in a while it would come back, my need to know. But I never asked. I knew how much it would hurt her, and I just couldn't do it. Once I was an adult I put it away. I told myself it didn't matter.

"Until that day when she told me how lucky I was to inherit something everyone covets. Something inside me snapped. She'd always acted like she was the lucky one to find me. She was the one person in my life who'd never told me I was lucky to be adopted. I don't think that's what she was doing then, but that's what it sounded like to me. It's what I heard." He's breathing hard, and his skin has turned chalky, drained of color.

"So you asked her about your birth mother."

"Yes." After a long beat of silence, he reaches into his pocket and extracts a white silk pouch.

He offers it to me, and I take it and open it. Inside is the exact same ring we returned to Reva. The other half of the set.

"She gave me this ring. It was the only thing she knew about my birth mother. It was the only thing my birth mother left with me when she abandoned me. I was livid at Mom for keeping it from me for so long. For not showing it to me sooner. I told her I'd never forgive her." Tears shine in his eyes. "Then she was gone. And that's what she took with her."

He squeezes the bridge of his nose, and a soft sob trembles out of him.

I wrap my arm around him. It's just for a moment. He gets himself together and looks at me again. "When she first gave it to me, I started to scour the internet for information. I was determined to use it to trace the person who'd given me away. Then the accident happened, and I never wanted to see it again. Until your video showed up in my feed almost exactly a year after Mom's death."

I press a hand into my mouth.

"I know. It's a lot. All of it," he says.

I just said those exact words to myself yesterday. I look over my shoulder at the town house with the rainbow steps. The uncomfortable interaction between Krish and Reva yesterday suddenly makes sense.

I look down at the ring in my hand. "You think she's the one who gave you up? You think Reva is your mother?"

"My mother is dead. She died last year," he says with some force.

I'm sorry, I want to say, for forcing him into meeting her. But I'm not sorry. Not even a little bit.

"I understand if you're angry that I didn't tell you. But you were a complete stranger."

It's not an apology. He's simply addressing the issue. Also, he said *were*, and that of all things is what feels significant.

I don't tell him it's okay that he lied to me. I'm not sure yet if it is. Two days ago I would have said it anyway.

"What do you want to do now?" I say instead.

The look he gives me is split somewhere between surprise and gratitude, but he neither apologizes nor thanks me.

He glances down the street at the house. "I guess we have to go back and find out. Obviously she has no interest in reuniting with me. I think she recognized something in me. Maybe I look like my birth father or something?" He sounds sad but not distraught.

I put the ring back in the pouch and return it to him. We can either sit here and second-guess this, or we can find out for sure. I stand up. "Let's go."

Instead of arguing with me, he stands too, but he doesn't move. "What if she's not home?"

"Let's find out. Come on."

We march back to the house and up the stairs.

"Knocker or bell?" he says.

"Decisions, decisions," I say.

He knocks and I ring.

It's a shock to see Reva when she opens the door. She's almost unrecognizable. Completely different from the woman we met yesterday. Her eyes are red rimmed and swollen. Her almost-all-salt-with-a-sprinkling-of-pepper hair is in a lopsided ponytail, and she's wearing an embroidered powder blue caftan much like the ones every auntie I know wears to bed. There's no sign of the casually athletic badass from yesterday. Her gaze lands on Krish.

His jaw works. I think he's following the breathing technique we just used. In for four and out for six.

She reaches out and touches his cheek. "You look just like her," she says.

He looks at me, then back at her. "I have no idea who you're talking about."

Her chin trembles in confusion. Her eyes cloud with it. She steps aside. "I think you should come in."

We follow her into the kitchen and to a breakfast nook nestled into a bay window overlooking a garden. It reminds me of Rumi and Saket's place, and yet it's completely different. There's more history here than hope.

There's a wooden box on the table. It's filled with what looks like folded-up letters. A few of the letters are spread open, as though they're in the middle of being read. Wadded-up tissues litter the table and the floor. Reva plucks a fresh tissue from a box and blows her nose and wipes her eyes. Then she gathers all the balled-up tissues and takes them to the trash under the sink.

"I'm sorry I'm a bit of a mess this morning." She's trying her best not to stare at Krish, but her eyes keep returning to him. "How can I help you?"

"The other ring you told us about, did you leave it with a baby when you gave him away?" That's the question Krish chooses to open with, and it's as good a question as any, given the circumstances.

Reva's head snaps up, and a million emotions flash across her face. My pain scale registers another ten-plus reading.

Without answering, she drops into a chair. "Have a seat, please. Can I offer you some tea? Or coffee." She points to a very complex coffee machine, much like the one Druv is addicted to.

"I'll make myself some tea," I say. "Can I make you some?"

She shakes her head and points at a cup on the table.

"Krish?"

"You sit," he says. "Let me make the tea."

He obviously needs something to do, so I pick out a black tea bag from the tea box, hand it to him, and sit down next to Reva.

He fills the kettle, turns it on, then picks up two cups from the drying rack and puts tea bags in them.

Time hangs. Every action of his seems to take up all the attention in the room. The muted tapping of a woodpecker feels loud and close in the silence.

"The milk is in the fridge," Reva says finally. "I wasn't the one who had the other ring."

Krish pauses in the act of pouring milk into the tea. Then continues to finish the job and brings the cups to the table.

Reva picks up one of the letters, and a tear slips from her eye. I notice that the ring is back around her neck, on a plain black thread this time.

"Her name was Vasu." Her voice does a painful wobble.

I take the cups from Krish, and he drops into the chair next to me.

Reva's eyes skim the letters. "The rings belonged to her grandmother." She takes a breath. "We grew up together, in a tiny town in India. Back when . . . it was like a different planet back then. I'm sure it's still hard, but back then it was . . ." She looks at Krish like she's gathering strength from his face. "My mother worked for Vasu's family. A live-in maid. We lived in the servant's unit behind the grand house. Vasu's father was a minister—something like a senator here—the wealthiest, most powerful man in town. Vasu and I did everything together. The family sent me to the same school as her. We studied together, played together, ate together. She was . . . she was my best friend, my . . . she . . ."

I hand her a tissue, and she dabs her cheeks and thanks me before continuing. "When we were eighteen, Vasu's father sent us away to college. She went to Pune, and I went to engineering college in Mumbai. For two years we survived the separation by writing letters. And then . . . then everything changed." Her fingers stroke the pages spread across the table. "The way we felt . . . we had no idea it was even possible. The world was so different then."

On the buffet is a framed picture of her with a woman, their arms wrapped around each other against a turquoise beach. "It was stronger than anything I've ever experienced, our love. It came out of the blue, but also, it didn't, you know." Her voice cracks again, and she takes a breath. "I don't even know why I'm . . . why I'm such a mess. It's been so long. I guess it's the letters. I haven't read them in years."

Krish makes a sound, and I think he's going to push her to spit out the rest of it. He doesn't. He just waits, his body utterly still.

Reva is obviously not his mother. But she knows who is. It's very likely this Vasu she's talking about is. How is he able to bear this? I want to hold his hand, but I don't.

"What happened?" I'm the one who speaks, because they're both frozen.

Reva shakes her head as if to clear it. "Vasu's family found out. They convinced her to get married to some distant cousin from an equally powerful family. The last I heard, she was still with him. When I was admitted into a master's program here, I wouldn't leave without her, so my mother visited her. She told my mother she'd made a mistake with me and she was ashamed. She even returned my letters. If not for the returned letters, I might not have believed it. The pictures of her with her family that my mother brought back were happy. My mother had lost her job, I had to support us, and there was nothing left in India for me. So I left."

Finally Krish speaks. "And the second ring?"

"She still had it the last I know. You obviously know where it is. Did she send you? Is she okay? Please, just tell me."

"I don't know her," Krish says. "I was adopted. From India, thirty-eight years ago. My birth mother left a ring with me when she gave me away. It seems like it's the other half of the set yours belongs to."

Reva's hand squeezes her temples. "That's impossible. I suspected you were hers. But why would she give you up?"

Krish takes the ring out of his pocket and places it on the table between them. Reva removes hers from around her neck and with shaking hands fits the two rings together. It's a perfect fit. The puzzle pieces lock together like they were never separated. The shree symbol on the inside matches exactly. Line to line, stroke to stroke.

Reva squeezes the rings in her hand, presses them to her chest, and folds over. For the longest time no one says anything. When she straightens and wipes her eyes, something in them feels shattered, cracked open. I can see all the way into her pain, old and calcified but fresh again. She gives Krish back his ring and reaches for the letters in the wooden box and starts rummaging through them. At the bottom of the box is a stack of pictures.

She shuffles through the faded sepia-toned prints and finds one that looks like it was taken in a studio, and hands it to Krish. The woman looks uncannily like him. The same thickly lashed beer-bottle eyes behind glasses; the same dimple in the center of one cheek; the same lighter coloring, wide lips, and square jaw. She's wearing a purple-and-gold sari and heavy gold jewelry, and she's holding a baby. Next to her, a man in a turban with a handlebar mustache looks proudly at the camera.

"Is that you?" I ask, because the baby looks nothing like Krish.

He shakes his head. "That's not me."

"But you're obviously related to her," Reva says. "Looking at you is like seeing her ghost."

Krish says nothing.

"Why would she put him up for adoption if this picture were real?" I ask. I pick up the picture and study it. Something in the way she's holding the child doesn't fit.

"I don't know," Reva whispers.

"Did you never reach out to her again?"

"I didn't want to put her in danger. It wasn't safe for us back then. Her father had already fired my mother, burned down her house, and sent goons after me. He also hurt Vasu. I believed my mother when she told me it would ruin Vasu's life if I didn't let her go. I told myself she'd made peace with the situation. She'd made her choice."

Except they'd probably lied to Reva.

"So she betrayed you, and she gave me away. Sounds like a peach," Krish says, and Reva looks like he's kicked her.

Something isn't right. I don't think Reva is lying to us, but the story doesn't fit. I say nothing because it feels like a cruel thing to say to either of them right now, when the pain of age-old wounds is so tightly wrapped around them.

"If we were to try and find her, where would we start?" I ask.

"We're not going to," Krish says and stands. "Thank you for your time."

Reva looks at me, and I can't tell if that's hope in her eyes or fear of what we might find, but it's fierce and desperate and I can't look away. "I think her husband's name was Namdeo Sawant. My aie passed in 1990, the year I got my PhD. Just before I was supposed to move her here. Her funeral was the last time I went back to India. I tried to reach out to Vasu then, but she wasn't interested. She didn't answer my letters or take my calls. Her parents have been dead for years now, and her older brother is a politician like her father."

"Do you have an address for her in Mumbai?" I ask.

"What are you doing, Mira?" Krish says.

"I can find it for you," Reva says.

"That won't be necessary," Krish says. "Let's go." He picks up the cups and puts them in the sink and heads to the door. "Thank you again for your time."

Reva doesn't move. "Thank you for returning the ring." She puts the ring back around her neck. There's something reverent about the way she does it.

"Why do you still wear it?" I ask.

There's exhaustion in her eyes and a deep sadness that feels as permanent and irreversible as the passage of time. "A matter of habit, I guess," she says. "And so I never forget who I am."

CHAPTER TWENTY-SIX

This is the third dinner party I'm attending in the two weeks since I got back from New York. Druv's mom threw one to welcome me back. Then my aie threw one to thank her for throwing that one. Then today, Druv's mom's girl gang is throwing one to bid us farewell before we leave on our shopping trip tomorrow.

The greatest miracle is that Druv has taken the day off. He wanted to spend time with me before I leave for India for two weeks. This morning he whisked me away for brunch in Chicago. After a leisurely feast of eggs and pastries at the Drake, we walked along Lake Michigan all the way from Navy Pier to the Adler Planetarium. It's my favorite walk. The familiarity of Chicago is comforting after the adventure through the unknown that was New York.

I've been resisting the comparison, but when Druv asked which of the two cities I prefer, I had to give it some thought. I don't think it's about the cities so much as who I am in each of them. I got to do something remarkable in New York. I've never given Chicago a chance to be anything more than what I was told it was.

When I said that to Druv, he laughed. "Who are you, and what did you do with my fiancée?" It's not the first time he's said that since I got home.

After our walk, he came home with me and hung around in my room while I packed. We never did this before I went to New York, just hang out in each other's presence. He's been around a lot more since I came back. For the first time in our relationship, I feel pursued. Even though he is being less overtly pursuing.

"You don't seem stressed about the trip at all," Druv says and takes a sip of his scotch. We're sitting on the deck of his mom's friend's house. It's weird to see him this way, relaxed, attentive in a different way than I'm used to. He's even wearing a golf shirt instead of his usual laundered button-downs. "You're so different since you came back from New York. Should I brace myself for who my future wife is going to be when she returns from India?"

His smile says that the question is rhetorical, so I respond with a smile.

The aunties and uncles are inside, possibly giving us privacy and winking at each other about it. The other "kids" in his parents' friend group are in the basement, playing pool or planning some sort of surprise dance for our wedding.

Druv decided to stay with me when I stepped out on the deck to check my messages. Reva sent me Vasu's husband's address last week, and I've been waiting to see if she can find Vasu's brother's number before I leave tomorrow.

I haven't heard from Krish since we said goodbye two weeks ago. I've seen the three dots in his messages a few times, but he's said nothing after our last exchange, just after we raced to LaGuardia from Reva's home with my bag tucked recklessly between us on the bike and miraculously made my flight.

I haven't told him yet that I plan to keep searching for Vasu when I'm in India. I need to before I leave, so I open up our chat on my phone and see our last texts.

Me: Thank you for the ride to the airport

Him: Sure

Me: You okay?

Him: Yes, thank you

Me: Don't you think there were holes in Reva's story?

Him: I know you think I should care. But I don't

Me: Vasu might be your mother

Him: Really? No way! How did you figure that out?

Him: I don't care, Mira

Me: Reva messaged me saying she can find Namdeo Sawant's address

Him: Can you respect my wishes and let this go please?

Me: What if I can't?

Him: You're on your own then. Can you at least do me the kindness of leaving me out of it?

Me: Fine

I've kept my word, even though I don't think leaving him out of it is doing him a kindness.

"Mira?" Druv says. "What's going on? Is it Reva?"

I've told Druv about Reva and Vasu. I've told him about Krish too. The parts where we combed the jewelry stores of New York. Even the New York speed sightseeing and the motorcycle. But not MoMA. And not the parts about Krish's connection to the ring. That's not mine to tell.

"No. She hasn't found Vasu's brother's number yet."

"Shouldn't it be easy enough to google it?"

I give him a pointed *Don't you think I've tried that already?* look.

He looks delighted. If my being assertive makes him this happy, why did he get together with me in the first place? Because I wasn't like this with him before.

"What's the matter? What did I say?" he asks.

"Nothing. I just feel like you're different, too, since I got back."

"Really? How?" But his face tells me he knows what I mean.

"We've been engaged for six months. We're getting married in three months. Why does it feel like we're only really talking now?"

"Isn't that natural? Don't all relationships evolve?"

He's not wrong. It's not his fault that I'm feeling all these things. That I feel so different. "Can I ask you something, Druv?"

He nods.

"Why me? Why did you pick me?"

I know that makes him sound like some sort of mythical prince who had his pick of a bride from the ladies at court, but I'm not sure that wasn't true, albeit in a somewhat modernized form.

He opens his mouth, but then he stops and gives it some thought before answering. "You're kind, and you listen, and you were truly interested in understanding me."

"That sounds like the bare minimum. The least amount of trouble. Someone who fit in with the life you wanted with minimal work."

"If that were true, why would I be so happy that you've come back like this?"

"Like what?"

"More open. More comfortable in your skin. Accessible. It's not like I didn't try before. But you were closed off. I didn't want to scare you away. You were"—he pauses—"skittish."

God, he's not wrong. I did feel skittish. I've felt like that for a very long time. I try to access that always skittish part of me, and I can't quite find her.

"Why didn't you try to find out what made me skittish?"

"I thought I knew."

"Tell me what you thought."

"It's what you've said before. Your childhood. Your parents are great, but they didn't have it easy, and they didn't make it easy on you. I remember how quiet and reserved you were in high school. I also remember the natural kindness and dignity you had about you. Something none of us had at that age. I think I was struck by it then, and when I met you at Shubha's wedding, I was struck by it again. There's always been something about you, Mira. It came back to me, and it soothed me. You calm the restlessness inside me. You feel like an answer to questions I don't even know I have."

That might be the most beautiful thing anyone's ever said to me. I blush. Because I might feel different, but I'm essentially the same dork.

"Can I ask you something too?" he says.

I nod.

"What happened in New York? Was it just the ring?"

"A lot of it was the ring. But . . . I spent some time with Rumi." I wait for him to react. Rumi's reputation in our town isn't exactly stellar.

"Isn't he in jail?"

"What?" Every bit of warmth I'm feeling vanishes.

"Sorry. I'm . . . you never talk about him. That's what your aie told Mom. Or maybe Mom made that assumption based on something your mother said. You know how the moms work."

"You went to school with Rumi. How could you think such a thing about him and not ask me about it?"

"Your brother's choices have nothing to do with you."

Does he think he's being generous right now? "How can you say that? Does Ariana have nothing to do with you?"

"It's not the same thing."

"Why? Because Brown Town gossips about Rumi and he isn't here to protect himself?"

"Mira, can we slow down for a minute? Please."

"No, Druv. This is not about my speed. Rumi is an architect who works on designing sets for the theater in New York. One of his plays was nominated for a Tony last year. He's not a criminal. He never was. This town basically chewed him up and spat him out because of their bigotry."

Druv takes my hands in his. "I'm sorry. I really am."

"You know all of this."

"Not in the way that I'm seeing it now. I'm glad you got to spend time with him. Was that what was bothering you before you went to New York? Your estrangement from Rumi?"

"I was never estranged from him. My parents are. My relationship with him was strained because I never stood up for him. It isn't anymore. So yes, the trip was great. I feel like I have my brother back."

He tucks a lock of hair behind my ear. I started straightening it again after I got home. He seems genuinely happy for me. "That's great. Ariana and I are ten years apart, and I can't imagine being distanced from her. I'm sorry you had to go through that."

"I think I like our evolved dynamic," I say, and he smiles.

"Me too. Are you really planning to search for Vasu when you're in India?"

"I have to find out what happened to her. You can't tell Aie and Ma. I can't handle them being involved."

"Does that mean I can blackmail you for favors?" His eyes are shining with warmth.

I think mine might be too. "I'm already taking the trip with them by myself and doing all your shopping for you. I thought you were favored out."

"Not the favors I had in mind."

I blush again, and he smiles.

"Will the journalist be there?"

"No," I say. "I think he's done with the story."

CHAPTER TWENTY-SEVEN

Full disclosure. I'm going to look for Vasu in India, I text Krish before we board the flight at O'Hare. Our route is Chicago to New York, then New York to Istanbul, and then to Mumbai.

Please don't. I see his response just before we take off out of Chicago.

I wasn't asking. Just letting you know, I type. I know you asked me to leave you out of it but I would feel wrong doing it without letting you know. Then I send him my flight and hotel details anyway.

He doesn't respond. Not even the three dots, and I turn my phone to airplane mode.

There's no response from him when we land in JFK, where we have to change planes. It's a short connection. Just two hours. In that time, Aie and Druv's mom want to try on every perfume in duty-free and get my opinion on each one.

They're in full Girls' Trip mode. They're dressed in matching pink kurtis over jeans. I don't remember ever seeing my aie this relaxed. Romona is so good for her.

I try to focus on their steady stream of excited conversation. Women are supposed to be the ones who dream about their wedding day from when they are girls, but I think Indian mothers dream about their children's weddings from the day they're born. Aie and Romona obviously have. I have to work hard to not let on how distracted I am. Reva sent me some information about Vasu's brother while we were in the air, and

I'm trying to use this time on the ground to do some research about distances in Mumbai and such. Our flight does not have Wi-Fi.

"What do you think, Mira?"

I smell the paper stick Romona holds out and make the mistake of letting out an impressed sound. Immediately she holds out three others and asks me to choose.

"I like the one that smells like jasmine. That one." I point at the only smell that won't give me a headache with its intensity.

Romona pays an absurd amount for the biggest bottle they have. Then Aie spends even more on a cologne for Druv. Which she makes me select. A vision of the two of them trying to outspend each other for the next week flashes in my mind.

By the time they've shared all the details about our plans, complete with pictures and names of designers, with the salesperson, it's time to board our next flight.

Krish hasn't responded to my last message. I know he told me he's done with this, but my eyes still search the boarding area. Even after we've taken our seats—the Two Moms next to each other in the row in front of me and me in the window seat behind—my gaze keeps straying to the stream of already tired-looking passengers as they shuffle through the aisles. Obviously, he's not on the plane. That would be an absurd thing to expect.

Our stop in Istanbul is uneventful. We eat our way through kababs and baklava in the lounge and can't wait to get back on the plane and sleep.

Landing at Mumbai airport, on my first trip to India, is at once nothing like I expected and everything I should have imagined. Druv had used the word *overwhelming* to describe the experience of visiting with his family when he was a child (unlike us, the Kalras visited almost every summer). *Overwhelming* is certainly one way to put it. It feels a little like stepping into the eye of a storm, a sensory storm. The airport is grander than any I've seen before. Intricately detailed canopied pillars inspired by peacock feathers hold up an endless ceiling from which light fixtures hang like giant lotus blooms. Ornate statues and dramatic pieces of art are scattered everywhere.

Despite the air-conditioning, it's humid and faintly dusty, and filled with people. So many people. I can feel my own skin—there's a mist layered over it. I'm aware of my breathing without trying to be. I feel a strange rightness. Like I'm meant to be here. But also completely out of place in the most backward, sideways, upside-down way. This is the first time in my life that I'm in a public place of this magnitude where almost every person is racially like me.

I push our luggage trolley out of the airport into a blast of heat, dust, sound, and smell. Aie's eyes fill with tears. She leans into her cane and just stands there for a moment. Romona squeezes her hand. Their bodies are not processing the sensory overload the way mine is. When Aie gives the taxi driver our hotel address, something about her is entirely different. Not even in our home or in the store has she ever seemed this natural, this unselfconscious. Her body language is so different she looks like a stranger with my mother's face.

My gaze, which has been searching the crowd, sweeps it one last time. Krish hasn't responded to my last message, and I don't know what I'm expecting, but it's not this kind of disappointment. I'm going to have to do this by myself.

"How does it feel?" Romona asks, cupping my cheek as the three of us settle into the cab.

Aie is silently sobbing as she takes in the sights. My parents have been back here only once since they bought the store and got their citizenship. I think about all the years—almost my entire lifetime—that she yearned to visit and couldn't. She never got to see her parents before they died.

"It's intense," I say. "But it's very exciting to be here."

"It's so different from when we grew up," Aie says.

Romona and she go off into raptures about how much India has changed over the past thirty years. Gigantic steel-and-glass buildings give way to shanties and crumbling buildings in an endlessly alternating pattern.

When we arrive at the JW Marriott on Juhu Beach, I'm in a strange state. My body should be rested from twenty hours of sitting, but it's also exhausted from it. There's a buzzing in my brain that's part excitement and part disorientation.

Romona's sister's son heads the hotel chain's operations in India. The moment our cab drops us off, a uniformed employee greets us and leads us into the lobby, with its pillared view of the ocean across a network of pools. She informs us that this is one of their most premium properties. We're handed tall glasses of coconut water, told how honored the staff is to have us, and upgraded to a luxury suite. Which means instead of two rooms, one for Aie and me and another for Romona, we'll share a unit with a living room and two bedrooms with two bathrooms and a terrace overlooking the ocean.

I don't know if I'm more relieved that I won't have to be stuck in one room with my mother for a week or more stressed about living with my soon-to-be mother-in-law for that long.

"You okay with this?" Romona asks me. "I know you young people need your space."

"Of course she's okay with it!" Aie says. "It's going to be so much fun."

Romona waits for me to answer.

"Aie is right. It's going to be great."

They both smile wide happy smiles, but they also look travel weary. It's eight in the evening, and we left home more than twenty-four hours ago.

The attendant tasked with welcoming us has already sent our luggage to our room and asks if we'd like a tour of the hotel.

The Two Moms politely decline. They announce their need for a shower and a good night's sleep. We have an appointment with the first designer at nine tomorrow morning.

I'm in need of a long shower, too, but I'm restless. I want to talk to Druv, let him know we've arrived safe and sound, but I want to do it without an audience. So I tell them that I'm going to take the tour and join them after.

Radha, my guide, picks up on my mood and makes it quick. Naturally everything is gorgeous and state of the art, and I'm totally not following along about the details.

Suddenly there's a ball of panic in my chest. I thank her for her time and tell her that I'd like to stay on the deck and enjoy the ocean view for a moment. My hand is shaking when I call Druv. He's in surgery.

What am I doing?

I've traveled all the way across the world to shop for my wedding. I should feel so much more invested in that than I do. My mind is entirely taken up with tracing a stranger's lost love. I shouldn't feel so incredibly invested in that. I have no idea how I'm going to get away from the Two Moms to manage it. The heat and humidity and twilit sky press against my senses. I've never felt like this in my life. I can't reconcile all these feelings: balance and imbalance, belonging and disconnection, freedom and feeling stifled, all together, all at once.

I spin away from the pool and ocean, needing to move, and stop dead in my tracks.

Krish is leaning on a wooden column, hands dug into his pockets, heavy vibe of disapproval overlaid with something else I can't quite place.

"Hi." I shouldn't sound so excited. I shouldn't feel so relieved.

"What are you doing?" he says, jaw tightly clenched.

I step up to him. "Finishing what we started."

"We did that already . . ." He trails off and looks away from me and then back. "Why are you doing this?"

"Because Reva wants me to."

"You barely know Reva."

"I barely know you." It sounds like such a lie.

"I thought we were friends."

"Are we?"

"Of course we are."

"Then as my friend, tell me why you don't want to do this. Why you don't want to find out what happened to Vasu when she might be your mother." I catch his expression and correct myself. "Your birth mother."

"Because she gave me up. She tossed me out like a piece of trash. Why would I go looking for her?"

"So you're here to talk me out of this. Not to help me."

"Can I talk you out of it?"

"No."

"Why is this so important to you?"

"Because I know without a doubt that she didn't toss you out like a piece of trash."

His frown dimple makes an appearance. "You have no way of knowing that."

"I know it, though. She's a person who someone loved enough that they've worn her ring for forty years." That's the piece that won't leave me. "I've seen bigotry and hatred in my own home. I saw the pain of a life destroyed in Reva's eyes. Reva got away. Rumi and Saket live in a time when they could escape it. What if Vasu wasn't able to?"

"So this is about your brother."

"I don't know what it's about, Krish. But whatever it's about isn't simple, and I can't imagine that it was fair. I have to know what it was."

Before either one of us can say more, I hear the last voice in the world I want to hear right now.

"Miru?" my mother calls. "What's going on?"

"Aie, what are you doing down here?" Her bobbed hair is wet, and she's changed into a T-shirt and yoga pants, but she still looks exhausted.

"You were taking so long. Romona and I were starting to worry, so I came looking for you." She throws a glance Krish's way. "Hello?"

"This is Krish Hale," I say. "He's a journalist from New York."

Krish offers her a hand, and she shakes it, confusion obvious on her face. "You know each other from before? You just ran into him by accident?" Her voice is filled with all the suspicion that defined my childhood.

"I'm working on a story," Krish says. "Mira had no idea I was going to be here." Two truths that add up to a lie.

"Mira is here to shop for her wedding outfits," Aie says pointedly, polite but cold.

Her tone is wasted on Krish. Distant and cordial is his default setting.

"Do you know Druv?" Aie continues. "He's an orthopedic surgeon. Specialist in spinal surgery."

"That's nice." Krish looks impressed enough, albeit in his signature distant way, and Aie relaxes a little. "I actually know your son," he says with a little more deliberateness. "He's an impressive designer. His work on *The A Game* was brilliant. That play totally deserved the Tony nomination. You must be so proud."

My heart has been stuttering in panic at my mother's appearance. Suddenly something warm blooms around it. Warmth slides down my limbs. I wrap my arms around myself.

Krish slides me the barest look, but he misses neither my relief nor my mother's stiffening.

I place a hand on my aie's arm. "Druv's mother must be wondering where we've disappeared to. I don't want to worry her. It was nice running into you, Krish."

"Likewise," he says in his old-world way. "Good luck with finding the perfect wedding dress."

"She has to find six," Aie says, glaring at him with a mix of scorn and pride. She holds up a hand and counts off. "For the haldi, mehendi, sangeet, wedding, reception, and brunch. Aren't you Indian?"

I can tell Krish is trying not to raise a brow at me that says *Apple, tree.*

"We have to go," I say and drag her to the elevator.

"Does he think you're marrying in a church that you need only one wedding dress?"

I really hope Krish didn't hear that, but I don't want to turn around and check. "He's a guy, Aie. You know men don't give much thought to weddings and clothes."

"Thank God," she says. "Imagine if we had to listen to men in that as well."

I can feel Krish's amused gaze follow us as we get into the elevator, and I wonder if he sees the relief filling my lungs like the heavy humid air.

CHAPTER TWENTY-EIGHT

The first lehenga I try on is gorgeous. It's emerald green silk with intricate gold threadwork that makes me feel like I'm draped in some sort of celestial garden. I never dreamed of a wedding dress, but if I had, this would be it.

"This is perfect," I say. "Let's go with this one."

Both Romona and Aie look shocked. Preeta Vaid, who's supposed to be one of India's leading wedding stylists, beams. The Two Moms scoured the internet and sat in on endless hours of Zoom calls before selecting Preeta as the designer for all our wedding needs.

"Preeta has five more picked out for you to try," Romona says. "In color palettes that complement your skin tone."

I open my mouth to say I've made my choice, but Aie widens her eyes at me and nips it in the bud.

"Mira's always been so easy. Always trying not to be a bother. This is your time, Mira. Don't think about us." What she means is: *Think about us. We want to play dress-up for a week. You cannot take that away from us.*

I try on all six of the lehengas. They're all lovely. After spending hours on draping and discussing each one, over masala chai, filter coffee, and cocktail samosas, I select the first one I tried on. Although, to be fair, I would be more than happy to wear any one of them. When we get home after a day of immersive shopping, the moms can barely get through dinner (room service) before passing out.

The next day, we rinse and repeat the process for the reception lehenga. This time I try not to react to the first one I see—a shimmery burgundy organza sprinkled with Swarovski crystals—but it is the one I like most, and it's the one I pick in the end. By the time I escape to the bathroom after we're done, so many messages have collected on my phone it almost feels heavy in my hand.

Yesterday, while I let the moms play dress-up with me as their doll, Krish went in search of Vasu's husband's home and found that the building has been torn down for redevelopment. Last night, as the moms slept, Krish and I texted and came up with a plan. He's going to ask around the neighborhood to see what he can find, and I'm going to meet him there as soon as I can get away.

I speed-read through Krish's texts. We're in Juhu, and Namdeo Sawant's address is in Shivaji Park. It's a distance of barely six miles, but my phone tells me it's going to take about an hour with the traffic.

Krish: I've been asking where the people who lived here have gone but no one on the construction site understands me

Me: Aren't you Indian?

Krish: Haha. When are you getting here so you can speak Indian to them?

Me: Aren't you a fancy journalist from a fancy journalism school? There's no language called Indian.

Krish: Really? Why don't they teach that in fancy journalism school? Damn.

Me: Maybe it's not that fancy after all?

Krish: Definitely Barely Fancy. When do you get here?

Aww, you miss me! I type. Then delete it.

Me: Just convinced the moms that I want to see some of Mumbai. Thank God they're too tired and jet lagged to join me. They're going back to the hotel. Be there in an hour.

Krish: Should I come get you?

Me: Only if you have a motorcycle. This traffic is the worst thing I've ever seen.

Krish: I created a monster.

I'm smiling when I shut down his texts, get a cab, and call Druv, who's just woken up for an early surgery.

"I miss you," he says. "Why does it take seven days to choose clothes?"

"Because they've been obsessing over wedding clothes for months, and they want me to try on everything that's ever caught their fancy. For hours and hours. I may never come back." Who knew trying on clothes was this exhausting? "Sorry that sounded terribly ungrateful."

"They get to watch you try on clothes for hours while I sit here imagining it? Feels particularly cruel."

He's not even here, and I feel my cheeks burn.

"Can you at least send me pictures?"

"I've been warned against that by the moms. Apparently, even if I describe the dresses to you, we'll be struck by bad luck."

"Isn't that a Western superstition?"

"You know our mothers embrace all global superstitions with equal zeal."

He laughs. "Please, please, when you choose my clothes, don't let my ma go overboard."

"I'm thinking a fluorescent yellow."

"Have mercy," he says, laughing.

"If you wanted a vote, you should have come along."

"So you do miss me."

"I do," I say softly.

"Thank you," he says, "for saying that. I needed to hear it. Have you had a chance to reach out to Vasu's family?"

"There's something I need to tell you," I say. "Krish is here."

"The journalist guy? How come?"

"I told him I'm going to keep working on finding her."

"You asked him to come."

"I gave him that choice. It is his story."

"How are you handling the Two Moms?"

"My aie met him. She wasn't happy. I really don't want them to know I'm doing this." The moms barely know what happened with the ring. They know I had "a little adventure in New York," but they're too preoccupied with the wedding to care.

"Let me know if you need help with them." He wants to help, and it's the sweetest thing.

"I will. Thanks. Today fortunately they're knocked out from the shopping marathon." I fill him in on the torn-down-building situation. "Thanks for being so understanding about this, Druv."

"I can tell it's important to you, Mira. I want you to have your answers. I'm invested, too, now. I want to know what happened to Vasu too. I love you," he says.

"Same," I say. My aie is right. I am lucky to have Druv.

~

The black-and-yellow cab drops me off next to a huge open park surrounded on three sides by concrete buildings. Across the street is the ocean, obscured by another row of buildings. If I focus, over the honking and traffic noise, I can hear the waves. I turn to the statue of the

Maratha emperor Shivaji astride his horse. Beneath the statue, Krish is waiting for me.

He's wearing a white T-shirt and jeans. I'm wearing a white kurti over jeans. We look like we're in some sort of plainclothes detective uniform.

"That was the building." He starts without preamble, pointing to a construction site across the open park. His eyes are hidden behind the aviators he was wearing the first time we met.

We make our way across the park. Children perform gymnastics on bars, and runners sprint across marked tracks. A group of older people laugh loudly, then stop, then laugh again as they practice laughter yoga.

We get to the construction site, where mounds of rubble surround the half-built building where steel rods poke out of concrete slabs. Women dressed in threadbare cotton saris draped like pants between their legs carry cement and stone back and forth on their heads. Cement mixers churn, and a crane tries to place a steel beam amid shouts from construction workers. A cloud of dust hangs in the air, and the sun blazes down on us.

When Krish and I approach, the women carrying rubble on their heads barely spare us a glance and keep working. A man in a hard hat and a gray polyester safari suit approaches us.

"What do you want?" he asks Krish in Marathi, ignoring me.

"We're looking for someone who used to live in this building," I respond in Marathi. My parents are most comfortable speaking their mother tongue, so growing up, Rumi and I exclusively spoke it at home. I still speak with my parents primarily in Marathi. They also had no patience with us accenting our Marathi, so we speak it with no accent.

Something about being able to speak the language makes being here easier. It makes the foreign-seeming parts a degree less foreign.

"Are you their relative?" the man asks.

"Yes." I slide a glance at Krish. "He's come from America. His uncle used to live here."

Krish nods without having any idea what I'm saying.

"What's his uncle's name?"

"Namdeo Sawant."

"Oh yes. This building belonged to him. Now it belongs to his son, Vishal Sawant." He turns to a man who's giving instructions to the women lugging the rubble. "Oy, is Vishal sir still in the office, or did he leave?"

"I didn't see him leave. I'm not his keeper, though," the other guy yells back.

"Where's the office?" I ask, and he points us in the direction of a trailer down the street, where a few other construction projects are in progress.

I translate what was said for Krish as we make our way past old art deco buildings that stand between the construction sites like remnants from a past era. We knock on the door of the makeshift office.

Fortunately Vishal Sawant hasn't left yet, and he speaks English.

"Where in America are you from?" he asks when we introduce ourselves. "I went to Ohio State for grad school. Architectural design."

When Krish tells him he went to Columbia, he thumps him on the back. "My wife is from NYU. Wait till I tell her I met someone from her rival school. How did you guys know my dad?" He calls to one of his employees and asks them to bring us coffee.

I search the guy's face. He looks nothing like Krish, but that might have to with the fact that he's fifty pounds heavier and his hairline is receding. I study his features but still can't find anything in common with Krish's angular face and brown eyes.

"Actually," Krish says, "we're trying to find someone named—"

"You're Namdeo Sawant's son?" I interrupt. Something tells me it's not a good idea to mention Vasu yet.

"Yeah," the man says as a young boy hands us paper cups of coffee.

"Can we speak to him?" I say.

The man's eyes sadden. "Baba died ten years ago. That's why I came back to Mumbai to take care of the family business after him. The responsibilities of being an only son are heavy indeed," he says directly to Krish.

"I'm sorry to hear that," I say. "How about your mother? Can we speak to her? My mother thinks she might be her childhood friend."

"Really? Is your mother from Varanasi? My aie never mentioned a friend who lives in America."

"Really? My mom can't stop talking about Vasudha."

Vishal's coffee cup freezes an inch from his lips. It takes him a moment to unfreeze. "Vasudha?" He stands up. "I've never heard of anyone by that name."

"Are you sure?" Krish and I say together.

"Vasudha Patil, then Sawant?" I add.

Vishal's face goes a strange shade of red. Every piece of friendliness vanishes from his demeanor. He looks at his watch. "What did you say your names were again?"

We remind him of our names.

"And you're here looking for this person?"

"Yes. Can you tell us what you know about her? Please," I say.

"I told you I've never heard of her."

That's obviously not true. "We know she was married to Namdeo Sawant who lived at this address," I say, "If that's your dad . . ."

"You have the wrong information," he snaps. "My mother's name is Amita, and she was married to my father thirty-seven years ago. I'm thirty-six."

"Is it possible that your father was married to Vasudha before that?" Krish says.

"Don't you think I'd know it if my father had another wife?"

"We have proof that your father was married to Vasudha," I say.

"Proof?" He stands. He's a big man, and the look in his eyes turns ice cold. "Around here we don't walk into people's places of work, enjoy their hospitality"—he looks at the empty coffee cups—"and threaten them." It's like he's a whole different person. He presses a button on his desk.

"I'm sorry. That's not what we were doing," Krish says. "As she said, Vasudha was her mother's friend, and her mother wants to reconnect. That's all."

Vishal laughs. "I love how you Americans think everyone other than you is stupid. If indeed she was your mother's friend, then I'm going to assume your mother had no idea what kind of woman she was." He lets out a disgusted scoff.

"So you do know her?" I say.

He gives me the most menacing look, but I don't care. "My father was tricked into marrying her. He left her when he found out what she was. Around here we still value decency."

The door opens, and three men who look like gangsters right out of a Bollywood film walk in and stand behind us, really close behind us. A sour combination of sweat, tobacco, and alcohol fills my nostrils.

"Our family has been eminent in this part of Mumbai for seven generations. My father's name means something around here. We're respectable and God fearing. That doesn't mean we're weak. My boys here have served us for decades. They don't like anyone messing with the family name."

One of his "boys" puts a hand on Krish's shoulder. Another one moves so close behind me that I feel his belt buckle against the back of my neck.

I jump out of my chair, and Krish does the same and moves closer.

Vishal raises his hand, and the men back up a step. Then he points to the door. "Make sure we don't hear of you using that filthy woman's name around here again."

CHAPTER TWENTY-NINE

I stumble out of the trailer, Krish right behind me.

I can't remember the last time I was this angry. "What an a-hole!" I never swear, and it feels weird in my mouth. I want to spit.

I speed walk across the park, not knowing where I'm going. Puffs of hot breath pump from my nose. Tears burn in my throat. My fists clench and unclench. Krish keeps up with me as I cross the street and keep walking. I'm so angry I can't make words. He's silent too.

Suddenly we're facing the ocean. The beach is mostly rocks, with small sandy patches where groups of children are building castles.

Anger is still raging through me. It's getting bigger by the minute, and I can't seem to calm myself down. Using my hands and legs, I climb a cluster of rocks jutting into the ocean and keep going until I'm at the very end, where a gigantic rock forms a low cliff over the water. I sit down on it and let my legs hang above the waves.

Krish sits down next to me. "You're right," he says. "What an a-hole."

Despite my anger, I smile.

"They did something to her," I say. I recognize the kind of hate that makes people think it's okay to hurt someone. I've seen it up close. In my own home.

Krish says nothing.

"Do you have the ring with you?"

He takes it out of his pocket and hands it to me. He seems calm, and that makes my own anger worse.

I hold it up against the setting sun. I'm going to find out what happened to Vasu. No matter what, I'm going to find out.

"What you said about being thrown away like trash. If that were true, why would she leave the ring with you when it was obviously a sign of such love?"

"We don't know that it was a sign of love for her. We don't know that she felt the same way Reva did."

I stare up at the sky and make a frustrated sound.

"Please don't say you just know. You can't know. You can't know that she loved Reva back, and you sure as hell can't know how she felt about giving me away."

"But I do know." I squeeze the ring in my fist and press it to my chest. "I do know what it's like when there's a child inside you and you didn't . . . you weren't even part of . . . it's not . . . it's not always simple. How can you not see that? Didn't you hear the things that man said? Don't you want to know what happened before you judge her? Not all pregnancies result from a choice the woman made. Sometimes it's thrust upon them, shoved down their throats." My heart is beating so hard that I'm shaking with it.

"Mira?" His voice is a whisper, but it sounds loud in my ears.

I don't answer. I've said too much already, and all I want is to take it back. I want to get up and run. I want to slide limblessly into the waves. But I can't move. I can't move.

"What happened to you?" That's even softer, his voice almost too gentle to bear.

The question isn't gentle, though. Nothing about any of this is gentle. "Isn't it obvious, based on what I just blurted out?"

"Do you want to talk about it?"

"Not even a little bit." I squeeze the ring harder. I want it to break skin. It must be the jet lag because I can't believe what just happened. What I just let out.

Two skinny boys run into the water in their day clothes and start playing in the waves as their mother shouts after them to be careful.

For a long time I watch them, unable to say more, unable to stop shaking, cold in the heat. They loop over the rolling water, under it. They let their bodies go. Give themselves up to the power of the ocean, the waves playing with them as much as they're playing with the waves.

Finally Krish breaks the silence. "You know how you asked yesterday if I had come all the way here to talk you out of looking for Vasu."

"Did you?"

"No."

"Then why did you come?"

"Because the only way I'll have the courage to do this is with you."

There's a good foot between us, and I'm so very grateful for it, because if he were closer, I'd let myself fall into his arms and cry. "Why am I so filled with the pain of this stranger?"

"Maybe it's not her pain you're filled with."

A giant wave crashes against our legs and soaks our jeans.

Neither of us moves.

That's when I know. I know why I'm here.

"I was seventeen." I say it with some force. I can't start there. That's not where it starts. "It's really hard to explain my childhood, but it was restrictive. Like living inside a cage. At seventeen, I had never been to a party, a sleepover, not even a playdate, really. My parents didn't trust anyone. They didn't trust us to not be influenced by other people's homes and lives and still be controllable. It worked. At least it worked with me."

He says nothing. I don't want him to say anything.

"The more they controlled us, the more uncontrollable Rumi became. The more uncontrollable Rumi became, the more responsible I became. He hated it, obviously, the fact that I kept making myself smaller, tying myself tighter. He goaded me constantly. He wasn't popular, exactly, but by junior year he hung out with a bunch of kids who were considered edgy. Some of his friends were dealers. They were invited to the parties at the cool kids' homes. Not in Brown Town, of course. Brown Town was too closed of a circle. This was true of all the communities, all these bubbles that were supposed to keep you safe. There was rarely any mixing between the racial groups, except a couple kids who were able to hang out across the boundaries.

"One night my parents were at a dinner party, and a boy I had a crush on invited me to a last-day-of-school party. Rumi was at a different party. He'd already mocked me before leaving. I'd done really well that semester, but some other Indian kid won the academic award, and my parents were incredibly disappointed. I was so angry, and so tired. I snuck out. I wanted out of the cage."

Now that the words are coming, I can't stop them. It feels like snakes slithering out of my throat. I want to stop them, I want them gone, but the sun is being swallowed up by the horizon, the waves are getting higher and higher, and for the first time in my life, a friend is listening by my side, so I let them out.

"The rest is almost like the plot of a bad teen film. The party got wild. The guy I'd gone with disappeared to hook up with some other girl when he realized what a prude I was. I wasn't drinking. I was too scared I'd get caught. Almost as soon as I got there, I wanted to go home, but there was no one I could ask to take me. I must've put my Coke down for a minute. Someone put something in it. The next thing I remember, I was throwing up in the bushes. The party seemed to have ended. There wasn't anyone else around. One of the Indian girls in my Young Feminist Leaders club found me. I had blood on my clothes and crusted down my legs. She tried to take me to the hospital, tried to get me to report it. I couldn't remember anything but flashes of ugly feelings and wanting to struggle. Nothing else, not the faces of the boys, not if there was one or more. I begged her not to tell anyone. I told her my parents would kill me if they found out. She sneaked me into her own house. I showered there, borrowed her clothes, and had her drop me home."

The thing I remember most about that day is the certainty with which I knew that my life was over, and how Priyanka's kindness felt like a lifeline.

"In a couple weeks I missed my period. My mother tracked my periods—remember what I said earlier about trust? When I didn't get them for a couple weeks, she confronted me. I told her what happened."

I can still feel the force of my father's hand slapping me across the face, I can hear his voice calling me a whore. I can't say that out loud even now. Not even to this person who doesn't know my parents. It's probably why I'm able to tell him this much. Or maybe I'm telling him because I had the choice to get rid of a pregnancy I did not want and that would have ruined my life. I need him to understand that maybe his birth mother didn't have that choice.

"My mother took me to San Diego. It was the farthest I'd ever been from Naperville until I came to Mumbai. We didn't know anyone there. She didn't want to take a chance on anyone finding out. I was told never to speak of it. I made the mistake of telling my mother who helped me that night. Unfortunately Priyanka had a reputation. My mom found out through the grapevine that she smoked weed in the toilets with some of the white kids. My mother reported her, and she was suspended and lost her position as the president of the club.

"She was totally discredited in the community. Which obviously was my aie's intention. So if she said anything about me, no one would believe her. She never did. I think it's the worst thing I've ever done to another human being. I was paralyzed by fear. I was scared everyone would find out. I was scared my parents would throw me out. I was scared of ever leaving the house again. But I wasn't forced to carry a child, and I didn't have to give a child up."

It's no surprise that I'm crying. But it's not cathartic. I feel like I've betrayed everyone I know. My parents, Druv, his parents. I squeeze the ring so hard it cuts into my palm.

Krish doesn't say a word. He knows not to, and that's the only reason I survive it.

CHAPTER THIRTY

Last night Krish and I sat on that rock until we were soaked to the bone and the sun was completely swallowed by the ocean. Then Krish brought me back to the hotel. We barely said a word. I felt like my skin had been peeled back from my body, leaving me raw and bleeding, exposed.

"I'll wait for you to text me," he said as we separated in the elevator.

When I got back to the suite, the moms were fast asleep. I pulled on my pajamas and fell into bed, fervently grateful for that.

This morning I woke up with a fever.

While Romona is on the phone with her nephew, arranging for a doctor, Aie lectures me about toughening up. "We're two women in our fifties, and we've handled the travel without getting sick. You can't let your in-laws think you're so weak."

I don't react. I feel like I've been beaten. Like something inside me has been scooped out and burned.

The doctor comes to see me and diagnoses exhaustion and asks me to stay in bed for the rest of the day. I tell the moms to carry on without me and get their own outfits taken care of. We were supposed to do Druv's clothes today and theirs tomorrow. We can just switch that out, since they don't need me to make their selections. Thankfully they agree to leave me.

The day passes in a haze. I don't look at my phone. I feel nothing but emptiness. I just lie there. Not awake and not asleep, my mind more feelings than thoughts.

At the end of the day—which passes in a flash—the two moms come home and show me all the saris they've bought for themselves and the sherwanis and kurtas for the dads. I smile and nod and hope those reactions reach them through the thick fog of my nothingness.

We're invited to dinner to one of my father's cousin's homes, but I'm still running a fever. Aie pushes some acetaminophen into my mouth and tells me to snap out of it. But Romona insists that I need more rest and declares that I'm staying back in the hotel.

"What's wrong with you?" Aie keeps asking when Romona is out of earshot, her whispers laced with anger, and not worry.

I shamelessly wait for Romona to be around so I can use her as a shield and not answer. And there's nothing Aie can do to make me. When Romona is in the shower, Aie begs me to promise that I will pull myself up and get back to normal by tomorrow.

My phone has been lying on the nightstand all day. I haven't been able to touch it. I imagine both Druv's and Krish's eyes glaring out at me from it, and I don't have what it takes to deal with that.

Romona hands me her phone. "It's Druv. He's been trying to get through on your phone. He's worried."

All my life I've lived with a feeling of being pushed into a corner. Now I feel like someone is hammering me into it. I know it isn't fair. I know that's not what Romona is doing. I know that's not what Druv is doing, but all I wanted was one day.

I take the phone.

"Mira? Sweetheart?"

"Hi."

"I'm taking the next flight out."

"Druv, please. It's nothing serious. I probably picked up something on the plane. The doctor thinks it's exhaustion. Not even an infection."

"Then why do you have a fever?"

"It happens to me sometimes." When I'm sad. "When I'm overwhelmed."

"Mira?" He sounds so very scared. "Is something wrong? Did I do something?"

"No." I should laugh to emphasize that, but I can't make the sound.

"I'm telling Ma to select my clothes herself. You're not leaving that hotel room until you're good and ready. It doesn't matter what I wear. I don't know why Ma insisted on going to India for the shopping. There's plenty of stuff right here in Chicago."

I want to sob, but Aie and Romona are both listening while pretending to get dressed. I should get out of bed and shut the door. Maybe tomorrow. Definitely tomorrow.

"Please don't be so nice, Druv," I say, and the moms exchange gleeful glances. "I'm looking forward to picking your clothes out."

He makes a joke about fluorescent-yellow clothes. I respond appropriately, but in the end, when he hangs up, I feel like I've sprinted a long-distance race. The moms order food for me. Dal and rice, my favorite. They want to stay to make sure I eat. I assure them that it's wholly unnecessary, that I will eat. That I'm famished (the thought of food feels impossible). Finally the fear of Mumbai traffic gets them out of the door and on their way.

The relief of being left alone is immeasurable. I know I must get up. I must shower. I must not let whatever is happening inside me win. I've done this before. I've beaten this kind of sadness.

I find my phone. It's bursting with notifications. I can't handle those right now. I just need to hear one voice.

"Miru?" Rumi answers on the first ring. "What's wrong, honey?"

I don't know how he knows something is wrong, but he does.

"I just wanted to hear your voice," I say.

"It's going to be okay," he says. "Just get out of bed and go to the balcony. Can you do that?"

"I will." Soon.

"You don't have to get married to him if it doesn't feel right," he says.

"That's not it. He's the best thing that's ever happened to me."

"You're the best thing that's ever happened to him, if anything."

"You think so?"

"I know so. Not just him. Anyone. Anyone would be lucky to have you love them. Ask me how I know."

I laugh. "Saket has been so good for you."

"You sound a hundred years old. Which makes me feel a hundred years old."

"I feel two years old. Like I can't do anything."

"Your body is rejecting your emotional hypercompetence."

"Did you just make up that word?"

"Maybe. Is it Vasu?"

"I think I met someone who knows who she is. There was just so much hatred in this person when he talked about her. He didn't even know her. Just the association of her name. I think they hurt her. How could they?"

"People are dicks, Miru. Society has given them permission to be dicks as long as their evil is focused on those who can't protect themselves."

"I don't think I can deal with it anymore. I don't think I have it in me to learn how to live in this world."

He's silent for a moment. It sounds like agreement. Then he speaks. "Do you know how many people would have put that ring on their own finger and gone about their lives? Or thrown it away? You found this woman. That's something no one else would have tried to do, let alone actually done. I don't think you have any idea what you have in you."

Before I can respond to that, there's a knock on the door. "Gotta go," I say. "That's room service."

"I'll stay on the phone until you get it."

"I'm not going to stay in bed and wait for them to go away, Rumi," I say when I was intending to do just that. "I'm getting up, I promise. Thank you."

"Good girl. You got this." He lets me go.

I force myself out of bed and open the door.

It is room service, but standing behind the waiter is Krish.

I can't deal with him right now. I turn around and go back to bed.

"Just leave the food by the door. Thank you," I call to the waiter. "I'll sign the check later."

"Can I come in?" Krish says from outside the door.

"Please don't."

"Do you mean that?" He sounds so far away. He's still outside the door.

"No," I say. "But you don't have to do this."

I close my eyes and hear the door close.

"I'm inside," Krish says. He's still by the door. "I can leave. But I'd really like to see you for a minute."

Something in the region of my heart wobbles. "There's nothing to see."

"Okay." He pushes the trolley with the food into the bedroom.

The way he looks at me hasn't changed after what I told him yesterday, and my breathing eases. It's like the ugliness I vomited all over him has been washed clean. He's as fresh as he always was.

"I can't eat."

He takes the dome off the dish. "Okay. Can you drink?" He holds a spoon of dal out.

It's my first actual laugh of the day. "Gosh. Are you seriously even Indian?"

"What? One drinks soup."

"It's not soup. It's dal, and you eat it with the rice."

"Interesting," he says, and I don't know if he's teasing me or if I really just taught him how dal-rice is eaten. He mixes them together and holds the spoon out to me.

I take it from him, but I can't make it move to my mouth.

"It's the first bite. That's the hardest one. The first step. That's the hardest one."

"You've done this before."

He nods. "I told you my mom struggled with episodes of sadness when I was young. It was depression. Dad always knew what to do."

"I don't think we're allowed to say that word in my house."

"Depression?"

"Shhh." I press a finger to my lips. Then I put a spoon of dal-rice in my mouth and chew and swallow.

Krish takes the spoon, fills it again, and hands it back to me. It takes a few spoons, but finally my body registers that I'm hungry, and I take the bowl from him and start eating. "Have you eaten?"

"Yes. The buffet at the hotel is something else. I think I might never leave. They have an entire table filled with hot sauces."

It's strange to be reminded that there's a world outside what I'm feeling. I try to smile but can't manage it.

I get through half the bowl and try to put it back.

"There's not much left. Let's finish it." He nudges the bowl back toward me.

I start eating again. "What are we going to do next?"

"Maybe a shower. Those really help. A walk on the beach before the moms get back?"

"Funny. About Vasu."

He studies me, gauging what I can handle.

"I want to know," I say with the first spark of life I've felt since we got off that rock.

"Let's go to the balcony." He holds out his arm. "I need some fresh air. I'll fill you in there."

I go, mostly because I don't have the energy to fight him.

We sit down on the wicker swing that faces the ocean. Another sunset hangs over the horizon.

"I checked the archives at the Asiatic Society Library for wedding announcements," Krish says. "And Namdeo was definitely married to her in March of 1984."

For the first time today my brain kicks into gear, and I sit up. "I knew it."

"I think I might have tracked her brother down. I'm going to Yevla tomorrow. To see what I can find."

"Why didn't you tell me?"

"I did." He glances at my phone.

Then I remember Vishal's menacing face. "Could it be dangerous, do you think?"

He shrugs. "I'll be careful."

"I'm going with you."

"Let's get better first."

I already feel better, but the idea of leaving the hotel room still feels daunting. A trip out of town feels impossible.

"Plus that would mean telling your moms."

That's totally out of the question.

"Let me do this by myself. I'll keep you posted the entire time. Hourly updates."

"How are you going to talk to people?"

"I've been using a translation app on my phone. But most people understand English, if I tweak my accent."

"Fine." There's no choice anyway.

"Focus on getting better," he says. "I have a good feeling about this. I think we're going to find her. I just know it." He smiles, and his impression of me is so spot on, I smile too.

"Thank you."

We sit there, staring at the ocean. When I can finally get up, he pushes me into the shower. When I come back out, feeling almost human again, he's brought me ice cream from some place the internet insists has the best mango ice cream in the world.

The internet is not wrong. "I want this to be the last thing I eat before I die," I say as I eat the entire bowl of hapus mangoes and cream and crawl into bed.

It's the first time in my life that I remember someone tucking me in.

CHAPTER THIRTY-ONE

To my aie's great approval and relief, I get out of bed the next morning before she and Romona do.

My insides are still a little wobbly, but I'm able to ignore that. I can put one foot in front of the other, and that's enough for now.

We eat a hearty breakfast of roughly one hundred breakfast foods from around the world (with the most delicious hot sauces and chutneys I've ever tasted), then make our way to the next store to select clothes for the bridesmaids. These will come "off the rack," Romona tells me. The moms are sensitive about how much they push me today. When I choose something, they immediately say yes instead of leaning on me to look at fifteen more options. The day goes off without a glitch, except that I'm waiting for communication from Krish, and I haven't heard from him at all. So much for hourly updates.

My texts have gone undelivered. I try to convince myself that it's because he probably doesn't have service and not because something bad has happened. Nonetheless, I can't stop checking my phone.

It's late in the afternoon when we get back to the hotel to squeeze in some rest before leaving to have dinner with a group of Aie's childhood friends. I try to call Krish but get a message that his phone is switched off.

Druv has texted me through the day, checking up on me and sending me jokes and pictures from the operating room. I'm grateful for the distraction.

The evening is uneventful. My mother's friends are clones of her. They talk solely about their husbands (in worshipful tones even when they're being critical), children and grandchildren (who are all at once superstars and projects who need daily motherly labor). They commiserate with Aie about my being almost thirty and single and share in her great relief that all that is about to change. They ooh and aah over Druv's pictures and fawn over Romona like she's some sort of foreign celebrity. She winks at me and is gracious, albeit a bit out of her depth, with their dated fashion choices. I see it all from a distance. I smile politely when they can't get enough of how well I speak Marathi and how un-Americanized I seem. Aie beams with pride.

When I crawl into bed at night, I'm restless. I cannot fall asleep not knowing what's happening with Krish. I imagine him being robbed, then eating something that gives him food poisoning and ending up in the hospital all alone. I imagine him trying to talk to people and being misunderstood, that stoic politeness doing nothing to protect him. I tell myself that there's no way for Vishal's goons to know where Krish is, but I picture them chasing him.

Just before midnight I get a text from an unknown number. This is Krish. Power outage in the area. No cell signal. Found this guy who's got service and let me use his phone. I'm safe. Don't worry. Met Vasu's brother. Not a good meeting but have intel. Check with Reva about Pune Safehouse ASAP. Don't text back on this number. Deleting your contact. I'll text when I have service.

That's it?

What does "not a good meeting" mean? At least he's safe. He's safe.

I get out of bed and tiptoe to the terrace. The night is balmy, and the hotel grounds twinkle with endless lights strung on trees, their reflection bouncing off the ocean and pools. I shut the sliding doors behind me and call Reva. I haven't spoken to her since we got here.

It's midafternoon in New York. She answers on the first ring. I tell her that Krish is in Yevla without phone service and ask what he could possibly mean about the safe house.

"Vasu's music teacher," she says. "She was part of a network that ran safe houses for women on the run. Her name was Ashatai Athavale. Her friends helped my mother and me hide when Vasu's father threatened us. Why do you think he's asking?"

I didn't want to tell her this next part until we knew more. "Because we met Namdeo's son. It seems like Vasu left her husband a year or so after they were married."

She gasps. "That's not possible. Where did she go? Why didn't you call me?"

"Because we don't know anything for sure yet. We're trying to figure it out. I promise I'll let you know as soon as we find out anything concrete."

"I should be there. I should be the one looking for her."

I imagine her in Vishal's office and protectiveness rises inside me. "I don't think there's anything you can do yet."

She takes a moment to absorb that. "You're right. Thank you. If she left her husband, then Ashatai has to be the one she went to. Let me find her address. Hold on."

I hear her blow her nose and imagine her trying not to cry. Then I hear her moving around. "I just sent it to you. It's from forty years ago. But people often don't move out of their family homes in India, so it might still work." She sounds deeply sad.

"We're going to find her," I say. "It would all be an awful waste of coincidences if we can't."

A small watery laugh escapes her. "You know what the hardest part is? The regret. I can't stop thinking about what I could have done differently. Could courage have changed everything? Was I too scared?"

I think about Rumi's bleeding shaved head and the unhinged rage in my father's eyes. I think about myself on that rock, letting out years of pain. About how I feel right now: lighter, free to be angry. Like the fury gathered inside me is something I earned the right to.

"You did everything you could. You had to survive. You can't judge your courage in a different world based on the world you're in right now."

This time her laugh is a little less sad. "You know, that's something Vasu would say. I'm so glad I dropped that ring," she says. "Someday I'll share her letters with you. I think you'd like her."

I already love her. I don't understand it, but I do.

~

The next morning we repeat the exact same routine. I rise before the moms, shower and dress in white cotton palazzos and a light cotton blouse. The heat is too oppressive for anything else. Then I video call Druv and go to another absurdly overstocked breakfast with the moms.

Just as we're waiting for our taxi to take us to yet another day of shopping, I get a text from Krish.

> Still spotty service. No good news. Vasu's brother says she's dead, but there are no records of her death. I think he's lying. He made Vishal seem like a teddy bear. I'm going to Pune tomorrow to track down the safe house. Heading to Mumbai today. Talk when I get there. How are you feeling?

I ignore that last question, and I hate that he had to ask it. I want to tell him I'll go to Pune with him. I want to ask what exactly happened with Vasu's brother, but Aie and Romona keep up a steady stream of conversation. They go down the list of close relatives on both sides, all of whom will get clothes as gifts from us that we have to pick out in the next three days.

Call me as soon as you have service, I text Krish.

It shows up as undelivered.

Our stop today is a store that exclusively sells wedding wear for men. The first thing they show us is a yellow sherwani, and I send a picture to Druv.

He insists he must have it. We choose it for the haldi, which is going to be a daytime event. We pick out all Druv's outfits and also those for his best man and four groomsmen.

"I need one more sherwani," I say to the salesperson. "In shades of powder blue that match my bridesmaids' colors."

"Who's that for?" Romona asks.

"My brother, Rumi."

Aie's body goes very still. She glares daggers at me over Romona's shoulder.

"Of course," Romona says, hiding her confusion. My parents' estranged-black-sheep narrative has made it easy for everyone to act like Rumi doesn't exist. "I'm so glad he'll be able to join us."

"Yes," I say. "We weren't sure if he and his fiancé were going to be able to make it, but they are."

Aie looks like she might spontaneously combust.

"Do we need to get his fiancée something too?" Romona asks kindly.

"Oh, look at this," Aie says a little too loudly. "Do we want to send a picture of this one to Druv? I like it better than the navy one we got him for the sangeet."

"I'm not sure what Rumi's fiancé will want to wear," I say. "I'll take some pictures for him today, and we'll see. He's something of a fashion icon, so he might want to choose his own clothes. Rumi is easier. I know what he'll like. So let's get that."

Aie makes a strangled sound.

"I didn't realize Rumi was engaged to a man," Romona says, making the effort to not sound judgmental.

"I think Saket identifies as nonbinary," I say.

"Oh," Romona says.

"You know kids these days. All sorts of phases they go through," Aie says, making a valiant effort to hide her panic and failing. "I'm sure they won't actually come to the wedding. Rumi's always been unpredictable."

"They're coming to the wedding," I say with some finality. "Druv was upset that they weren't going to," I add.

They both look like that settles it, and I don't know what comes over me. "Actually, that's not true. Druv isn't the one who was upset. I don't want to get married without my twin brother there."

Aie and Romona exchange glances.

"Are you still feeling sick?" Aie says. "Maybe we should go back to the hotel so you can get some rest."

"I think I do want to go back to the hotel, Aie. But first I'm going to pick a sherwani for Rumi."

"Of course," Romona says and starts filing through the hangers.

Aie remains silent and leans into her cane.

He's your child! I want to scream at her. But I mirror her and ignore her. A radical act for me. I select two powder blue sherwanis, one with silver flowers and the other with pearlescent beads. I send Rumi and Saket pictures of both, asking them to choose. I can imagine Saket's delight, and it makes me smile. I can imagine Rumi and him endlessly dissecting which one to go with, and my heart feels even lighter. I text them to let me know soon and also send me measurements, because all the clothes will be custom tailored and shipped to America in two weeks.

Aie and I ignore each other until we get back to the suite. Romona has taken her cue and hung back at the lobby shops to buy a gift for the cousin we're visiting tonight.

"What was that?" Aie says as soon as the door to the suite closes behind us.

I finally say it. "He's your child, Aie!" I'm done skirting around the issue. I want to dive straight into the heart of it.

She steps back in shock. Her surprise makes me sick to my stomach.

"Not anymore."

"I don't think that's how having children works. You gave birth to us, you raised us. You can't just give us back because we're not exactly what you wanted."

"Where is this 'us' business coming from? Your baba and I have always supported you, no matter what you've done. Has your brother turned your head so much that you've forgotten what we've done for you?"

I have a soul-deep urge to scream. If I let it out now, I'll never be able to stop.

"I was assaulted, Aie! I did nothing wrong except leave my house. At seventeen. I should have known how to leave the house. I should have known how to navigate the simple act of going to a party. What to do if I was in danger. Taking care of the pregnancy and encouraging me never to leave the house again until it was to marry a man of your choosing wasn't something you did for me. It was something you did for you."

She steps up to me and raises her hand. I'm so angry I grab it and push it away.

She stumbles back and starts crying. There's horror on her face, but I'm the one who's horrified by what I just did and by the fact that my mother thinks slapping me is the answer to anything.

"I knew we should not have let you go to New York. Don't you see he just wants to destroy your life the way he's destroyed his own?"

"The only part of his life that's destroyed is you and Baba. The rest of his life is beautiful!"

"Does this have to do with that boy Krish? Who has been filling your head with this nonsense?"

"What part of this is nonsense? That my brother, your son, should be at my wedding?"

"Don't you think I want that? But how is it possible? How can we let him shame us in public by doing those things? Already, I don't know what Romona is thinking. You shouldn't have said what you said in front of her without warning me."

"Aie, he isn't doing anything. Saket and he love each other."

She presses her hands to her ears, dramatic as ever. "How dare you speak that person's name around me? There is no way on earth Rumi can bring another boy to the wedding." She looks like she's going to throw up. It's the same sickened face I saw on Vishal Sawant in that trailer. "Your dad will kill them. Or die himself."

"What about you? Why is it always about Baba? You are our mother. Why does Baba come between you and every feeling you have about us?"

She closes her eyes and says a desperate prayer. "God is punishing us for leaving our family and moving to a different country. If we'd raised you children in India, this would never have happened. My mother told me that if I abandoned her, my children would abandon me too. It's a curse."

"Aie, stop. Rumi isn't the one who abandoned you. You're the one who abandoned him. This has nothing to do with where we grew up."

"It does. Such dirty things don't happen here in India."

That's it. That's all I can take. I have to get away from her. "I don't know much," I say, "but I do know that nothing about Rumi and Saket's love is dirty. They're beautiful together. Also, not only does it happen in India, but it happens in every corner of the world, and it has forever, because it's human. Tens of thousands of people attend pride parades in Mumbai every year. It's people like you who've been trained to think it's wrong and forced people to hide. It's people like you who have turned everything ugly." I open the door to leave. Romona is standing outside the door.

"Where are you going?" Aie says behind me.

"I need some air."

"But we have to go to Druv's uncle's for dinner," Aie says.

Romona studies me.

"I don't feel great. I'm not up for a dinner party."

Romona steps into the room where Aie can see her and touches my forehead. "Are you feeling sick again?"

I shake my head. "I'm just exhausted. I'm sorry to miss it."

"You won't be missing anything. My cousin is a world-class bore," she says with a wink.

Aie's gaze bounces from me to Romona with abject apology. "I don't know what's come over her. I'm sure she'll be fine when we're back in Naperville. I think she misses Druv." She rushes to me and puts an arm on my shoulder. "There, there. Come on. Come inside, drink some chai, and get dressed. Let's go."

I remove her arm from around me, gently but firmly. "I said I need air, Aie, and I'm not going." With that I turn to Romona and squeeze her hand. "Thank you for being so understanding."

All my life my parents have been lovely to everyone else and terrible to Rumi and me. Am I doing that same thing?

"Don't say that, honey. Weddings are overwhelming. Our culture doesn't make it easy. There's too many people's feelings to consider. Just know that you come first. It's your day." She smiles. "Well, your four days."

I hug her. My heart is filled with affection for her and deep envy for Druv and Ariana. Surely it isn't hard to be a parent who doesn't put what they want first all the time.

I turn to my mother. "Also, I'm going to Pune tomorrow to take care of something."

"Pune!" both moms say together.

I guess now's as good a time as any to lay it all out there. "There's something I didn't tell you. Remember that ring I found in New York? I found the woman it belonged to. Turns out it used to belong to another woman who is missing. A journalist friend and I have been trying to track her down here in India."

Romona steps back in shock.

"It was a coincidence, a sign. I'm here anyway, and this is a person who shouldn't have been forgotten. We have a lead in Pune. You can choose the gifts for the guests tomorrow. Please. I love everything you two pick. It's just one day."

We have two more days of shopping left, after which Romona is going to Delhi for a week and Aie and I are going to visit her sister in Nagpur. Then we're heading back home.

"You cannot go traipsing off in a foreign country with some man three months before your wedding," Aie says, looking horrified at having to say it in front of Druv's mother.

Now it's a foreign country? Until five minutes ago it was the home she should have raised me in. My weariness turns heavy.

"There won't be a wedding if I don't do this, Aie," I say, because it's the only thing I can think of that will get her to back off. "I have to go. I have to do this."

CHAPTER THIRTY-TWO

"Are you rethinking marrying me, Mira?" Druv's question falls on me the way a knife's blade nicks a finger, entirely unexpected and shockingly painful.

"No! Why would you say that?" Even as I ask, I know exactly why. The Two Moms have obviously relayed my threat from yesterday. "Okay, I know why. But what I said to my aie had to do with her giving me a hard time about going to Pune." Thanks to the threat, I'm on a train headed to see Ashatai Athavale with Krish. So I'm not sorry for having used it.

"That's what I thought," Druv says. "But I think Ma's really worried."

I know he doesn't mean that as an accusation, but it falls on me like one. I throw a glance at Krish, who is fast asleep next to me. There are deep shadows under his eyes and an angry bruise on his cheekbone. Unlike Vishal, Vasu's brother acted on his threats. He set his goons on Krish, and Krish had to hide in the back of a freight truck full of live goats to escape. The thing I can't figure out is why these men are still so afraid, all these years later. What did they do to Vasu that they don't want exposed?

When Krish called me this morning, he was headed to Dadar station to take the train to Pune. He tried to convince me that he could do it alone. No way was he doing this without me. This is my search too.

"Mira?" Druv snaps me back to our conversation.

"I didn't mean to worry her. I'm almost thirty, Druv. I shouldn't have to use threats to be able to do what I want."

"Of course. But you always take care of everyone's feelings with such empathy. It's one of the things I love most about you."

Is navigating everyone's feelings at the cost of my own really empathy? Nonetheless, Romona has done nothing but be kind to me, and she doesn't deserve to be worried. "I'll talk to Romona Auntie again and set her mind at rest."

"Thank you. You know how much she loves you, right? That's why she's so freaked out at the thought of you changing your mind."

No one ever freaks out about losing me. It's me who's universally considered at risk of being abandoned lest my good luck run out. Druv doesn't sound like he feels that way, and neither did Romona when she wished me luck this morning. I'm not sure I like how worried they are.

"Everything's going to be okay, Druv." That much I can feel in my bones. "Please don't worry."

"I know," he says. "So long as I have you, I know it is. Will you take care? You've never been to India. I don't know how you're so calm about traveling everywhere alone."

I'm not alone, though. Saying that feels cruel, so I don't. Druv knows I'm traveling with Krish. Maybe it's time to tell him why this is important to Krish. But Krish and I have been able to share things with each other because our lives only intersect at this one point where we're two individuals, able to share the unspeakable because no one else we know has any interest in the other's secrets. I can't break his confidence.

Instead I give Druv another truth that has surprised me. "It doesn't feel like I've never been here. It's overwhelming and chaotic, but I don't feel lost here. I feel like I can navigate it. Please don't worry about me."

His answer is a laugh. "You're part of me, Mira. How can I not worry when you're not with me?" With that he lets me go.

Krish is frowning in his sleep, and I feel a bolt of something tender, almost maternal. Behind him mountains blanketed in green race past the train window. His neck falls forward at a painful angle. I'm about to straighten it when I hear aggressive voices and look up. Two men carrying field hockey sticks enter the train. They're all the way across the compartment, and they're making no effort to hide the fact that they're looking for someone.

"Krish," I whisper and poke his leg.

His eyes fly open, but he doesn't startle.

"Some men just entered the train. They seem to be looking for someone."

His gaze slides to them.

"Move very slowly," he says and stands up, hooking both our back-packs on his shoulders.

I take mine from him, and as casually as we can, we start walking in the opposite direction.

As we go from this compartment to the adjoining one through the rickety connecting tunnel, I hear the men speed up behind us. Krish grabs my hand and starts to run. We race across the chugging train, past bored-looking passengers, as the cars get more and more crowded and noisy. When we enter one of the connected compartments, the aisle is blocked by a group of women sitting on the metal floor with baskets filled with vegetables.

They see Krish and shift their wares to let him through, but they're too busy ogling him and giggling to notice me.

"Sorry," I say as I stumble over a basket.

A woman smacks my ankles. "Can't you see where you're going, you witch!"

I throw a glance over my shoulder. The commotion causes the men to notice us.

Krish tugs my arm. "Come on."

I run for my life.

We're approaching the end of the train. I've never been so scared in my life.

"In the bathroom," Krish says just as the train slows down and enters a station.

"They'll find us in the bathroom."

A crowd of passengers rises from their seats and rushes toward the exit. I pull Krish into the crowd. "Don't let go."

He presses close, and we start pushing with the crowd toward the tiny door. Thanks to the women with the baskets, our pursuers are all the way across the crowd. The moment we hop off the train and onto the platform, we grip hands like our life depends on it and start running.

We weave through the crowded platform, then up metal stairs that creak under the weight of the crowd and onto a bridge over the tracks. We push through the cracks in the crowd across the bridge and run down another flight of stairs, and we find ourselves in a market street. It's lined with handcart vendors selling vegetables and ceramics and shoes and plastics and clothes. Sounds and smells and humid heat engulf me so tight my head spins, but we keep running.

We don't stop until the crowd thins and the shanty town ends and we're on a dirt road surrounded by open fields. There's a lone structure at the edge of the road, four walls and a corrugated roof. We go around it and collapse against a wall, hiding in its shadows. It takes a good five minutes of catching our breath before we can talk again.

"What the hell happened in Yevla?" I ask.

He'd looked so exhausted when we met at Dadar station and got on the train that I'd decided to let him rest before he got me caught up. That was because I didn't know we were going to be chased by thugs with hockey sticks.

"I didn't think they'd find us here. I'm sorry." He throws a look up and down the dirt road.

"I think we lost them. Tell me what you found out."

He mops his forehead with his sleeve and fills me in. "A year or so into her marriage, Vasu told her husband that she wanted to leave him to be with the woman she was in love with and threatened to tell everyone if he didn't let her go. Namdeo's family, terrified of the scandal, took her back to her father, who was up for reelection." His eyes continue to scan the surroundings for our pursuers. "Her parents locked her up while they came up with a plan to deal with her, but she escaped and disappeared. They hushed up the matter by announcing that she'd died in a road accident in Pune."

"They didn't even try to find her?"

"Why would they? It saved them the trouble of figuring out how to get rid of her." He's distracted with scanning our surroundings, and so am I, but anger gathers inside me.

"How do you know all this?"

"There was a journalist who, according to Vasu's brother, was paid by their father's political opponents to chase down the story. To try and scare me off, the brother told me how they shut journalists up. So, naturally I went looking for him. I found him in Nashik."

"Wow."

"Yeah. Barely fancy journalism schools have their advantages." The sardonic dimple makes an appearance. "It's been so long, it was amazing that he even remembered all this."

"What does he think happened to her?"

The sun is bouncing off Krish's glasses. He's not wearing the ones that darken in the sun, and I can see his eyes. They're burning with the same anger I'm feeling. "He believes they had her killed. The last place she was seen was Pune, at a safe house for women. She was never seen after that."

"If that were true, how were you born?"

He makes an *exactly* face. "She disappeared in August of 1985, and I was born in February 1986."

"So she obviously didn't die."

"Or she did and she isn't my birth mother."

"And the fact that you look exactly like her and have her ring is pure coincidence?"

He shrugs.

I point to his bruised face. "And the guys who hurt you?"

"Vasu's brother trying to scare me into giving up on digging around in his family's business. The same old story: family's shame needed to stay buried, their honor intact. He has an election coming up. To prove he means business, he had some guys slap me around." He touches his cheek.

"The a-hole!" I say. "All of them! A-holes!"

That makes him smile, of all things, which punches a hole in my anger. I'm about to smile, too, but then we hear shouts and footsteps approaching and turn.

The two men from the train charge straight at us, hockey sticks raised, and there's nowhere for us to run.

CHAPTER THIRTY-THREE

Shock flashes through my system. Everything slows down. My thoughts freeze into frames. One part of my brain wants to duck, another wants to run, another wants to fight. It wants to charge at our attackers, yank the hockey sticks from their hands, and beat them back.

Krish throws himself in front of me. That snaps terror to the top of everything I'm feeling. One of the men pulls him off me and slams his face into a wall. I scream.

"Shut up!" the other guy says in Marathi and holds the hockey stick up. "Shut up or I'll bash his head in."

"Whatever he's saying, listen to him," Krish says, utterly calm.

There's only two of them, and they're both shorter and smaller than Krish, but they have those sticks.

"What do you want?" I say. Suddenly I feel utterly calm too.

"Shut up," the man shouts again. He has the thickest mustache I've ever seen. It covers his entire upper lip. "What we want is for you to shut up so we don't have to break your face."

They duct tape our mouths shut, then bind our hands behind our backs with it. Krish steadies me with his gaze. He's not struggling. I take my cue from that and stop struggling. They drag us inside the room. It isn't until we're inside that I realize it's a public restroom. An unfinished one. The walls are unplastered, the floor is half rubble, and a urinal hangs crookedly on the wall. Obviously that hasn't stopped someone from using it because the smell is so caustic it's like being bashed in the head with a hockey stick.

The men push us to the floor and tape our feet. Fantastic. We're on the floor of a public toilet that smells like rotting feces soaked in ammonia.

When they're done, the man with the mustache grabs Krish's hair and looks at me. "Tell him he's lucky we're not breaking his bones. If we find out he's poking his foreign nose into things again, there will be no more warnings."

I narrow my eyes and make as loud a sound as I can with a taped mouth.

"She's right," the other guy says. "We can't deliver the message we were paid to deliver if he doesn't understand what we're saying." He reaches out and yanks the tape off my face. It feels like he's ripped my skin with it. "Tell him what we just said."

I do. Krish nods.

"If I hear you screaming, I'll come back and bash his head in."

I squeeze my lips together and give them my most terrified look. They buy it and leave.

"A-holes!" I say the moment they're gone.

Krish's eyes smile.

I notice for the first time that they aren't just one shade of brown. They're filled with flecks of every shade, and every fleck is filled with relief as he looks at me.

"The first thing I need to do is take the tape off your mouth." I try to stand, but it isn't easy with my feet and arms bound.

He scoots closer to me, and I use his body to prop mine, and finally I'm up. I turn away from him and hop closer. "Can you get your face close to my hands?"

He moves around behind me and finds my hands with his face. I wiggle my fingers and feel for the tape and find the edge.

"This might hurt." My face still stings, so I'm gentle, and it takes me a minute to get the thick tape off.

"Jesus!" he says and blows out a breath. "Shit. Thank you."

I bunny hop to face him.

He stands up with substantially more grace than I did.

"Are you okay?" we both say together and smile.

I look around the filthy room. There's just one door and one window all the way near the roof that light is streaming in through. I hop toward the door, and he follows.

Moving around with bound legs is much harder than it appears to be. The door is locked but rickety.

Krish turns and tries to pull at the handle. It rattles but stays shut. "If we could grab that handle properly, we could break it open."

"Okay, I'm going to scream for help."

"What if those ass . . . a-holes are still out there?"

"Well, we can't do nothing," I say. Apparently near-death experiences make me reckless. "Help!" I say tentatively at first, because even when I'm reckless I'm careful.

"Help," Krish says, also tentatively.

Then we're both shouting at the top of our lungs. "HELP! ANYBODY OUT THERE?" Over and over and slamming our bodies into the door.

I scream it in Marathi. Then in the little broken Hindi I know. Nothing.

"Now what?" I say.

"We have to get out of here," Krish says.

"Really? Why didn't I think of that?" Evidently near-death experiences make me snarky too.

"Funny, Mirabai."

"Thank you, Krishna."

"You have to untie me."

"Oh, okay. Easy peasy."

He lets out a laugh. He hops around this time until we're back to back. "Let's see if we can get each other's tape off. The way you did for my face."

I move until our hands touch. He struggles to rip the tape off me, but he can't seem to do it. Then I try him, but the tape is too thick and too tight, and with neither of us able to see what we're doing, it doesn't work.

"Can you use your nails?"

My nails aren't really long, but I give it another try.

No luck. Wiggling my fingers around so much with my wrists taped is making me lose sensation in them.

"We need something sharp to cut through the tape." As soon as he says it, both of us twist our necks to look at each other.

The ring.

"Where is it?" he asks. He left it with me for safekeeping when he went to Yevla.

I told him earlier that I'd put it in a safe place. Our backpacks are gone and so are our phones. The goons took them.

"Is it back in the hotel?"

Nope. I shake my head.

"Please tell me it's on your person."

"Yes. It is." Embarrassment blooms inside me, and I squeeze my eyes shut.

He hops to face me. "Mira?" He has a way of using my name to say entire sentences.

My cheeks burn. I know this is not the time for my dorkiness. We have to hurry. Who knows if our captors will return. This smell has to be taking years off our lives.

The impatience in his eyes turns helpless.

"Just tell me. It's okay," he whispers.

"It's . . . it's in . . ." My eyes drop to my breasts. It's 2024. I work with human bodies day in and day out. How can I be embarrassed by such a basic word? It's not just embarrassment, though. I'm painfully self-conscious of how my body suddenly feels around him and mortified by it.

I conjure up a picture of Druv in my mind. *Think about Druv. Think about the fact that we're trapped here. Think about the fact that we could end up dead if we don't free ourselves.*

"In my bra," I say, forcing myself to be an adult.

He meets my eyes. "That was actually really smart. To hide it there."

He sounds genuinely impressed, and now I want to laugh. Men. "My mother grew up in Mumbai. Before we landed here she trained me"—with several physical demonstrations, I don't add—"to tuck all valuables in there. I also have ten thousand rupees and a credit card tucked away with the ring."

He laughs. I laugh. But that doesn't help anyone.

"So," he says, "how do we get it out of there with our hands tied behind our backs?"

I can feel the ring dig into the side of my breast. I wiggle my shoulders and suck in my breath, but it's ridiculous to think I can magically pop it out of my bra by sheer force of will.

"You're going to have to do it," I say finally.

"Do what?"

"Get the ring out."

"Oh that? Easy peasy." His tone is teasing, but he swallows. Then he lowers his voice and leans toward me. "I hate to break it to you, but my hands are tied behind my back."

Well, I'm tired of that metaphor being the story of my life.

"You can move your fingers," I say with all the rage that's rushing back inside me. I shuffle until my front is facing his back.

There's a moment of silence, but I can hear him thinking the word *Mira?*

"Focus," I say to the both of us. "This has to work. Reach back." I lean over, working hard not to think about the fact that I'm trying to get my boobs into his hands. *How is this happening right now?* a voice screams inside me. I tell it to shut up. We are not dying here in this filthy room.

It takes him a second, but Krish figures out what I'm trying to do. Without a word, he stretches back his arms and pokes around until his fingers make contact with my chest. I ignore every single thing except the fact that someone chased us down and tied us up because we're trying to find Vasu. We're going to find her no matter what.

I stretch and twist until I literally cup myself into his searching hands.

"I'm sorry," he says, and it's such a kind, such a humane thing to do, my embarrassment eases. In everything he's ever done, he's considered my feelings. Even when we didn't get along, he considered me. No one has ever done that for me before.

Everyone should be making you feel special, Mira. Because . . . well, because everyone deserves that. His words in Central Park feel eons away but also like he's saying them now.

"It's okay," I say. God, how I wish I was cool enough to make funny quips in a situation like this. "You're . . . umm . . ." I swallow. "You're going to have to poke around to find it." I can't believe I just said that.

He laughs. "I get that a lot."

I can't help it, I start laughing too. It's weird to laugh when I'm in a half-forward-fold yoga pose with someone's hands on my breasts. "I'd draw you a map, but I'm tied up at the moment."

We're both laughing now. "Just tell me what you want, and I'll give it to you." He hams up a sexy voice.

I bump his back with my head. "Shut up." But I do tell him what to do.

Between adjusting myself under his hands and a few "a little higher, a little to the left" instructions, his hands find the bump of the ring, which, dear lord, is all the way on the outer underside of my right breast.

For a second the awkward silence returns as we both realize what has to happen next.

"Just do it," I say.

"Like ripping off a Band-Aid," he says.

"Yes." I try not to be weird, but the word catches in my throat.

"I'm taking no pleasure in this. I swear, Mira." His voice is sincere now.

"I know," I say. "I know."

"I'm going in. Brace yourself," he says, and I laugh again.

Despite my best effort, my laugh hitches when his hand brushes my nipple. To my horror, it puckers. He doesn't linger, not even for a breath. I can feel him working hard to be as clinical as possible as he pokes around blind and finds the metal and tugs it out.

I pull back. He pulls back.

We catch our breath.

"Done," he says before things get any more awkward. "You okay?" He doesn't turn around, giving me the time I need.

It's a moment I know I will remember for as long as I live. A moment when Krish Hale showed me exactly the man he was, exactly what every man can be if he chooses. I've been violated without my consent, and I've been blamed for it my whole life. It stole the person I was from myself and turned me into someone else entirely. It made it impossible for me to ever trust anyone again, to trust myself again.

A little piece of my ability to trust snaps back into place. A little piece of me snaps back into place. And I know that little piece of me will always belong with Krish Hale, here in this filthy room.

CHAPTER THIRTY-FOUR

I wait as Krish jabs away at the tape binding my hands with the sharp protrusion of the ring. Finally something gives, and he's able to rip it off. Blood rushes to my fingers. I turn around and shake out my arms.

I'm still feeling an odd awkwardness, and it makes it hard to face him. I remind myself to keep my focus on getting us out of here. He hands the ring back to me, and I push it back into my bra because that's still the safest place for it. Then I free Krish's arms before getting the tape off my ankles.

He makes quick work of his own and helps me. He doesn't avoid my eyes, and that makes the awkwardness melt away. We help each other stand, then use the wall for support as circulation returns to our limbs.

"Let's get out of here," he says and grabs the door handle and tugs it. The door rattles but doesn't open, so he gives it a few more yanks.

There seems to be a single slide bolt at the top on the outside. It's barely holding the door shut. I grab the handle, too, wrapping my hands around his, and we put every bit of our joint strength into pulling it open.

After a few hefty tugs, it swings inward, and we're thrown back. We find our balance and step gingerly out into the sunshine.

I tiptoe to one side, and he goes to the other, scanning the area for our captors. There's not a soul in sight. We make our way to the dirt road. To our right is the station where we got off the train, and to our left only fields.

"I don't think we should go back to the station," I say, still nervous. "Maybe if we keep walking in the other direction, we'll get to a major road where we can find a ride."

"That's as good a plan as any," he says, and we start walking.

Without GPS, we have to get somewhere where we can ask for directions.

The dirt road leads us through a field. It looks like sugarcane. I know because we used to sell sugarcane at the store when stock came in from Hawaii. After Baba bought the store, he installed a juicer, and for a while fresh sugarcane juice was one of our most popular items.

This is my first time in a sugarcane field, and I'm glad to discover that the cane grows tall and tight enough to hide adult-size humans. I press close to the sugarcane.

"If they planned to follow us, I don't think they would have left us alone," Krish says, picking up on my discomfort, but he also sticks close.

After a good mile of walking, there's still no road in sight, and I'm thirsty.

"Have you ever tried sugarcane?" I ask and grab a stalk to test if I can break it. "It might be the most delicious thing in the world."

"More delicious than hot sauce?" Krish says.

I try not to smile and attempt bending the inch-thick stalk. After some heavy-duty bending, it cracks, but the fibers still hold on, keeping it attached to the plant. Krish takes one end of it and I hold the other, and we twist and pull until it breaks free.

I whoop and high-five Krish. Then I bite into the broken end, grip the thick green-brown peel with my teeth, and pull it off in strips until I've exposed the fleshy fibrous inner stalk.

Krish looks impressed.

Wait until you've tasted it, buddy.

I bite off a piece of the exposed meat and start chewing to release the sugarcane juice, which tastes like liquid sweetness, nectar made by angels for the dying. The sugary high fills me, and I try not to, but I moan.

Once I've sucked out all the juice, I spit out the husk, bite off another chunk, and hand the cane to Krish. He mirrors me and bites off a chunk and starts chewing. Surprise widens his eyes.

"Damn," he says sucking the juice out of the husk in his mouth.

We start walking again and hand the stalk back and forth until the entire thing is gone—not a quick activity, since sugarcane makes you pay in effort to taste its magic. Just as we finish, we hear a car approaching.

We run to the middle of the road and start waving our arms about. A fluorescent-green vehicle, which can't technically be described as any form of the automobile, sputters past us and bounces to a stop in a cloud of dust. It looks like a cross between a rickshaw and a stunted minivan, in a state so decrepit it has to be a hazard on a public road.

"What's happening?" the grizzled white-turbaned driver asks in a thick rural dialect of Marathi I barely understand.

"Where are you off to?" I ask in my more urban dialect.

"How is that your business?" he says.

I'm not sure if it's rude to smile, but a smile escapes me. "Our car broke down back there. We need a ride into the closest town so we can get a mechanic."

"Do I look like your uncle?"

"No." I turn around and pull a thousand-rupee bill from my bra and turn back to him. "But if you were my uncle, I wouldn't have to pay you, now, would I?"

The guy leans over and pushes the passenger door open. "Consider this your uncle's Tempo."

Krish and I squeeze in next to him on the cracked vinyl seats and ask where he's going. He tells us he's headed to Pune, but our deal was to get to the next town, which is Vadgaon.

"The deal can be adjusted if you take us to Pune," I shout over the metallic racket of the motor as we start driving.

"What about your car?" he shouts back with a wink.

"We'll get it later," I say.

"I'll bet," he says. "Just make sure your family doesn't come after me for helping you run away with your lover." He throws a look at Krish, who smiles politely.

The driver goes off into the story of how he ran away with the village beauty when they were fifteen as the Tempo makes sure every bone in our bodies vibrates at a different frequency.

"Are you still together?" I ask.

"I'm not lucky enough to be rid of her," he says. "Even though all you women turn from roses into cauliflowers once you have us. Good thing your man doesn't understand Marathi, so I can't warn him."

"There is a God," I mumble.

The man talks without stopping the entire way. He even talks in the background when Krish and I discuss how we're going to find Ashatai Athavale without GPS.

Krish, naturally, remembers her address because I forwarded it to him when Reva sent it to me.

"Ask him if he has a cell phone," Krish says over the rattling motor and the man's relentless monologue. "And if we can use his maps."

"I used to be a rickshaw driver in Pune for thirty years," the man says when I ask. "I don't need maps." He taps a finger to his temple. "The GPS is here."

"You don't need to translate that," Krish says when I open my mouth to do just that. "*Real men don't need directions* transcends language."

I'm still smiling as Krish rattles off the address and the man navigates a network of narrow lanes and takes us there. He drops us off on the coziest tree-lined street with the most charming buildings. I thank him and the GPS in his brain and hope he hasn't just dropped us off at some random place. He hasn't, because a painted sign on the building gate says **Laxmi Nivas**, and the street we turned on did say Tenth Lane Prabhat Road.

We take the stairs up to the second floor and find the door with a polished brass **A B Athavale** nameplate.

"I love that the buildings have names here and people put their names on their front doors," Krish says, which is exactly what I was just thinking. "Ready?"

I haven't noticed until now that he doesn't seem out of place here the way he did in Jackson Heights. Either he's changed or the way I see him has.

"Just a minute," I say. The bruise on his cheek has turned an angry purple. "You have some dirt on your face and a few bits of hay." I point to his curls, which aren't tied back today. "May I?"

He nods and makes the effort to keep his expression flat.

I wipe his cheek and make quick work of the mess in his hair.

"Thank you," he says and points to my face.

Obviously, I'm a mess, too, and I have no idea how bad it is. I start wiping my cheeks. "Fine?"

He lifts his hand, then pulls it back.

"Just do it," I say.

He hesitates only slightly before stroking my jaw with his thumb. Then he pulls a few leaves out of my hair, which is a full-blown hornet's nest. I pull it out of the ponytail, smooth it back, and tie it up in a high bun.

He nods. "As presentable as we're going to be."

He rings the doorbell and I knock.

A woman in a white cotton sari opens the inner door and stares at us through the wrought iron bars of the outer door. The word that springs to mind is *frail*. Her face is covered in a network of lines so fine it's like her skin is made of crushed chiffon. Her thinning all-gray hair is pulled back in a barely there braid. "How can I help you?" she asks, voice shaking.

"We're looking for Ashatai Athavale," I say in Marathi.

"She's dead," she says, and then watches unblinking as our faces melt into confusion. Before we can recover from that, she points at Krish's bruise. "What happened to your face?"

Naturally he doesn't understand a word, but before he can tell her that or I can translate for him, she does it herself.

"Who boxed your face?" she asks in perfectly clipped English.

"The guys who didn't want us to find Ashatai," Krish says, meeting her gaze head-on.

She laughs. "I like you. What do you want?"

"To talk to Ashatai about Vasudha Patil."

The change in her eyes is imperceptible, but she pulls the door open. "Come on in. I guess you found Ashatai."

Then, before our very eyes, she transforms from frail to fierce, no tremor in her hands, a hard alertness in her eyes, her spine straight, her steps quick.

We follow her in. The apartment is dimly lit and cozy in the way of an ancient library, walls lined with books, cement mosaic floors worn to smoothness. It reeks of history and buzzes with stories.

"You look hungry." That's the first thing she says, and she leads us into the kitchen, where huge stainless steel pots of rice, dal, and ghee and a jar of pickle are laid out on the heavy teakwood dining table.

"Go wash up before you eat," she orders and points us to a sink.

I've never given soap much thought, but scrubbing my hands and face makes me grateful for all the simple things we take for granted.

When we're done, she orders us to sit down and help ourselves.

We do as she says. Turns out being chased, bound, and robbed is great for the appetite, because we eat as though we haven't in days. It's possibly the most delicious dal I've ever eaten in my life, and there's a lot of it.

"I live by myself, but I never got out of the habit of making enough for my music students. Now it feeds some of the children who work in the neighborhood market."

"I'm sorry," I say. "We didn't mean to eat their food."

"We're all eating each other's food on this earth, child. Never feel guilty to eat when you're hungry. Just remember to feed the hungry when you can. Now tell me everything."

As we scarf down the food, we do exactly that. We tell her every single detail except the part where Krish has the second ring. We pass the story between us like a baton. She listens like a sari-clad Yoda, heavy lidded and meditative, hands folded in her lap.

When we reach the part where we knocked on her door, she sighs out a breath.

"I don't know who Reva Smith is. But based on what you're telling me, it sounds like she's Sureva Bhalekar. Who was Vasu's lover." She says the word *lover* with some satisfaction, and Krish and I exchange a glance.

Her gaze slides between us. "I don't know why people associate that word with the physical. If you're in love, if your hearts recognize each other as a piece of themselves, you're lovers. When will people stop using lust to devalue love?"

I look at my hands. I have no response to that. I think of my parents devaluing Rumi and Saket's love because they can't see anything but the physical aspect of it. Or they choose to see only that so they can call it ugly based on what feels physically natural to them. If they saw Rumi and Saket together, if they saw how they care for each other, how they glow in each other's presence, if they let themselves see the love, that would make it impossible for them to believe the things they believe.

"Now tell me the parts you left out," she says, breaking the silence.

Krish's jaw tightens.

She fixes him with a look. "I never forget a face, and yours is almost exactly the same as hers."

Krish holds out his hand to me. I remove the ring from my bra and place it in his palm. Then he tells her how the ring was left with him when he was given up for adoption.

"I remember it." She takes the ring from him with reverence. "Vasu would never have given it up for anything."

"Is she really dead?" Krish asks, and for the first time he lets pain escape into his voice when he talks about her.

A lump gathers in my throat.

Without answering, Ashatai leaves the room.

I want to comfort him, but I can't get myself to reach for him.

It feels like an age before she comes back out, an envelope in her hand. "I haven't seen Vasu in almost forty years. But some five years after I last saw her, she sent me this letter to give to Sureva, in case she ever came looking for her."

CHAPTER THIRTY-FIVE

Vasudha Patil
Yiga Choeling Monastery
Ghoom, West Bengal
February 1990

Sureva Bhalekar
c/o Mrs. Ashatai Athavale
215 Laxmi Nivas
10th Lane Prabhat Rd., Pune

Dear Suru,
It has been seven years since I've heard from you. Everyone wants me to believe that you sold out our love and took a deal from Appa to pay for your education in New York in return for forgetting me. At first this broke me. But somewhere in my heart I've always known that they were lying. They've only ever lied to us. When they told us they loved us, when they told us they were taking care of us. They were only ever interested in keeping the world exactly as it is. Safe only for them.

They cheated us, Suru. I don't know what they told you, but they worked together to tear us apart. Your aie, my parents, my dada, all of them. They wanted us to believe that we had betrayed each other.

When your aie came to visit me, I told her everything. I told her how they forced me to marry Namdeo, how my appa paid him millions of rupees, how they threatened to put you in jail for stealing the ring and hurt you if I didn't consent to the marriage. They would've had you thrown out of college and caused you to lose your chance of going to America. Taken away your life. I was so scared I married him, I let him touch me, violate me. All the while hoping a way out would show up.

When your aie came to see me, I thought my escape had come. I was obviously wrong. Something tells me your aie never told you anything I told her. I should have known because she tried to convince me that I was lucky that Appa had found me a way to save myself from sin and given me a chance at repentance. When I wouldn't listen, she begged me to save you by letting you go, because Appa had threatened to kill you if you didn't forget about me.

When I told her I couldn't, when I begged her to help us, she took your letters from me, saying it was the only way to convince you that she'd seen me and that I was waiting for you. I made Appa give me those letters back when I agreed to marry that man. I had that bit of leverage, and I used it to get your words back. Then I gave away the one thing of yours I had. You know I remember every word, but I've missed touching your beautiful penmanship every single day.

I waited and waited for you to reach out, but at least I knew through Ashatai that you had left for New York. Once I knew you were safe, I ran away from that prison they wanted me to die in and call that death life. I couldn't let that man touch me again. I knew I wouldn't survive if I stayed.

You know how powerful Appa is, and Dada will do anything to prove himself a worthy successor. Namdeo's family will also use any means necessary to keep their name unsullied. So I ran from them all.

Thanks to Ashatai's network, I was able to make my way across the country, too far out of the sphere of their influence. Too far to be a threat to their public image. But when I got here, I found out that the worst had happened. I was carrying a child. That poor child, growing inside a body with a broken spirit. I felt nothing but sadness for him. I did not have it in me to feel anything else.

Four years ago to this day, I gave birth to him in the monastery where I've lived and worked since then. The doctor assured me she would make sure he had a good home. An American couple was looking for a baby to complete their family. I was told they lived close to New York, so I let them have him. I sent him to New York so at least one little part of me might be close to you. And I gave him our ring. Sometimes I think if I had held on to the ring we would be together. Maybe I invoked a curse by giving it away. But I needed a piece of me to be with him. You've always accused me of being fanciful, and I dream of a day when those rings will bring us back together again.

Why is there a cruelty to friendship? All my life I had this need to come first for you. Now I would gladly be standing all the way at the end of your priorities if only I could see you one more time.

I've often wondered if the life you gained when we lost each other was worth it. I suspect there is no easy answer to that. I know you've done amazing things already and you will do more. There are too many fatal diseases that are only fatal because you haven't found a way to stop them yet. I can see it already. Work you'll do. Machines you'll create to break down cells that kill us. Magic you'll make to heal the pieces that make our bodies breathe and hurt and bleed.

I can see the trance in your eyes as you dig and push and inhale entire libraries so you can move something into place. The nights you stay up, the days you forget to eat. That's the life I imagine you living. I hope there's someone there telling you how beautiful you are, someone to cherish the force of nature you are, someone to scold you to rest. Another jealous and brutal piece of me wishes it's me still, who sits on your shoulder, who makes you care for yourself because you can't bear to upset me.

I am there, you know. On your shoulder. As you are on mine.

If there is happiness in this world it is knowing that we have that forever.

When you live in a monastery (isn't it ironic how I ended up in one of the coldest parts of India when I hated the cold so very much) you get to think a lot about what happiness is. Even after everything, I do believe that our families who separated us did want us to be happy. They just couldn't define happiness as anything outside of what they were taught to define as normal. I've questioned almost everything in my life. I've questioned the intentions and character of every person I've ever met. Including yours and mine. I've hated that you left me. But I've never questioned that our love was right, that it was powerful, that it made me feel my own humanity more than a single other thing I've ever experienced.

If you are reading this letter then I hope it follows that the only thing I've ever desired in this lifetime is about to come true. I hope that it isn't after our entire lives have gone by. Even if it is, I'll take it because I will not leave this earth without seeing you again, Suru. My soul cannot carry the burden of so much unfulfilled wanting to the next life.

Waiting for you.

Always only yours,

Vasu

CHAPTER THIRTY-SIX

Reva asks us to open the letter and send her an image of it. It's the fastest way to get it to her. So I take a picture on Ashatai's phone and send it to her.

"Thank you," Reva says when she calls us after reading it. Her voice is raw with tears. "I can't believe you found her."

We haven't yet. The letter is thirty-four years old. No one mentions that. It doesn't matter because we're close.

"You can read it," Reva says. "In fact, Krish, please read it."

"I'm okay, thank you," he says and leaves the room and steps into the balcony. He hasn't said a word since he asked Ashatai if his birth mother was dead.

"Mira?" Reva says.

"I got him," I say. "What do you want to do?"

"I want to come there. I'll be there as soon as I can. What are you planning to do next?"

"The only way to find her is to go to Darjeeling," I say, and Ashatai squeezes my shoulder in encouragement. "We'll have to go to Mumbai first." We need our passports to fly to Darjeeling, where the monastery is located.

Reva promises to let me know her travel plans, and I promise to keep her posted on ours. It's late, and the phone stores are closed. It's a good thing Ashatai is the most resourceful person I've ever met because she hands us a burner phone and arranges for a taxi to take us to Mumbai. I think I might be done with trains for life.

Ashatai agrees with Krish's theory that the fact that we were attacked but not really hurt means whoever set those thugs on us—very possibly Vasu's brother—just meant to scare us. Going to the cops will only alert him to the fact that we're not ready to let things go and will send him after us again.

"Don't worry about him anymore. I know people who can warn him off," Ashatai says with chilling finality, and I feel the entire weight of all the people whose lives she's changed.

As soon as we get in the cab, I call Druv at his office. I don't know his cell phone number by heart, and his office number is easy enough to find on his website.

Obviously, he's frantic with worry because my phone has been unreachable all day. I can't believe it's been just one day. It feels like at least a week. Finding the ring feels like it was a lifetime ago. I feel nothing like that person who was knocked down by a child on a New York sidewalk. I tell Druv that we were robbed but that we're safe. Thankfully the only things in my backpack other than my phone were a change of clothes and toiletries. I obviously leave out the abduction. He's having a hard enough time with the robbery.

"Are you done with this now?" he asks.

"I don't know."

He sounds upset, and I don't want to have this conversation around Krish so I ask him to let the moms know that I'm headed back to the hotel and promise to call him once I'm there.

When I'm done, I offer Krish the phone. "Do you need to call anyone?"

He shakes his head. No one knows he's here.

I'm holding the letter, and his gaze falls to it. I hold it out to him. "This confirms she was your birth mother. I think you should read it."

After hesitating for a moment, he takes it. I look out the window, giving him privacy as he reads by the dim light of the cab. Outside, the moonlight turns the mountains into silhouettes. I've read the letter. There is no number on the pain scale that could measure how I would feel if I were him.

When I look back at him, he's folded the letter and is holding it in his lap. "I don't think I can do it. I don't think I can go to Darjeeling."

"How can you not go now? You came this far looking for her."

"No. *You* came this far looking for her."

That's fair and unfair at the same time. "I did. But I didn't make you come."

He swallows. "Fine. But I should be able to decide when I stop."

"Okay."

For a long time neither of us says anything. I realize that this feels like the end of a search for me, like reaching a destination. That's not true for him. No matter what we find, it's not going to be the end for him. It's going to be the beginning of something possibly incredibly painful. Something he may never be able to put behind him. This will never be over for him.

Just when I think he may not speak for the rest of the drive, he does. "You know the thing about being adopted that sucks?"

The question is not one I have any authority to answer, so I wait for him to say what's dancing like pain in his eyes.

"That everyone had a choice—your birth parents, your adoptive parents—and you had none, and you're the one who has to live with the consequences of everyone else's choices."

"Isn't that true of all children? All babies?" I say without thinking. "My parents chose to have Rumi and me. They gave birth to us, then for the rest of our lives they made us feel like we had to make ourselves worthy of all the hard work they had to put into raising us so they could give us this life that they wanted, not just for us but for themselves. How one approaches parenting is about the person you are. The parents you get is a game of chance for everyone."

"And yet when you're adopted, you're just someone your parents could give away."

"You're also someone your parents chose because they wanted you that badly."

Those words seem to jolt through him. He doesn't respond. He just sits there staring at his hands, then turns his gaze on me as though he's waiting for me to say more.

"How are the millions of children whose parents had them without ever giving it a thought more special than someone for whom their parents stayed on a waiting list for years, praying, proving, bettering themselves? If Vasu had stayed with Namdeo, if Vasu had kept you in that ugliness, would that really be better?"

"I don't know." His shoulders start to shake. He swallows.

Then he reaches over and collapses against me. From the depth of his soul, he lets his pain out in heart-wrenching sobs. Krish, stoic, indomitable Krish. Krish, who hasn't shown me a sliver of emotion in the time I've known him, is crying in my arms as though he's been waiting his entire life to be able to cry.

I wrap my arms around him. For those minutes, I'm what holds him up. What makes it possible for him to keep breathing through the pain that's choked him for so long. In being that, I'm also what I've wanted to be for as long as I can remember: someone whose humanity is complete because they're connected to others. Someone who feels undamaged and enough. Someone with the power to make the unbearable bearable.

When the sobs stop, we sit there like that, his forehead pressed into my shoulder. Another moment when we've breached a wall with each other that has kept us safe from everyone else.

When he pulls away, his face is wet. That, combined with the swollen, bruised jaw, makes him so vulnerable, it's like he's stripped down to his soul. He takes off his glasses and wipes his eyes. "You should have seen the look on my mom's face when I said those things to her. I see her face in my dreams every night. I gave her that. In return for a lifetime of love, I gave her that."

I squeeze his hand. "You were horrible to her one time. You were obviously a wonderful son all the other times. Do you think she took only that one conversation with her? Do you think she forgot the lifetime of love that you remember so well, that's such a part of who you are? I've been awful to you. Is that what you'll remember when you think of me? Is that what's imprinted on your soul about me?"

He pulls my hands to his chest. "No," he whispers. "It's the hot-sauce breakdown."

We both smile.

"And the motorcycle freak-out?" I say.

"And ripping sugarcane with your bare teeth. And how badass you were when you refused to be afraid of the guy who tried to steal the ring in New York."

"You mean how I toppled over when he gave me one push?"

"That too. And how you feel everyone's pain as though it's your own."

"Yes, it's super fun being a pain magnet!"

"And yet you race headfirst into it."

I pull my hand away. That's a lot. All of it.

"I'm willing to bet my life that the last thing your mother wished was that you wouldn't carry the guilt of that last conversation with you on top of your grief. I'll bet she would give anything to let you know that it didn't touch the love between you."

"Thank you," he says.

Then he looks at the phone, so I hand it to him.

He dials a number.

"Dad?" he says. "It's Krish."

CHAPTER THIRTY-SEVEN

For the first time in my life, my mother doesn't yell at me when she's angry. I'm so grateful to whoever invented the silent treatment, I send up a prayer to rest their passive-aggressive soul.

Romona seems worried about me. My heart warms at her care. Both she and my aie were waiting up for me when I got to the suite a little after midnight last night.

Romona hugged me tight and told me she was glad I was safe. "Don't worry about the phone. Things can always be replaced."

I did thank Aie for teaching me the bra-as-a-bag trick, and she cracked a little and patted my shoulder. All they know is that we were robbed on the train, and they're aghast that we chose to go on to Pune anyway. Neither of them has asked if we found Vasu.

We have another day of shopping left, and I really have no interest in it. That's one of two difficult pieces of news I need to break to them as we make our way through another endless cornucopia of international breakfast foods. I need something simple and comforting today. I pour good old-fashioned American maple syrup on my waffles and top it with an extra serving of whipped cream and carry it to the table.

The moms watch me expectantly. I start with the easier piece. "I need to spend the morning getting a new phone today. Is it okay if I skip shopping?"

Aie slams her teacup on the table hard enough that a few of the neighboring tables look over. "Is this Romona and my wedding, Mira?"

The truth is that Druv and I are getting married but the wedding is Romona's and Aie's more than it is ours. I don't say it. Naturally Aie hears that I think it.

"I'm so grateful for all the work you're both doing for the wedding. If I didn't need to take care of this, I would love to look at jewelry with you."

My mother throws me a look that says *If your mother-in-law wasn't at the table, I'd smack you.*

Instead of making me angry, this amuses me. I'm not afraid of her anymore. I don't think I ever was. I was afraid of hurting her feelings. But she's an adult who's just as responsible for how she treats me as I am for how I treat her.

"Don't you want to choose the sets you will wear at your wedding?" Druv's mom says. "Those look very different worn than in pictures."

That's a fair point. "Maybe you two could narrow down the choices while I get the phone taken care of, and I can come by and try them on to make a final choice?"

Romona brightens. Aie doesn't give an inch.

"That works," Romona says. "I also wanted to go to dinner at my cousin's favorite chaat place to celebrate getting everything done."

"I think I'm flying out to Darjeeling this afternoon."

They freeze midchew.

Aie stands up. "I'm so sorry, Romona! I would not blame you if you reconsidered making her your daughter-in-law."

Romona gasps. Anger speeds up my heartbeat.

"Don't say that, Ajita. At least hear her out."

"You've been so patient with her," Aie says. "But I can't pardon such selfish behavior. We've spent months trying to make your wedding perfect for you, and you want to run around looking for some stranger?"

"You're the one who wanted an elaborate wedding. I wanted a simple ceremony. I know I did agree to it, so I am grateful, and I came here with you, but none of this is about making anything perfect for me."

They both gasp now. Then Aie turns around and makes a grand exit, her cane thumping dramatically next to her.

Romona and I sit there. An awkwardness between us for the first time.

"I'm guessing whatever is happening in Darjeeling is important."

I reach over and squeeze her hand. "Druv and Ariana are so lucky to have had you as a mother."

She gives me a look that blends commiseration with sympathy. "Well, I had it easy. I didn't have to struggle like Ajita. The important thing is how hard she's worked for you. She loves you. She'd do anything for you."

Our family's theme song.

"In that case she'll come around to being okay with me going to Darjeeling instead of Akola with her. That would be doing something for me."

Nonetheless, she is my mother, so I go back to the room to try and soothe her. I fail. She threatens to not pay for the wedding if I go to Darjeeling.

"I'm going, Aie. I'm also happy to have a small wedding that Druv and I will pay for ourselves. So, it's your call."

"That poor boy. He didn't know you would change into this selfish person when he decided to marry you. I feel pity for him for having to deal with this new version of you for the rest of his life."

Meanness. Another thing that has always sliced me to pieces. Now I see it for what it is. A weapon I've allowed her to wield to control me.

When I don't answer, her response is to call Baba and start screaming, while sobbing, about how I've lost my mind. I feel like I'm in one of those Indian soap operas Aie used to watch when I was growing up. As if to add to that theme, Romona comes back to the suite and starts to placate her.

I feel the kick of humiliation I'm so used to. I gather my things, write down Romona's number, then promise to call her when I have my new phone and leave.

The second the door shuts behind me, I want to crumple to the floor. Instead of powerful, I feel sick to my stomach with guilt and anger. It's like I don't recognize the person who's taken over my body, and I want the ease of my old self back. I'm a bird who's never learned to fly, toppling out of my nest. I can't fit in the nest of my old self anymore. All I can hope is that my wings will find a way to hold me up before I crash to the ground.

The feelings of guilt and anger don't go away as I take a rickshaw to the mall, but the feeling of rightness does return. The act of growing a spine hurts, but it doesn't seem reversible. I don't want it to be reversible. I wish I could go back and tell Aie that I love her but I need her to treat me like an adult. I need her to listen to what I want. I want her to see who I am. I want to have a conversation with my mother that isn't a lecture, a monologue, or a transactional list of favors. A simple conversation between two people who respect each other. And I want that for both Rumi and me or not at all.

It takes over an hour to get my phone set up and download everything from the cloud. It's like those bastards never stole it. It's all in my hand again. I'm guessing Krish has bought a new phone by now too and had it set up. I text him.

Me: I have a new phone

Him: No!

Me: Good to see you have yours too. Don't you love technology?!

(Silence accompanied by three dots.)

Finally, him: I have our ticket options.

After that change of tone and topic, the rest of the conversation is spent deciding between leaving in three hours so we get there this evening or leaving first thing tomorrow. It's a three-hour flight to Bagdogra, then a two-hour cab ride up the Himalayas to Darjeeling.

We decide to leave today. I don't think I'm going to be very productive in Mumbai with Aie. Suddenly, I need to put this behind me so I can return to my life.

I call Romona, then stop at the jewelry store and try on jewelry. Five sets for my five main outfits. Romona oohs and aahs. Aie is grumpy but nods along with Romona's reactions. Then I tell them that I'm going to the airport from here, and Aie freezes over like a statue again.

After we're done, I drop them off at the hotel, pick up my bags, and head to the airport, where I'm meeting Krish.

Ten minutes into the drive, Druv calls. I feel like one of those superheroes holding multiple laser beams at bay with both hands.

"I no longer want you to do this," Druv says without preamble. "You've already been robbed, and you found out what happened to Vasu. Why can't the journalist guy do the rest by himself? He's the one who's going to benefit from the story anyway."

"This means something to me, Druv."

"That's what I don't understand. I get why you got excited about it. Why it took up your imagination. You had never left home. This got you out of your family's shadow. It gave you adventure, a sense of satisfaction. I'm sure it's been great, but now it's getting in the way of our real life."

"What is that supposed to mean?"

"Mira! I'm not your enemy. Your mother is no longer speaking to you, three months before our wedding. Ma has gone to bat for you. She's completely okay with your brother bringing his cross-dressing boyfriend to the wedding. My *grandmother* is going to be there. A bunch of people who aren't as liberal as us are going to be there. She's still doing this. For you. Because it means something to you. Don't you think that's amazing?"

"Actually, no, Druv. I don't. This is not about being liberal or not being liberal. This isn't about Romona Auntie being okay with Saket.

This is about you thinking that being okay with Saket is a choice you get to make, let alone something you have to do for me. This is about the fact that we're even having a conversation that reduces real human beings to an issue you're compromising on."

"I didn't say that."

"You said exactly that."

There's a moment of silence. I'm so angry, my skin feels hot. I'm ashamed that it has taken me this long to understand what I was doing to my own brother.

"I'm sorry," Druv says finally. "You're right. I never saw it that way."

I feel like a hypocrite. Less than a month ago I would not have seen it this way either. I would have been grateful if Rumi got to attend my wedding with Saket. I would have thought myself lucky to have a family who was so *tolerant*.

"I know," I say. "Thanks for listening."

"Are we okay?"

"I think so. But I'm still going to Darjeeling."

CHAPTER THIRTY-EIGHT

There's a deep despondence wedged inside me when I get to the airport.

Krish is leaning on a pillar, hands pushed into his pockets. His Henleys have been replaced by white lightweight cotton T-shirts here. The shiny watch he used to acquire a motorcycle for us in New York catches the light, and a new backpack hangs on one shoulder. He straightens imperceptibly when his eyes find me.

If he asks me what's wrong, I will snap his head off.

He doesn't. He doesn't take my bag from me or try to help. He simply waits for me to walk past him and falls in step next to me.

There's a long line to get into the airport. Unlike at home, here, there's a security screening to enter the airport building.

We've been standing in line in silence for a few minutes when Druv calls again.

"I feel like shit about what I said. I really am sorry," he says.

"It means a lot that you'd say that. Thank you for understanding," I say. Then I tell him I'm in line and have to go.

I shouldn't look at Krish's face, but I do. "What?" I ask because he's avoiding my gaze and staring away into the distance with an odd expression. Actually, it's not odd, it's downright judgmental.

"I didn't say anything."

"Words aren't the only way to say something."

"Let's not do this. Not when you're this upset."

Wow. "I'm not upset."

"I thought we didn't lie to each other."

I laugh. "Really? I thought we started out with you lying to me about why you were interested in the ring."

It's a mean thing to say. I shouldn't have said it. Obviously, I understand why he didn't tell me. What I don't understand is this restless anger I'm filled with, and I can't get myself to apologize.

"Why does it matter what I think?" he asks, and that same restless anger shines in his eyes.

Because it does. But I don't say that out loud.

His eyes have a way of intensifying when he's struggling to decide if he should say what he wants to say. I wish I hadn't asked. I no longer want him to answer.

He does. "You talk to him like you're talking to a stranger."

I step back and into the person behind me. Lines in India aren't like lines in America. The person behind me is inches from me. It's a full-body collision. I apologize, and she steps back. She's kind about it, but I feel trapped.

The line moves forward, and I move with it. Krish remains a step behind me, buying me space.

"I'm sorry. I shouldn't have said that," he says.

I nod. He shouldn't have. And it's not true.

We make our way through this security checkpoint in silence. Then once we're inside, through a few more checkpoints. I try to focus on the fact that we live in a world where planes being blown up by bombs is a real thing and preventing it requires billions of dollars across the world. Hate is everywhere. Borders are supposed to make us feel safe, but they feed hate and make us less so. Life is fragile and safety tenuous at best.

I think about the fact that I left my mother in a state of rage. Krish lost his mother after having broken her heart and carries the pain of it every day. We're looking for Vasu thirty-eight years too late. We have no way of knowing if she's even alive. Krish might be about to lose another mother.

"How is your dad?" I ask when we make it to the gate area and find a corner to wait in.

My question seems to pull him out of his own spiral of thoughts. He looks surprised. I don't know if it's because I'm speaking to him again or because I asked about his father. Or both. "He's great. I spoke to him for a long time last night after getting back to the hotel."

"Did you tell him what we're doing here?"

"Yes. He said he supports me in whatever I need to do. We apologized for not being there for each other after Mom's accident. I told him no matter what I find, he and Mom will always be my parents. He said he knew. He said Mom knew."

I have tears in my eyes. It's a good thing we're all the way in a corner and everyone is staring at their phones.

"Did you have a fight with your mother about going to Darjeeling?"

I nod. "I think she's afraid I'm changing my mind about the life I want to live."

"Mira," he says, turning the full force of his sincerity on me, "do you want to change your mind about this? We haven't boarded the plane. You can go back, and everything will be as it was."

That's what one part of me wants, more than anything. Another part knows that's no longer possible. Nothing will ever be as it was. I don't know if I want it to be. So much feels crystal clear inside me, and yet everything is somehow more tangled up.

"Is that what you want, Krish?"

"Isn't it obvious what I want?" he asks, and I catch a wild yearning blazing in his eyes for the first time.

I want to look away, but I can't. I'm reeling from shock but I'm also not.

No, this is not the first time I'm seeing it. I've just been trying not to see. He makes no effort to hide it now, and I feel like someone just pulled the floor from under me.

"I meant about Darjeeling," I say with a firmness I want to feel. "Do you want me to go?"

He takes a breath, swallows back what he was about to say. "I want you to do what you need to do."

"Krish! Do you want me to go to Darjeeling with you or not?"

"Yes," he says too quickly and fiercely. "Even if it's one last thing. I don't want to do this by myself."

"Then I'm coming." Far too much relief blooms in his face. I feel that relief, too, all the way in my bones, and I don't like it. "But my relationship with Druv is off limits."

Just like that, the restless anger is back in his eyes. He doesn't accept that immediately, and my restless anger returns too.

"Why?" he asks. "Why do you want to be there so bad? Why are you doing this?"

"You just asked me to."

"So what? Why do you care?" There's an almost harsh deliberateness to his words, and my irritation spikes so sharp and fast my heartbeat gallops in my chest. Never before I met him did my heartbeat, my pulse, all the beating parts of me react so riotously. Up, then down. Up, then down.

"Maybe because I'm a caring person. I care about things," I say with all the frustration I'm feeling. "Even for people who glower at the world relentlessly and for no good reason."

His jaw works. His eyes soften. Up, then down.

"What?" I say. It comes out a hiss.

"I can't argue with that." His answer is a whisper. How can someone so guarded and in control turn so vulnerable I can see all the way inside him? Absolutely nothing separates us.

Suddenly he straightens. An odd resolve tightens his body, his face. His expression is so intense I can hardly bear to look at him. "There is something else."

I don't want to hear it. Already, I want to erase this conversation. He gives me time to ask him not to say it. But I can't get myself to.

"Since you've already accused me of being a liar, there is something else I've kept from you."

This time my pulse slows. Time slows because our gazes are locked and there isn't enough breath entering my lungs.

"I should have told you this earlier. I shouldn't have waited so long to say it. I have a girlfriend. We've been together for a year."

Pain lances through my heart. A knife slicing in and twisting. *Turn around and leave,* a voice inside me says. *What do you care that he has a girlfriend?* another voice says, but pain paralyzes me and pins me in place.

His lips press together. He takes a step away from me and raises a finger, pointing at my face, then at his heart. He opens his mouth but struggles with words. "That. How you just felt. That's how I feel every time you say his name. There's no one else in my life."

Relief floods through me. He isn't with anyone else. Then anger so violent I want to explode with it. Then shame. I'm getting married in a few months.

He's breathing hard, seeing right through me. Why would he do this to me?

His hand goes to his temples and squeezes. "When we first met, you were right about me. All through my childhood I learned not to show my discomfort when I didn't fit. Because I've never fit. Not until now. For the first time in my life, I fit. I fit in my skin, in this world, in my own discomfort. I'm not a stranger when you're with me, Mira. And I've been a stranger to myself all my life."

The silence that follows his words rings in my ears. "Why are you telling me this now?"

"Because it wouldn't be fair for me to not say it before we get on that plane."

"Krish, I can't just flip my entire life over."

For one second the words *Why not?* burn in his eyes.

He knows why not, just as much as I do.

"I don't ever want you to do anything that feels like it's flipping your life over." I hate how articulate he is. How he doesn't just throw words out without choosing each one carefully. Even more than that, I hate how much those words pierce me.

The gate agent calls boarding numbers over the PA system. People start scanning their boarding passes and moving toward the bus that will take us to our plane.

What do you want from me? I want to say, but I have nothing to give him. I don't want to have anything to give him.

"I'm not asking for anything, Mira," he says too gently. "I just had to tell you. It means nothing if you don't want it to." He hooks his backpack over his shoulder. "I'm going to board the plane. Take your time. If you choose to go with me, I will not take it to mean anything more than us finishing what we started. I will never do anything to make you uncomfortable. And if you choose not to come after what I just told you, I'll understand." With that he joins the line to board the bus and disappears through the sliding doors into the waiting crowd, leaving me to make my choice.

CHAPTER THIRTY-NINE

We land in Bagdogra just as the sun is starting its descent over the Himalayas. I was the last person on the plane. There was a moment when I almost turned around and went back to the hotel. It was a short-lived moment. I almost called Rumi and Saket, even Druv. Needing a sign, a piece of advice to tell me what to do. To know what was right.

In the end what made me heed that last boarding call was the realization that no matter what Rumi, Saket, or Druv said to me, I would get on the plane. I was looking for validation, for permission to do something I already knew I was going to do.

Krish's expression when he saw me come down the aisle is something I'll remember till the day I die. Everything that's happened this past month is going to stick with me forever. Krish was right in clearing the air because now I can relax. He's developed feelings for me, which, given the circumstances, is natural. Every time I take a patient's chronic pain away, they get emotionally attached to me. That's how humans work. People meet for a reason. Krish and I met so Vasu and Reva would be reunited and Krish could know his birth story. Druv is my fiancé. My life is in Chicago.

Finding the ring and tracking it to Reva and Vasu has given me back parts of myself I had buried so deep I'd forgotten they existed. Not finishing that journey is not an option.

Ever since I got on the plane, Krish has kept his promise. He's been friendly while giving me space. It's almost as though we didn't have that conversation. We're friends again, and our friendship feels like the bedrock we're going to need to stand on to get through what comes next.

We find a taxi at the airport to take us up the mountain roads. Even in the waning light the magnificent scale of the Himalayas is almost impossible to wrap my head around. The winding road takes us up seven thousand feet in two hours. The road is narrow and the pine trees majestic and abundant. Rhododendrons grow to full-size trees, twenty feet tall, and dot the slopes with flaming-red blooms. Thick pine forests break at intervals, giving way to endless terraced slopes covered in velvety green tea gardens.

Our taxi driver, Norbu, keeps up a steady stream of conversation, naming trees and settlements and giving us historical anecdotes from when the British colonizers settled this area as an escape from the heat of Calcutta and started tea plantations to combat China's tea production. He fills us in on why Darjeeling tea is the world's most flavorful, his voice filled with pride and belonging. We stop at a tea store on a cliff so we can try some, and Norbu demonstrates how tea tastes better when you make slurping sounds when you drink it because of the extra air that oxidizes the tannin. He's right, and I wonder how I'll ever go back to sipping tea soundlessly.

As we enter the Darjeeling area, the air turns light and misty, ambient twilight paints the skies, and the temperature drops a good twenty degrees. Krish pulls a Columbia Journalism sweatshirt from his backpack and hands it to me. "I'm sorry it doesn't say *Barely Fancy Journalism School*," he says.

"It does, though," I say.

I want to not take the sweatshirt, but the other option is to let my teeth chatter, so I pull it over my head and try not to notice how comforting it smells.

As we pass the town of Darjeeling and enter Ghoom, the roads become narrow enough to barely fit one car. There's a train track almost touching the side of the mountain and taking up part of the road. I can't imagine how a train could possibly fit on a road this size. The mountains feel as magical and majestic as the fantastical lands from the books I read as a child. The town wedged into the slopes is wretchedly decrepit, but that does nothing to take away from the mythical quality of floating above the world on clouds. As we pass homes and shops along steeply sloping streets, our cab almost touching the walls and verandas, ruddy-cheeked children wave at us and old people with lined faces smile at our bafflement at being mere feet from them in the car.

Just as the layered scallops of a pagoda come into sight and Norbu tells us we're looking at the Ghoom monastery, the car stops. There's another car on the road. Norbu and the driver of the other car stick their heads out of their windows and devise a strategy of reversing and navigating so the two cars can pass each other. I've never known driving to be a team sport, and it fills my heart with something I've never felt before.

A little girl in a faded blue sweaterdress watches me with fascination from the veranda of her home. A thickly furred stray dog sits next to her and watches her with worshipful eyes. She waves to me, and I wave back. Emboldened, she reaches out and touches the window, and I lower it. She smiles and touches a springy curl that's escaped my ponytail.

"Noodle hair," she says, then points at Krish's hair. "Noodle hair," she says again. I laugh. Something about her sweetness brings tears to my eyes. Her own hair is straight as silk.

"Silk hair," I say, and she smiles.

Our car moves again, and we wave goodbye. My heart feels wobbly. Krish looks at my wet cheeks and looks away.

I want to reach out and hold his hand. I don't. And I never will. My time with him feels close to its end, and suddenly my heart squeezes painfully at the thought.

The car bounces to a stop next to a crumbling arch that's blocked by bamboo scaffolding. Every building in town appears to be unfinished and in need of repair, but the purity of the air makes the state of the buildings seem insignificant.

Krish pays Norbu and takes his number so we can call him for our return.

"Ready?" Krish asks, and I feel like it's been an age since I heard his voice.

I've never felt this exposed and defenseless. We've made it here and something about that makes it impossible to hold on to my shields. Everything I'm feeling is reflected in his eyes, and I step closer. "You?"

He shakes his head. He's not ready, but he's going to do this anyway. Whatever is happening in my heart, I don't think I'm strong enough to bear it.

There's a narrow gap between the arch and the scaffolding, and we turn sideways and slide through it. It's not safe, but it's the only way to get inside the monastery compound. There's an open courtyard with two low buildings on each side of us and a temple with a pagoda roof on the far side. Its walls are lined with rotating brass bells.

There's not a soul in sight. Clouds hang low over the golden steeple. The silence feels spiritual.

We walk toward the temple. Just as we get there, a monk in maroon robes with a shaved head steps out.

He bows, and we bow back. "Time closed," he says in English.

"We're looking for someone," Krish says. "Vasu Sawant?"

He looks blank.

"Vasu Patil?" I say.

"Time closed," he says again and points to Krish's watch.

"Vasudha?" Krish says. "We're looking for a Vasudha Patil? Sawant?"

Still nothing.

"Maybe she goes by a different name now," I say. "Reva used to be Sureva. So maybe Vasu goes by, I don't know, Sudha now?" I say to Krish. It's common in India to use parts of names and turn them into nicknames. "Sudha?" I say to the monk.

His eyes narrow. "Sudha?" He says it differently than I did, elongating the *u*. Then he shakes his head and makes a tsking sound. "Ati dhila."

"We don't know what that means," Krish says. "Where can we find her?"

The monk closes his eyes and makes a dead face or a sleeping face. Krish and I exchange a glance.

He studies Krish's face, and something in his expression changes. He grabs Krish's arm above his elbow and starts walking.

We take a path past the building to the left of the courtyard and follow a dirt trail along the edge of a cliff that drops into an endless abyss. I'm struck yet again by the scale of these mountains. What must it feel like to live in the shadow of something so untenably vast?

I feel insignificant, and it's a beautiful feeling.

The monk's steps are quick. The walk isn't a short one.

I'm a step behind them, and Krish throws a look over his shoulder every few steps to make sure I'm still there. I don't know if it's the thinness of the air or the idea that the monk might be taking us to Vasu, but I'm short of breath. We come upon a cluster of cottages with clay roofs, plastered walls, and cement verandas. A young woman in a sweater and what looks like a cross between a sari and a sarong is standing outside one of the cottages.

The monk and she start talking. The word *Sudha* is repeated a few times. It's the only word I recognize.

Finally, she turns to us, and the monk walks away. "Can I help you?" she says in perfect English.

"We're looking for Vasudha Patil," I say.

"For what reason?" she asks.

Krish and I look at each other. If there ever was a question that didn't have an easy answer.

"Her childhood friend has been searching for her," I say.

"You are her childhood friends?"

I smile. "No. We're helping our friend. Her name is Reva. We think Vasu . . . Sudha knows her as Suru."

The woman gasps. "You know Suru?" she asks with some force. "Where is she? Did she come with you?" She sounds almost desperate.

"Not right now. But she's on her way. We've been looking for Vasudha. We wanted to make sure we found her before Suru made the trip."

The woman's eyes fill with tears. "Come." She starts walking, and we follow. "Tell your friend to hurry. There isn't much time."

I reach out and hold Krish's hand, and he clutches mine like it's a lifeline.

"Is she sick?" I ask.

The woman turns around, and there's pain in her face. We approach a small cottage. Like all the other cottages in this cluster, it's white-walled with a gray veranda and a red clay roof. This one has a bright-yellow door.

"The doctors said Didi had six months to live. That was two years ago. A month ago, she collapsed and has been in and out of consciousness. She hasn't left her bed, and she barely talks. But she asks for Suru day and night."

"Can we see her?" I ask, because Krish has gone utterly silent. He's holding my hand in a vise grip.

With a nod, she leads us in through the yellow door.

A woman, so thin and slight she's the size of a child, lies on a wooden cot. There's an IV stand and a food trolley pushed against a wall. A faded plaid woolen blanket covers her lower half. Her face is skin and bones, and there's a smattering of silver tufts of hair on her head. An astringent smell fills the air.

"Didi?" The young woman uses the term of affection and respect for a big sister. "Look who's come to see you."

Vasudha opens her eyes and turns her gaze on us. "Suru?" she says, and it's the most heartbreaking thing I've ever witnessed in my life.

Her eyes, even in their sunken sockets, are beautiful. Every shade of gold and brown, and wide and heavy lidded. Krish's eyes. They flicker from me to Krish.

"She didn't come with you?" she says in Marathi.

"Nahi." I tell her she didn't. "She's on her way."

A thin smile pulls at her lips, and a crinkle of a dimple sinks into her hollow cheek. Then she closes her eyes and drifts away again.

Krish just stands there looking at her.

"Is it okay if he sits with her while I call our friend?" I ask the woman, who tells us her name is Janet.

"Of course." She pushes Krish into the bed. "She likes when people sit with her. The villagers usually come sit with her for hours. They believe Didi's presence will make everything better."

Krish sits, and Janet takes his hand and places it in Vasu's. At first he hesitates, but then he grabs it with both of his, and a tear slips from his eye.

I leave him and step outside to call Reva.

~

It takes Reva just over twenty-four hours to reach Darjeeling. Krish and I spend almost all that time sitting by Vasu's bed. She doesn't open her eyes again. Janet and the other people in the monastery community bring us food. A doctor comes by and connects her IV to fluids. Janet and a few others clean out her bedpan and sheets. Someone drags in another cot from one of the other cottages and puts fresh sheets on it so we can sleep. We take turns. I sleep first, then force Krish to sleep while I sit with her.

Throughout the day people stop by to visit with her, hold her hand, talk to her. The ones who can speak English tell us stories of how no one really remembers when she came here or from where. The local legend is that she's always been here. She raised the children who were left at the monastery orphanage, like Janet. She led the chants at the monastery every morning and evening for as long as anyone can remember. Her singing voice is legendary. She cooked with the monks to feed anyone in town who needed food. When people got sick, she sat with them, and they always recovered. When people were suffering, they came to her for advice. It's like she's the soul of this place. Like she's imbibed the power of these mountains.

When the doctor comes by, she tells us that it's a miracle that Vasudha's lungs are still pulling in oxygen, but no one here is surprised by it.

A month ago the doctor declared Vasu's time was at its end.

A month ago Vasu told the doctor that she's not going anywhere until Suru comes.

A month ago is when I found the ring.

CHAPTER FORTY

When Reva arrives at her side, Vasu opens her eyes and smiles again.

"You came," she says, raising her arm to touch Reva's cheek.

"What have you done to yourself?" Reva says, sitting down next to her and stroking her cheek too.

"But look at you. Still beautiful enough to slap Marilyn Monroe in the face."

"Marilyn's dead, Vasu," Reva says.

Vasu makes a sound like a laugh. "In that case I take it back. Your aie would have scolded us for comparing ourselves to the dead, wouldn't she?"

"True," Reva says and starts to cry.

"You learned to cry," Vasu says.

"Forty years ago. I should have come looking for you. I should have tried harder."

"You came now, when it matters. Because I wasn't going to die without seeing you again. These poor people were getting a little tired of caring for me."

"I owe them everything. But I'm taking you home with me."

Vasu laughs. "My home just came to me."

"Oh, Vasu." Reva leans over, puts her arms around Vasu, gathers her up, and cries like I've never seen anyone cry before.

Vasu strokes her hair.

They lie there like that, their bodies entwined, as though there's no one but them in the room. No one but them in the world.

I step closer to Krish and put an arm around him. He leans into me, wipes my tears, and places a kiss on the top of my head. That's when I know exactly what he meant when he said he fit. I fit in my skin more than I ever have. I'm filled with pain, but I'm no longer a stranger to my own pain. I'm no longer a stranger to myself.

~

The next morning, Krish and I wake up early to watch the sun paint the Kanchenjunga golden. It's the most beautiful sight I've ever beheld. The snowcapped peak floats over the clouds and catches the first orange rays of the rising sun and turns to fiery gold.

I shiver in Krish's sweatshirt, but my heart has never been warmer.

"I'm going to stay," Krish says. "Is that okay?"

"Of course." I don't ask him how long he plans to stay. We both know Vasu doesn't have much time left. I want to stay, too, but I've done what I set out to do, and I have to return to all the things I've neglected since the ring came into my life. My real life. "I have to go, though."

"I know."

We go back to Vasu's room. Reva hasn't left her side except to use the bathroom. Vasu's been mostly asleep, but Reva has been sitting there, holding her hand and watching her face and talking to her.

When we walk in, Vasu and Reva are laughing about something.

Vasu seems more awake today, like life's been pumped back into her. Yesterday felt like it belonged to Reva and Vasu, but today I see longing in Krish's eyes when he looks at her.

Vasu holds out her hand, and Krish goes to her and takes it. He kneels next to her bed.

Reva asks Vasu if she knows who Krish is.

"Yes," Vasu says. Her voice is stronger today too. She studies him, and her thumb strokes his hand. "Were they good to you?"

"The best," Krish says. His eyes are shining. "But I still missed you."

"I know," she says. "I missed you too."

"You did?"

"Like a phantom limb. Even when I didn't understand it."

There's so much heartbreak in his expression, I want to go to him again. He pulls her hand to his lips and drops a kiss on it, an act of forgiveness so generous it destroys me. "Thank you for saying that."

"Will you tell me about them?"

"Of course. I'm not going anywhere."

Her smile is wet and filled with relief and gratitude, but the thing that catches in my heart is the pride. I feel it, too, a deep pride in the person he is.

Vasu turns to me, and her expression changes to confusion. "You're leaving? Why?"

"I'm getting married in three months. I need to get back to my family and fiancé."

She looks with some surprise from Krish to me. "You're not marrying each other?"

"No," Krish says.

"Why? Is your family forcing you?" she asks me.

I shake my head. "No one's forcing me."

It's like she can't believe what she's hearing, and I imagine her young and baffled at the ways of the world. "Are you sure?" she says. "Sometimes it's not easy to know when they're forcing you."

No one says anything.

"It's time," Krish says, but he doesn't look at me.

"I just wanted to say bye," I say.

Vasu lets go of Krish's hand and reaches for me. I go to her. "Thank you for finding me." The ring is hanging around her neck on a black thread. We returned it to her yesterday, and Reva put it on her.

I nod. My throat feels raw. There's so much I want to say, but I can't speak.

"I know," she says. "It is hard to do the thing you want when you've been taught that doing what others want means loving them. But you came here to find me. You do know how to do what you want." She places her hand over my chest, where my heart hurts. Her hand is cool, but heat gathers beneath my skin under her touch. "When you're true to yourself, even when something hurts, it feels good. When you're betraying yourself, even when something is supposed to feel good, it hurts."

When she pulls away, I feel shredded. And so seen it's like she just stripped me. It hurts. And of course it feels good.

Reva hugs me tightly. "You will stay in touch?"

I nod. "Will you take care of him?" I whisper.

She opens her mouth to say something, then nods. "Of course."

"You sure you don't want me to take you to Bagdogra?" Krish asks as he walks me to the main monastery compound. To the scaffolded arch where Norbu dropped us off two days ago.

"I'll be fine." He needs to be here right now. "Will you be okay?"

He digs his hands into his pockets. "You don't want me to answer that."

He's right.

And wrong.

I do want him to answer that. But I shouldn't.

Norbu is driving me to Bagdogra, but he's not here yet.

This is the last time I'll ever see Krish. So I say it. "I do want you to answer that. I have to know that you'll be okay."

He steps close to me, but he doesn't touch me. From the very bottom of my being I want him to. I want to wrap my arms around him. I want him to drop a kiss on my head, where my hair parts and my nerve endings gather. I want to feel that feeling one more time before I die. I want to know what his lips feel like when they smile against mine. I want to be able to cry in his arms, have him cry in mine. "Tell me you'll be okay, Krish."

He takes a breath. "If returning to your old life will make you happy, I will be okay. As long as you feel seen and cared for, I'll be okay. As long as no one makes you feel like you're lucky to have them, I will be okay. As long as you promise never to put yourself away again, I will be okay." He presses a hand to his chest, and I wish I didn't see how much he means every word. "As long as I know you're happy, I will be okay, Mira."

I want to tell him to take the words back. But I don't. I want to tell him I feel the same way. But I can't. I don't know how I feel.

Liar. That's the word that rings in my ears when I hold out my hand. He looks at it, then shakes it.

A handshake, that's what I leave him with, and a whispered "Thank you."

When I get in the car and drive away, he stands there watching me go.

CHAPTER FORTY-ONE

It's been two days since I spoke to Druv, but I've barely noticed. It's been two hours since I saw Krish, and I feel like a part of me is missing.

I make it through the many security lines in a haze, my brain spinning cobwebs around itself, trying not to think the things it keeps thinking.

When I get to the boarding gate, Krish's absence is so harsh, so sharp, I can't bear it. I call Rumi.

"Wow," he says when I tell him everything that's happened since I last spoke to him, including being attacked and how frail Vasu's body looked yet how strong her spirit is. "Who are you, and what did you do with my twin sister?"

"I think I left her behind in Central Park, or maybe in front of Van Gogh's *Starry Night* at MoMA. Or maybe in a sugarcane field. I don't know. I think I want her back. She always knew what to do."

"Fuck her. She was a wimp. I've been waiting for you to leave her behind."

"I know. You've said that a lot recently. Stop repeating yourself and tell me what to do!"

"Miru, you already know what to do. You're just freaking out because you've never blown shit up before, and this is going to be Oppenheimer level."

"I think that might be a problematic thing to say," I say, and he laughs.

"Sweetheart, this shouldn't need to be said, but you're supposed to marry the person you love."

"You're also not supposed to go back on a commitment because someone newer and hotter shows up."

"So you admit hot reporter guy is hot."

An electric buzz spasms in my belly when I think about how hot he is. "Of course he's hot. Is it possible to be in love with two people at the same time?"

"I'm sure it is. But do you really think you are?"

"They're both good men."

"That's not what I'm asking."

"But they are, and I could have a good life with either one of them. Then why would I do such a terrible thing to Druv?"

"You tell me why."

"Because my definition of a good life has changed." When I think about my life, another forty, fifty years, or as long as I'm lucky to be alive, who I will be in each marriage is two versions of me.

"I have to go," I say. "I'll call you back."

"You got this, Miru," he says.

We have no way to predict the future, but the star in Druv's life will always be Druv. The thing that's changed is that I no longer want to be part of the Druv story, and I can see the labor I'll have to do to shift our relationship from that to the Druv and Mira story or the Sometimes Mira and Sometimes Druv Depending on the Situation story.

With Krish, we're already there. I'm already part of a *we* with him. *What are we going to do next?* We've already thought that together countless times in our short time together. He's driven already by what I am where I am and who I want to be right then.

As long as I know you're happy, I will be okay.

He's intimidatingly honest and too intelligent for me to ever hide from him, and I can see that being exhausting, too, and infuriating, and terrifying. I'm used to hiding and contorting.

With Druv, who I'll be is who I've trained at being all my life: first a wife, daughter, daughter-in-law, mother.

With Krish, my conditioning digs into my skin. My shields block my view. With him I'm Mira first. I'll be Mira, who's also a wife, a daughter, a daughter-in-law. Mira, who's also a mom and a pain management therapist. Mira, who has to learn a new way without a guarantee of how it will feel. Exhausting.

Why would you want that? my mother's voice says in my ear.

I don't know. I don't know why it matters that Druv and Krish are already that. Druv, who's also a son, son-in-law, surgeon, husband, and someday a father. Krish, who's also a writer, a son, a man in love with me. Why does it matter that their being themselves is not in competition with all the other things they want to be?

But it does matter. I want me to be me first too. I want to not have to say "But being a mother comes first," the way I've heard all the aunties say over the years. Over and over again. I might still put others first sometimes, but I want to have a choice, a real choice. Not one that makes me feel halved and quartered.

I call my mother. She doesn't answer. Thanks a lot, Aie.

The gate agent announces that the incoming flight is delayed and our flight is going to be late.

It's not a sign, I tell myself. But it is.

I call Druv.

"I can't do this, Druv," I say. "I don't want to get married."

"Did you sleep with him?" Of all the responses in the world, that's the one he chooses.

"You did not just ask me that."

"If you give it some thought, you'd know it's a logical question."

"If you give it some thought, you'd know that it means you don't know me at all . . . but I'm actually glad that you asked me that. Because

I made the effort not to even touch him that way. I worked hard not to even let myself think about it. If I were a person who did things without thinking, I might have."

One of the reasons I went out with Druv and thought marrying him was a good idea was that the thought of sex with him was not repulsive. But Krish is the first man with whom my body feels different. It feels wide open. I want him to touch me. I feel like he's already touched parts of me no one else ever has.

Maybe it's not just about who I will be with him but who I already am.

"Our wedding is in three months, Mira! Our families, our friends, everyone has been working their asses off for it. You have been working your ass off for it." There's an edge of panic in his voice, and my heart hurts.

"I know. I know. But that should not be a reason to get married. That is the only reason I would marry you now, Druv. And I can't do that to you or to me. I am so very sorry."

"You can't do this. Does it not matter that I love you? Exactly the way you are, Mira? The parts you've told me, the parts you haven't. I've never cared about anything but who you are." He sounds desperate and angry but also sincere. He truly believes what he's saying, and it's filled with pieces of truth.

"But don't you see, you don't know who I am because I wasn't able to be who I am with you."

"Then tell me. We can work this out. I'm okay with whoever you want to be."

"It doesn't matter that you're okay with it. What matters is that I couldn't." I think about sitting on those rocks and letting the worst experience of my life out. I could tell Krish. I wanted to tell Krish. With him I was the person who could say the words, access the person it was so painful to be. I can access pain around him. I can access me. "You are one of the best men I know, Druv. I was the one who didn't know how to be who I am. I didn't even know who I was."

"Are you giving me the 'it's not you, it's me' speech right now?"

"Actually, it's us. We're both settling for the bare minimum. Not the bare minimum in terms of the people we are, but we're choosing a situation where we have to do the least work. Have you ever been with someone or done something that makes you feel like you're being tossed off your feet by a gigantic wave and taken under? I hope you have. To be with that person, you have to wake up parts of yourself that are terrifying. You have to be your whole self. Or maybe you don't have to. But I want to. I hope you'll forgive me."

"And I hope you'll forgive me for not understanding how you can break our parents' hearts. How you can leave them to face the censure of the community where they're so respected. They've spent hundreds of thousands of dollars already, Mira. How can you let all of that go to waste?"

I have thought about all those things. I have thought about them so much I almost chose to relegate myself to a life I don't want. "I'll pay them back." One advantage of working since I was sixteen and being too afraid to go anywhere or do anything is that I've saved a lot of money. "And the censure will be mine. I'm the one to blame." Also, is respect that's so easily lost really respect? But I don't say that. I've said all I can say. "I'm sorry, Druv. I truly am."

He does not forgive me. He probably never will, but he will thank me some day. That much I know for sure.

I call Norbu back, and he returns with the biggest smile on his face.

The mountains already feel familiar. The heaviness in my heart settles but stays. It hurts, but it also feels good.

Krish is sitting on the steps of Vasu's house when I get there.

His head snaps up when he sees me. His gaze floods with relief, like the world reorienting itself in his eyes.

"Vasu?" I ask.

"She's still here. Reva's with her." He stands up and comes to me, not stopping until he's so close I can feel the warmth of his body. "She gave me this to give you when you came back." He presses the ring into my palm. "She wants you to have it."

I wrap my hand around it and press it to my chest. "I'm sorry I left you when you needed me."

"You didn't, though. You're here." And Vasu knew I'd come.

"Yes, I am. And I'm not leaving again." I slip the ring on my finger. It's a perfect fit.

I look up at him, and he pulls me close and drops a kiss on the top of my head, right where my hair parts and all my nerve endings gather. Sensation cascades down my body.

I wrap my arms around him and stand there like that, holding him, soaking up how he feels. Soaking up how I feel in his arms.

There's something about me when I'm with him. And I think it's that I really like who I am.

He pulls me closer. *You're here,* his body says to mine. *You're here.*

From one breath to the next, the rush of comfort turns to need. Heat pools in my belly. I go up on my toes. He looks down at me. The pinkening sky swirls above us as our lips meet. It's the softest touch. He breathes me in. Twin shocks of awareness vibrate through our bodies. All the desire that's been dancing on the edge of my consciousness flares at once and melts through my body. I reach up and into the kiss, parting my lips, opening myself, wanting to feel him, to take him in, all the way, everywhere. He grabs my face with both hands and presses into the kiss with everything he is.

I fall so hard and free it's like I've never done anything but this. Never been anyone but this. His breath and mine, his hands against my skin, in my hair. A fever where our tongues touch, where the softest parts of our mouths slide and fit and search for the things they've never tasted before, never felt. My lips, my breasts, all of it friction and heat, sparking hunger deep in my womb. Our bodies press so close there isn't an inch left untouched, not a speck of me left unchanged.

When we pull apart I'm in pieces, and all the ones I've never let out before are clinging to him.

I open my eyes and wait for him to open his. When he does, I see the entirety of our life together flash in them.

"My home just came to me," he says and pulls me back into the tightest hug.

Krish Hale is a hugger. Who would have thought?

I smile against his chest. And it feels so good, it doesn't even hurt.

EPILOGUE

Two years later

There are lobsters on Rumi's sherwani and a jeweled ocean floor on Saket's anarkali. *Go obvious or go home* is the theme for this wedding, obviously, and the twenty guests at the ceremony are fully on board with the symbolic deliciousness of it. Krish and I are hosting, of course, on the terrace of our apartment overlooking Central Park. *Nana Nasty*, as Saket and Rumi call Krish's grandmother, knew how to plant an urban garden, and it's everyone's favorite place to hang out.

Turns out her plants, like her grandson, have my whole heart. I spend so much time in this garden with my hands in the dirt, it's like I was born into it. I love my job at NewYork-Presbyterian, working with children in pain, but after a full shift, I need this garden to put me back together. We haven't used a single flower for the wedding that I haven't grown myself, and the terrace is blooming like the joy on Rumi and Saket's faces.

"Was this rooftop garden always so gorgeous?" Karl Hale asks Krish as we watch the guests admire the view and the wine while they generously ignore the delay and wait for the ceremony to start.

"Not to me," his son says and rubs my shoulders to relieve the tension gathered there.

Karl's looking dapper in a black Pathani suit with lightning bolts on it, and his girlfriend, Linda, has on a caftan dress with lightbulbs.

Saket's mother has kathak dancers embroidered into her lehenga, and his stepfather has musical instruments on his sherwani. They join us with a plate of pakoras that are being fried on an open flame by the bar.

It wasn't easy to keep Krish from frying them himself, because his obsession with Indian cooking is a little out of control. He's insisted on cooking the biryani himself. It's Reva's special recipe that she helped him perfect when we spent four months in Darjeeling with Vasu. Four months that were miraculous in every way. Vasu let us soak up her spirit, and we carry it with us every day.

Reva is wearing a white sari with a wide pink border of pagodas. It's the first time I've seen her wear color since Vasu left us a year and eight months ago to the day. I squeeze her in a hug. "You okay?"

She nods. "I'm fabulous." Like the rest of the guests, she's being patient with the delay. We've already made all the Indian Standard Time jokes. "Love the lehenga, by the way," she says. "I get that those are rings, but are you going to tell us what Krish's kurta is supposed to mean?"

"It's an inside joke," I say.

"She's not telling you, either, is she?" Saket comes over and kisses Reva's cheek. "Come on, guys? As the person who brought you together, I have the right to know. Rooh, can't you use your twinsies thing to figure it out?"

Krish wraps his arms around me from behind and nuzzles a kiss into my cheek. "It's not that complicated, people. The pocket on my kurta is made out of duct tape."

I start laughing. The memory of Krish and me tied up in that stinky room should be a terrible one, but instead it's one that never fails to warm my heart. It also belongs to us alone.

"Duct tape and rings, that totally makes sense," Rumi says. "If you're into bondage."

Wine spurts from my mouth, and I punch my brother.

Everyone's still laughing when the doorbell rings. Rumi's gaze flies to mine, and I see everything I'm feeling reflected in my brother's eyes, hope and nervousness but also wholeness that feels unshakable no matter what's waiting for us on the other side of the door.

Krish squeezes my hand. I haven't seen my parents since I went to Naperville to give Druv back his ring after coming back from Darjeeling. He didn't meet me, but Romona did. We still follow each other on social media and like each other's posts every once in a while. She's never made me feel small, and she did text me a few months ago when Druv got engaged again to his childhood friend Priyanka Joshi. I texted back my congratulations. Something tells me Priyanka is just the person to make Druv feel like a gigantic wave knocked him down and took him under.

"I hope you're happy now that you've shamed us" were Aie's last words to me.

"I am happy, Aie," I said. "But it's not because you feel shamed. It's because I learned how to be happy."

Last month Rumi and I let Saket and Krish talk us into inviting our parents to the wedding. Baba refused to talk to us, but Aie asked why we were calling when we'd already abandoned them.

"Because life is too short," Rumi had told her. "And because Miru is hosting the ceremony in her beautiful home, the likes of which you've never seen, and because it would mean a lot to Saket and me if you came."

Until yesterday we believed they weren't coming. Then yesterday Aie sent me a text requesting the address and then ignored my response and questions about whether she needed a ride or a place to stay.

It's been over an hour since the ceremony was supposed to start, but Saket and Rumi wanted to wait. Now Rumi and I stand at the door, too nervous to open it.

When I pull it open, it is her. She looks even more nervous than I'm feeling.

She's wearing a silk sari and leaning heavily on her cane. A suitcase stands next to her. "I couldn't convince your father to come," she says. "I'm sorry."

Rumi takes her bag, and I help her in. It's the first time one of our parents has apologized to us for anything. It is the smallest thing, but deep in my heart I know that everything is going to be okay.

ACKNOWLEDGMENTS

Writing acknowledgments after finishing a book is one of my favorite things. For one, I get to thank all the people who made it possible to take this book from a wild idea to a meaningful story. For another, I'm still wallowing in the incomparable high of finishing a story and being wholly submerged in my love of the characters and their world. I don't know if this is true of all authors, but for me every time a new idea shows up I'm completely at a loss for how it's going to turn into a full-length novel. Going from that moment of terror to this moment of utter gratified delight involves relearning every step of the process. And the only way to get through that is to rely on my community inside and outside the publishing industry.

First and foremost I'm grateful to my editor, Alicia Clancy, and my agent, Alexandra Machinist. As always, this story came from my need to say something about what baffles me about this world. But when I started out, it was a bunch of ideas with no spine to stand up on. If my editor and agent hadn't spent hours brainstorming with me, and if my editor weren't the most generous, inventive, badass person in the world, I would never have that spine, and consequently, I would never have Mira. So thank you, Alicia, for handing me your ring for this story and letting me fly with it. And to Alexandra Machinist for helping me chart my flight path even when it isn't easy.

Through all the ups and downs and blocks and doubts that followed, my writing sisterhood held my hand, as they have done for years now. Barbara O'Neal, Virginia Kantra, Jamie Beck, Liz Talley, Tracy Brogan, Sally Killpatrick, Priscilla Oliveras, Kristan Higgins, Christina Lauren, Alisha Rai, Susan Elizabeth Phillips, Nisha Sharma, Annika Sharma, Melonie Faith Johnson, CJ Warrant, Clara Kensie, and Robin Skylar, with you I always have someone to go to, and what is a family if not that? You are my writing family, my brains to pick, my shoulders to cry on, my cheerleaders, and my kick in the pants when I need it. Thank you for every single thing.

Another invaluable step in getting my messy drafts honed is relying on my beta readers and subject experts. Swati Bakre, Nishaad Navkal, Jamie Beck, without you, the things that matter most to the story would never feel real to me. So thank you for holding my hand and sharing your experiences and knowledge with such generosity.

Thanks also to the amazing editorial, publicity, and marketing teams at Amazon Publishing and Lake Union. Without you, my books would not make the final, most vital, leg of this journey. They would not turn into the shiny pennies that beckon readers. Jen Bentham, Rachael Clark, Allyson Cullinan, Adrienne Krogh, Kimberly Glyder, Elyse Lyon, Katherine Kirk, I am more grateful than you can imagine for your tireless efforts and innovative brains.

To Manoj, Mihir, Annika, Mamma, and Papa. You are here through the hardest bumps and the highest highs, and you hold me exactly as steady as I need to stay, always. Thanks for all the hugs, laughs, meals, trips, and limitless love and just-right levels of drama. You are my inspiration and my reason. Basically, you're everything.

And finally and most importantly, thank you from the bottom of my heart to you, my readers. Without you, the parts of me I pour into my stories would have nowhere to go. Thank you for reading, reviewing, sharing, discussing, opining. Thank you for bringing my stories alive with that final, most crucial ingredient: your hearts and your perspectives. Thank you.

BOOK CLUB QUESTIONS

1. Part of the reason Mira found herself so drawn to the mystery of the lost ring is her love for classic rom-com films. Do you have a favorite classic rom-com? Which one, and why?
2. As a physical therapist, Mira finds herself keenly attuned to other people's pain and able to help them move through it. So why do you think she has such a hard time facing her own pain from her past?
3. Mira's parents sacrificed and worked hard to give their children new opportunities in the United States but also seem to hold those sacrifices over Mira and Rumi in order to control their choices. Did you have similar experiences with your own parents? Are you able to empathize with their parents in any way?
4. Mira found herself making excuses for her parents' bigotry toward her brother to try to keep the peace. Do you believe that sometimes we have to overlook flaws in our loved ones to hold family together or that doing so is more harmful than helpful?
5. Rumi, Vasu, and Suru face hate, violence, and bigotry for who they are and who they love, even generations and continents apart. Why do you think people target them? What do you think can be done to right these wrongs?

6. The idea of wedding themes features several times throughout the novel. If you are married, did you have a theme, and if not, what would you have wanted it to be? If not, would you have one, and what would you want it to be?
7. Mira believed that by going along with what her parents wanted, she was protecting her brother from their scrutiny and holding her family together. Have you ever changed your own behavior for other people?
8. Being true to oneself is a major theme in the novel. Do you feel like you are able to be your authentic self? If not, why do you think that is?
9. The idea of fate is a thread that runs throughout the novel. Do you believe in fate? Why or why not?

ABOUT THE AUTHOR

Photo © 2018 Ishita Singh Photography

USA Today bestselling author Sonali Dev writes stories that explore the experience of being a woman in today's world. Her novels have been named Best Books of the Year by *Library Journal*, NPR, the *Washington Post*, *Cosmopolitan*, BuzzFeed, PopSugar, and *Kirkus Reviews*. Dev has won the American Library Association's award for best in genre, the *Romantic Times* Reviewers' Choice Award, and multiple RT Seals of Excellence. Other honors include being named a RITA finalist and being listed for the Dublin Literary Award. *Shelf Awareness* calls her "not only one of the best, but one of the bravest romance novelists working today."

Sonali lives in Chicagoland with her husband, two visiting adult children, and the world's most perfect dog. Find out more about the author and her work at https://sonalidev.com.